God's Bastard Sons

A

SBI

PUBLICATION

distributed by

A&B DISTRIBUTORS INC
BROOKLYN, NEW YORK
11238

Published by
SBI

STREBOR BOOKS INTERNATIONAL
P. O. Box 10127
Silver Spring, MD, 20914
http://www.streborbooks.com

ISBN 0-9674601-9-0

LCCN 2001090576

Distributed by
A&B Distributors Inc
1000 Atlantic Ave.
Brooklyn, NY 11238
(718) 783-7808

Cover illustration: © *Andre Harriss*
Typesetting & Interior design: *Industrial Fonts & Graphix*

Manufactured & Printed in Canada
01 02 03 04 05 06 10 9 8 7 6 5 4 3 2 1

God's Bastard Sons

D.V. Bernard

Dedication

For my sisters, Corinthia and Antonia

—Antonia, if you taught me one thing, it's the importance of dreaming big—no matter the consequences

—Corinthia, I can still remember you reading to me as a kid and giving me my first reading lessons. You didn't even seem to mind reading my first horrible stories. I'm eternally grateful that you're my sister

...Every one (of us is) a drum major leading a parade of hurts, marching with our bitterness. And some day—the armies of bitterness will all be going the same way. And they'll all walk together, and there'll be a dead terror from it.

John Steinbeck, *The Grapes of Wrath*

Prologue

Louisiana, Mid 1980s

The morning that Roland Micheaux finally opened his eyes to the world had seemed like the beginning of any other hot, muggy New Orleans summer day. He had sauntered over to his bedroom window, as he usually did upon awakening, staring outside dreamily as the sun rose above the neighboring tenements. As it was the middle of July, by now he had fallen into the rhythm of summer vacation. There had been no rush—no place to go or be. But as he yawned and stared out at all the litter and filth on the streets, a frown had suddenly come to his face. It hadn't been some newfound feeling of revulsion at the sight of the crumbling and burnt-out buildings of his neighborhood; it hadn't been the sight of an old man pissing against the side of one of the graffiti-covered tenements; nor had it been the stench from the toppled, dog-ravaged garbage cans just below his second story window. On the contrary, those had been the only things about the place that he recognized—and therefore, the only things that had the potential to give him solace.

He had taken a tentative step closer to the window, his frown deepening as his eyes moved warily about the landscape. He had been seeing these streets for all 13 years of his life. He knew how they hardened you inside, and distorted even the simplest perceptions. But whatever was out there had been something new entirely, which seemed as though it would take an entire lifetime to unravel. His mind had tried to go to it, but the single-mindedness and urgency necessary for the task, were quickly undone by his morning drowsiness. In fact, he had been just about to yawn and return to bed, when his eyes finally came to rest on the pale morning sun.

And the worst fears aren't those with faces that we can name, but those that hang over us like a faint ether that we can just barely sense. He had stood there numbly, staring up at the sky as though he had never seen it before. The pale morning sun had seemed dead somehow—without warmth: without *life*. And everything bathed in those suspect rays, had seemed drained of its essence—*fake*. The bricks and concrete had seemed only like dull shapes painted against a canvass. Even the sounds in the air—a honking horn from down the block; a blaring television from a neighbor's apartment—had sounded hollow and "canned." It was as though something had come while he was asleep, sucking the life out of the world. He had stood there confusedly, wondering what all this could mean, until the sudden realization of what day it was, made him shudder and back away from the window....

Eight hours later, Roland once again emerged from his thoughts; but this time, instead of the ghetto streets, there was a lonely stretch of Louisiana highway. He glanced to his left then, to the driver's seat, seeing the profile of the state trooper's grim, immutable face. They were driving west, and the dead sun of that morning was before them. Roland felt lost and dazed; but in the distance, he could clearly see their destination: the prison....Everything was coming full circle now: all the things he had ever wanted to know would be realized when he reached that place; all the things he had known, but forgotten, were coming back to him; all the things he had suspected, but been unable to prove...it was all there before him, in the huge, ugly prison complex in the distance.

They had been driving for two hours now; yet, even with the prison in sight, Roland felt as though he had been caught in some side channel in time. It was as if he were only drifting on a memory, *daydreaming*, and that his body was still at his bedroom window, trying to make sense of the world. Only after this daydream had run its course, would he be snapped back into his real self, and the real world. Everything seemed *off—suspect*...The state trooper had a country music station on, and the crooning voices, which were barely intelligible through the static of the AM station—not to mention the droning of the car's engine and the howl of the wind as it blew past the open windows—produced an eerie, unreal effect...Across the highway, for as far as the eye could see, there was marshland, with towering grass waving in the wind with a gracefulness that made Roland think of the evening tide, but there was suddenly something troubling about that peaceful ebb and flow: about the prospect of peace, itself.

And with the flatness of the landscape, he had been staring at the approaching prison for 15 minutes now. At first, it had been a jagged speck on the horizon; now, it stood off to his right, only 50 meters beyond the chain-linked fence. It was huge and dark, with a macabre air that made him think of some vampire's castle at sundown. The realization that he was going to be entering that place within a matter of minutes, made Roland quake inside. He looked over at the state trooper pleadingly then, part of him wanting to beg the man to bring him back to his mother's home. But as he watched the white man's badly sun burnt face, he kept his silence. It was too late for entreaties now. And besides, there was something about this place that was slowly and completely draining his will. With all that had happened, Roland was a tired old man masquerading as a boy; and like an old man, all that there was to do, was make his peace with the world.

He took a deep breath to calm himself. But just then, the change in the pitch of the car's engine told him that they were slowing down; and as he looked ahead and saw what lay before him, his breath got caught in his throat, making him choke. He tried to get his bearings, but he was utterly lost now. Somehow, he had been staring at the prison so intently, that he hadn't noticed the chaotic scene unfolding at the front gate. It didn't seem possible, but there were *hundreds* of people and scores of vehicles ahead. He could make out the state police and prison guards, who were already clad in full riot gear. The crowd seemed like a huge churning mass—like a cresting wave, about to engulf him. And yet, even here, there were contradictions. Some of the people were holding signs and yelling chants of protest; some were making cookouts and laughing, as if it were a tailgate party at a football game. The dozen or so camera crews added energy and motion to all of the contradictions. Their news vans and satellite dishes formed a phalanx along the fence, like some kind of battalion. Even the network anchormen were here—this thing had become that huge! Reporters were already posing in front of cameras; cameras were already rolling; interviews with the various factions within the crowd were already going on. The reminder that this was all a media circus triggered, in Roland, a daunting stream of flashbacks: recollections of how he had had to stay inside for days, because reporters and camera crews had camped outside his door; recollections of him having to fight his way through them, and *run* from them. He heard, in his mind, their high-pitched, indecipherable voices; he saw his own harangued image on television, his madness reflected back at him as he ran from the people who would not leave him alone: who always had to ask him what he was thinking…if he was sorry…if he wanted to give a statement to the press…! His reaction to the sight of them was that of a soldier who had barely survived the last battle and who, patched up and returned to the front lines, quaked at being sent back into the clutches of death. He felt betrayed by the world—and by his own inability to account for all that he now saw and felt. It again seemed impossible that he was only now noticing it all; but as his gaze returned to the dead sun, he nodded and bowed his head, like a pagan acknowledging the works of his god….

The state trooper made a right-hand turn when they got to the front entrance, then started driving up the crowded prison driveway. The sea was spreading slowly before the car, engulfing them. The car's windows were open and Roland could hear them: the *din* of them. Many of the people were yelling incoherently; some were singing softly, but their words were just as indecipherable. And then, all of a sudden, a scrawny white man with a bushy beard ran up to the passenger side of the car with a sign that read: "Abolish death row! Kill them all now!" The man was yelling gibberish; but for some reason, Roland stared at him, trying to understand. He tried to read the man's lips, but all that he could see was a glob of spittle on the man's beard, where he guessed that his lips were supposed to be—

And then, the state trooper slammed on the brakes and began honking the horn. Looking though the windshield, Roland saw that an old white woman was standing in front of the car. The strange thing was how peaceful she looked as she swayed rhythmically to the soft song that she was singing. As she swayed, she held a candle in one hand and a rosary in the other; and standing there like that, in a long, white flowing dress, she looked like one of those statues of

Saints from the church, so that Roland frowned. It was all so strange...and a steady stream of curses now flowed from the trooper's lips as the woman, caught in some euphoric place, continued to sway peacefully and sing. She seemed to be in a place so insular that Roland, in his current state of mind, both longed for it and was terrified by the prospect of it. The trooper was banging on the horn as if it were a surrogate for the old woman's head. Roland watched him warily for a moment: the man seemed as though he were going to *explode*. But other state troopers were coming about now. In a millisecond, the woman was quickly and gruffly pushed to the side by one of the riot-gear-clad troopers. And then, as the woman fell to the ground, one segment of the crowd let out whoops of approval; while amongst the other, there were shouts of anger and outrage. A man from the latter camp stepped up and kicked the offending trooper in the chest. A baton came out; more troopers flooded into the area; and instantaneously, everywhere, people were yelling and fighting and running. The cameramen and sound crews were soon mixed in the fray, seeming just as insane as their subjects as they clambered for the best vantage points. There were jeers and shouts of agony; and, in the midst of it all, an inscrutable kind of laughter, which rose in the air like the wailing of cicadas.

Roland stared ahead blankly, overcome by the fears and uncertainties that had had a hold of him all that day—all his *life*, it seemed. Just then, he realized that the trooper was yelling something; and startled, he read the man's lips as he screamed: "Close the fucking window!" His hands trembling, Roland did as told. But as he glanced outside, he saw a man running past the car, screaming, his face bloodied and gashed open....

Roland closed his eyes, yearning for the illusion of peace and solitude that he had had in his mother's home. That place seemed so far away now...He thought back to earlier that day, remembering how he had sat on the edge of his bed, numbly waiting for the trooper to arrive. The window had been to his back, showing another muggy New Orleans summer day, with dilapidated tenement buildings the type of which could be seen anywhere from New York City to Los Angeles; and with his back turned to the world, Roland had seemed to be shunning it all. On the pavement, he had heard the neighborhood children playing, and had been reminded of his hatred of them. Their laughter had been unbearable, wafting up through the air like the stench from open sewers. Like so much in his world, it had been another thing to be borne. It had been like the Louisiana heat: best endured if taken with an acceptance akin to passivity. So he had taken it all—the midday heat, the wafting laughter...—waiting for the trooper in the scratchy stuffiness of his Sunday suit.

In the next room, he had still heard his mother clanging pots and moving around the furniture in her quest to find hidden dirt. She had been trying to preoccupy herself with tasks that didn't have to be done, but there had been no peace for either of them. All that day, the thing had been in their eyes: it had bent their frames and brought inevitable frowns to their faces. For the last *eight years* of their lives, in fact, the thing had been there, eating away at their souls. They had moved around restlessly in the cramped space of the apartment, like soldiers who knew that this was going to be their last battle: that they would either survive and be sent home as heroes, or die and lay forgotten in the muck of this foreign land. Those two choices—literally, life and death—had loomed large in their world. Because of this, neither of them had really been able to come to grips with the reality of what this day would bring. That reality had not confronted Roland during those chaotic weeks, when everyone had run after him, desperate to know his life story, or to tease him, or to spit in his face—as an old woman had done to him once. Only now, as Roland looked past all the chaos of the riot, and up at the grim walls of the prison, did he feel the full weight of it: somewhere within that huge, ugly complex, was his father; and in a matter of hours, the man was going to be put to death—

Someone threw something—*a brick!*—against the windshield of the state trooper's car. In the closed vehicle, the noise was like an explosion. All at once, a mass of concentric circles and snaking lines appeared on the windshield. With the riot going strong, people were now bumping into, and being thrown against, the car. Roland was beginning to feel seasick. As for the trooper, the man seemed like some trapped beast. He had gotten out his gun, his eyes darting about wildly. Roland scrounged down in the seat, looking up pleadingly at the man again; and as he stared up at the trooper's sun burnt, pealing face, Roland was reminded that the man had had to bring him here, because his mother, and everyone else but him, had refused to see his father. His coming here had been his first true act of defiance against his mother. It seemed as if he had sacrificed everything for this last chance to...he didn't even know what. He had driven across three parishes and borne the silent disapproval and disappointment of his mother, just for the chance to eat a final meal with the man whom he hadn't seen since he was five years old.

But to say that he had never known his father belied the fact that the man was now a national celebrity. His father's picture was all over the news now—especially as the Supreme Court had denied his final appeal. There would be justice at last, or so the pundits were saying. This week alone, there had been at least four network specials done on the implications of his father's execution. Conservatives were touting the curative effects that the execution was going to have on a nation that had "lost its moral compass." Liberals were lamenting what they called the misguided bestiality of capital punishment and working hard for a last minute pardon. However, the governor, whose re-election campaign always seemed to be in full swing, was lobbying to be the one to pull the switch!

As for Roland, his father's act—the man's *crime*, in fact—had been the defining element of his life. Supposedly, they had found his father's semen inside of that hacked up white woman. Her blood had been splattered all over his clothes when they found him stumbling down the block in that drug-induced daze. His scratched skin had been underneath her fingernails; his bloody fingerprints had been all over her rummaged apartment; and finally, not only had several people seen him exiting from the woman's apartment, but her wallet had been in his pocket when the policemen picked him up. The brazen stupidity of the crime was somehow responsible for feeding the fervor over it. Beyond the state trooper's car, the battle lines were clearly drawn. There were those who, having viewed the "evidence" were convinced that his father was the Devil and should be handed over to mob justice. Others, confronted with the same "evidence," were convinced that it was all a frame-up by those desperate to get a conviction and mollify the white community. Among this latter group, there were even those who saw the pithiness of the case as proof that he *couldn't* have done it.

As for Roland, however, he had never really asked himself if his father was guilty. He had *said* the words to himself of course, but he had never *felt* them. Thousands of times over the years, he had found himself wondering about his father's innocence the way that he wondered about the existence of God and Eternal Life. For both, he had come to the conclusion that if it were so, it would be great, but that it just seemed, in the face of everything, either unlikely or irrelevant. Maybe irrelevant described his mindset better. It wasn't that he didn't care, but that he wasn't yet at the stage where he *could* care. There was so much that he had to battle before he could reach that stage. It was as if he were at the bottom of the ocean, staring up at the dim orb of the sun. That orb was his caring. He would drown down there in the depths, swallowed up by a sea of resentment and fear and shame, before he would ever be able to care.

And others didn't really care, either. They were fascinated and obsessed with the case, but they couldn't really *care*. Their seas were filled with a gossip's intrigue about the sensationalized events of the case—maybe not even that. Maybe not even the events, themselves, but the prospect of what they could become. There was a strange hopefulness in their eyes, even when whispering of the more macabre details of the case. They were like oil speculators who had found a few barrels of oil near the surface and sank dozens of wells down into the depths of the earth, hoping insanely for more. There was some perverse wealth to be garnered here. Roland now saw it in the eyes of the people fighting beyond the state trooper's car—and the cameramen who rushed to cover it all. Added to this enveloping chaos, sirens wailed in the air—from ambulances and police cruisers and the prison, itself. The world was mad; but worse than that, it seemed as if that madness were keeping it all together. It was like the stock market: millions of people driven by greed and hope and fear and uncertainty and rumor and a thousand other neuroses that Adam Smith and the other shamans of the faith had deigned to call Rationality. Sanity would destroy the tottering house of cards that had been built up, willy-nilly, by generations of unquestioning madness….

The riot outside the car was finally dying down. As shots were fired in the air and reinforcements were called in, the more violent of the offenders scrambled away—back towards the highway. Looking up in a daze, Roland saw that a column of troopers in riot gear was now outside the car. A trooper was knocking on Roland's window, trying to get his attention; and with all of his protective gear, the man at first stuck Roland as Darth Vader: as some fictionalized character impinging upon the real world. Roland sat there in a daze, staring at the man until the latter's tapping turned into annoyed banging. Coming to his senses, Roland unlocked the door with the same nervous haste with which he had locked it. He was trembling so much that he almost collapsed when he tried to step out of the car. His legs didn't feel like his own. The trooper that had driven him here, came around and held him by the shoulders. The others formed protective flanks on either side of them, then they all began walking towards the entrance—which was about 20 meters away. Even more armed, grim-faced troopers were protecting the entrance: it stood in the shadows of the shadows, towering above his head, like a wide-open mouth about to chomp down on him.

There was a pall in the air. The crowd, beaten back, stood their distance and watched the troopers like cornered animals looking for a chance to strike. Most of them had fled back towards the highway. But the reporters, realizing whom the kid surrounded by the troopers was, began running towards Roland. Roland looked about warily as a barrage of indecipherable questions came from beyond the wall of troopers. The reporters were trying to yell over one another. Cameras and microphones were being inserted between the phalanx of troopers; a couple of the reporters were gruffly pushed away, but seemed undaunted. And soon, the crowd, which had been subdued just seconds ago, became raucous again. They were once again organizing themselves into their camps, yelling their slogans over the sirens that continued to wail in the air. As Roland stumbled along, the rhythmic chanting reminded him of the neighborhood children taunting him with:

Roland's papa killed a cracker
Roland's papa booty scratcher

How he hated them all—all the reporters, the protesters, the policemen: even the mildly interested bystanders and those flipping by these images on their television screens! It made no difference to him what their stances were. Those claiming to sympathize with and speak in favor of his father were no different from those who, in their hatred, wanted to rip the man apart. They were all killers, whose touch and thoughts—whose very claim of interest—was a death knell. Just then, Roland looked to his left, where a white woman and her camera crew were trying to get his attention. All those bastards, chasing after him to (it suddenly seemed) *reap* his shame...Why wouldn't they just leave him alone! The hatred surged within him then, like vomit threatening to choke him. He despised everything at the moment—and himself most of all, for continuing to feel shame. And swept up in this self-loathing, he found himself fantasizing that he were a kind of kamikaze, and that the hatred inside of him were a kind of bomb, which would explode and engulf the world in fire. He was hopelessly lost in this fantasy now, seeing all the filth purged, all the shame and worries dissolved in flame...but the trooper's grip on his shoulders was tight; and soon, he was inside of the prison. The contrast with the outside world was so stark, that it was almost violent. He looked around in confusion, unable to get over the dark vastness of the place—and the eerie silence....

Most of the guards and troopers were staying behind to restrain the media and the resurgent crowd. It was only the three of them now: Roland, the trooper and a prison guard. The trooper's grip was still firm, somehow embedding him in reality. But the man was leading Roland deeper into the prison now; and with each step, he felt himself unraveling. His eyes were open, yet he could barely see. The lighting seemed at once dim and blinding—maybe it was the contrast with just having been outside....They were taking him through labyrinthine cement passages, which had locked steel doors about every 30 meters. The guard had to yell out to a remote station for the electronically locked doors to be opened and closed. The stench of industrial floor polish was nauseating. The floor was so shiny that he could see the reflection of the overhead fluorescent lights in them. The feeling of loneliness overwhelmed him once again. The silence, in contrast to the din of the mobs, was still eating away at him. The silence left him time to think about his father, and he couldn't stand that. The thought that he would be seeing the man in a matter of *minutes* almost made him collapse. The added fact that the man would then be put to death that night was too...*unreal*. But what could death possibly mean to him? Death was a reified thing, pumped out of the media with the same intonations used to sell soap. Death on the ghetto streets was a colorful spectacle, with flashing emergency lights and sirens. It was a chance to stand around and watch the show, giggling at the half-naked, swooning mothers who ran out into the streets to find their murdered sons. It was all a joke: a spectacle made unreal by the frequency….

In the next corridor, there was a prison cleaning detail. Two old black men—both well over 65—were mopping the floor. They stopped and looked up when Roland and his guides entered. The two men had probably been in prison for most of their lives, because in their eyes, was the defeated look of an old dray horse. All about them, there was the aura of an animal that had been broken and *knew* it. Their frames were bent and frail, as if from a lifetime of heavy labor. Now too old for that labor, they were good for nothing but these few menial tasks. Roland suddenly found himself wondering if his father was like that now. The resurgent anarchist side of him, fed by his newfound hatred, hoped not. It hoped to find his father a defiant bastard who would curse the world with his dying breath: who would remain, even when strapped into the death chair, fearsome and fearless. Yes: better for his father to be a despised nigger than a lap dog. He suddenly needed to find the man strong and unbroken: as unrepentantly evil as everyone was saying. For some unaccountable reason, *his* manhood, or whatever passed for it, depended on his father's strength. All of his life, his father had been little more than an abstraction, looming above his world with the ominous threat of a rotten ceiling. The imminence of the meeting was giving flesh to the man now. Maybe the man would greet him with the force of that collapsing ceiling; but for just that one moment, he didn't care….

They entered a small cafeteria that could seat no more than 40 men. By its size—and its emptiness—Roland guessed that it probably wasn't for the general population of inmates, but was perhaps only for the guards. From an adjacent chamber came the aroma and sounds of something spicy being cooked. But in the face of all that had passed that day, and that *would* pass, the prospect of food was suddenly nauseating. The trooper was saying something: Roland's father had been summoned and would arrive in a matter of minutes. The words and their meaning probably didn't register in Roland's mind until minutes later, by which time the trooper and the guard had wandered over to the other side of the cafeteria by themselves, leaving Roland sitting alone. A rhythmic chinking sound brought Roland to his senses. He looked about confusedly before realizing that it was coming from down the corridor. At first, it terrified him simply by its echoing loudness; but then, as he realized that the clinking was from chains—from *manacles*, in fact—the renewed awareness that his father was coming, made him panic. He looked over his shoulder, but the trooper and the guard were still talking on the other side of the room. It was only he. He was alone. He got up nervously, then sat back down as the trembling proved too much for him. And the chinking was getting closer—

Two guards came in with the man—*with his father*! The man's eyes were bright, almost beaming, as he saw the boy—*his* boy—sitting there. Roland couldn't move. The man before him seemed fatter and softer than he remembered. The man was older and more…*benevolent* than the man on the mug shot that was always being shown on television. His hair was now in one of those James Brown perms, which, in the parlance of the streets, made him look like "an old faggot." Or at least, this was what came into Roland's mind. And while the guards unlocked his father's manacles, the man smiled and stared at Roland with an intentness that left him uneasy and shy.

The last meal was being brought out of the kitchen now. Two cooks were bringing it out in huge metal cartons and placing it on a table deeper into the room. From the scent, Roland knew that it was gumbo and the kind of spicy Cajun food that his grandmother cooked down on the bayou. His father had been unrestrained—he was coming over now! Roland didn't know what to do! Somehow, he managed to stand. The man was putting out his hands! He was *hugging* him now! Roland let the man hold him. The reality of the man's body next to his was unnerving. The *warmth* of it—the *fullness* of it—made him panic inside. This man would *die* today! Roland hadn't seen him in eight years, and all that would be left were these purloined moments. What *was* this man? Roland suddenly wondered. Was there even time to know him? Forgotten were all the moments of shame and resentful hatred. Forgotten were all those broken childhood promises—some of which had been due to drunken forgetfulness, but most to blatant lying and indifference. This man, holding him tightly, was his father. And maybe he didn't love the man—*couldn't* love the man, in fact—but he could, like countless others, love the *thought* of loving his father, and of *being* loved. The fantasy was there, making the tears well up in his eyes. He was coughing on his tears now. An entire lifetime had come down to this. His father's death: what did it mean to him? What *could* it mean, in the face of all that had happened…?

His father was detaching from him now, holding him at arm's length so that he could take him in. "You've gotten big, praise the Lord!" the man boomed.

Roland didn't know what to say, so he nodded. He looked up into the man's bright, searching eyes, still not knowing what to think. But then, Roland suddenly noticed a big silver cross around his father's neck; and as the man saw his son's glance, another smile came to his face.

"We all gotta have the Lord in our lives, son," his father started in a gleeful tone. "The Lord's with me now. He's holding my hand now!" he said with more urgency. And then: "He's *forgiven* me, son!" he shouted with a strange ebullience. "He's been so good…[Roland stared, a frown slowly building on his face.] *Pray* with me, son!" the man cried. "Only the Lord can save you! You, me…we all sinners, son! Only in Him is there life!" he rejoiced. Then he grabbed Roland's hand, holding it so tightly that Roland let out an inadvertent yelp at the pain. "*Pray* with me son!" the man demanded once again, raising Roland's throbbing hand above his head like the evangelists did. "Oh God!" the man suddenly broke down, "I couldn't help the madness, son—sin coming down on me, *burning* in me like hell, itself…driving me to evil. Satan had a hold on me, son! You can't resist the Devil on your own—you need God's help for that! Surrender to God, son! You're useless on your own…!"

The man began praying then, screaming out his subservience and gratitude to God, while Roland stared on in bewilderment. For those first few moments, Roland was only aware of his squeezed hand—of the *pain!* He was lost…*confused*, but then he looked up at his father, seeing the man's tears—his *fear*—…seeing, for the first time, what a defeated bastard the man was. Roland had wanted to see defiance, not this! All that he saw was some scared nigger feigning redemption because he was afraid of burning in hell. The realization made new tears well up in his eyes; and then, when he could stand it no more, he wrenched his hand from his father's vise grip and pushed the man to the ground. In two steps, he was at the door, darting wildly down the corridor as he heard, in the maddening recesses of his mind:

Roland's papa killed a cracker
Roland's papa booty scratcher

Book One

1

World on the Verge of a Nervous Breakdown

New York City, the early 2000s

Months later, Roland would point to the events of this night as the beginning of his slow descent into madness; but while he was in the moment, he was in paradise. His woman straddled him in the spacious luxury of his Mercedes Benz's back seat, taking pains not to damage the fragile material of her $2,500 evening gown. The gown had been a gift from Roland. They were in an underground parking garage, supposedly on their way to the Mayor's banquet. Needless to say, they had gotten somewhat sidetracked. The woman, Candice Parker, was on top of him now. In the darkness of the parking garage, her expression seemed either lusty or demented; but at the moment, Roland didn't care which. He was burying his face in her ample cleavage, deftly unzipping the back of the gown…and he was *free*. He was beyond the world for those few moments: beyond its problems and the expectations his social success increasingly demanded of him. In a matter of days, he was to give his opening statement in a huge class action suit worth *millions*; and being just 33-years-old, he was not only a kind of golden boy within his firm, but amongst the general public and the media—both of which loved celebrated winners. He was rising in society faster than he had ever thought possible—he had even appeared in *People* magazine!

Still, at times, he would be acutely aware that this public self was not himself. A case in point was the story in the news a few weeks ago, about him being one of the ten most eligible bachelors in the city. They had created an entire mythology around some movie-star-like romantic entity and put Roland's face on it. They had interviewed him for the piece; and yet, those words hadn't been Roland's words. It had all belonged to some marketable doppelganger, in whose shadow the real Roland Micheaux lived.

And what made it all seem so unreal was that only three years ago, he had been an overworked, underpaid attorney with the Public Defender's Office. If his present life was a fantasy, then the five years he had spent as a New York City Public Defender had been a nightmare. He had dealt with every conceivable form and byproduct of scum: from those who seemed to have demons within them, to those who seemed to lack genuine evil and the impetus to commit crimes, but were either in the wrong place at the wrong time, or victims of that invisible current which saw black and minority men swallowed up by the booming prison industrial complex. Roland felt as though he had escaped from that nightmare—even, at times, that he had sold out in order to feast and grow fat at the trough of corporate law....The fact of the matter was that he had gone into law with that naïve, "I want to save the world" mentality; but being around so many wasted lives—lives that he had in time come to realize that he had no chance of ameliorating—had not so much killed his idealism, as blinded him to the true scope of societal evil. In a sense, the more disheartening the things he had seen, the less he had absorbed into himself. He had gone about his cases with the same uncompromising drive as before, but with a mental and spiritual detachment that had been his only shield against the bloated, fatally flawed judicial system.

But all of that was years behind him in time, and seemed like a whole other reality—*like someone else's life*—in terms of his current attitude and place in the world. It also explained why the feeling of peace seized him as he held his woman in the solemn darkness of the parking garage: she drove away the restless spirits and the marketable doppelgangers; and, in a strange sense, she allowed him to be alone with himself. Moreover, no world, no matter how wonderful or troubling, was a match for the touch of a good woman. Roland could be himself when he was with her—or he could surrender to the abyss that came with their lust, and be nothing at all. In fact, it wasn't so much lust, as a kind of nirvana, which canceled out all the entanglements of the world and left him at peace. He breathed in the delicate fragrance of her perfume then, feeling somehow that he was pulling her into him: that he wasn't simply breathing in her scent, but her *essence*. As he continued to unzip the back of her dress, it wasn't simply that he was disrobing her, but himself and the concerns of the world. And it was so wonderful that they were the only ones there: there were no media or courtroom expectations to be met, no cultural mores to defer to…nothing but the smooth softness of her body in the darkness. He unconsciously smiled to himself at that moment; however, it was then that Candice laughed out suddenly, startling him as she breathed heavily into his ear: "You're a *killer*, Roland Micheaux!"

"—*What?*"

"You have a murderous heart, Roland Micheaux," she whispered in her sultry Caribbean accent. When Roland only looked up at her like a dazed child roused from a good dream, she giggled and continued, "*Sex*, Roland…women can *lie* with it—can do one thing and have their minds on something else, or on nothing at all; but with men"—she kissed him on the tip of his nose and he recoiled slightly—"it's their only moment of honesty. If they're in love with you, you can tell it in their sex; if they're tired of you, you can tell that as well. You, Roland Micheaux, are a *killer*."

"…What the hell are you talking about?" Roland said in bewilderment. But he was momentarily distracted by her exposed nipple; and as he looked at it, she giggled and slipped off of him, moving to the far side of the back seat. She then zipped herself up with the agility of a contortionist and sat there, amused by his confusion. He looked at her for a moment, totally baffled; then, watching her smile of sexual triumph, he sat back and chuckled to himself. There was something about young, beautiful women that was not unlike gas station attendants who knew that their gas station was the only one for hundreds of kilometers. Due to the forces of economics, those gas stations always had the nastiest bathrooms—and the worst service.

With the magic of their session broken, Roland's strange nirvana departed, like the contours of a dream after the day had begun; and still chuckling to himself, he started buttoning up his shirt—

"You don't like my philosophical musings anymore?" she said

with a smirk, crossing her legs seductively. "I thought my philosophizing was the only reason you've been with me so long."

"Right you are," he teased her in the playful manner that he always fell into when he was with her, "—my goal in life is to figure out the mysteries of the universe."

"Is *that* what you were looking for under my dress?"

He looked across at her and smiled.

"What has it been?" she went on in the same playful tone,"—a month now since you met me at that party? Me: a poor Grenadian girl with an expired student visa; and you: the great Roland Micheaux, lawyer *extraordinaire*, rated one of the ten most eligible bachelors in the city…I amuse you, that's why you keep coming back for more."

He stared at her for a good three seconds before he shook his head and smiled. Their strange way of talking to one another—as though they were characters in a 1930s melodrama—was a kind of foreplay. It turned him on not only sexually, but on a level that approached spirituality. In a sense, it was her singularity that made her real to him. She wasn't like all the other women he had met, who looked the same and dressed the same and talked the same and even *smelled* the same. She was an individual, in a world where people—particularly the young—seemed to get their personalities out of the latest fashion magazines and music videos. For some reason, it felt good to be around her; he felt for her something visceral—something *tangible*—which wasn't as mundane as love or as shallow as desire. When he was with her, he felt as though he would figure out some grand cathartic mystery. Of course, he wasn't entirely conscious of all this, and it mostly manifested itself as a feeling of comfort.

Whatever the case, he again smiled to himself; but remembering the banquet, he held up his watch to the fluorescent light outside and looked at it fixedly. It was approaching nine-thirty: they were already fashionably late, verging on being boorishly late. Resolved to leave for the banquet at once, he began putting on his bowtie. However, when he looked up at Candice, he realized that she was still smirking at him.

"Oh-oh," he laughed, "what are you plotting in that head of yours?"

"Just thinking about you."

"You seem to spend an inordinate amount of time doing that," he joked, still putting on his bowtie.

"Well, you're an interesting subject."

"*Subject?*" he laughed at her phrasing, "—and what is your prognosis, professor?"

"Some minor neuroses, but nothing that a few years of intensive therapy won't cure."

"I see," he laughed. "And what is your proposed method of treatment?"

"First, we have to uncover the roots of your murderous heart."

"My *what?*"

"Like I said before, you're a *killer*, Roland Micheaux."

"Are we on this again?" he groaned playfully.

"Yup," she said, moving closer to him and lowering her voice to a sexy whisper, "—so tell me, when is the last time you thought about killing someone—"

"What are you talking about?" he returned, instinctively putting up his hand to keep her at bay.

"Don't try to tell me you've *never* thought about it," she said, smiling at him oddly; then, in a nonchalant manner: "I think about it all the time."

"*Killing* someone?"

"Yes."

He looked at her calm, seemingly affected expression then burst out laughing. Shaking his head, and ready to put the entire thing out of his mind, he checked the breast pocket of his tuxedo to make sure that he still had the invitations. However, when he glanced up from this task, he realized that she had been staring at him fixedly all that time, as though coming to some conclusion—or waiting for the right moment. When their eyes locked, she spoke up in the same nonchalant manner, saying, "I've *killed* someone, you know."

"...What?"

"I've *killed* someone—you're the first person I've ever told. I guess you're one of those men that women want to unburden themselves to."

"...What the *hell* are you talking about?"

"I'm a killer as well," she said, serenely.

He stared at her for a while, as she sat there with a smirk on her face; and then, dubiously: "Who'd you kill?"

"My first lover."

For some reason, he burst out laughing.

"He wasn't a *real* lover," she protested.

"Of course," he chuckled.

"...He was about 60—a big, fat, sweaty man. [Roland looked up sharply, his smile replaced by an expression of uncertainty.] He lived right next to us—back in Grenada—up on a mountain. He started with me when I was 12. [Roland sat up straighter, his frown deepening.] It was off and on—probably about three times in all. Months would go by, and I would convince myself that nothing had happened. It was like a dream: the longer you're awake, the less real it seems; and after a while, it seemed so unreal that I couldn't believe that it had happened. He would come and visit my parents, joking with us all...and I would think to myself: Nah, I must have imagined it.

"But that day...I came home from school and saw him walking up the lane with my little sister, to his house. I followed them up there, and when I saw for myself, I knew, right then and there, that I had to kill him. It wasn't a murderous rage or anything: it was calm—a *logical* conclusion. His car was in the driveway; and as my father was a mechanic, I had picked up some things. It was all so perfect, as if God had mandated that I do it, because a toolbox had been lying right there. I cut the brake cable on his car. Grenada has a lot of mountains, see. The lane from his house led right down into a deep ravine; and without brakes to make the turn...well, that would be that.

"When my sister came home, I saw it all in her eyes: the same shock that I had felt that first time....But everything was going to be fine. I lay in bed and bided my time; and that night, while I was lying there, looking out of the window at the moon, I finally heard the crash and loud explosion as his car dropped into that ravine. With the fire, there wasn't enough of him left to fill a shoe box....Justifiable homicide, Roland?"

"*What?*" he whispered when she said his name and broke the spell that had held him. Her voice had had a strangely hypnotic quality: he shook his head to be free of it.

"You think they'd convict me?" she asked him earnestly.

"You *serious?*"

"Of course. Was it justified or not?"

"...I don't know what your laws are," he said evasively.

"Screw the laws—what do *you* say?"

"I say you're a dangerous woman," he said, trying to smile.

"Isn't that what men want," she laughed in return, "—a little hint of danger in their women to spice up their sex lives?"

"Only the self-destructive ones want that," he laughed. It was nervous laughter, but he was so desperate to be free of this strange discomfort, that the laughter soon consumed him, somehow leaving him convinced that her story of childhood murder had been nothing but a joke: another of her female tricks to get into his head. And yet, she was scrutinizing him with a look that he couldn't quite gauge; and regardless of whether or not he thought she was a murderer, he had the unsettling feeling that she was seeing through him, reading his thoughts—

"What do you want from me, Roland Micheaux?" she asked abruptly.

He hated it when she used both of his names: it reminded him of his mother, who was now dead—and therefore doubly sacred. But when he looked at Candice, he saw that there was again a smirk on her face; and something about it, and the way she was sitting there, made him laugh, "What makes you assume I want anything?"

"Men always want something," she purred, "—it's in their nature."

"What about women, don't they want anything?"

"Women don't have wants, they have *prerogatives*."

"Thanks for clarifying that!" he laughed. "Anyway, why bother asking me anything? According to you, a woman can tell anything she wants to know by *screwing* a man—"

"That's not what I said!" she protested.

"Didn't you just say that a man is only honest when he's screwing," he teased her, "—and that I'm a killer? Since I'm a killer and you're a killer, we can have a little death orgy: put one another out of our misery."

"...Maybe," she mused oddly.

He frowned imperceptibly, having detected something unsettling in her voice. He went to ask her if she was all right, but instinctively retreated; and besides, he was suddenly weary of their exchange. It was a war of sorts: a battle royal between the sexes; and at the moment, they both seemed to be taking unacceptable losses. Again looking at his watch, he sighed and shook his head at nothing in particular. "Look, let's just get going," he said then. But as he glanced at her in the darkness, he was suddenly disturbed by the smirk that had been on her face for most of that evening. He quickly opened the door and went to exit, when:

"What are you running from, Roland Micheaux?"

He sat there, with the door open and one foot outside; then, slowly and deliberately, he turned around and looked at her. She was still smirking. His voice was low but emphatic: "Stop it, okay. Just *stop* it." He took a deep breath, inwardly angry with himself for having allowed her to get under his skin: she had won that battle. "—Look," he went on quickly, "let's just go and have a good time. We've got invitations to spend the evening at a banquet with the Mayor of New York City—"

"And all the other social elite."

"...Candice," he began, his tone more contentious, "if you don't want to go, I can get you a cab back home."

"Stop being such a grouch," she giggled, caressing his shoulder.

He watched her for a while, then groaned again as he exited the car and walked around to her door. "I don't want to talk about murder anymore," he warned her as he opened the door for her. "And I've heard enough of your 'philosophical musings' to last a lifetime." But by then, she was standing before him. She was tall and statuesque, and her beauty and poise made his annoyance and misgivings ebb away. She was a weird woman—perhaps even a *disturbed* one—still, he couldn't help thinking that there was something magical about her. Beauty is a horrible thing in a crazy woman, he thought with a smile. How many fools, over the eons, had died for it: had felt compelled to give up their lives in defense of it; how many otherwise intelligent men had made stupid decisions for the sake of it? She stood there posing for him with one hand placed seductively on her hip, and he almost laughed out loud at the entire game: the farce that was the mating ritual. There she was, playing the role of the classic vixen: a carefully contrived combination of sexual aggressiveness, mystery/nuttiness, and, to win over that macho streak in all men, a tinge of defenselessness. For the first time, it occurred to him that her seeming originality might just be an act. Or maybe it was only that her story of childhood murder was still percolating in his mind, setting off alarm bells. She seemed somehow different to him now; and, as was so often the case when a once-perfect lover was shown to have a blemish, the relationship was thrown into crisis—not by the flaw, itself, but by the debilitating blow that came with the loss of the *illusion* of perfection. His vessel of nirvana was somehow lost to him, so that he wasn't merely losing his woman, but his *religion*. And now that he thought about their one-month relationship, he allowed himself to acknowledge that he had always been somewhat wary of her. At first, he had thought that that wariness was what women referred to as "a fear of commitment." But he now realized that what he feared wasn't belonging to her, but losing himself within her. Nirvana could only be wonderful in passing—as a respite from the world. But continuous nirvana was death; and every time he was with Candice, he came away with the feeling that there was an abyss within her: a vast void of nothingness, waiting to suck him in. Even when having a simple conversation with her, he would find himself tumbling into her depths, falling deeper and deeper into her nothingness. And again, with her story of childhood murder percolating in his mind, his sense of inner panic couldn't be denied. He looked at her uneasily then and nodded to himself, knowing that his time with her was drawing to a close.

It was perhaps to shelter himself from the specter of a nettlesome breakup, that his thoughts gravitated towards the imminent pleasure—indeed, the social triumph—of attending the Mayor's banquet. Strangely enough, he and the Mayor were locked in a titanic struggle—a gentleman's fight to the death. It was all the result of a case that Roland had won three years ago. It had been his last case with the Public Defender's Office; and with his mental detachment almost complete, he had cared less about whom he was defending. The defendant had been a middle-aged white supremacist who burst into City Hall one day, ran up to Mayor Randolph—a Republican who had the quirky distinction of being a black man—and declared that the Mayor was "a dirty, no-good nigger!" After the man was arrested, the case had of course been seized upon by the media. And suddenly tossed into the spotlight, Roland had seemed perfect for television: poised, handsome, giving impassioned homilies about freedom of speech and "The American Way." When he won the case, the Mayor had invited him to a diplomatic banquet—and had been inviting him to dinners and social events ever since. It had seemed like a friendly gesture, but Roland rightly saw it as a declaration of war. *We'll see who breaks first*! the Mayor had seemed to be saying. But Roland's career had taken off after that. With all the media attention from the trial, the young, dynamic firm of Rosencrantz and Associates had quickly retained his services; and after being on a legal team that won a $50 million settlement against a negligent automaker, his reputation and future had been guaranteed.

For whatever reason, Roland again smiled to himself and felt at ease. Despite the uneasiness Candice's story had inspired in him, he now took her by the hand and led her away. A confrontation with her was imminent, but he didn't want it to be tonight. Right now, the only thing that he wanted was peace from his thoughts. And there was something almost magical about the dark, eerie emptiness of the parking garage, where their steps echoed in the darkness and left him with the feeling that they were the last two people on earth. He liked the solemnity: the sense of peace and well being that came when one was with someone and there was nothing to be said. They walked along like that for a few moments, until Candice looked up abruptly and said:

"Do you ever think about the world ending, Roland?"

"*What?*" he said, at once alarmed and irritated that she had broken the spell of peace.

"—Ever think that all the craziness in the world might be a sign from God?"

"…Not particularly," he said, giving her an odd look.

"I mean, *think* about it," she went on. "You turn on the television and all you see is death: people going to work—and kids going to their schools—and gunning down dozens of people. People starving and desperate in every corner of the world…People butchering one another in wars…*AIDS*…And in New York, we even have our own kind of craziness: trigger-happy cops sticking plungers up people's asses…mothers leaving newborn babies in garbage cans…and then there's that crazy Hair Jacker, or whatever he's called, running loose for the last two years, shaving people's heads. The world's *mad*, Roland. Something's wrong somewhere—something's *sick*!"

Roland's sense of inner panic began to surge within him again. Her words struck a sensitive cord in him—*disturbed* him, in fact; and all at once, his previous compulsion to get away from her, seized him again. But she had stopped and was staring up at him imploringly; and as he looked into her eyes, he felt, for perhaps the first time, that he was seeing into her: seeing the *real* her. He didn't quite know what to make of it, but he felt something inside of him melting. At first, he wondered if this was another one of her tricks to get into his head, but as he continued to look into her, there seemed to be genuine disillusionment in her eyes; and like a fool, he found himself thinking: She has big, puppy dog eyes. She seemed young and naïve to him just now, and Roland was overcome by the self-destructive male urge to protect and comfort her. He took her in his arms then, holding her tenderly. But just as the spell began to envelop him again, she blurted out:

"I knew one of his victims, you know."

"*What?*" he groaned, releasing her.

"One of my friends got her head shaved by that Hair Jacker guy," she went on. "She had this long hair weave, and he snuck up behind her one night and shaved it all off. Why do you figure he does it?"

"Who *cares*," he groaned, annoyed with her again. He started to walk off; but oblivious to his snub, she came up to his side and looped her arm though his.

"They say it might be more than one man," she went on, "—a whole cult of them. Almost 300 people have had their heads shaved in the last two years—that's a hell of a lot for one man—"

Roland was about to lose his cool and tell her to shut the hell up, when a wretched-looking black man suddenly stepped out of the shadows—actually, from behind one of the concrete columns. The man said nothing: the gun that he brought from his pocket did all the talking. The man was shorter and slighter than both Roland and Candice, but a gun elevates even the lowest weakling to mystical proportions. Roland abruptly stopped and raised his hands. Candice merely stopped by Roland's side and looked at the man with her strange nonchalance.

"Empty your pockets!" the wretched-looking man demanded. He looked like a starved stray dog. His clothes were all *caked* with dirt—as though he had fallen asleep somewhere and been buried alive when he was mistaken for a corpse. The man even *smelled* like death.

Taking all this in, Roland took out the cash from his wallet, handed the wad of bills over to the man, then went to put the wallet back in his pocket.

"Gimmie your wallet!" the man demanded.

"My credit cards will be canceled in 15 minutes—"

"Not if I blow your fucking brains out!" the man pointed out.

Roland couldn't deny the man's logic. He extended his suddenly trembling hand to give the man his wallet; but when the man, who held the gun in his right hand, stretched out his left hand to receive the wallet, he let his right hand, and the gun, drop somewhat. Instinctively, something was triggered in Roland; and before he even knew what was going on, he knocked the gun out of the man's hand! For a second, they both stood there in shock. But it was Roland who let that vicious left cross fly, breaking the man's nose and knocking him back into the concrete column. A brutal left-right combination followed, and the man was on the ground. Roland was kicking the man now, stomping his head mercilessly with the hard soles of his dress shoes. The man wasn't moving anymore. In truth, the man had been knocked senseless by the initial blow, and the subsequent 15 seconds of vicious blows were all superfluous. It was Candice who stopped Roland: who brought him back to his senses. She came up and tapped him on the shoulder; and when he looked over at her, he was both startled and confused: first, to see her standing by his side; and then, to see the bloody, unmoving form lying at his feet.

"*See*," Candice said with the same disconcerting smirk that had graced her face all that evening, "I *told* you you're a killer...."

* * *

THE NIGHT WAS COLD FOR MID MAY. Roland was shivering—or maybe it was only the dawning realization of what had just happened: of what he had just *done*. Candice was leading him across Park Avenue, to the banquet hall. He was suddenly frail and dazed...*lost*—

Candice wrenched him back, just as an angry cabby zoomed past, honking his horn. He and Candice were in the middle of the wide avenue, and he was suddenly terrified. He felt like a deer startled by headlights. Zooming cars seemed to be everywhere, their headlights blinding. Candice tugged on his arm again and they finished running across the avenue. Roland was panting when they reached the pavement. He looked back in horror, towards the parking garage:

"You think he's *dead*?" he whispered.

"Probably," she answered, still with that godforsaken smirk. He instinctively drew away from her, but she looped her arm through his and steered him towards the other end of the block, where the banquet hall was. "Nothing to worry about," she purred to him again. "It was simple self-defense: you were justified. *See*," she laughed, "I don't need to know what your laws are to make my decision. There is a natural law—fighting for survival: defending yourself against those who threaten you. I'm right, aren't I?"

"*God*," he said anxiously, as though the thought had just occurred to him, "why the hell did we run—we should have called the police!"

"*First* of all," she corrected him, "we didn't 'run' from anything. Secondly, why should we take our time to call anyone about that fool? Why waste more time on him and let him ruin our evening? I mean, really: *think* about it. If you step in shit, do you call someone to report it? No, you wipe your shoe off as best you can and go about your business."

"I guess," he said, distractedly. Then, looking back warily: "You think anyone *saw*?"

"Of course not—there was no one else down there: that's why he was there. And besides," she laughed, "You're Roland Micheaux: the golden boy—everyone loves you. In fact," she said with a chuckle, caressing his chest, "I bet you could get away with *murder*—"

He cringed at her laughter, stopping abruptly. *What's wrong with this woman*! But she only laughed louder when she saw his expression.

"God, you're wound up tight!" she said, shaking her head. "Get a hold of yourself, man," she went on, taking his hand once again. "It was self-defense, Roland. It's as simple as that. And in a while, someone's going to come upon the body. They'll see some scrawny black bum with a gun. If he's dead, they'll check his fingerprints…probably find out he has a record as long as my arm. And so another black criminal will be found dead…quickly forgotten. There's not even anything to link you to him. I wiped the gun down, didn't I?—just in case you got any fingerprints on it—and we took your money back. People won't know what to make of it. We took care of everything, didn't we?"

"Yea," he said, his voice strangely hoarse; and then: "I was forgetting that you've done this before."

She burst out laughing; and, for the life of him, he was startled to find the ends of his lips rising and a kind of chortling laughter escaping from his chest. But there was something about laughter which drained one's strength and will; and instead of feeling relieved, he felt more dazed and disillusioned....They continued walking. His legs felt wobbly, but Candice was there, helping him along. Candice was there, both supporting him and draining his strength....

"We'll just stay here for an hour or so," she began. "We'll go in and act naturally: you can flirt with as many old white women as you want," she joked again. "By then, somebody would have found the body and there won't be anything for you to worry about...."

They were nearing the building. About half a dozen police officers were in front of the door; and when Roland saw them, his guts seemed to knot themselves. A crowd of about 50 eager celebrity-seekers was waiting eagerly; and behind a barricade, a flock of paparazzi had their cameras at the ready, in expectation of the next celebrity. When Roland and Candice were about 20 meters from the entrance, a limousine stopped before the awning, and from it emerged a celebrity couple—whose name escaped Roland at the moment. The couple waved at the crowd and walked ceremoniously up the red carpet, into the building; and as they did so, the cameras of the paparazzi went off like machine-gun fire. Roland froze!

"Cameras!" he gasped, gaping at Candice. "You think that garage had surveillance cameras!"

"Don't worry about it," she assured him again. "Even if they do, that'll only prove that it was self-defense. You're Roland Micheaux—"

"You have *any* idea what can happen to us!" he yelled. "Footage of me knocking some guy's head in would *ruin* me! I may have just *killed* a man—doesn't that mean anything to you! I'm a goddamn lawyer...and I fled from the scene of a crime! We wiped the gun clean and ran away!"

"What are you talking about? You're *famous*, nothing—"

"America *hates* celebrities!" he raged, his mind instinctively going to the never-ending stream of celebrity scandals. "*Look* at them!" he ranted, pointing to the people standing before the entrance. "You really think they give a shit about me? They're freaking *vultures*!"

"Calm down, Roland!" she said, seeming concerned—and *sane*—for the first time. Some of the people in the crowd were looking in their direction, but it was dark; and despite his tuxedo, Roland looked too harried to be a celebrity of any importance, so they turned away.

"*Relax*," Candice cooed to him once again, to which Roland nodded nervously. "Come on," she said, coaxing him towards the entrance when he seemed to have collected himself. "You have those invitations?"

"Yea," he said, getting them out. His mind was blank, which was odd, since it was racing on at a feverish pace. Everything was passing him by. It was Candice who took the invitations and showed them to the police officer when they got to the entrance. It was Candice who waved and smiled at the crowd, positioning Roland so that they could pose for the paparazzi. The attention and applause was all proof that he was a rising star, but he was too preoccupied to care. For the first time in a while, he was thinking about his father. And Candice was wrong about the parking garage: at *first* he had merely defended himself, but then something had taken over. Some horrible instinct had possessed him, and it had felt good: had felt *natural*. There was a taunting, ever-present voice of vengeance in his soul, and that voice was his father's. Somewhere out there, his father was lying in wait, plotting his revenge, both against the world that had killed him, and the son that had deserted him in the moment of death. His father, finished with the forgiveness of God, was waiting to be released from hell on furlough—

Get a hold of yourself, Roland...! But he felt like a hapless fool who had gone too far down a treacherous road: there was no turning back. A man was lying back at the parking garage—*and that man could be dead*! There was still a chance to save the man by calling an ambulance, and yet Roland was doing nothing. He felt suddenly filthy—and irredeemably so. He had made a wrong turn, and was now falling helplessly into the gutter....

Candice and he were beyond the entrance now, passing through a grand anteroom, but he was too numb to notice such things anymore. There was an opening at an oblique angle from the front entrance; and through it, they could see and hear the banquet. About five hundred elegantly dressed people were milling about inside, and the sound of their laughter and conversation seemed to be an extension of the music that the live jazz quartet was playing. It all seemed so idyllic: as though that were some other world. Roland even saw the Mayor: the man was only about 10 meters from the door, surrounded by about 20 people, who looked at him eagerly, laughing uproariously at his punch lines—

But just then, in the direction of the front entrance, there came an even louder noise. It was like the undulating roar of a lion—a *pride* of lions. Roland and Candice abruptly whirled around; even those laughing at the Mayor's story stopped and turned in that direction. The noise crested in the air, confusing them all. It was almost supernatural in its intensity. Candice instinctively went to see what was happening; and Roland, like an insecure child that was terrified of losing his mother, followed her back to the front entrance.

When they got there, they saw that dozens—perhaps *hundreds*—of black people were now on the sidewalk. *How*, Roland couldn't even begin to explain it. It was as though time had gone haywire again. The people were *everywhere*, stopping traffic and displacing all the celebrity-seekers from the pavement. And they were chanting, "No justice, no peace!" with such vehemence that it was as though their voices would bring the world down. It was yet another thing for Roland's overburdened mind to account for. It was as if they had appeared out of the nothingness: been beamed there, straight from some netherworld. Roland felt as though he were unraveling from within; he was lost in a world of random violence, seeing corpses lying in the darkness, felled by his own hand; and now, here were these people, standing in the night like some satanic cult, chanting the words—the *incantations*—which would bring down the world. He couldn't take it anymore! He needed to stop and clear his head—press some cosmic pause button—but the world was marching on wildly—

And in the meantime, while the people chanted, the cameras of the paparazzi went off with the same machine-gun-like explosiveness. Network camera crews were now on the scene, also joining in the fray; and while all this went on, the six police officers stood before the door, desperately calling for backup. The chaos all reminded Roland of going to see his father that day; and placed in that light, the body in the parking garage was an omen of coming madness. He had killed, just as his father had killed; and like his father, he had looked at the work of his hands and fled like a scared nigger—

"No justice, no peace!" the people screamed into the night. And as he fought to make sense of it—or at least to protect himself from it by giving it some tangible form—Roland realized that the protest was most likely for some unarmed black youth that had been killed by the police a few nights ago. It all came back to him from bygone gleanings of the news. Four undercover officers on a drug sweep had shot the kid 27 times—some inconceivable number like that—thinking that his cell phone was a gun. The police shooting had been all over the news for *days*: was *everywhere*. One couldn't look up without hearing comments from the police commissioner or the Mayor or the victim's crying mother. Even Roland had felt himself being swept up when the story first came out, but one couldn't honestly be outraged by something that occurred so frequently that it was clearly systematic; because one couldn't honestly talk about "the system" anymore, without sounding like a nut from the 60s, or a deluded conspiracy theorist, trying to get everyone else to see ghosts. The reality was that most people would look at the story for a while then become confused and frustrated—or bored and annoyed; and to get rid of the discomfort, they would allow themselves to forget, with that well-cultivated, "who the hell cares" attitude hovering in the back of the American consciousness, and move onto something that they understood, like the latest celebrity gossip, or the NBA playoffs.

But while the people in front of the banquet hall chanted, Roland felt as though his head were being pried open, and that all the politics and gossip and self-destructiveness of his society was being shoved inside. He was drifting further away from reality now. None of it seemed real anymore: not the corpse in the garage, not the chanting crowd...He felt, strangely enough, as though he were trapped in someone else's dream, forced to make sense of her delusions and neuroses. Roland was about to retreat into the banquet hall when he detected footsteps at his back; and looking over his shoulder, he saw the Mayor followed by *dozens* of people! He felt trapped again—*trapped within the randomness*. In desperation, he quickly moved to the side—as if fearful of being trampled. Several bodyguards were trying to restrain the Mayor now, yelling that it wasn't safe, but Randolph scoffed at this, especially when he looked into the night and saw that the protest was being led by Charles Marenga. The latter was a tuxedo-clad, rotund black man about 55, whose history of flamboyant protest had made him a kind of laughingstock—particularly to the mainstream. In fact, Randolph instinctively smiled when he saw the man.

As for Roland, he felt *sick*. He put his hands to his ears, futilely trying to block it all out. He tried telling himself that he was Roland Micheaux, Millionaire Corporate Lawyer, etc., etc.; but no matter what he tried, he kept seeing the body lying in the darkness of the parking garage; and there was his father's grinning face, and countless other maddening images; and now, on top of everything, the strangely melodic chants of the crowd made him want to scream out and run away, betraying to the world that he was no longer sane. The world seemed to be swirling before his eyes: he felt like he was only moments away from passing out. These seemed like the last moments of his life; but just then, when he happened to glance up, Randolph, who was still on his way to the entrance, winked at him—their usual greeting. Roland barely managed to nod....

Mayor Alexander Randolph was a tall 48-year-old, who had been a star athlete in his youth; and as the man stopped in the doorway, looking out boldly, he seemed so heroic that cameramen scrambled to get a shot of him. Added to the sudden outburst by the media, Charles Marenga stepped up as far as the police officers would allow him. He brought with him a microcosm of black rage—if not black insanity; and at the sight of Randolph, the people's chants intensified. It was again as though their words would bring the world down—make buildings crumble at their foundations...cause streets to rip open and buckle as if from underground fault lines. Marenga was waving his hand wildly in the air now—they all were. He and his gangly sidekick, Botswana Glade, were urging the people on to even more hatred and outrage and madness...and it only seemed to be a matter of time before the world crumbled around them.

Still, despite all of that, Randolph seemed perfectly at ease as he surveyed the situation and inquired in a booming voice: "What's the problem?" Strangely enough, the chants stopped. Some people—particularly those from the banquet—naturally relaxed and smiled, because that was Randolph's catch phrase: the slogan which had led him into City Hall four years ago, and which was constantly being repeated in his re-election commercials. In the sudden silence, Marenga screamed back:

"You and this racist system are the problem, Randolph!"

"*Yea*!" Botswana Glade and the rest of the protesters screamed in unison. [Roland's head was swirling!]

"A young, *unarmed* black man has been shot by the police!" Marenga screamed. "—*Murdered*! Ruthlessly gunned down by 27 bullets! And you have the *nerve* to be holding a banquet!"

"*Yea*!" the protesters yelled once again.

The tension in the air seemed palpable; some cosmic explosion seemed imminent—at least to Roland. Nevertheless, Randolph merely looked on with pursed lips, then smiled as he said: "Do you want to come in, Marenga?"

"...What?"

"I see you came in your tuxedo," he said, and there was laughter from the people at Randolph's heels, while Marenga and his protesters looked on confusedly. It was while Marenga was standing there, somewhat disarmed by Randolph's question, that Randolph walked down, past the six officers, and gripped the much shorter Marenga by the shoulders, saying:

"Come in, come in..." There was something compelling about Randolph's manner; and he was so decisive, that in a matter of seconds, he brought Marenga though the entrance, leaving the rest of the protesters standing there ineptly; and as easily as that, the protest was over. Botswana Glade and the rest of Marenga's cronies looked like puppies watching their master go. There was something sorrowful and pathetic about them now.

"We'll talk later," Roland heard Randolph say to Marenga as they walked past him. "Man can't live on politics and conflict alone," Randolph laughed in a louder voice; and then, poking Marenga in his pendulous gut, "—see how bloated it's gotten you!" Everyone again laughed as Marenga, scowling slightly, was whisked away. But despite the scowl, there was a look of hopelessness on his face as he seemed to ask himself how in the hell Randolph had managed to do it to him!

Roland looked at it all, and was acutely aware that the world was mad.

* * *

ALL THE GUESTS WERE RETURNING TO THE MAIN HALL now, most of them talking excitedly amongst themselves—like children after a Saturday matinee. Even while aftershocks from the parking garage continued to eat away at him, Roland was relieved beyond reason that the protest seemed to be over. Just the sound of their voices had been maddening. As such, while the other guests returned to the banquet hall, Roland wanted to stand there by himself and recover his composure. And the dark images of the parking garage were now taking on supernatural dimensions. It was not even criminal prosecution or his own conscience that he feared anymore, but something more amorphous and dire. He had to find a way to reconcile those dark realities—to purge his soul of them—before they drove him mad. He was just beginning to convince himself that he would eventually master the situation, when Candice—whom he had forgotten about entirely—once again looped her arm through his and pulled him along. He took a few unsteady steps towards the main chamber of the hall when, all at once, a voice boomed:

"Micheaux!"

Looking up in alarm, Roland saw one of the partners from his firm: Dallas Phelps! Just the sight of this man, who was so indelibly associated with all that Roland had spent the last 20 years building—*and all that he stood to lose*!—pushed him towards the edge again. He felt his mind lurching off wildly once more, conjuring more horrors as it went. Phelps was a white man in his 40s with premature gray, almost *white*, hair, who always reminded Roland of Steve Martin. The man came up to Roland, giving him a hearty handshake and patting him on the shoulder. Roland, feeling himself drawing closer and closer to the edge, had to bite his lip to keep from screaming. Alarm bells were going off inside of him. He kept seeing the body lying on the dusty concrete of the parking garage.

He had *killed* a man, and now there was no going back: no way to purify the evil and reclaim his soul. For the first time in years, Roland felt helpless before the world—wanted to *run* from it. He again had an urge to scream and rant—and vent all the irrationality surging within! He looked at Phelps' smiling face and knew that self-preservation meant getting away: *fleeing*...But somehow getting in touch with the remnants of his reason, he knew that in the interim, he had to play along; and pooling all his will, he forced himself to smile: to effect the intonations and expressions of the world in which he was currently stranded. He felt as if his face were going to crack—his smile, or whatever passed for it, felt that phony. He didn't know how much longer he could keep it going. However, just then, as though offering him a reprieve, Phelps, in that annoyingly cliché social way, looked at Candice and asked, in the third person:

"Who is this *beautiful* young woman?"

Roland distractedly introduced Candice to Phelps; she quickly took the lead and introduced herself.

"I like your accent," Phelps declared, smiling down at her.

"Oh, you like talking, do you?" she joked in her usual fashion. "You must be one of those new sensitive men."

"I ain't too sensitive," Phelps howled, "but I've been known to bruise easy!"

While they laughed, Roland found them both insufferable. He had an urge to leap at them and strangle them both!

Control yourself, Roland!

"Hey, Dallas," Roland broke in, his voice strangely winded, "why don't you take her to get a drink—I have to use the bathroom."

"It would be my honor," Phelps said quickly, offering her his arm. And without further ado, they walked away together, into the hall. Phelps, Roland just then remembered, was married to one of those blond, Barbie Doll wives. As Roland watched Phelps sauntering away with Candice, he suddenly doubted that the wife, Cindy, was here. But he also didn't care. To hell with them all....

He needed to rest: to get away and clear his head; but now that he was alone, another of the aftershocks from the parking garage drained more of his strength and will. The banquet that he had once thought of as a social triumph, now had a macabre edge to it. The banquet was a wake; the music that was playing, was a dirge, and the corpse about to be lain at their feet, was his own—

Get a hold of yourself, man!

Just five or ten minutes alone in a bathroom stall should be enough for him to compose himself. Looking around for the bathroom, he saw that the jazz quartet was playing on a dais on the far side of the room; and that next to that dais, there was an archway, above which were the icons for the bathrooms. He took a step in that direction when, all of a sudden, a skinny black man of middle age, with a bushy afro that was way out of style, stepped before him.

"Ah, Mr. Micheaux," the man said in a deep baritone that was out of proportion with his gaunt frame, "—I *knew* you would be here!" The man then pat Roland on the shoulder, looking up at him as though they were old friends.

Roland again bit his lip to keep from screaming! It was as if something had exploded in his head! He couldn't take it anymore! An entire world of random idiocy! It was driving him mad. He had a sudden impulse to bash the man's head in; and as he realized this, more of his precious strength was drained away! *Relax, Roland*! But even that plea—and the desperation evident behind it—only drained more of his sanity. The man was still staring at him knowingly; and Roland, marshaling his strength, blurted out: "—I'm sorry—do I *know* you?" But even as he said it, he avoided eye contact with the man, anxiously looking in the direction of the bathroom.

"You've been trying to know me all your life," the man responded matter-of-factly.

What...? Roland felt as though the room were swirling! The feeling of hysteria again welled up inside of him, so that he felt himself even closer to screaming and ranting. Desperate to get away, he made a curt nodding gesture with his head and went to leave, but the man again stepped into his path.

"—What the *hell* do you want!" Roland cursed, no longer even pretending to remain calm. He stood there panting like a beast, while the man laughed and shook his head in a self-deprecating manner.

"I'm sorry," he laughed, seemingly oblivious of Roland's outburst—of the murderous rage in his eyes. The man again patted Roland on the shoulder, going on: "I got so excited that I forgot to introduce myself. My name is Jasper Kain, Mr. Micheaux. I am a statistician for the Mayor." Kain stretched out his hand then, and

Roland shook it confusedly.

"A pollster?" Roland said, fighting to understand—and to *focus*.

"Yes. I do calculations and give probabilities."

"—You said you were expecting me?" he went on quickly. He was taking deep breaths to calm himself—and it seemed to be working.

"Yes: you are part of a survey I've been keeping."

"*Me*?"

"Yes."

"I…I don't understand." And he didn't. He was so far gone that he didn't know if that lack of understanding was a result of his mind being unable to decipher Kain's words, or because Kain's words were indecipherable. A side of him suspected that his mind was skipping over entire sentences, discarding huge chunks of vital information—

"Everything will be made clear tonight!" Kain suddenly exulted—or so it seemed to Roland. "Ever since you won that big freedom of speech case," the man continued, "I've been keeping an eye on you, Mr. Micheaux. You're an inevitable byproduct of these times. Since back then, I *knew* that we were all going to be here on this night—all the big players: you, Marenga, Randolph, Botswana Glade…Probabilities are becoming certainties, Mr. Micheaux!" the man said, smiling triumphantly.

"What are you talking about?" Roland said from the depths of his frustration. And just then, he abruptly looked in the direction of the quartet—the music seemed strangely cacophonous just now; the surrounding laughter all at once seemed disconnected and unsettling. It was all a warning for him to get away. He felt as if the ground were falling away beneath him. And as another of the aftershocks from the parking garage hit him, he shuddered, as though a jolt of electricity had gone through him. The image of the corpse lying in the darkness, and Phelps's good cheer, and Marenga's shouting match with Randolph, and all the other random events, were swirling in his mind. He definitely couldn't take much more. The world seemed to be going out of focus; and for a moment, he found himself wondering if Kain, with his bushy afro and his disconcertingly deep voice, was even real. Maybe the man was some delusion cooked up by a mind that had long cracked. He shook his head to drive away those thoughts, but everything seemed useless now. He was losing his grip, disappearing into the darkness within himself—

"You've been thinking about the end of the world," Kain said—again seemingly out of nowhere.

Roland stared at him for a long while: it took him that long to focus himself—to re-imbed himself in reality. "...What?"—and then, remembering his conversation with Candice—"Did Candice send you over?"

"No one *sent* me, Mr. Micheaux. I'm here because of your madness: I was *drawn* to you."

Roland stared on confusedly, his face creasing as he tried to make sense of it. "...What is this, some joke?" he said at last. It *had* to be a joke: that was the only thing that made sense. Grasping at straws, it occurred to him that maybe Candice—or some playful colleague at work—had put the man up to this; maybe all of it, including Candice's annoying weirdness and the beating in the parking garage, was some prank that was spiraling out of control; and suddenly desperate for the great punch line which would release him, he eked out a twitching grin and blurted out: "It's a joke, *right?*"

But Kain only shook his head solemnly. "Why is it that people only ask that question when it is clear to them that nothing funny has been said? I am here because of *madness*, Mr.—"

"Stop it!" Roland demanded. "Look, I don't know who put you up to this, but it's not funny anymore."

"I'm not here to *amuse* you, Mr. Micheaux."

"I don't give a shit *why* you're here!"

"—Of course you do," Kain laughed, still calm. "Thanks to your father, you've been trying to understand madness all your life—"

"*Stop it!*" Roland screamed hysterically; several people in nearby groups looked up at him sharply. "*Shut up!*" Roland repeated.

But Kain continued to laugh softly, seeming satisfied. There was something murderous in Roland's eyes—he could have easily snapped the man's neck; but after a second or so, he found himself snickering nervously. It *had* to be a joke! He looked around expectantly for Candice—or even Phelps—still waiting for them to come out and yell, "Gotcha!" He needed to laugh—*needed to think that it was all worthy of laughter*—but he was suddenly out of breath...Had Kain mentioned his father? Of course not...nobody knew about his father—not even the media (as hard as that was to believe). He had always been able to deflect their questions about that aspect of his past, saying simply that his father had died when he was young. Nevertheless, he suddenly realized that he was sweating profusely. It was all collapsing around him, and he didn't know how much longer he could keep himself together. He once again looked around for Candice—this time in desperation. However, in the end, the great climactic joke remained unrealized; and like before, the only point of reference he had in the world of men, was Jasper Kain. Kain was his reality. He looked desperately at the man, part of him still wondering if the man was even real; and then:

"I thought you said your goal in life was to figure out the mysteries of the universe, Mr. Micheaux?"

Roland looked up sharply! As Kain looked at him coyly, a cold, creepy feeling went down Roland's spine. *That's what he had said to Candice back in the parking garage*! How the hell could the man know about that! A hundred irrational thoughts went through his mind in the blink of an eye, all of them draining a little more of his strength.

But Kain laughed calmly then, going on: "No need to be distraught, Mr. Micheaux: I'm not a mind reader."

But how else could the man know what Roland was thinking! Roland had taken another one of those blind steps into the nothingness, and now everything seemed to be turned on its head. He had lost all perspective, so that the man now standing before him was a creature of infinite dimension and possibility. And, on top of everything, Kain's continued ease tore away at something vital in him. The man seemed to know him—seemed to be his *master*—and it was while Roland stood there, feeling as if he were on the threshold of something horrible, that the man again laughed softly, saying: "The fact of the matter is, Mr. Micheaux, that I followed you tonight—"

"*What*!"

"I know everything that happened in the parking garage—quite inadvertently, of course. [Roland's jaw dropped!] I'm not normally a snoop, Mr. Micheaux. But as I said, I've been keeping a survey, of which you're a part. I had already parked in the parking garage and was walking out to the banquet, when I saw you driving into the parking garage with your girlfriend. Candice, right?" he said, frowning, while Roland stood before him like a frail old man. "Like I said, I didn't mean to spy," he went on with a chuckle, "even though the evidence does make it seem so. See, I had intended to walk down and introduce myself to you right then, but when I got there, you and your lady friend were too preoccupied. [Roland twitched.] I must admit that I was rather like a snoop when I crouched by the door and listened to your conversation; and then, when you were getting ready to leave, I snuck behind one of the columns. Thank goodness Candice asked you what you were running from: that gave me time to make my escape. I didn't want us to be introduced on those terms, with you thinking that I was a garden-variety peeping tom. I stayed in the shadows...and I saw it all; and now, I'm even more convinced that you're just the man I need."

Roland exhaled forcefully! (He had unconsciously been holding his breath.) "What do you want from me!" he managed to whisper, looking pale and distraught. "—You want money!" he said with a suddenly hoarse voice. But Kain only laughed out then, again with his usual calmness, going on:

"First of all, I wanted to point out a simple fact to you, Mr. Micheaux: people are all too willing to believe in the supernatural when facts dictate a more mundane answer. I profess no powers other than those of quiet observation and attention to detail. Those skills will serve you well as I tell you about the facts of the world, Mr. Micheaux."

Roland could only stare; his mind kept repeating, *He knows*! For a moment, he was again overcome by the urge to bash the man's head in. But he shook his head to chase away those thoughts. He had to figure out what to do! Of course, with his mind a wreck, nothing came to him; and to bide his time, and keep Kain occupied until he could figure something out, he instinctively blurted out: "*What* facts?"

"Like I said before: the facts you've been trying to understand all your life."

Sensing where Kain was going, Roland shook his head, like a fool begging his attacker for mercy. "Look," he pleaded then, "I can't really talk right now—" And as he said it, he looked around nervously for Candice and Phelps. But Kain shushed him as if he were a disagreeable baby, going on:

"I know you, Mr. Micheaux, because I know myself—and I understand madness."

"—I'm not crazy!" Roland blurted out, perhaps somewhat defensively. The sweat was streaming down his face now, and he was a mess. Still, Kain's only reaction to Roland's outburst, was to again laugh calmly—the way someone laughed at a child's foolishness.

"Don't misunderstand me, Mr. Micheaux," Kain started with his usual ease and self-possession. "When I talk about madness, I am not talking of that sensationalized drivel you see in tabloid news broadcasts. One shouldn't confuse chaos and madness. You turn on the news today, and all you see is chaos: murder, rape, self-destruction…

"On the other hand, " Kain continued, while Roland looked on in utter disarray, "the madness you have inside of you—*true* madness—is subtle. Unlike chaos, it doesn't have to bare its wares garishly, like an old whore on a street corner: it sneaks up on you, so that you don't know it's there. You become comfortable with it; *it* becomes your reason, and you start using it to make decisions. [Roland was trembling!] It takes over everything, Mr. Micheaux, and you never realize it. In fact, when men like yourself, Randolph and Marenga—and God only knows how many others—become endowed with enough of this madness, the world of chaos and self-destruction is *bound* to come crashing down—"

"Look, I'll pay whatever you want!" Roland cried in desperation, but Kain only looked up in surprise, then pity, before laughing:

"You think this is about money?"

"Look, I'm ready to talk reasonably—I'm sure we can arrange something."

"You think I'm trying to blackmail you for a couple bucks?" Kain laughed then, in genuine disbelief.

"Then what do you want from me?"

"I want your *soul*, Mr. Micheaux."

"My *what?*" And, for some reason, he snickered, "Who are you supposed to be, the Devil?"

"Of course," he said, matter-of-factly. At first, Roland snickered, but when the man didn't smile, an eerie shiver went up Roland's spine and he retreated to another level of numbness—

"You know what's wrong with the world?" Kain went on with a sigh, as Roland sunk deeper into the depths. "Everyone prefers mystery and romanticism to facts. [Roland went to shake his head—] That's what's wrong with the fucking world," Kain cursed now, seeming to grow annoyed for the first time. "Everybody's like cigarette smokers. They smoke the goddamn things for 40 years, knowing full well how filthy they are, and then when they get cancer, they sue the tobacco companies, saying that they were duped. That's the great loophole of stupidity, Micheaux: seeing your problems as the result of someone else's scheming."

"Look," Roland tried to plead with him—

"No, *you*, look!" Kain raged. "I've been patient with you, Micheaux, but I have some things to say to you, so shut the hell up! [Roland cringed like a scared puppy!] And stop that goddamn shivering!"

Roland, for the life of him, nodded compliantly, wiping away a stream of sweat from his forehead.

"Okay," Kain resumed, trying to refocus himself. "...Let's get to the heart of the matter, Mr. Micheaux. It felt good to kill that man, didn't it?"

"*What*!" he peeped, feeling yet another wave of alarm going over him.

"It felt good to beat that man with your bare hands! Don't lie to me now!" he warned when Roland began looking around nervously, as though trying to hedge. "You got off on it, didn't you? *Well*!"

"—Yea, I guess," he blurted out, responding more to the insistence in the man's voice than anything else.

"You *guess*?" the man laughed, now with a certain amount of derision. "You've never felt such freedom before. Even now, what worries you, is not the act, itself, or the consequences, but that you enjoyed it so much: that you were able to slip into it so easily and totally."

"No—I'm not like that!" he cried defensively, looking even more distraught.

"—Come off it, Micheaux!" Kain laughed. "That was the single greatest moment of your life! [Roland shook his head feebly.] You've done something that most people only *dream* about! In a few seconds, you've seized the power of the gods, and are now ready to take your rightful place in society."

—Roland again shook his head: it was the only thing he could manage—

"You're a *killer*, Micheaux," Kain continued, "just like Candice said. [Roland was still shaking his head feebly.] *See*," Kain laughed now, "even she could sense the greatness in you—and sense the wonderful madness to come. That's right," Kain continued, fully in the throes of his rant, "all the self-destruction you see out there on the streets is a sign that we're on the path to greatness—"

"What are you talking about?" Roland mumbled, looking dazed and wretched.

"I'm answering all your questions, Micheaux: cueing you in on the business side of death and madness. In fact, self-destruction is the most successful product that our society has ever produced, Micheaux. Every time you see a 13-year-old gunning down his classmates, you see a successful business transaction. That child has bought a product he has seen advertised all his life! But not only has he bought the product, he *becomes* the product—and we in turn become the consumers! We don't tune in to the news merely to be *informed*—but to be *entertained*! You said it yourself when you saw those people waiting outside the banquet: They're *vultures*, waiting around for scandal and death! That's how fucked up we've become as a society: we're reassured when somebody else's life is more fucked up than ours! But that's the beauty of capitalism, Micheaux: everything can be commodified—even death and suffering!"

"—What are you talking about!" Roland moaned again, but:

"*And take note*," Kain's voice rose above his, "I'm not talking about people being brainwashed by TV or being desensitized to violence—none of that insipid shit! I am saying that they *need* it, like we've come to think we need a BMW. In fact, we are no more brainwashed than one is brainwashed into buying a pair of Nike's!"

Roland blinked slowly—as though doing so required effort—

"And while there have always been murders and rapes and all of that, with *TV*, we have added a new, perverse element, Mr. Micheaux: an *audience—a vital consumer base*! [Roland nibbled his lower lip nervously, wondering how the hell he was going to get away.] In fact," Kain continued, "if death were on the stock market, its stockholders would be rich beyond reason! People are talking about the Internet Revolution: we're in the midst of the *Death* Revolution!"

"—What are you talking about!" Roland groaned in frustration, repeating the phrase that had become his mantra.

"—Why do you think the lead story of the evening news is almost always the most violent story, Micheaux? That pulls in viewers—*consumers*! In fact, all the crime and violence and self-destruction you see on TV are no different from McDonald's hamburgers and Diet Coke! They are *products*, and everyone's buying!"

"—*What are you talking about*!" Roland screamed in frustration, unable to take it anymore. "I have no idea what you're talking about!" he cried, looking as though he were on the verge of tears. "Nothing you're saying…*none* of it makes sense! What do you want from me?"

"I'm telling you the facts of life, Micheaux! I'm talking about shit and piss and all the mess you got inside of you! I'm talking about a society that's *buying* its own destruction: consuming its own filth, and yet can't understand that it's poisoning itself!"

"—So *what*!" Roland ejaculated. "What does that have to do with anything—or with *me*! [People in nearby groups were still looking at them oddly; Roland lowered his voice and leaned into Kain.] Look, if you're going to blackmail me, *blackmail* me already!"

"Okay," Kain laughed maliciously. "You want to be blackmailed? Shut the hell up or I'll tell everyone what you've done! [Roland's face went blank and he seemed to shrink away.] How is that for blackmail, Mr. Micheaux?" Kain laughed. "Close your fucking mouth and listen to what I have to say or I'll ruin your goddamn life! How is that? Do you understand me now?"

Roland stared at the man hopelessly for a moment, then nodded. A stream of sweat went down his temple again, and he wiped it away nervously.

"Okay, Mr. Micheaux," Kain went on with a sigh, "you asked what this has to do with you. Obviously you haven't been listening to me, but I'll tell you one more time. This society loves raising people up, and loves tearing them down—look at all the celebrity scandals. It's like a kid with those building blocks: building becomes part of the process of destruction—and of pleasure. This is our new national pastime—which is where you come in. You're like Michael Jordan, Mr. Micheaux: you can do no wrong—the perfect media object. The only thing is that nobody suspects the madness you have inside. [Roland went to shake his head, but was suddenly too weak to do even this.] You've always been at odds with the world, Mr. Micheaux," Kain continued, "—even before they killed your father—but you're going to be the seed that brings all the chaos crashing down. You're a new paradigm, Mr. Micheaux—a new *product*: a kind of Trojan Horse, ready to deliver our blessed madness to a society that is already devouring you whole. You, Marenga, Botswana Glade, Randolph—even Charlotte McPrice, Randolph's opponent in the upcoming election...*all* of you are part of it; and all those fools out there are going to gobble you up before they even realize what you are—"

But somehow, miraculously, Roland was laughing again. He put his head back and laughed helplessly. At first, he laughed simply because it occurred to him that Kain was mad. But then, he became lost in the laughter—*trapped* within it. It sounded and looked horrible: was more like the baying of a wild animal, than human laughter. It shook his entire body, seeming as though it were rending his insides. He had gone too far; and now, he was being consumed by the laughter, the way a lunatic was consumed by his delusions. He now had no idea what was going on around him—no way of even making sense of it.

As expected, Kain stood there calmly, smiling as he watched Roland being consumed by the madness; and suddenly realizing that he had lost control, and that he had absolutely no idea why he was laughing, Roland stopped abruptly. When he looked up, the nearby people were frowning at him. Roland had to get away: flee while he still realized that he *should* flee! In a last-ditch effort to save himself, he tried to walk off—

"You're not going anywhere!" Kain laughed mordantly, gripping Roland's arm. "You've wanted to talk about this all your life," Kain went on. "You've been brought up in madness—*nourished* by it—"

"*Shut up*!" Roland begged. But Kain held him there, seemingly with little effort.

"—Just a little bit more," the man explained, "then you can go...[Roland shook his head feebly—like a toddler trying to exert its will.] I'm about to go and do something now, Mr. Micheaux," Kain went on, still holding Roland's arm, "and you need to know why—"

Roland shook his head, again looking as though he were going to cry—

"*Listen* to me, Mr. Micheaux!" Kain demanded, to which Roland looked up in dismay and helplessness. "...There's no reason to fear violence—no matter how self-destructive it seems. Death never killed anyone," he said with a chuckle. "In fact, this is a joyous time," Kain continued. "The foundation has already been set; now, all I have to do is play my part and hook them in. *Yes*," Kain said, while Roland looked on, feeling his substance and sanity being siphoned off, "I'm going to talk to them like your father talked to them. [Roland recoiled!] I'm going to inject myself into the intravenous tube that's filling their veins with the self-destruction and scandal they crave. And being a student of this society, I know that a guaranteed way to get people's attention and hold onto it for at least a few weeks, is to *kill* [Roland shuddered!]—slaughter as many people as I can—just like those 13-year-olds! That's *guaranteed* to get people's attention, Mr. Micheaux—guaranteed to attract *consumers*!

"I'm going to be the ultimate product, Mr. Micheaux," Kain went on, his face horrible, "—and I am going to do it through the very violence they're addicted to. And when they gather around to consume me, I'll rip their goddamn heads off! I'll set off the explosion that will clear the way for you and all the others to finish off the job! I'll be everything they want—let them gorge their filthy bellies on me. But I'll be too pure for them," he laughed, "—like heroin right out of the vat. They'll overdose on what I've got: puke out their goddamn guts and burst their veins with what I got!"

And then Roland shuddered as the man began to laugh. It was as though Roland had been hit by a cold breeze that reached some inner place that he had never even known existed. Still, Kain only smiled when he saw that Roland—on some level—understood. It was then that the man released Roland's arm. Looking suddenly peaceful, the man smiled and walked away from Roland then, navigating his way through the banquet. Roland, numb beyond reason, followed Kain with his eyes, shuddering when the man looked back to make sure that he was still watching—

At that moment, the music stopped. The Mayor stepped up on the dais and was waving his hands to get everyone's attention. Something churned in Roland's gut as he realized that Kain was walking straight for the Mayor! Roland started off in that direction himself, rudely pushing past old ladies as he looked nervously from Kain to the Mayor. The Mayor was talking on the microphone, telling a chaffing story about Charlotte McPrice, his Democratic opponent in the election that fall—

"Roland?" It was Candice. She and Phelps were standing in his path, looking at him oddly. But he pushed past them and continued on his way. His eyes were on Kain, who had reached the dais; and just as Randolph was about to give his punch line, Kain leapt onto the dais. Randolph looked over at Kain confusedly; the bodyguards at the foot of the dais, who were used to seeing Kain around the Mayor, also didn't know how to react. But just then, when Roland was no more than 15 meters from the dais, Kain gripped the stunned Mayor around the neck with one hand, while taking a shiny metal object from his jacket pocket and putting it to Randolph's head, with the other. Kain had had to wrench Randolph's head down, because of the man's height. Some people, like the jazz quartet, instantly realized what was happening and darted for cover; others, perhaps succumbing to the morbid streak Kain had raved about, craned their necks for a better view. Several screams pierced the air now. Roland gasped, unable to move from the spot. *Kain was actually doing it*...! The bodyguards went to attack, but:

"Stand back or I'll do it!" Kain yelled over the microphone, giggling to himself as they all backed away grimly. Everyone stared up at him in the sudden silence, unable to quite believe what was happening. Roland was beyond numb. *This is it*! he kept thinking. This was the coup de grace of his descent into madness. Kain made eye contact with him at that moment, as if to confirm this. Kain was about to blow the Mayor's brains out, but it was nothing but Roland's final rite of initiation. This entire night—Roland's entire *life*, in fact—had been nothing but a rite; and beyond this moment, there would be nothing but death and madness. He had the feeling that he was floating in an ocean—drifting on the current—and that there was nothing around him for hundreds of kilometers. He felt as though he were slightly out of phase with the surrounding reality—and Kain had done it all! Kain was about to kill the Mayor of New York City, and only seconds earlier, the man had been standing with Roland—*touching* Roland; Kain, who continued to grip the quailing Mayor around the neck, was Roland's only link to the world, and that reality confirmed the truism he had discovered on the day he went to see his father: madness was keeping the world sane—

But just then, when he thought he had figured it all out, someone near the front looked up at Kain and whispered, "What the hell is that in his hand?" And in response to this, everyone looked up at the implement in Kain's hand, frowning. They had all thought that it was a gun, but—

"It's *him!*" someone whispered in frightened awe.

"*Who?*" several more people whispered in confusion.

"It's the Hair Jacker!" an old man squeaked, just as Kain flipped a switch and started up his clippers. The man laughed out triumphantly then, sounding like a cartoon villain; and then, in two deft swoops, the quickness of which no one could believe, Kain shaved the Mayor's head, leaving only a stubby, misshapen Mohawk.

Jasper Kain is the Hair Jacker…? Roland tried to understand it, but it was all happening too quickly for him. The accumulated bizarreness of the night was too much for his system. Indeed, they all seemed caught in that place, unable to move or make a sound—

But presently, not far from where Roland stood in his dumbfounded daze, there came a booming fit of laughter. Everyone looked to see Marenga squealing with delight. Indeed, the man seemed barely able to remain on his feet. While the Mayor's two burly bodyguards tackled the grinning Kain and dragged him off, and Randolph stood ineptly on the dais, feeling his butchered head, Marenga watched it all, squealing in delight. The man was now holding his pendulous gut as though it were going to burst. Tears now rolled down his cheeks as he pointed at the horrified Randolph and laughed at the beauty of the thing. All Randolph could do was stand there, looking like a naked man who didn't know how to get away from a crowd of onlookers. It all proved to be too much for Marenga when a conscientious old lady tossed Randolph her flowery church hat; and making do, Randolph pulled it low over his head and made a hasty—but utterly unglamorous—exit by way of the bathroom. Marenga practically doubled over at the sight of it; and by now, dozens of others were forcing back laughter themselves….Unfortunately for Marenga, just before the incident, while he was brooding over being thwarted by the Mayor, he had taken a mouthful of hors d'oeuvres (which had been tumbling from his mouth as he laughed); and as expected, some of them inevitably went down the wrong way, and he promptly began to choke. A doctor standing nearby recognized all the signs and ran over to help, but Marenga's gut was too big for him to perform the Heimlich Maneuver; and panicking, and weak from lack of air, Marenga fell to the ground, where he lay choking. Seeing him in that position, the doctor decided to improvise, and promptly did a kind of professional wrestling high dive onto Marenga's gut. There was a disconcerting squishing sound, the sound of Marenga hacking, and then the sight of the well-meaning doctor getting up with his face and tuxedo splattered with lumpy green paste.

On that ignominious note, the banquet was concluded.

* * *

ROLAND DIDN'T KNOW HOW HE HAD GOTTEN OUTSIDE: he simply became aware of it. It was as if he had been sleepwalking. He was standing against the outer wall of the banquet hall when wailing sirens from police cars startled him into consciousness. The sidewalk was packed with people from the banquet, curious onlookers and members of the media. A paddy wagon took off from the curb, sandwiched by two police cruisers, and as Roland watched the awe-stricken crowd, he was vaguely aware that Kain was in that paddy wagon. From the haze of his memories, he recalled how the police had put Kain in there: how everyone had come out to look, standing on the sidewalk as though mesmerized.

Now Kain was being driven away, disappearing down the block. Everyone stared at the procession in wonderment—perhaps none more so than Roland. Jasper Kain had gone on about violence and madness, and the end of the world, assuring Roland that he was to be the conduit for it all. Kain had clearly been mad—the fact that he had gone around shaving people's heads for the last two years was proof of it—but Kain was a part of him now. Kain had touched him—not only physically, but *spiritually*. It was as though Kain had *known* him: he couldn't get over that. And so, even while Kain's words were quickly becoming jumbled in his mind, Kain's madness was clear to him. He remembered how he had tried to laugh at Kain, but the madness of others was only reassuring when one thought one's self totally insulated from it. On some deep level, he understood Kain. There was a strange familiarity there, like déjà vu. He didn't believe in destiny or second sight or any of that, but there was something about Kain that troubled him, simply because it seemed so close to him—so *natural*.

And looking around at the huge crowd that continued to linger outside, even in Kain's absence, he knew that Kain had triumphed tonight—and not only over those in the crowd, but the millions soon to be swept up by the scandal and spectacle of the famous Hair Jacker's capture. Kain had worked his magic, and they were all trapped in his spell. Camera crews were now zipping around, interviewing people and trying to understand what had happened; but all at once, it occurred to Roland that what he needed was not understanding, but oblivion. Kain, and the events of the parking garage, and Candice—and *everything*, it seemed—was systematically draining the strength and will from him. He felt as though he needed a long, relaxing bath—and *sleep*. His was the kind of exhaustion that could only be counteracted by total inactivity. He didn't want to think anymore; he was tired of trying to make sense of and reconcile events that seemed as though they had sprung up from hell to confound him. And as he looked around, he felt like a newborn child watching a world whose points of reference were still meaningless to him. All that he had to guide himself, were instincts and fears and a lifetime of distrust—

"There you are!" someone cried; and startled, Roland looked up to see Candice and Phelps approaching. There was a tingle of excitement in Candice's eyes—as there seemed to be in everyone's eyes. "We've been looking everywhere for you," she went on. "Can you believe what just happened!" she said with a little laugh. "And remember how we were just talking about that Hair Jacker, too—how's that for a coincidence....You all right, Roland?" she said at last, detecting something in his forlorn expression.

"Just tired," he replied. And as he watched them, he knew that he couldn't be around them right now. "...Dallas," he started in a new voice, "you live in Brooklyn, don't you?"

"Sure."

"Can you drop off Candice for me—since you're both going in the same direction."

"Of course!" Phelps said with his usual good cheer. "My limousine is waiting on the corner right now."

"You sure you're all right?" Candice went on. "Didn't I see that Hair Jacker guy talking to you?"

"Yea."

"What'd he say?"

"Just a bunch of nonsense." But even as Roland said those words, it occurred to him that the danger of madness wasn't its departure from reality, but its veneer of plausibility. Kain had talked of violence and the world tearing itself apart: things which seemed, in retrospect, *trite*—

"Hey," Candice continued as something occurred to her, "I'm sure the TV guys would love to hear what he said—"

"*No*!" Roland said with too much force. When the other two looked at him oddly, he quickly went on, "I just want to go home and get some sleep." And then, to Phelps: "You sure dropping off Candice won't put you out?"

"Of course not."

"You don't mind, do you, Candice?" Roland asked.

"...Roland," Candice started again, still looking unsure, "...Since Dallas has his limousine ready, maybe we should drop you off or something—you can pick up your car tomorrow..."

"I'll be fine," he said. He was so desperate to get away from them that he didn't realize what Candice was saying about the parking garage. "I'll be fine," he said again—regardless of whether or not he thought that was true. "I'm just going to go home and get some sleep...Rosencrantz has been a slave-driver lately," he tried to joke. When nobody laughed, he simply nodded abruptly and walked off. Candice and Phelps stared after him, but he did not look back....

There were so many emergency vehicles and news vans parked in the street—not to mention curious onlookers—that traffic was hopelessly snarled. At the curb, sitting in the back of an ambulance, a disgruntled Marenga was receiving treatment, while camera crews videotaped the entire thing. With the traffic jam, Roland was easily able to make his way across the street. He needed to get away. He was running at last, jogging down the block. A kind of numbness came over him, and he was happy for it. It wasn't until he was in the parking garage, riding down the empty elevator to his sub level, that something vital occurred to him: *What if the body's still there*!

When the elevator doors opened up, he froze. Perhaps a good five seconds passed as he stood there, staring out into the dark, cavernous chamber. The body wasn't there! At least, it wasn't where they had left it. They had left it right by that column over there, but it was gone. A side of him, suddenly unable to believe in anything without concrete proof, began wondering if the incident had ever even happened; now that Kain was gone, he no longer existed, either—*only the truths of his madness*.

Roland stood in the elevator so long that the doors began to close. He threw out his arm to trigger the sensors, then he stepped outside. However, when the elevator closed behind him, he felt trapped—and *alone*. The body was gone, but the eeriness of the place remained. His car was parked on the far side of the chamber—next to the ramp and the stairs that led upstairs—and the thought that he would have to walk all the way across the dark, cavernous chamber by himself, was a little unnerving. As he began walking, his steps echoed horribly in the dark, empty expanse of the place. He kept looking around anxiously, as though expecting some monster to leap out of the shadows. It all reminded him of when he was a kid, visiting his grandmother out on the bayou. Her place had been in a dark, isolated enclave of the swamp; and upon occasion, when she sent him to the store, he had had to walk the nine kilometers by himself. Sometimes, it had been dark when he was coming back and he would be terrified of the eerie loneliness of the bayou. At those times, he would run all the way home, constantly imagining that he heard footsteps behind him. Every noise would seem like a prelude to death. He would always be running at full speed when he finally reached his grandmother's house, his exhaustion superseded by terror.

And now, back in the darkness of the parking garage, he realized that his pace had speeded up, and that those same childhood fears were coming over him. *Get a hold of yourself*! he cursed himself for the hundredth time that night. He was nearing his car, trying to get himself to relax, when he suddenly heard a moan; and looking fixedly at the staircase, which was right by his car, he realized that a man—*the* man—had collapsed in front of it! Roland froze. In a sense, it was like a nonbeliever seeing the face of God: all doubts fell away, and there was only fear and trembling. He wanted to run away, but something held him there—just like Kain had held him. For the first time, he wished that Candice had come along—even Phelps. He didn't want to be alone; but at that moment, a loud moan from the man made it clear that he wasn't. The moan had the strange effect of stunning him back into consciousness; and before Roland could think about what he was doing, he walked over to the staircase. The man was lying prone, just at the foot of the staircase. He was lying there, dying like an animal, and Roland suddenly knew that he couldn't just leave him there—regardless of all Candice had said to the contrary, and what might happen to himself. This, it suddenly occurred to him, was his chance to redeem himself—to prove that he wasn't some frightened lunatic in the making. This was his chance to fight off Kain and Candice and the ever-present specter of his father, and be a *man*.

Looking up, he noticed an emergency call box by the stairs. He walked over and picked it up; and when a man on the other end of the line answered, Roland calmly stated his name, his location, and the nature of the emergency. When that was concluded, he nodded to himself and replaced the receiver on the phone.

* * *

JASPER KAIN, IN HIS ERSTWHILE considerations of the world, had found himself thinking that the entire history of man could be related in a single sound: the loud, guttural growl of a beast. That growl subsumed all of its love, its altruism, its hatred and jingoism—everything that had allowed the perpetuation of the species. It was that growl which he now heard as he sat, chained in the darkness of the speeding paddy wagon; and it was that growl, suddenly resounding in the surrounding darkness, which reminded him of his mission. The paddy wagon was his universe; the eerie growls now rising around him, were a beacon back to a place that was pure and beatific. He sat there contentedly, reveling in the sensation of suffocating—actually, of being buried alive. It seized him for a moment, before passing into the triumphant daze that had come with his capture.

The paddy wagon's siren had a sick, unreal sound to it as it wailed in the night. He was chained into his seat, sitting erectly and proudly. Every time the speeding vehicle hit a pothole or swung around a corner, he was jostled and wrenched in the cold metal seat. The manacles were tight, cutting into the soft flesh at his wrists and ankles. But he liked the sensation somehow: liked the *realness* of it—especially after all that had happened over the past few years. This was it: the final step in his two-year plan. Now, they would all want to know why he had done it.

In fact, the media circus had already begun. The image of Kain holding his clippers to the Mayor's trembling head had been captured by a stationary camera from the banquet hall's balcony. The story was quickly becoming national news. Reporters were still broadcasting from the site of Kain's triumph, getting eyewitness reports. Considering the scope of what Kain had done, and to *whom*, in the end, he had done it, they would no doubt throw the proverbial book at him. Still, as he sat in the back of the speeding paddy wagon, Kain's sense of contentment was complete; if anything, he felt a sense of peace at the thought that there would be no more hiding—no more *running*. In fact, close at hand was the day when there would be no more running for any of them. One way or another, the spell of self-deception that kept society going, was going to be broken; all the invisible strings of their society, were finally going to be shown for what they were; and in getting himself arrested in this high-profile manner, Kain had insinuated himself into those strings—which connected everything, from the teachings of God to the ravings of politicians and the carefully researched high jinks of Ronald McDonald.

Kain looked at the world through the prism of his madness and it all became clear to him. Millions of people were out there now, marching in step with those invisible strings. They thought that they were modern men and women living in a logical universe, when everything they did, was a pagan tribute to the devil-gods that were torturing them. The gods of their society were even now whipping them up into a fury, shaping their dreams and ideals and souls through all the gossip and scandal and useless fluff that filled the airwaves.

Their gods appeared every fathomable guise—dangling happiness before their eyes. And this strange happiness demanded the latest cars and houses and high-tech gadgets, so that happiness not only had a price, but a corporate logo. And this strange happiness required that there was always something else to be attained and *consumed*—so that attaining happiness meant that one was never *content*. And to get the latest tantalizing products required power for factories, mines and vast tracts of land for raw materials…all the infrastructure and politics and inherent conflicts that went into pumping oil out of the ground and finding populations willing to work for the lowest possible pay. All this, just so that prices could be kept low enough that the factories could afford to run and people could afford to buy. And in their drive to attain this strange happiness, people had developed religions and party affiliations and television shows and commercials to tell them that they were doing all right, or that they could do better. And something was good if it made money, because that meant that someone was being made happy. And the proof of God's existence was in a gaudy billboard, flashing, "Buy me!" And those who didn't approve, were heretics; and those who realized that they were unhappy, were sinners; and those who set out to find happiness beyond the arbitrary dictates of the economy, were un-American, unwise, unrealistic dreamers who had no idea what kept the world running. And those who rebelled against at all the invisible strings, were either mad or in jail or looked upon pityingly by the rest of society as fools who didn't *deserve* to be happy. All this, Jasper Kain saw, and all this, he saw coming to a crashing end, either by his own hand, or through the logical dictates of the cosmos....

The wagon swerved around a final corner, then came to an abrupt stop. After the jolt of pain to his wrists and ankles, Kain waited patiently in the darkness. The sick wailing of the siren continued for a few seconds, then was cut off, leaving a horrible void. Kain could hear his own breath now; his heart, while not racing, was beating loudly and steadily. He waited. And then, suddenly, the doors at the back were hauled open, and into the great void rushed light and motion and sound.

The sudden chaos brought by the presence of so many agitated people, was like a violent explosion. There were now about a dozen blinding camera lights trained on him. The news had already gotten out that he was going to be there, and all these people had rushed over to get a glimpse of him. The voices of the reporters—and of the dozens (in his mind it seemed like *thousands*) of people in the crowd beyond them and the vigilant policemen—rose clangorously in the air. It sounded more like the banging of pots and pans than human voices; nevertheless, the din of them was like music to Kain's ears; the sight of the frantic crowd filled him with joy. Seeing what his two-year rampage had instilled in them, he was again at ease.

Presently, two policemen came in and unstrapped him from the seat; then, pulling him up gruffly, they hauled him out into the world. The dark, ugly precinct house was to his right as he exited. But the spring breeze was nice and cool on his skin. He smiled at the sensation, seeming like a drunkard as he stumbled along in his manacles. Finally in the light, his beaten, bruised face could be seen. The hematomas beneath his black skin, from when the bodyguards tackled and restrained him, made him seem even blacker—even more threatening. His afro was now a disheveled mess; and as the bystanders looked at the rest of him, they saw that the Hair Jacker wasn't as big and muscular as some of his victims, in their post-traumatic ranting, had claimed. He was actually of average height, and below-average weight. But as he had ascended to the status of media star, claiming all the mythology of a desperado, there was some unaccountable power about him. The dozens of cameramen were maneuvering for the best vantage points now, seeming like snakes wrangling with one another in a pit. A few of them, in their eagerness, tripped and fell to the ground, almost becoming trampled by their onrushing colleagues. Kain walked proudly before them—the way a general walked before his troops. True, they were still possessed by chaos, but if his plan went well, they would be co-opted by his madness. These were the ones who would go out into the world and spread the seeds of madness that he had been preparing. These were the future missionaries of his religion....

The reporters were now yelling an endless stream of questions at him. Their questions passed him in a meaningless blur—as did their faces; but then: "Will you plead insanity?" a reporter yelled, finally managing to crack the barrier of Kain's consciousness. Still stumbling along, Kain thought about it for a while, then laughed to himself—laughed *insanely*, they would report the next day.

He was still smiling when they finally marched him into the precinct house, and beyond the reach and sound of the mob stirring outside. He was satisfied, even though he knew that he and the world would never truly be at peace. He had done everything he could; and now, all that he could hope, was that it would be enough, and that his missionaries would be true ambassadors of his faith. In the end, human beings, all those fools out there, could only be moved by blunt force—by fear, anger, hatred...He wanted to suck the entire world into his madness—push it towards the precipice, and into the oblivion waiting beyond those craggy cliffs; but in a sense, he was like an arsonist who wanted to burn down an entire forest with one match: the placement of the spark was tantamount—and there were still random factors, like the wind and rain…and Roland Micheaux.

He was being marched through the building now. There were curious police officers standing in the corridors, looking on with the same awe as everyone else. They came out of their offices to get a look at him. There was a strange silence about the place—even other criminals, waiting to be booked, looked at him in awe.

In time, he was brought to an interrogation room. Two middle-aged white cops were there. They were both overweight and stood there with their shirt sleeves rolled up and cups of coffee in their hands. They were scrutinizing Kain closely, as though trying to come to some conclusion about him. Kain's escorts made him sit down in a seat before the two cops, then they left. The two cops were still observing Kain closely; after a while, they looked at one another and shrugged their shoulders: obviously he wasn't what they had been expecting—

"Lieutenants Franklin and Parks!" Kain laughed. The men again looked at one another, wondering how Kain knew them. "You're the leaders of the famous squad set up to capture me. Congratulations are in order, gentlemen!" Having said that, Kain sat there smiling at them; actually, on the wall across from Kain, there was a huge mirror, no doubt masking an observation room on the other side, and Kain looked at himself in the glass. His smile was so strange and unsettling, that one of the officers quickly spoke up:

"You've been apprised of your rights, sir?"

"I have—everything was aboveboard and legal."

The two men again exchanged an odd look as Kain sat there smiling at them.

"Can you state your name for the record?"

"My name is Jasper Kain."

"Are you really the Hair Jacker?" one demanded, jumping to the chase.

"Of course I am."

The two men's faces brightened.

"Did you have any accomplices?"

"Of course," Kain declared matter-of-factly. "My lawyer will tell you all about it."

The two men suddenly seemed crestfallen.

"Your lawyer? Things might go more smoothly for you if we did this without a lawyer."

But Kain only chuckled to himself before declaring: "I have no interest in making things go smoothly—I want as many entanglements as possible."

The two men again looked at one another confusedly.

"Okay," one groaned at last, "who's your lawyer?"

"Roland Micheaux, of course."

* * *

MAYOR RANDOLPH ARRIVED BACK AT Gracie Mansion, the Mayor of New York City's official residence, in a daze. The driver dropped him off at the door, and he walked in by himself. There were officers at the front door; he usually joked with them, but today he ignored them and walked in. What had just happened to him didn't seem conceivable! He headed for the luxurious dining room, where he would fix himself a drink. The TV was on in the room, and assuming that one of the servants was watching it, he was about to ask the offender to leave, when he looked in and saw his wife sitting there. She was an English professor and had left a week ago for some symposium or another. It was as though he had forgotten that she existed. She was still in her business suit—as though she had just arrived. She was a good-looking woman, but this sparked no reaction from him; even her presence sparked nothing in him but surprise.

"The symposium ended early," she said, staring at him intently.

He nodded; and as he looked over at the TV, he realized that the episode with Jasper Kain was already airing! When he shook his head, he realized that his wife was still looking at his head intently—and that he still had that old lady's flowery hat on. When his wife saw that he realized this, she started snickering.

"You think this is a joke?"

"Even you have to admit that it's a *little* funny."

He grunted noncommittally. She got off the couch and walked over to him:

"Let me see your head."

At first, he tried to keep her away, but with a deft grab, the hat was off. Instantaneously, she burst out laughing. He watched her sullenly for a while, as she stood there squealing with the same delight as Marenga, then he walked over to the couch, sitting down dejectedly before the television.

"Come on," she said when her laughter subsided, "you're overreacting."

"Am I?" he said in annoyance. "Kain was my *head* pollster! When that gets out...! I can see the headlines now: Randolph's policies steered by nut case."

After a while, she shrugged her shoulders, seeing the logic behind his words; taking one last sly glance at his head, she sat down beside her husband, watching the TV as well. "By the way," she went on, "Lester just called."

"And what does our wonderful son want? More money to blow on frat parties? Isn't school over yet?"

"Yea—he's going to Mexico with some friends for the summer. Anyway, that's not why he called. He saw the Hair Jacker thing on TV—"

"In *California*!"

"Yea, it's showing on CNN."

"*Goddamn*!"

"Alex...look, the story will go away eventually. It's only because they've been chasing that guy for two years now. He's become a kind of folk hero all over the country."

"It's on *CNN* already!" he said in disbelief. "Images of me getting my head shaved by a man who was not only a lunatic but a trusted aide, are being shown all over the goddamn country—"

"It could be worse."

"How could it *possibly* be worse! Why in the hell do people say stupid shit like that. 'It could be worse.'" he mocked her.

"I'm just trying to be helpful, okay."

"Well you're not helping!" he said, getting up and going over to mix himself a drink.

"Well..."—she searched for something hurtful to say—"the world doesn't revolve around you, Alex!" she screamed then, getting up and marching out of the room. Looking at her go, it suddenly occurred to him that he had never loved her. It wasn't that he hated her, but that he didn't have any intimate feelings for her. Twenty years ago, he had married her because she was the type of woman a man should marry: beautiful, intelligent...but he had never really loved her. He had married her for the same reason someone bought a Volvo station wagon: more out of considerations of security, than passion. They had acted towards one another the way married people were *supposed* to act; but in the end, it had all been an act. This realization, coming as it did on the heels of all that had happened that night, was both harsh and debilitating. For a moment, he wondered if he was simply being heartless—if this entire Hair Jacker thing had pushed him over the edge in some way—but he knew that it wasn't so. On some level, the reality of his marriage had always been clear to him. It was only that now it was being exposed at last—like a huge, ugly boulder uncovered by a flood. For the first time, perhaps in his entire life, he was overcome by a feeling of loneliness—and *fear*. This Hair Jacker thing had brought him to a place that he, the glib, confident politician, had never been before. Political necessity required that he get out and have a press conference as soon as possible—to put a political spin on the events of the night—but all he wanted to do was stay here and have a few drinks in private. For the first time in decades, he looked at the world not as a politician looking for votes, but as a man in search of his soul—and *truth*. It was this sudden deviation from the reasoned dictates of his life that put him on the path to ruin.

* * *

ROLAND GOT UP FROM THE GROUND when he heard the sirens coming down the ramp. He had been sitting on the ground—in his new tuxedo—staring at the shabbily dressed man. The latter had been lying there, breathing shallowly; in fact, Roland hadn't even been sure that the man was breathing at all. He could have checked somehow, but he had suddenly been terrified of touching the man. The man had seemed like a reanimated corpse, returning to death. It had either been that something unnatural was being corrected, or that nature was unraveling before his eyes. Lying there, prone before him, had been the reality of life—and of *death*. Life, the most powerful thing in the universe, had been showing itself to also be the most fragile; and it had suddenly occurred to him that human beings, who were perhaps destined to understand all there was to know about the stars and galaxies, were doomed to return to the great nothingness in what, in celestial terms, wasn't even the blink of an eye. Human beings, who, as they did on Earth, might one day possess the ability to destroy the very universe, had been of no consequence. But therein, had been the nature of man. It was only in destruction that he had power, and only in his ability to destroy the things around him, that he was able to cloak himself in the illusion of power over the nothingness within....

The ambulance came down first, followed by a police cruiser. Roland glanced at his watch: it was a little after 11 o'clock. As the paramedics rushed out, and the two police officers strolled up to survey the situation, Roland instinctively stepped away from the body.

"Do you know the victim?" a paramedic asked as he rushed to examine the body.

"No—he was lying there when I got here."

Looking at his tuxedo, one of the officers asked: "Hey, you just come from the banquet across the street?"

As Roland nodded, the man's partner said: "It's a madhouse out there! It took us 15 minutes just to get down this block alone."

Working frantically—but with a precision that came with practice—the paramedics turned the guy over and placed him on a stretcher.

"Goddamn!" one of the cops ejaculated. "Somebody really fucked this guy up!"

"—Hey," the other cop ejaculated, scrutinizing Roland, "ain't you somebody famous?"

The first cop looked at Roland as well, his face brightening: "Yea, he's that lawyer guy: Roland something or another—"

"Roland Micheaux," his partner corrected him. Roland nodded distractedly while the officers smiled at their accomplishment. It was as though they had just won at charades. In the meanwhile, the two paramedics, oblivious of what the other men were doing, were still working frantically—

"We found a wallet," one of the paramedics declared suddenly.

"Give it here," said one of the officers, "—I'll run a check on him." The officer took the wallet and was about to go back to the cruiser to do a check, when—

"He's got a *gun*, too!" announced the same paramedic. Roland only then remembered that Candice had put it in the man's pocket after she wiped it down—

The officers were suddenly sober. The officer who had started to walk back to the cruiser, came back; they looked at one another anxiously. Roland felt as though he were going to faint—

"Any gunshot wounds?" an officer asked the paramedics.

"Not that we can see—but he's really messed up. His pulse is weak."

And then, turning to Roland, an officer asked: "You see anybody else when you got down here?"

A wave of alarm went over Roland! "No, only him."

"He say anything to you?"

"No, he was just moaning—that's the only reason I noticed him."

"Well lucky for him that you came along. He looks like—"

The paramedics had ripped the man's shirt open; the officer's partner had been frowning at the man's bony chest, on which there was a tattoo. Suddenly, his eyes grew wide: "Hey, Vinnie! I think I know who that guy is!" He pulled an ID out of the wallet in his hand, his eyes growing even wider. "It's Lamar Smith!"

"*The* Lamar Smith?" asked his partner, "—you sure?"

"Yea! Look, that's his tattoo," he said, pointing at the tattoo of a 1970s pimp with a fuzzy, wide-brimmed hat and bell bottoms. "And I got his wallet—his *driver's license*."

"*Jesus*!" the man said, realizing it himself.

"What…?" Roland said, confusedly.

"This guy is about the biggest drug dealer on the east coast," one of the officers declared then.

"*Him*?" Roland said dubiously.

Just then, the Paramedics, in their own world of urgency, rushed Smith and the stretcher to the ambulance, leaving the other men standing about.

One of the cops went on: "Yea, we busted his entire operation last week, but he managed to escape somehow. We froze all his assets, arrested about 50 of his gang members, and have been keeping tags on everyone he knows. He's been wandering about, trying to hide and survive…robbing people."

"I guess he wasn't a real good mugger!" his partner laughed.

"I guess not! This is a damn good night: first that Hair Jacker weirdo, and now this guy!"

"You have a knack for being around big arrests," one of them laughed to Roland.

Roland nodded his head, exhausted beyond reason.

The two officers were still laughing between themselves; but seeing that the ambulance was getting ready to go, they started for their cruiser. One of them turned back then:

"Hey, you have a card or something—in case we have to get in touch with you for testimony?"

Roland numbly got a business card out of his wallet.

"Thanks a lot!" the officer yelled, then rushed to the cruiser to follow the ambulance.

Roland was left standing there by himself. But he didn't want to be alone again—especially down here. He quickly went to his car and pulled out after the police cruiser. Was it over, he wondered? Probably not…there were so many complications. A world of maddening complications…*And what if they called him to testify at Smith's trial*…! He was still somewhat proud of himself that he had called the ambulance—even though he had lied to the policemen. Still, the *complications*…! If there was any consolation, it was that Candice had been right about the police reaction to Smith. Once the men saw that criminal record, nothing else had mattered….

At the front entrance of the garage, the nervous-looking attendant waved the ambulance and police cruiser through. Roland drove up to the man slowly and stopped to pay his bill.

"Nothing like this ever happened before!" the attendant moaned. It was a pimple-faced white kid, probably just out of high school. "We have a pretty safe garage."

Instinctively, Roland found himself saying: "Don't you have surveillance cameras or anything?"

"Nah," the kid said absentmindedly, "—too much space to cover I guess."

Roland nodded his head equivocally. "…How much do I owe you?" he said, handing over the ticket.

"It's on the house," the nervous kid replied, distractedly looking in the direction of the street. "What a crazy night—the street's still blocked from that Hair Jacker thing."

Roland nodded again, then moved on.

And like the kid had said, the street was totally blocked. He couldn't believe it: thousands of other people had joined those already there, so that the entire block seemed to be a solid mass of traffic and people—neither of which seemed to be going anywhere.

After honking his horn for about five minutes and getting absolutely nowhere, he looked up to see the two cops from the parking garage coming through the crowd! He froze, like a fugitive seeing his captors closing in. His first thought was that Smith had come out of his stupor and told the police everything—and now they were coming for him! But as the men neared his vehicle, Roland saw that they were smiling, waving at him.

"Thank goodness we caught you! On the other hand," the officer went on, gesturing over his shoulder, "you weren't going anywhere anyhow."

All Roland could do was stare.

"The call just came over the police radio," the other officer continued.

"What?" Roland managed to mumble.

"You're wanted at the police precinct."

Roland felt *sick*! *So this was it*!

"Yea, something to do with the Hair Jacker."

"*Kain*...!" Roland whispered. Had Kain told them what Roland had done in the parking garage!

"Sorry about this," one of the officers laughed, confusing Roland in the process. "Just follow us out—we have the cruiser waiting—we'll give you an escort."

"What about Lamar Smith?" Roland managed to ask.

"Oh, *him*," one of the officers said in an offhand manner, "he's dead."

"*What*!"

"Yea, like I said before, somebody really fucked him up—but no bother."

"Just follow us," his partner continued, "—we'll get you out of here."

Roland nodded....

Smith was dead...Roland had murdered a man...! It was too unreal to be true. He had killed a man, and now the police were taking him to see Kain—who knew his secret!...He felt sick to his stomach; his hands were trembling so much that he could barely hold onto the steering wheel. The two cops were directly in front of his car, waving people out of the way, and Roland had a sudden impulse to stomp on the accelerator and run them all over: not only the officers, but as many people as possible. It was all falling apart! People were everywhere, and he felt suddenly claustrophobic. *And he had killed a man*! That realization ripped through him again; and just like when he was standing over Smith's body in the parking garage, he was beset by thoughts of death—and the fragile meaninglessness of life. And the realization that he was on his way to see Kain, almost made him retch. All the hysteria of the banquet hall was coming over him again. There were too many things to deal with at once, and it only seemed to be a matter of time before everything came crashing down around him...!

The police had led Roland out to their cruiser, and now he followed their car as they inched their way through the crowd. He felt like a condemned man following his jailer to the scaffold. What the hell did they want him for! What had Kain said to them! He was again overcome by the need to get away; and the knowledge that Kain was still manipulating him like a puppet (even behind prison walls) made the shivers come back....

They were free of the crowd at last. Roland didn't know whether to be relieved by the freedom or disconcerted by the fact that that freedom only meant that they would reach Kain quicker. The only chance for him again seemed to be flight: escaping while he still had the chance. He had an impulse to make a turn at the next corner and zoom away from the police: to do anything to keep Kain from touching him again. In fact, Roland couldn't help thinking that Kain's mark was already on him. Like Cain of the Bible, Roland seemed marked by the inescapable will of God—and was doomed. An hour or so ago, when he left the banquet, he hadn't thought that he could feel any more drained and disillusioned, but he was falling into a bottomless pit, and the depths were inexhaustible—as were the horrors....

Roland flinched when he saw the huge crowd waiting outside the police precinct. It was as though they were all waiting around to see a rock concert. There were even vendors along the sidewalk, selling ice cream and T-shirts and all sorts of incomprehensible things! He realized, all at once, that these people had come to hear Kain's words—just as the man had said they would! Most of them would probably be happy if they simply caught a *glimpse* of the man! Kain had done it all—everything he had said to Roland; and now, right on cue, Roland was being summoned as well.

They parked in front of the building; and just like in his childhood memories, Roland was given an armed escort up to the entrance. The crowd was huge; camera crews were everywhere. They came up to Roland, yelling questions, but the officers pushed them away—and Roland was too dazed to decipher what they were saying. He stumbled along, seeing the excitement—indeed, the *madness*—that Kain had already inspired in these people; and he knew, all at once, that somehow or another, he had to stop Kain from speaking to them. He had to *silence* Kain. He couldn't let Kain touch those thousands—indeed, *millions*—like he had touched him. Roland was that wounded soldier who instinctively threw himself on a hand grenade in order to save his unit. The thought set off more hysteria and alarm bells in him…When the hell would it end! It was now a quarter past 12, and the night had no end in sight….He was finally marched through the entrance. Officers were standing there in full riot gear….Roland walked through the police precinct in a daze. The two officers finally brought him to the observation room—which looked out, through the one-way mirror, on the interrogation room that held Kain. There was a camera set up in the observation room, taking in Kain's every motion. There were also about five men sitting around in the dim lighting, watching Kain in awe. Kain was the only one in the other room, smiling contentedly as he stared into the mirror. It was as if there were no partition, and the man could see them all clearly. Roland glanced at the man, then looked away nervously.

"Roland Micheaux?" one of the men in the room asked. All of the men were getting to their feet now, as if awakening from a trance.

"Yes," Roland replied, swallowing deeply.

"Do you know why we called you?"

"No…" His voice was horribly hoarse.

"Do you know Jasper Kain?"

He again swallowed deeply: "No…not really…" He groaned

nervously, and the realization that he had no poise, made him quake inside. Still, he went on: "He came up to me at the banquet tonight—that's the first time I met him."

"So you aren't his lawyer?" one of the men said with a hopeful smile.

Roland paused for a second; but seeing the lieutenant's smile, he instinctively smiled as well. "*Me?*" he said.

The men in the room were laughing now. "—Just what we figured, Mr. Micheaux."

Roland looked at them confusedly; but then, one of the officers asked: "What did Mr. Kain talk to you about?"

Roland's stomach convulsed; he felt slightly faint, but he forced himself to remain calm. He took a deep breath of air, releasing it slowly. "He said that I was all part of some plan," he began when he had scrounged together enough composure, "—and that he had been keeping an eye on me for two years....And then he went and shaved the Mayor's head."

The men in the room suddenly looked at one another and began to chuckle amongst themselves. Roland again looked on confusedly, until one revealed: "Kain seems to be under the impression that you were one of his accomplices—"

"*Me*," Roland peeped; and as the other men continued to laugh, he suddenly found himself joining in. Like back at the banquet, he needed desperately to laugh. His mind worked feverishly, telling him that he could use this: that the more insane he made Kain seem (and the man had obviously been insane to begin with) the less they would believe the man if he told them about what Roland had done to Smith. He felt so very filthy then: he had killed a man, and now he was lying to protect himself. Still, despite everything, he allowed himself be lulled into a feeling of relief—or whatever this was. He laughed louder now—along with the officers. It was the way he had laughed after Candice told him that she was a murderer: he was pulled in by the thing, both terrified and relieved by his surrender.

When the laughter began to die down, and the other men began talking amongst themselves, Roland walked up to the glass and stood watching Kain—who was still smiling confidently. *What the hell are you planning, Kain*! Roland wondered, his old feelings coming over him again. There was some incomprehensible power about the man.

Roland couldn't deny that. One only needed to look at the man to see it. And then, all at once, it was as though an avalanche thundered over him: there were just too many parallels here—too many fears realizing themselves at once for him to ignore it....Kain was like a long lost father, a *prodigal* father, returned from debauchery and sin, not in the form of a regretful man, but a restless, insane spirit. He couldn't think of Kain as a man anymore. Kain wasn't flesh and blood: he was a vapor, an aroma, which worked on those present by rekindling memories of far-away places and distant, long-forgotten dreams—

"Don't let him speak," Roland blurted out then.

"What?" the men said at his back, looking up confusedly from their conversation.

Roland turned to them: "Don't let Kain speak," he repeated. "He's only doing it for the attention—that's one of the things he told me. All he wants is the publicity...he's *nuts*." And then, when the cops smiled to themselves: "I think he was stalking me or something," he went on quickly.

"Yea, exactly what we figured!" one said, and they began to laugh again.

But Roland couldn't be intoxicated by their laughter anymore. He glanced at Kain nervously; and then, to the officers: "You think he's going to get out of jail?"

"*Him*?" one laughed. "In my opinion, that guy will be spending a couple of decades in a nut house! We just called for a psychological evaluation."

The man next to him laughed: "And I wonder what the tests are gonna tell us!"

Even Roland laughed along to that one....

"Thanks for coming to see us so promptly," a detective started in a tone which said that the interview was over.

"Actually," Roland laughed, "I got a police escort."

"Well, we spare no expense around here. Have a good night, sir."

Roland was getting ready to leave, when he was called back: "Hey, you have a card or something—some way we can reach you if we have any questions, or need you to testify?"

A wave of numbness came over him. "Sure," he said, getting out his business cards for the second time that night. When that was done, the detectives again gave their thanks. But as he was walking out of the room, he glanced back at Kain, who was still sitting there patiently, smiling. *What the hell are you so confident about*! Roland wondered....At least they were going to lock Kain up. Something about the idea of Kain locked away somewhere, unable to wander the streets, calmed him somewhat. But then, while he walked down the corridors of the precinct, a hysterical internal voice asked him if a restless spirit could be confined by walls.

The daze that had gripped him several times that night, seized him once more. A quick flashback of all the night's events drained even more of his strength. He was acutely aware that he wasn't the same man he had been just six hours ago. He had *killed* a man; and as he walked through the precinct, the very proof of his madness was the fact that even now he feared Jasper Kain not as a man, but the reincarnation of his father....

The crowd outside was still boisterous—and it seemed to be growing. A few reporters, seeing Roland coming out of the precinct, rushed up to him, but he had nothing to say. He was exhausted beyond reason. He drove off aimlessly, his mind in the obligatory daze of the night. It wasn't until he was halfway across the Brooklyn Bridge that he realized that he was going to see Candice. He didn't want to be alone tonight. He'd said that he did, but he'd only been fooling himself—

All at once, something unsettling popped into his mind. About a week into his relationship with Candice, they had been making love. It had been their second time in all, and the entire act had still been heightened by the excitement of nuance. She had been on top of him, riding him with wild abandon, when she cried out, in one of those growly voices which came only when one was having sex: "You want a slut, don't you—a real cheap whore!" Before he had been able to say anything, she had moaned, "Well, I'm the bitch for you: no strings, a real good fuck...so you can get your rocks off!" She had said all of this while she galloped on top of him, and when her words finally reached him through the shroud of sex, he had instinctively pushed her away.

"What's wrong, baby," she had purred, "I'm only being what you want."

"That's not what I want," he'd said, gruffly.

"Oh?" she'd said, smirking....

The entire sequence of events probably passed through his mind 10 times as he drove down the Brooklyn streets. And as thoughts of pathological sex swirled in his mind, he suddenly found himself remembering how he had lost his virginity. A loud, obnoxious ghetto girl had seemed to do it out of spite, groping him in the fetid basement of their tenement. It had been early fall, a few months after his father's execution. That same afternoon, right after they were finished having sex, she had gone out of her way to tease him before all the neighborhood children and make fun of his sexuality: of the very notion that a woman would ever see him as a sexual prospect. While the neighborhood children laughed, and her triumphant, vindictive eyes bore into him, it had occurred to him that it was not even that their moment together—their supposed intimacy—meant nothing, but that she had allowed it just to point out this very nothingness. As he walked away, slumping back to his room to escape their laughter, it had occurred to him that receiving emptied the soul more thoroughly than taking; because in receiving, you were inevitably forced to let down your defenses and open up your soul.

What it all meant, however, Roland had no idea. The only thing that he knew for sure, was that he didn't want to be alone tonight. On this strange night of murder and madness, he had been reduced to the level of a child, afraid of the emptiness of his bed, and the ghost-like images that kept flaring up in his imagination. In fact, he was so desperate to drown his thoughts that he turned on the radio, putting up the volume so high that he could feel the music vibrating in the steering wheel….

His mind was relatively blank when he entered Candice's block. It was about one in the morning now. He turned down the radio and was looking for a parking space, when he looked up and saw a figure step out onto Candice's stoop. Roland, suddenly numb, drove past to make sure, but there was no doubt. *It was Phelps*! The man's limousine was double parked in front of the building; and for a moment, the man stood on the stoop with his tuxedo jacket held in his hand in an impromptu fashion, and his unbuttoned shirt hanging out of his pants sloppily. From the way the man's hair glistened in the light, Roland realized that he had just taken a shower—no doubt to wash off the scent of sex before he went home to his wife. Roland saw all this in a matter of seconds, and sped up the car to make the yellow light at the intersection.

2.

Random Acts of Violence

Two months later, it was now New York City's hottest summer on record; and with much of July and all of August still to go, it only seemed that things would get worse. Strange, dark clouds hovered over the city, composed not so much of water vapor, as a noxious cocktail of pollutants. Every day now for over a month, there had been reports of people dying from heat strokes and acute respiratory attacks. Everyone, suffering under the strain of the heat, was more short-tempered and on-edge. Passing incidents, which a few weeks ago would have at worst resulted in a shouting match, now regularly ended in deaths and trips to the emergency room. Scientists of all sorts emerged to offer theories about the heat. They warned of exhaust from car-jammed city streets, and drifting pollution from distant states. They demonstrated how the summer sun was cooking up all the airborne filth, producing chemical reactions that should have been left to test tubes. They designed elaborate computer models, showing how heat, which would have escaped back into the atmosphere, and space, was being trapped near the surface by the noxious clouds. But the longer the heat wave lasted, and the more the scientists talked, the less scientific people's conceptualization of the heat became; and as they looked up at the polluted sky, they all seemed to know that that which had been initiated by the hand of man was now utterly out of their hands.

People had gotten into the habit of whispering when talking of the heat. They glanced surreptitiously at the smoggy skies with all the frightened awe of pagans, and found themselves listening wistfully for rustling leaves and the delicate sound of rain—for *any* harbinger of change. But about everything, there was now a swamp-like stillness. Something evil seemed to be in the air, and it didn't seem to be the work of science alone. It was as if the heat were the punishment for some unrealized crime: some judgment literally being handed down from above; and faced with that possibility, it was not only the discomfort of the heat which was behind their uneasiness, but an unarticulated fear of God.

Even when nighttime came, and the sun and the smoggy skies faded into the darkness, the heat and uneasiness remained; because even at night, the sky was there to tell them that something was terribly wrong. With all the pollution, the night sky was a reddish brown, which grew darker and more menacing as the night went on. Scientists offered theories about this as well, talking about longer summer days and the illumination of the smog banks by the sun and the moon—but the people had lost their faith in science by then....

* * *

THE ODOR OF THE SMALL BROOKLYN APARTMENT was a nauseating combination of stale sweat, stale perfume, stale semen and whatever was rotting in the dark, unkempt recesses. The room, dark and cramped as it was, was like a coffin; the odor, heightened by the heat to the verge of putrescence, was like death. The place seemed to belong to no one; and like a city street, it seemed to have the discarded refuse of countless passersby. In fact, everything from candy wrappers to used condoms lay trapped in the dust piles on the floor. A stray sock and forgotten pairs of underwear could be turned up if one looked around. Still, no one entered the chamber because he or she wanted to see what was there. The men and women who were compelled to enter it, did not do so for its sights and sounds and odors, but to lose themselves in fantasy and forgetfulness.

Accordingly, as Nikolai Petrovich Andropov groped the whore in the sweltering darkness of the room, his great nihilistic fantasies welled up in his mind. All his love and hate, his dreams and his nightmares...everything was subsumed by his fantasies—and the whore's body. Six months ago, when he finally gave in to the urge to take a woman, he had told himself that he only came to this whorehouse in order to remember his wife—but that was a lie. His wife of 25 years, and their four children, were back in Russia; and after a year in New York, away from them, he knew that he could care less if he ever saw them again. This was not to say that he didn't love them, but that they now existed in a place that he couldn't easily bring himself to contemplate—much less *remember*. To him, memory, imagination and myth all combined into something that was beyond truths and lies; and after 45 years on this planet, he had come to the conclusion that reality was useless to him. Reality was too harsh—too *empty*—a thing. It was a grand anticlimax, leaving him stranded in a place cut off from the vital hopes and dreams that made life worth living. So nowadays, he spent most of his free time in this strange realm, where memory, imagination and myth combined; and with minimal effort, he would find himself young again—but taller and stronger and more vital and handsome than he had ever been in reality. His wife would be there too, looking graceful and more beautiful than she had ever been…and they would be making love.

In the strange idyll that his mind concocted, it was a summer day in the mid seventies, and he was an athletic teenager in Leningrad. The day was sunny and warm, and he took the object of his love to a beach on the Baltic, where they played coquettish games in the water and in the sand. Every touch, even those that seemed the most inadvertent, was in fact a prelude to their lovemaking. The beach was crowded, but it seemed as though they were the only ones there—the only ones in the *world*. Possessed by their passion, they sneaked away to a beach house and barred the door, surrendering to the maddening impulse that drove them. In that moment, it was as if the entire universe were theirs for the taking. Whole lifetimes seemed to pass in a kiss; but with all the time in the universe at their disposal, they surrendered to those decades with neither anxiety nor impatience. Through the act of love, they became gods in their own universe. They transformed the physical into something beyond the mechanical maneuverings of bodies. They only needed to think of pleasure, and it was so. They soared on the current of their shared, inexhaustible energy, until, with the passing of eons, stars collapsed and gravitational fields rented whole galaxies asunder; and in time, all that had ever been, became one churning mass; and then, when infinity seemed to exhaust itself, and all that had ever been known had outlived the knowers, there was an explosion; and after countless eons, there were once again stars and planets and galaxies; and somewhere, in all the chaos that had brought about creation, there was order and the wonderment of lovers....

That was how he liked to remember it. In reality, he, a scrawny, acne-blighted 18-year-old, had stolen a bottle of vodka from his father and taken a frail 14-year-old girl to a third-rate movie. They had gotten drunk, groped one another in the fetid darkness of the theater, then stumbled off to a smelly alley to do their business. Two minutes into their impromptu courtship, they had been set upon by the police; and in the police station, Andropov had discovered that his new girlfriend's father was a high official in the politburo, who demanded that Andropov make "an honorable woman" out of his daughter. So that, as they say, had been that.

Whether it was his party connections, or his scientific prowess, Andropov had eventually become a respected chemist, settling into a comfortable, though regimented, life. But with the crumbling of the Soviet Union, that had of course come to an abrupt end. The world had changed in an instant, unleashing a revolution that none of the paranoid officials of the politburo could have imagined. The Soviet Union had literally torn itself apart, and all the things shaken free by the upheaval had belonged to no one: had been strange refugees of the times. After his government-funded research lab was shut down and he found himself jobless and without prospects, his entire life had unraveled so quickly and easily, that it was as if none of it had ever happened. To survive, he had spent the last decade doing things like selling newspapers on street corners. It had all been like a dream, where everyone, putting his or her hopes in the proposition that none of it was real, was waiting around to awaken.

Still, Nikolai Petrovich Andropov had always been a dreamer. For most of his life, his great dream had been America, itself; throughout his life, his conceptualization of America had been like a 13-year-old boy's idea of the women in *Playboy* magazine. The promises of America had been like the smiling women spreading their legs within those glossy pages. Everything had been so simple—so beyond *thought*. Thus, perhaps still gripped by those masturbatory fantasies, a year ago, he had made arrangements to be smuggled into America by the Russian mob. Along with a thousand other hopeful immigrants, the mob had smuggled him across the Atlantic in the cargo hold of a rusting ship. But even in the cramped, filthy cargo hold, where disease and starvation swept through the population, there had been hope. He had kept thinking of all that he would do when he reached New York. He would be a chemist again, he had kept telling himself. He had kept telling himself that with all of his knowledge, he would quickly be granted citizenship. While people had lain prone beside him, retching from tubercular attacks, he had imagined the entire world rising to applaud his discoveries. Those dreams had been mesmerizing in their grandeur and complexity. It was for this very reason that he could not understand how he had gone from that, to this—

As he came to his senses in the sweltering darkness of the chamber, the whore now lying limply beneath him wasn't so much a mark on his conscience, as a jarring shock to his consciousness. As Andropov groped her, he was suddenly overcome by the unsettling sensation of seeping into quicksand. The layer of sweat between them seemed like sticky muck. Every few seconds, like clockwork, she let out a dutiful, "Oh yes," in the thickest Belorussian accent imaginable, and then returned to her corpselike rigor. Those two words of English were perhaps the only ones at which she was proficient—and the only ones that she would ever need to know. She had the face of some babushka-wearing peasant who, like generations of her predecessors, had once existed only to give birth to children and work the fields. But now, instead of the calming familiarity of thick forests and fallow fields outside her window, there were the Brooklyn streets, with their jarring but ever-present sounds of life and death. Through an opening in the curtains, the stray illumination from a streetlight highlighted part of her face; and as he continued the act from which he was supposed to derive pleasure, Andropov watched her indifferent expression, suddenly repulsed. It wasn't only the realization of his depravity, but an acute awareness of the realities that had brought them both to this room. The woman beneath him had probably only been in the country for a couple of weeks—maybe even *days*. They had perhaps both been fantasizing about that smiling contortionist within the glossy pages of the magazine; but now, in the face of reality, those hopeful fantasies were supplanted by a certain numbness. He recognized it all, because a day after he had arrived in America, still on-edge from his strange middle passage, the fantasies had come to an end when the mob demanded payment for its services. Looking down at the woman, Andropov now saw the same dawning realization in her dead eyes. In truth, few of those who had allowed themselves to be smuggled had given thought to the Russian syndicate for which they would spend the rest of their lives slaving. Andropov, with his knowledge of chemistry, now spent his time "cooking" various illicit drugs for the syndicate; the woman, who had nothing to offer but her body, was also required to make reparations to those that had delivered her into her fantasy.

Just then, the woman feigned pleasure by writhing beneath him and uttering another dutiful, "Oh yes." But as Andropov watched her, she seemed like some tortured spirit caught between life and death. He had a sudden impulse to put her out of her misery—to choke her and throw her out of the third-story window. The thought made him nervous, so that he pumped more savagely into her to trigger the forgetfulness. The bed was rattling horribly now. That din rose above the sickening sound of his sweaty body slapping against hers; and her droning cries of, "Oh yes," which were supposed to spur him on to the fulfillment of pleasure, only mocked him.

In the face of all of this, he did not initially realize that the pimp had begun to bang on the door, yelling at him in Russian. Maybe an entire minute passed before he acknowledged the voice and cursed: "I'm almost done!" But what was he done *doing*? Looking down at the indifferent whore, who was staring into the corner, no longer even pretending to moan in pleasure, it was obvious that neither of them was feeling anything. The banging on the door, and her continued indifference, made the panicky feeling grow within him. He had a sudden impulse to strike out; the thought of putting her out of her misery—of putting them *both* out of their misery—gripped him once more. He was pumping into her viciously now, and she accepted him the way a broken horse accepted its rider's urgings to go faster. The bed was creaking horribly; outside the door, the pimp was cursing loudly…but it was all without meaning—without *sense*. Andropov was now sweating so profusely that his entire body was slipping against the whore. Between that, and the creaking bed, and the banging door, the cacophony was an ode to ineptitude and madness—

"That's enough in there!" the pimp screamed. Andropov swore viciously and gnashed his teeth in a final, all-out attempt to derive some fleeting pleasure out of the whore's body; but a few seconds later, when he realized that his goal was nowhere in sight, he let out a final curse and rose from between the woman's legs. The whore, finally free of him, turned over and pulled a filthy sheet over her numb body.

The pimp was still banging. Out of breath, and slightly light-headed from having breathed the putrescence of the room for an extended period, Andropov almost passed out as he stood up and groped in the darkness for his things. The pimp's curses grew louder—

"I'm coming!" Andropov screamed in anger, then grunted at the annoying irony of the words. He needed to be away from the whore—away from this *room*. In a few seconds, he had on his pants and shoes; he was just buttoning up his shirt when he opened the door and looked out. The lighting in the hallway was dim—*shady*; the paint was peeling from crumbling plaster walls, creating a heightened impression of desuetude. The first face that he saw was the pimp's. The latter was an emaciated, middle-aged man about average height who had the pallid complexion and scheming eyes of a Gestapo agent. But to be an enslaver, one either had to be without conscience, or hate those whom one had to enslave; sometimes, one attempted the latter to achieve the former. Whatever the case, the pimp glowered at Andropov then walked away. Now stepping up were two men whose presence made Andropov's stomach twinge. The men had achieved the consonance of both looking like stupid gangsters and actually being that. They had everything from the black suits—notwithstanding the heat—to the slicked-back hair.

"What the hell do you two want?" Andropov demanded, closing the door behind him and stepping farther into the hallway. He glanced at the cheap digital watch that he had bought in Chinatown, seeing that it was just past 9 o'clock.

"We need someone to make a delivery," started one, producing a package which Andropov knew contained drugs.

"*Me?*" Andropov groaned. And as the feeling of outrage grew in him, he blurted out: "I was a university chemist!"

"—But now you're a delivery boy," joked the other goon, at which time both thugs laughed. Andropov glared at them with a snarled lip.

"Don't be angry, pops," jibed one of them. "We brought you a little present." And at that, he produced a smaller package. All of a sudden, Andropov's expression became more contrite. He first took the bigger package; then, with a guilty quickness, he took the other.

The two men watched him slyly, then smiled. One of the goons then proffered a handgun from his pocket. At first Andropov shook his head, but then he accepted it begrudgingly. Looking up at the two men, he had an impulse to put a bullet hole in each of their smug faces....

He walked out to the car—a huge, 1977, gas-guzzling *tank* of a Dodge. How the hell had he come to this? But no: he couldn't think about that now. He had to keep on going: keep rushing on, as if fleeing from thought, itself....The red, menacing night sky made him uneasy for some reason, so that he grimaced and walked faster, hoping to drown all his thoughts. However, plastered to the dumpster by the curb, were campaign posters for Charlotte McPrice—the woman who was to face Mayor Randolph in the upcoming Mayoral election. As he always did, Andropov stopped and looked down at the poster, somehow captivated by the comely woman on it and her campaign slogan. "We're Americans, damn it!" declared the inscription above her smiling picture. That had been the rallying cry that swept the woman to a landslide victory in the Democratic primary for Mayor; but as Andropov looked down at the poster, that smiling, comely face—like everything else in the world—only seemed to mock him. It was plastered across hundreds of streets, always there to remind him of what was unattainable; and the words, "We're Americans, damn it!" were only a burning reminder that this was a house in which he was an uninvited guest—a *thief*, in fact....

As soon as he had settled himself in the car, Andropov took out the smaller package and took a pinch of the white powder—just a little to tide him over: to bring the amnesia back. Outside, the night was sweltering, but nowhere near the hell of the apartment. The stench of the whore was still on him....When he sat back in the seat, the gun dug into his back. He took it out and looked at it oddly, hefting it in his hand....

When he started up the engine and drove down the block, he again felt the stirrings of something horrible in his soul. He couldn't even begin to fathom what impulse had brought him to the whorehouse. But what he was feeling now, wasn't the self-recrimination of someone who had sought out some sordid pleasure, only to be confronted by a pang of guilt—it was something darker. His mind hovered on the threshold of that darkness, then faltered. And besides, the white powder was beginning to work its magic.

Presently, he was driving through the Coney Island section of Brooklyn, where many Russian immigrants had settled. As the drug flowed through him, the streets all blurred together, seeming composed of flashes of multi-hued light, streaked against a backdrop of incomprehensible darkness. He smiled for no good reason and sat back in the seat, enjoying the sensation of vapidity.

But in time, he found himself driving through the slums, watching the blacks and Latinos lolling out on the sidewalks as they tried to escape the heat. With the heat wave going strong, those without air conditioners were almost compelled to stay outside—where the air at least had the illusion of circulating. To his right, some kids were playing in an open fire hydrant, dancing with glee in the heavy spray that flew into his window and wet his pants. Andropov looked at them intently, startled to realize that there was a strange kind of joy about them. He looked at their dilapidated tenements doubtfully, sure in nothing but that their joy—their *ease*, in fact—could only be seen as a sign of stupidity. Still, when a soul is dark and troubled, its keeper cannot imagine there being light and joy anywhere. And the thought that they—as ignorant and worthless as they appeared to him—were *rightful* Americans, whereas he was some kind of criminal, hiding in the shadows, filled him with outrage and hatred—

At that moment, a laughing kid ran out into the street, chasing a ball. Andropov's car was a good half a block away from him, so the boy's chasing the ball wasn't an act of utter recklessness. Andropov's mind was blank as he watched the kid's smile—and as he watched that smile die. In that strange moment, the only clue that the car was speeding up, was the higher pitch of its engine. The world again became a place of blurred lights against a backdrop of incomprehensible darkness. The impact of the car into the body of the frozen kid was also a sound. There was a low thud, then a louder crash as the body flew over the hood, splintering the windshield before disappearing back into the darkness. And then, again, there was only the whining pitch of the engine as Andropov sped into the night. The red light at the intersection of course meant nothing to him by now; and so, still locked away, Andropov crashed into the car that had the right of way. The sound was like an explosion; the steel and glass around him seemed to blow apart in every direction, leaving him toppling through a void. Even with his seat belt on, he banged his head against the steering wheel. The explosion of pain in his head was like the explosion all around him....And then, for a long moment afterwards, it seemed as if there were only silence—*nothingness*. It seemed so peaceful—and *sudden*—that he hoped that it would last forever. But soon, the driver of the other car—a brand new BMW—came around and started cursing him through the open window. It was a young black man. It took Andropov a long time to acknowledge the man; but when he did, he got out of the car with a calmness that the black man must have taken for shock—or contrition....When Andropov had shot the man in the face, he didn't exactly know. He was aware only of the echoes of the shots—and the sight of the bloody corpse, which he looked down at, still feeling nothing. This horrible numbness—the same feeling he had felt as he pumped his penis into that whore—was all about him now. For a moment, he thought that he would be trapped in it forever, but the angry mob was coming up the street now. It was as though the entire block, which, only moments ago, had seemed to find some measure of peace in the summer night, were now descending upon Andropov with hate and madness in their eyes. With cold efficiency, Andropov rose the nozzle of his gun and fired into the mob—into those worthless scum who had the nerve to be Americans! Some fell to the ground and others scattered in horror; but still others continued to charge, gripped by the injustice of it all. Against the backdrop of the red, menacing sky, the images were unreal. But soon, the gun was empty; and as the most incensed of the mob continued to charge, it was only a matter of time before they were upon him. Whatever it was that Andropov felt then, he did not exactly know. Maybe it was terror—maybe even regret at the realization that he had just killed several people and a child. Whatever it was, he was soon smiling as he felt the first blows of the mob and thought: *Yes, my friends, help me to forget it all!*

* * *

LITTLE DID ROLAND MICHEAUX KNOW that the seeds of his destruction were being sown in the events currently taking place in the Brooklyn slums. But the life cycle of seeds can be anywhere from a few minutes, to decades—even centuries….

In Brooklyn, the people who had just lost loved ones, seemed to go mad with the loss; or, in Kain's terms, they surrendered to the surrounding chaos. But in Manhattan, Roland Micheaux was sitting in the back seat of a cab with an ease that didn't seem fitting with either the shabby surroundings or the heat. He was off in a world of success and contentment; and perceiving the grin that now graced Roland's face, the Pakistani cab driver watched him suspiciously in the rear view mirror. The designer suit had at first put the driver at ease, but one always had to watch one's fares for the slightest sign of insanity. Working late nights in New York City, such vigilance was often the difference between life and death.

It was just after 9:30 when the cab darted somewhat recklessly down Broadway, towards Greenwich Village. But driving in New York City required a certain amount of recklessness. Drivers from Iowa had no business driving in New York City: they lacked the vital viciousness that the cabby was demonstrating with such panache. Three times, the man had almost crashed—twice into jaywalking pedestrians, who stared back with undaunted contemptuousness, as if a mere two tons of steel were no match for their New York brashness; and a third time, the man had almost crashed into a fellow cabby—whom had swerved across the road, narrowly averting two other accidents, just to pick up a passenger.

—While in the Brooklyn slums, people rushed out to take revenge on a world that had again shown them how cheap their lives were, Roland looked around and felt only joy. He was young and successful and *free*, and he felt as if he could do anything. It all had to do with the fact that just this afternoon—just *hours* ago—he had settled a huge, multimillion dollar class action suit! He had just left the press conference, where he had undoubtedly been the star. A nationwide hamburger chain had sold hamburgers tainted with E. coli bacteria, and 20 people, most of whom were kids, had died. The company had settled out of court for 100 million dollars, catapulting Roland into a new legal clique. Now was the time for celebration, and it was with this purpose in mind that he drove towards the little cabaret in Greenwich Village—where the men of his firm always congregated after a court victory.

Yes, Roland was undoubtedly a star now. Even more proof of it was that he was going to be appearing on network television tomorrow morning, as a featured guest! He was feeling *good*—invincible. Even Jasper Kain, and all that had taken place in the spring, was out of his system now. Kain was locked away in a nut house, and Lamar Smith had long been forgotten by anyone who matters. And with all of Roland's startling success, the events of that spring night seemed to be nothing but ghosts from a passing dream. Even as the cabby narrowly missed some pedestrians in the crosswalk, and zoomed through an intersection where the traffic light had changed from yellow to red a second before, Roland smiled to himself. That smile was still on his face when the cabby came to a screeching halt in front of the cabaret.

However, when Roland exited the car, the oppressive heat seemed to collapse on him like a building. His frame literally bent with the weight of it. And when he glanced up at the red, menacing sky, he frowned for the first time, probably only then noticing it. It was one of those weird signs, which we either ignore or heed as omens; and as in Roland's case this was the time for celebration, he put it all aside and smiled as he walked up to the cabaret.

From outside, the place looked like a fine restaurant, with an awning and a plush red carpet leading up to the door, but Roland smiled to himself, knowing the sleazy bacchanalia that lay within.

—While in the Brooklyn slums, terrified parents ran out into the streets, desperately looking for their children, Roland entered the establishment. The bouncer, a black man of gargantuan proportions, recognized him immediately and smiled. Roland shook the man's hand and walked on. However, on the threshold of the huge chamber, he stopped for a moment, just taking it all in. The most discordant thing was the strobe lights: everything seemed to be moving in slow motion. The place was as crowded as usual, with about 500 people, and Roland always felt somewhat claustrophobic upon entering it. There were several stages scattered haphazardly about the place, with women in varying stages of undress capering about as if in the throes of demonic possession; on top of that, scantily clad women were everywhere, either gyrating in the men's laps or serving drinks. The music, a cacophonous techo mix, was ear-splitting. On top of everything, there was a kind of panicky laughter everywhere, the likes of which had always unnerved Roland. He shook his head in bewilderment as he watched the hordes of drunken men and giggling lesbians (for this place didn't discriminate) as they either sat there in a daze, stupefied by drink, or screamed out and leapt about, as if they were having seizures. Those professing to be religious would call it a pit of sin; but from where Roland stood, it seemed worse than that. It was a pit of forgetfulness—of *make-believe*—where women pretended to be something that they were not, and men pretended to want something that in their heart of hearts, they knew was not real.

With the strobe lights, it was difficult to make out faces; but eventually, Roland's searching eyes came to rest on Dallas Phelps; and as they did so, he felt an uncomfortable twinge in his stomach. He had been feeling that twinge for weeks now—every time he came across the man. It seemed to be nothing but jealousy and resentment—things that were supposedly beyond a man of success—but it was more than that. That Candice had slept with Phelps didn't, in and of itself, really bother him anymore—especially since he was no longer seeing her. But the thing that troubled him was that he now suspected that Candice was Phelps's full-time mistress!

After he stopped returning her calls, Roland had thought that that would be the end of it; but about a month ago, at the office water cooler of all places, Phelps had come up to him and announced that Candice was now his daughter's nanny! Roland had spilled an entire cup of water on himself!

As for the coupling of Phelps and Candice—and their new living arrangements—that was just sick. In fact, it seemed too unreal to be true. He kept thinking that maybe he had gotten everything wrong: that there was nothing sexual between Phelps and Candice. He tried coming up with scenarios to explain why a freshly showered Phelps would be coming out of her apartment. Maybe Candice ("a poor Grenadian girl here on an expired student visa," as she had described herself) was just working for Phelps—and nothing more. He was almost desperate for it to be true. He didn't love Candice—and he didn't want her back—but he cared enough for her to know that he didn't want her to end up as some middle-aged married man's slut.

Roland sighed. In all honesty, his ultimate wish was that he could forget about it—like he was forgetting about Kain and Smith. But strangely enough, of all the things that had happened on that spring night two months ago, the image of Phelps coming out of Candice's apartment building, was the most vivid in his mind. As such, every time he looked at Phelps, he felt the discomfort of someone who knew things that he didn't want to know. Moreover, perhaps the sickest thing of all was that there was a time when Phelps had been a kind of mentor to him. Roland had gone to firm galas at Phelps's million-dollar brownstone in Brooklyn Heights, feeling genuine awe—even *envy*—at the opulence. Once upon a time, even Phelps's home life had seemed, for lack of a better word, "perfect." The man had a young, beautiful wife and a three-year-old daughter who was almost *sickeningly* sweet. In fact, Phelps's wife, Cindy, and their three-year-old daughter, Mindy, often dropped by the office to "see daddy" (so much so that Mindy had gotten into the habit of calling Roland, *Uncle* Roland!); and once upon a time, Roland had found himself thinking: *Phelps has everything a man can want.* But it was all lies.

—While in the Brooklyn slums, the rioters, like sharks at a feeding frenzy, inadvertently began to turn on their own, Roland looked through the crowd and knew that he definitely didn't want to be around Phelps tonight. Phelps's presence at what was supposed to be his celebration, turned the entire affair into a wake. Still, figuring that the rest of the guys would be close by—and that he could simply ignore the man—Roland began to make his way towards Phelps.

Phelps was sitting by himself, at a small table right in front of one of the stages, dancing in his seat with a bottle of beer in one hand and a wad of bills in the other. Once, that image, in contrast to the paragon of social etiquette and grace that Roland knew from the office and society affairs, would have been somewhat comical—if not shocking—but not anymore. Roland's face was grim as he walked towards the man; however, when he finally got there, he looked around in confusion. Phelps, happening to glance his way, smiled and went back to ogling the woman. Roland's frown deepened:

"Where is everyone else?" he said (he had to yell with all the noise).

But Phelps only gestured with his head for Roland to sit down next to him, in the seat that the man had obviously been saving. Then, after Roland had complied, Phelps leaned over to him, but kept his eyes on the naked woman as he announced: "I wanted you *all* to myself, Micheaux." The man's breath reeked of beer and his eyes were glossy and dilated from all the drinking he had already done.

Roland's face unconsciously soured. "*What?*" he said, fighting to understand.

"I sent everyone else away, Micheaux," Phelps replied, still ogling the woman on stage.

—While in the Brooklyn slums, one of those searching mothers was knocked senseless by a youth who, staring at her intently, finally recognized his own mother, Roland sat there confusedly. He definitely didn't want to be alone with the man—especially in this drunken state. And then, something else registered in Roland's mind: what had Phelps meant by, "I wanted you *all* to myself, Micheaux"? Roland frowned at the man as the latter continued to dance in his chair. Phelps was still staring at the stripper on stage with a simpering grin on his face; and instinctively following the man's gaze, Roland watched the gyrations of the huge-breasted, bleach blond woman, more amused than aroused by her nakedness. As for the strippers, they all seemed…*fake*. Their bodies were all so similar, that it was as if they had come out of some mold—or at least the same plastic surgeon's office. Eighty percent of them had breasts that were so obviously fake that it was, upon reflection, revolting to think that women were willing to have their breasts cut open and propped up with sacks of gel, just in order to get the dollar bills that these fools stuffed down their panties—

"Yes, indeed!" Phelps said out of nowhere, turning to look at Roland's startled face, "—the patron saint of our firm!"

"I beg your pardon?"

"Don't be bashful," the man laughed, "you doing us good, Micheaux."

Roland smiled in response, but mostly at the fact that Phelps's drunkenness had allowed his southern accent to slip out: the man had always sounded as if he were born and bred in Cambridge, Boston.

"Lawyers," Phelps started again, slurring his words slightly, "…nobody has faith in us: they're just waiting for us to fuck up.

Well, you know what I say?"—he leaned in closer, staring intently at Roland with his glossy eyes—"I say fuck 'em, too!" And at that, he howled with laughter. Phelps was apparently one of those good-natured drunks. Some men got morose when drunk; some, like Phelps, became congenial and talkative. The man patted Roland on the shoulder then, going on, "But you're not like other lawyers, Micheaux! I been keeping an eye on you. Yes, sir, you been moving up—both in and out of the firm. And you gonna be on TV in the morning, too!"

Roland had been looking on in bewilderment, wondering how he was going to get away; but at Phelps's prompting, he responded: "Yes, sir, that's right."

"Well, see now," Phelps said with a glowing smile, "that's just what we need: lawyers like you, doing pro bono work and such, helping out the community."

"I suppose."

"Don't be bashful, Micheaux!" Phelps said, patting him on the shoulder again; Roland winced at the repeated touch. "Now, if it's one thing I can't stand," Phelps went on, "it's bashfulness, especially in someone who has no need to be. You been hanging with these northern boys too long. You and me just two southern boys here with these Yankees. They're bigger and faster, but they ain't smarter, are they!" he laughed. "They don't know about the ways of the world, like us southern boys. These northern boys got all the tools," he howled, suggestively, "but don't know how to use 'em, do they!"

"I suppose not, sir," Roland responded flatly.

"Now what you looking so troubled for!" Phelps said, sizing him up. "This is supposed to be a *celebration*, ain't it!" he bellowed, patting Roland on the shoulder once again, this time with a lingering squeeze. He called over a scantily clad waitress then, belting some slurred orders at her. When he was done, he looked at the stage again, soon wearing the same simpering expression that he had had upon Roland's entrance. Roland was beginning to think that he had been given a reprieve, when Phelps again turned to him and said: "You ever read Edgar Alan Poe, Micheaux?"

"...Some," Roland said, unable to keep from smiling at the strangeness of the question in a strip joint. Roland wanted to say, Is that who you think about when you look at naked women? but checked himself.

"Brilliant writer," Phelps began, staring dreamily at the stripper again, "...wrote about *perverseness*—about folks doing precisely what they shouldn't do: almost about people going out of their way to fuck up their lives. A *brilliant* writer...would have a field day with our times. *Perverseness*—the desire to go out and do something you *know* is wrong. It's the ultimate thrill ride in modern times," he said, turning to Roland again. "It's like when you talk to some of the faggots today and ask them why in the hell they keep fucking one another up the ass"—Roland grimaced at the image—"...some will say some bullshit about they were born that way; but then, there are others who will be honest and admit it: who will say: 'Because getting pussy's too goddamn easy!' *Too easy*!" he laughed. "It's all a thrill ride, Micheaux: playing chicken with fate."

—While in the Brooklyn slums, the rage, like a fire burning wildly out of control, threatened to reduce the world to ashes, Roland fidgeted in his seat. But as if offering him a reprieve, the waitress came up with two drinks on her tray. Phelps salivated at the sight of the woman; and when she put the drinks on the table, he caught her and whispered something in her ear, so that she giggled. Phelps then felt her buttocks with one hand; and with the other, he reached into his pocket and brought out a hundred dollar bill. Roland watched as Phelps folded the bill with his free hand—Roland was actually quite amazed by Phelps's dexterity!—and inserted the bill in the crotch of her panties. At that, she caressed his face and walked off. Phelps stared at her retreating buttocks; Roland did as well, and not without appreciation—

"Come back here with me, Micheaux," Phelps said suddenly, getting up.

"*Sir?*"

"There are back rooms here—*you* know...more private."

Roland got up feebly, the consternation registering on his face.

"Don't forget your drink," Phelps called over his shoulder.

Suddenly numb, Roland picked up the bottle of beer and followed his superior. Behind a curtain in the far corner of the room, which was manned by a guard (who nodded knowingly at Phelps), there was a dimly lit corridor, lined with about eight doors. Phelps walked to the second door on his right and was about to open it, when the door across the corridor opened. Roland, who was standing at Phelps's heels, turned with Phelps when the door opened; and there, standing in the doorway, was a tall black man in an elegant suit that was now disheveled. Time seemed to stand still; Roland's jaw dropped!

It was Mayor Randolph!

Roland froze; Phelps, taking in the scene with a nonchalant shrug of his shoulders, chuckled: "How's it hanging, Alex!" And then, while Randolph twitched in shock and embarrassment, seeming as though he had been drained of life, a young bleach blond woman (they all seemed to be blond in this place) came out of the room. She was so petite that she easily passed by the rather tall Randolph, who still stood nervously in the doorway. Then the woman, perfectly at ease, winked at the leering Phelps and the dumbfounded Roland as she walked past them all and back into the main chamber of the strip joint. They all turned and watched her. When she was gone, Roland and Phelps looked at Randolph again; but as if fearful of their eyes, the Mayor fled in the opposite direction from the woman, and out the secret door hidden at the far end of the corridor. There was a brief glimpse of the alley as Randolph made his hasty retreat.

Phelps chuckled then, declaring: "Now I know why I voted for him!"

"That was the Mayor...!" Roland said in disbelief.

"Of course it was—and why shouldn't he be here!" Phelps said, as if outraged. "If President Clinton can get blow jobs in the Oval Office, why shouldn't our own venerable Mayor be able to get one in a strip joint!"

"...The Mayor," Roland said again, still numb. And then, as the reality of it filtered through his mind: "That's probably why his wife's leaving him."

"*Fuck* his wife," Phelps cackled as he opened the door with a practiced ease and walked into the small chamber. "Man wasn't meant to screw one woman all his life!" he went on.

But as he was still in shock, Roland wasn't really listening; accordingly, his mind was elsewhere as he followed the man into the room. The room's illumination came from a red light—no doubt to give it that perfect ambiance. But as it reminded him of the night sky, it only deepened his uneasiness. Something about the light was mesmerizing—or maybe it was only the residual effects of seeing the Mayor of New York City coming out of a room with a hooker. Whatever the case, it was only after Phelps closed the door behind them, that the voice of panic re-awakened within him. He looked at Phelps warily as the man walked calmly over to the couch against the wall—the small room's only piece of furniture—and sat down in a calm, leisurely manner. Still standing by the door, Roland felt as if he were caught in a bizarre nightmare. Now that he was within the cramped quarters of the room, its effluvium almost made him pass out. The stench of stale beer and cigar smoke, which was commingled, nauseatingly, with cheap perfume and vomit, left him feeling light-headed—

"Did I ever thank you for introducing me to Candice?" Phelps said from the couch.

Roland was seeing spots before his eyes now, squinting in the dim lighting to keep a wary eye on Phelps. "...No," Roland said at last, distractedly.

"—She's been a *godsend*!" Phelps said with a strange gleam in his eyes. Roland wondered if this was Phelps's way of boasting that he was screwing her. The man was smiling at him in the dim lighting, and the expression of ease and confidence on his face disturbed Roland. It reminded him of the smirk that Candice had had on her face all those weeks ago, and he didn't want to think about that night. He had to get the hell away from this place! He needed some fresh air—and *space*! And as the strangeness of the last ten minutes re-exerted its force, he again remembered what Phelps had said in the beginning, about wanting him alone. His mind tried to go to it, but he had neither the strength nor patience. He felt as though he were running out of time: that some cosmic clock were ticking, and that if he didn't get out of here soon, then he would be done for! It was the same eerie feeling he had felt when Kain gripped him that spring night. *Just get the hell out of here*! a voice screamed within him; he was about to take a step towards the door, when Phelps broke in:

"You ever had a white woman, Micheaux?" And at that, Phelps crossed his legs in a professorial manner and looked up at Roland earnestly. But the question was so abrupt—so strangely *unsettling*—that Roland was left dumbfounded. Phelps laughed at the expression on his face, saying: "Getting a white woman ain't nothing, Micheaux—not like in your daddy's day!"—Roland winced; Phelps went on—"In your daddy's day, a black man taking a white woman…now, *that* was perverse—in *Poe's* language, I mean. You ever think about that, Micheaux: taking a woman like your daddy done—"

"What the hell…!" Roland blurted out.

"Don't be so squeamish there, Micheaux," Phelps laughed—

But just then, two women—one of whom had been the waitress that Phelps groped—came in. The room was so small that when they entered, Roland was forced to move over to the other side of the room, where Phelps and the couch were; nonplused, he sat down on the couch beside the man, unconsciously cringing as he stared at the grinning women.

Phelps let out a drunken laugh then, declaring: "Yes, indeed, it's time to celebrate! All hail Edgar Alan Poe and *perverseness*!" And at that, he giggled and nodded to the women, who started slobbering over one another and grabbing one another's breasts.

A resurgent wave of panic and revulsion went over Roland, leaving him numb for those first few moments. While Phelps watched the women intently, Roland stared ahead blankly, feeling himself falling deeper and deeper into the abyss. It again occurred to him, with a jolt of panic that was so severe that it was nauseating, that he hadn't felt this way since that spring night. But Phelps spoke up then, an intense expression on his face as he gestured towards the women and declared:

"Here, it is for us, Micheaux: a perfect laboratory before our eyes. Now, why you figure they're feeling up one another like that?" he said, feigning confusion. "Lust?" he queried, before shaking his head. "Don't make me laugh…that's a human ploy: ascribing everything we don't want to understand—all *perverseness*—to emotionalism."

But at that moment, it was as if Roland were seized by the spirit of the Brooklyn slums. *He had had enough*! All the hatred and ghetto bestiality came flowing out of him. "—And what do *you* see, professor?" Roland growled in the darkness. "This is *your* laboratory, isn't it? That's *your* $100 bill she's got in her panties there. What are we learning: that all people got their price?" His voice became gruffer; it was the voice of the beast/soldier in him. "You trying to *blackmail* me with some bullshit about my father, Phelps!"

"—*Blackmail*?" Phelps laughed in genuine bemusement, while

the oblivious women continued their strange groping, "—about some shit your daddy done 25 years ago!" And he laughed out loud at the fatuousness of it; in fact, his laughter was so hearty that Roland, despite himself, felt foolish. "You been watching too many bad television mysteries, Micheaux!" Phelps went on, laughing so hard that there were tears in his eyes now. "In those shows, I always end up dead; and in the final scene, you end up being cross-examined by Perry Mason, just as he gets a note handed to him by his detective, revealing the strange consanguinity of your bank statements and mine. Nah, Micheaux," Phelps said with a strange zest, "this is about *science*: about the scientific method and experimentation. It's about that age-old question"—he leaned in closer to Roland, still reeking of beer as his hand moved up Roland's thigh—"why do people do the sick shit they do!"

The beast within Roland reappeared in a flash! Phelps was just about to burst out laughing, when Roland leapt up and hit him in the jaw with so much force that the man was knocked off the couch. The women, finally free of their strange lust, cried out and cringed against the wall. Phelps, his mouth bloody and hanging loose, tried to get up, but couldn't. He lay moaning on the floor while Roland, still trembling with rage, stood above him. And that was the same beast that was rising to ascension in the Brooklyn slums. Upon seeing it, the terrified women gripped one another in terror. Roland was in a realm of pure rage, where there were no consequences; the vengeful voice of the beast cried out for more blood. It yearned to leap at Phelps—to *obliterate* the man. The strangely euphoric voice of the beast wanted to say fuck it all! Fuck his career, his life—all of that bullshit, and *kill*. But glancing up then—and seeing the terrified women—some emergency brake was triggered in his mind. He looked about confusedly for a while, utterly lost. The rage that had fed him and given him drive, faded away and left a horrible void in its wake. *He had just knocked out a partner in his firm*! Something in him died away as the full extent of it hit him; and with that death, he was finally able to see the precipice before him. *It was Lamar Smith all over again*! Smith and Kain and his father were reincarnating themselves everywhere, and their madness and will were inescapable. Roland looked down at Phelps in horror, glanced at the cringing women—who screamed out again, as though fearful that he had intentions of coming near them—then he fled.

The rest of the strip joint passed him in a blur; actually, he escaped through the same hidden exit that Randolph had used, perhaps feeling all the horror that Randolph had felt; and then, he was out on the street, first walking, then running at full speed. *I'm running away again*! he thought in alarm, about two blocks later. He stopped then, leaning against a lamppost to support his suddenly frail body. He was panting and sweating profusely, trembling as the reality of what had just happened passed through his mind. But Charlotte McPrice's self-assured, smiling face was looking up at him from the poster on the lamp post, declaring that they were Americans, damn it! And seized by a resurgent wave of queasiness and dismay, he moved on with haste.

* * *

THEY PUMMELED ANDROPOV'S UNMOVING BODY, even as the police sirens sounded in the background. That pummeling seemed to be the only way to exorcise the demons—both within Andropov, and themselves. While both parties survived, there could be no sanity. Destruction was their only salvation. There was something otherworldly in the air: screams that didn't sound as though they could possibly come from human beings. In the despair of the people who ran out into the street and saw their loved-ones' unmoving bodies reduced to the level of gutter trash, there was something that seemed to transcend their pain and loss. What had been instigated by a hit-and-run killing of a young boy, was causing a chain reaction, escalating wildly out of control. They were setting cars on fire now. They attacked anything that was standing: that seemed to represent stability and "the system." An all-night diner across the street got a garbage can through its window; and then, some of the people rushed in and began raiding the cash register. It was like an orgy, where everyone was gripped by the orgasmic bliss that came with surrendering one's self to oblivion. The police found them in this state; the ambulances and fire engines arrived, but feared entering into that chaos. Those already maddened by the possibility of loss, now became incensed, because the paramedics were just standing there, refusing to help their loved-ones. And so, they attacked them as well, further escalating the chaos. The police, seeing this, pulled out their guns. But that didn't mean anything to the people anymore. Even Andropov didn't mean anything to them now. They left his bloody, unmoving body and ran off wildly, in search of more destruction. One man, who had just lost his son, was shot in the face when he ran up to a policeman with a baseball bat in his hand. Nothing could stop them now, but death. The people, like wild beasts stampeding, were going on a rampage. The white neighborhood was a few blocks over: they were going there now, to show those people what it meant to lose everything. The police, unable to get anywhere by firing into the air, and terrified by what they saw before them, lowered their guns and—just like Andropov had done—fired into the charging mob.

*   *   *

MAYOR RANDOLPH STUMBLED down the dark city streets in a daze, feeling, on some level, everything that the city felt: all the pain, terror and madness of the Brooklyn slums. Either he was going mad, or he was becoming sane so quickly, that the shock was too much for his system. His mind was a chaotic jumble; a mocking voice was blaring in his head, telling him that it was all over....Earlier that evening, when he sneaked away from his bodyguards at that mid-town charity benefit and made his way down to the strip joint, it had been as if some demon were whispering in his ear. He had run out into the night, transfixed on the idea of filth. He had wanted a *filthy* woman, as though desperate to hasten the end that was the inevitable consequence of the last few weeks. He had met the hooker at the strip joint through an escort service a week ago; and tonight, he had run to her, not merely driven by lust, but *madness*. He had called her on his cellular phone, and she had told him to meet her in the alley behind the strip joint. They had groped one another for a while behind a huge garbage dumpster. It was incredible how much the insanity of it had turned him on. There had been people walking out in the street just a few meters away, and rats crawling about in the garbage...It had been the woman who protested: who told him to come into the strip joint, where there were private, air-conditioned rooms. They had entered through the secret door....

Randolph felt sick! Of all the men to run into: Roland Micheaux and Dallas Phelps! *Wait until the media hears about this*! he kept thinking. In this scandal-obsessed country, it was only a matter of time before they brought him down. He felt like some deformed movie monster, fleeing from the village peasants. There was nowhere to go now—the entire world was against him. And yet, there was nothing to do, but flee and hide.

—While in the Brooklyn slums, police cruisers were being set on fire by the mob, Randolph, seeming to feel that heat, wrenched off his jacket and meandered down the street like a drunkard. He kept trying to figure out when he had lost it all; and every time he searched his soul, Jasper Kain sprang out from the emptiness within. In fact, ever since Jasper Kain shaved his head and made him a laughingstock, everything had come tumbling down. It was inconceivable how far he had fallen…! The image of Randolph standing on the dais in shock as he felt his shaved scalp, had been an *international* joke. For weeks after the fact, late night talk show comedians had done entire acts on him. Foreign dignitaries visiting City Hall had eyed his head—which, in the initial aftermath, he had shaved completely bald—with a knowing slyness. In the first two days alone, he had dropped 20 points in the polls to Charlotte McPrice! That tiny pebble had torn a gaping hole in reality, setting in motion a chain reaction; and now, boulders were rumbling down the mountain, bringing with them the mountain, itself. All of a sudden, *everything* had seemed to go wrong: his career, his marriage…the very values that had given him the drive and foundation to reach the heights from which he now found himself tumbling.

Still, he had tried to fight Kain's madness at first. Even when he saw all that he had worked for slipping through his fingers, he had laughed at those initial urges, telling himself that he would never act on them. He had laughed at himself the first time he called that phone sex line—and when, a few days later, he had called up that massage service. But the more he laughed and shook his head, the more his self-indulgent mid-life crisis had gripped him. And initially, that was all it had seemed to be: a mid-life crisis, triggered by the fact that he was now a laughingstock. As strange as it seemed, he had been reassured by the thought that he was only joining the ranks of those self-absorbed, bourgeois, middle-aged men that had achieved some measure of success and stability in their lives, but who were now eager to risk it all for something base and transient. Just before his wife came home early from yet another English symposium and found him receiving a massage from a Chinese "call girl"—*in Gracie Mansion*—he had explored filth with such utter carelessness, that it had been as though he were playing Russian roulette. When, a few days ago, he had called up that $10-a-minute phone sex line, and heard himself asking the panting woman on the other end of line what kind of panties she was wearing, he had known, while she breathed heavily into the phone, describing their laciness, and their sudden dampness, not only how ridiculous it all was, but that he was addicted to that very ridiculousness. Even after his wife left him and set a scandal in motion by filing divorce papers, he had been unable to stop. His only thought had been to fling himself headlong into the filth, in some desperate kamikaze act to either save himself from Kain's madness, or succumb to it totally and know the nullifying peace that lay within its depths.

But in reality, he had already sacrificed everything to Kain's madness. He no longer even tried to pretend that he was sane—he had gone too far for that. He was a true believer now, laughing at the fools that had tried to subject Kain to their laws. They had no idea of the man's power. No jail could hold madness. Madness was free, and its power was absolute.

...Every few seconds, he saw the stunned faces of Micheaux and Phelps, knowing that there was no going back....He groaned in the darkness and stumbled down the sidewalk....A bum sleeping in the mouth of the upcoming alleyway ended Randolph's reverie. As Randolph was about to pass by the alley, the man gave a resounding snort, then woke up, screaming: "Eureka!" It was a grizzled white man, who looked like some old prospector who had been up in the hills sifting gold for the last 20 years. The man looked around wildly, leapt to his feet, then ran up to Randolph, demanding:

"I need a dollar, mister!"

"...What?" Randolph said, distractedly.

"I need a dollar!"

Randolph looked him over, saw nothing but an old bum probably thirsting for a bottle of cheap wine, and went to walk off.

"I know you got money, mister!" the old prospector shouted,

stepping into Randolph's path. "Guys like you always got money!" He started patting Randolph's pants pockets—

"Get the hell off of me!" Randolph cursed, finally coming to his senses.

"Give me a dollar!" the old man demanded again. "I know you got it!" And then he went for Randolph's pockets again. There was something wily about him. Randolph was bigger and stronger, but the old man was as nimble as a fox. Randolph tried to grab him and fling him away, but the man kept darting out of the way and reaching for Randolph's pockets. Finally having had enough, Randolph lurched at the man and tackled him to the ground. But even then, the man leapt to his feet, leaving Randolph on the ground. Just as Randolph got back on his feet, the prospector took out an old rusty knife. The prospect of a street fight suddenly reminded Randolph of being a kid in the ghetto again: of being the kid who could take on anything—the star athlete, the magnet for the young girls—

Just then, the old man slashed at him with the knife! Randolph barely managed to leap out of the way, but the tip of the blade sliced him across his chest. He backed away, staring down at the cut in disbelief. It was a flesh wound, but as he was sweating profusely, it stung.

"You should have given me that dollar, mister!" the old man warned, coming at him again.

"A *dollar*!" Randolph screamed hysterically. "You want to kill me for a goddamn dollar!"

"We could have done this the easy way, mister, but you had to be all stingy!"

"What are you, a *crackhead*!" he cried in bewilderment, still backing away.

"Hell *no*!" the man said, as though outraged by the allegation, "I need it to buy a lotto ticket!"

"*What*!"

"See, I was dreaming just now," he explained, "and my Great Aunt Emelda, she gave me those numbers. Twenty-five million dollar jackpot this Saturday! Emelda, she was always *real* good to me...So I got to get me a dollar to buy that ticket!"

Randolph looked on in disbelief. "*Here*!" he said at last, hurriedly taking out his wallet from his jacket (which he still carried in his hand) and grabbing the first bill he saw. "Here's $20, buy *20* tickets!"

The old man grabbed the bill greedily, then a huge, hideous, toothless grin came to his face as he held it before him. Satisfied, he disappeared down the alley, whistling merrily. Randolph watched him disappear, then leaned against the wall in shock. He had almost been killed because an old nut wanted to buy a lotto ticket…! Maybe tomorrow—or whenever he was sane again—he would laugh at it; but in his state of mind, it simply seemed to be more of Kain's doing. Another devotee of Kain's madness had accosted him, and they had merely exchanged salutations.

There was in fact a world of madness out there; and strangely enough, the immensity of the city—and the *world*—suddenly left him with the assurance that he couldn't possibly be the only one thinking these thoughts. There had to be others like him out there—others at the vanguard of Kain's madness. Out there, in all that madness, there had to be a chosen few—soul mates of a sort—wandering about, feeling the same bewilderment that he now felt, trying to discover the route back to their sanity….

His chest was still bleeding, but to hell with it. He stumbled down the street, still unable to believe how far he had fallen. Was he the Mayor of New York City? It seemed too farfetched to be real. He was a man of the gutter now: a man who needed darkness and filth to survive. He saw a clean-cut young white couple coming down the sidewalk and crossed the street to avoid being seen. At the curb, a homeless man was collecting aluminum cans and bottles from the garbage can….Randolph moved on with haste.

—While in the Brooklyn slums, SWAT teams arrived to combat the spiraling violence, Randolph walked along, again realizing that he didn't have a home to return to. His wife had moved back into the townhouse, and Gracie Mansion was too big and empty to be of any solace. Still, like a criminal, all that he could think, was that he had to hide; and it now occurred to him that City Hall, which was about seven blocks away, was the only place he had to go. He set off down the block; but after a few quick steps, a feeling of inevitability came over him, and his pace slowed. He looked around at the world then—and up at the red, menacing sky—suddenly cowed by all that seemed to be ahead. Something evil was out there—he was certain of it now. Ever since this strange heat wave gripped the city, they had all been going mad; from the story of a mother beating her son to death because he had spoiled his dinner by eating a pizza, to stories of motorists getting out of cars and shooting one another, they were all degenerating into animals. Either the source of that madness was supernatural, or, like the pollution choking them on the streets, it had its provenance in the hand of man—

His cellular phone had already rung four times before he realized that it was ringing. He had forgotten that he was even carrying it. In fact, the only people who had ever called him on it were his wife and his little brother; and with divorce proceedings in effect, it had probably been about a month since it had even rung! That it could only be one of two people, set his mind off wildly. And with everything that had happened that night, he was so desperate for even the *illusion* of the love he had had with his wife, that he found himself praying that it were her—and that she was calling to reconcile. He was like the Prodigal Son in the Bible. He had explored filth, but now he was desperate to go back home to everything he had turned his back on. When he answered the phone—which had been in his jacket pocket—his voice was breathless and eager:

"*Hello?*"

"Hello," said a woman.

The voice was too high and young to be his wife's, and his spirits crumpled within him. "Who is this?"

"Don't you recognize my voice?" the woman said with a laugh.

After a frown, Randolph shuddered: *it was the stripper*! He recalled that he had given her the number after he met her through the escort service! It seemed hopelessly stupid to him now, but during those weeks of filth…! "What do you want?" he managed to whisper.

"Is that any way to talk to me?" she laughed, "—especially after the beautiful night we shared?"

"…Why are you calling?" he said. He stopped on the dark street, looking around nervously, as though someone might have overheard.

Again she laughed, and went on in a confident, menacing voice, "I'm calling because I like the sound of your voice, Mayor. I like talking to you."

He paused for a moment, more uneasy than ever. "What do you want to talk about?"

"I want to talk about my needs."

"Your needs?" he said in a faint, monotone voice.

"*You* know," she explained, "—the usual: a nice place to live, a little something in the bank for a rainy day..."

For some reason, Randolph chuckled. It was the laugh of a man at the end of his limits. "And if I don't?" he asked, a side of him genuinely curious.

"Well," she laughed, "you'll be surprised to hear that there are cameras in all those little rooms in the strip joint. That's why I made you come inside—to get some security. See, now it isn't simply your word against mine. I have *evidence*—"

The phone had slipped from Randolph's hand, but he didn't realize it at first. He stood there, with his empty hand against his ear, looking pale and distraught. The blow that came when he realized that he was totally at her mercy was so severe that he felt as though he were having an "out-of-body" experience. It was as if everything were going in slow motion, because he was able to look down in time to see the phone smashing against the pavement. He looked down in awe, seeing it shattering into half a dozen pieces. In fact, time was moving so slowly, that it was as if he had been standing there for minutes—for *hours* even—

So this is it! he thought at last. Indeed, he couldn't think of anything else. A side of him was probably relieved that the proverbial die had been cast, and that he wouldn't have to be afraid of ghosts anymore. But the horrible emptiness that came with knowing that it was all over (and the realization of the long, painful ride to total self-destruction) was like a dull blade slowly disemboweling him. He left the shattered phone where it was and continued walking on, now with a stiff, feeble gait.

—While in the Brooklyn slums, all the inadvertent devotees of Kain's madness rose up to destroy the world and themselves, Randolph stumbled across Broadway, finally entering City Hall Park. How the hell it had come to this! he wondered, like Andropov had wondered just an hour before. He was so numb, that it was now as though time had stopped. The outside world was like the blurry background of a dream. He heard nothing, saw nothing...was aware only that he was moving, and that his life as he had known it, was over—

"*Hey*!" a gruff voice screamed. Randolph had just climbed over the barricade, which, for anti-terrorist purposes, now surrounded City Hall. Two officers were now running up, their guns drawn.

Randolph stepped numbly beyond the barricade, as though he hadn't heard them. "*Freeze!*" the men screamed. But some hysterical voice was blaring in Randolph's mind, telling him to run—or move his hands aggressively—so that they would gun him down like that black youth in the news a few months ago, who had been shot 27 times just because, in the darkness, it had looked as if he were reaching for something.

"*Don't move!*" the officers yelled again, and Randolph, finally stopping, watched them disinterestedly. They came up to him, their guns pointed at his head. Randolph continued to look up at them with a bizarre nonchalance as they told him to keep his hands where they could see them; but just then, in turning his head, his face was at last illuminated by a street lamp—

"*Sir*...! We didn't know...!" The two men stood there trembling, making excuses that Randolph neither heard, nor cared to hear. He waved his hand in a distracted manner and walked into the building. Other guards, hearing the disturbance, came running; but when they saw Randolph walking by with his shirt bloodied by the cut, they only stared confusedly.

* * *

AS NEWS OF THE EVENTS IN the Brooklyn slums spread, Maria Santos sat on the edge of the news van's passenger side seat, watching her cameraman anxiously as he sped down the Brooklyn streets. Her anxiety wasn't because she thought that he was going too fast, but because she was sure that he wasn't going fast enough! They had heard the story over the police radio about 30 minutes ago—there was a full-blown race riot in progress! As she sat on the edge of her seat, she let out an inadvertent squeal of excitement that was almost orgasmic. What a perfect story it all was! There had been a story in the news the other day, lambasting the growth of violence on television—but to hell with that! It was sex and violence that made the world turn—*forget money*. Half the world was broke and starving, and yet in every destitute nook of the world, the women were popping out kids like crazy, while their men were off fighting one another. Sex and violence were the spice of life; and as she rushed through the Brooklyn streets, Maria Santos prepared herself for the orgy to come.

The way that they were rushing, it was as though they were paramedics making haste towards an accident scene. But in reality, it was death and dismemberment that she was chasing. She found herself hoping that the ambulances hadn't arrived yet: that she would get there in time to see the dead and dying lying on the ground. She found herself hoping that the police hadn't quelled the strife yet, and that the gleam of mob violence would still be in the eyes of the people.

It was like finding a treasure map and hoping that someone hadn't already dug up the treasure. But after 12 years as a roving reporter on New York's streets, Maria Santos knew all the tricks of treasure hunting. As she repeatedly reminded herself, she was not only a woman in a man's world, but a swarthy minority woman who was approaching middle age, in a youth-obsessed society that had as its ideal some anorexic, blond swimsuit model. So what if she had to "put out a little ass" every once in a while to get a story or placate her boss? What if she had had to have a couple of plastic surgeries—not to mention liposuction and a tummy tuck? This was the way of the world. You either had to *put* out or *get* out. It wasn't that she didn't have journalistic integrity, mind you, but that she was honest about what it was that she did. She was a slut, and her johns were the type of viewers who couldn't get enough of her hard-hitting investigative series on the disastrous mistakes of penile enlargement surgery. That one had been a masterpiece, producing her most memorable line: "Choose your doctor carefully, lest you end up with the short end of the stick...."

To Maria Santos, there were three kinds of viewers: those, luckily in the minority, who actually wanted "news," a substantially greater section of the populace, who wanted others to *think* that they wanted news, but who actually wanted scandal and entertainment, and an increasingly significant portion who wanted sleaze and scandal and didn't care who knew. It was the latter group that was her most loyal clientele—and towards whom she tailored her reports. Her exposés on suburban housewives turned streetwalkers, and the sex cult operating out of a city councilman's basement, had catapulted her to nationwide acclaim. There had been a story in the news the other day, about her going too far with her two-part report on a 20-year veteran of the coroner's office, who, according to her "evidence," was a necrophiliac. But Santos's worry was never of crossing some mythical line, but of not going far enough! Ratings were the only absolute in her business, and it was they that told her what to do. And besides, if she didn't do it, then someone else—someone younger and prettier and less constrained by social guilt—would. There was no room for conscience in this business. "Taste" arguments were for those who lacked the imagination and drive necessary to be successful in her world. She was a slut, and as she always said: I'm going to get fucked anyway, so I may as well "get mine" while I am at it!

As her sense of excitement grew, she looked over at the cameraman and barked at him to drive faster—to run red lights if necessary! A quivering smile came to her lips as she thought of all that was to come. It would be all hers—a perfect treasure, lying bloody and bullet-riddled on the filthy street!

Another grin was about to grace her lips; but just then, the cameraman turned the corner and they entered the blocks of the rampage. About five ambulances and fifteen police cars were on that one block alone—their wailing sirens were deafening in the air. About three fire trucks were there as well, extinguishing a burning building. The dizzying array of flashing lights made Santos squint as she looked gloomily down the block. The police presence was *massive:* they had definitely learned from the L.A. riots. They had hit the people hard and fast, with overwhelming force, so that the people wouldn't be emboldened by the freedom of rioting. Dozens of people were lining up to be put in paddy wagons. In the air, over the sirens and the lingering odor of tear gas, there were intermittent gun shots. And a few blocks down, it seemed like everything was engulfed in flames: cars, houses...Against the backdrop of the red, menacing sky, it would have all been perfect, if not for the fact that several other television crews were already on the scene. She saw them darting around, interviewing the stunned populace. On top of that, two news helicopters were hovering overhead, giving a bird's-eye-view of all the chaos. And just then, adding insult to injury, another news van swerved around Santos and her cameraman, and zoomed past.

"*Shit!*" Santos cursed out loud as she came to her senses and gestured for the cameraman to move in fast. As she looked at all that could have been hers, she shook her head in frustration, thinking, *Scraps again!*

* * *

FOR THE FIRST FEW MINUTES, Roland was in shock. He made his way down the city streets with the mortal terror of someone who had just seen the Devil. In the heat, he was down to his shirt sleeves now, and even they were soaked through. The sweltering air of the city was thick and foul around him, leaving an aftertaste in his mouth. His tongue felt as though it had been coated with muck; the membranes of his nostrils, as dry and chapped as they were, felt like mud that had hardened and cracked in the sun. He was walking up Broadway, somnambulating towards his midtown condominium, but it didn't seem as though he could possibly have a destination in mind. That mind was like a bird buzzing about a crocodile to drive it away from its eggs; the thing that had just happened—huge, fierce, and, it seemed, *unstoppable*—was the crocodile.

—While on television (this was *way* beyond the Brooklyn slums now) there were helicopter views of entire blocks engulfed in flames, and bands of looters breaking into cars and any open businesses, Roland's mind hovered over the reality that he had been on the verge of *killing* Phelps—*a partner in his firm*! He had knocked down Phelps like he had knocked down Lamar Smith; and, in the end, he had run from it all the way he had run from his father. But between Phelps and those men there was a world of difference. The world was eager to forget Kain and Smith and his father; but men like Phelps, with their money and influence, were the invisible power behind the world. Smith and Kain, at worst, could kill him, but men like Phelps destroyed men *totally*—stripped them of their dignity, their means of earning a living...*everything*—so that in the end, their lives weren't *worth* living. That was power. In a battle between Roland and Phelps, it was all too clear who the winner would be. Phelps would ruin him now—Roland was certain of it! Men like Phelps were petty and vengeful; the man had already proven that his depravity had no limits, what could ruining Roland's life possibly mean to him? Roland was sport for such men: a chance for them to experiment with perversion, not because they were lusty, but because they *could*!

—While on television, grainy images of life and death were broadcast over all the network feeds, Roland stumbled up Broadway, looking at all the passersby. As the events of the night continued either to warp his perceptions or to clarify all that had before been misperceived, the people on the street suddenly seemed suspect to him. They walked along quietly and seemed peaceful; but with all that had happened tonight, he was instinctively wary of them—and what passed for their peace. The strange thing about the city, was that a few kilometers away, in Brooklyn, there seemed to be another reality: another universe, with people acting in ways that didn't seem possible. That other universe had its own gravity: its own laws of physics—and its own possibilities. From block to block, one went from one reality to another, so that what was real in one place, was meaningless in another. And yet, at the same time, all those disparate places were joined by something not as cliché as human nature—but also, not as predictable. In the wake of all that had happened tonight, that thing seemed to have Phelps's face; and as he looked at the people on the streets, Roland instinctively wondered what perversions their hunger led them to; because in the end, this all seemed to be about hunger—emptiness that was so vast, that it drove one insane. Indeed, the world was full of perverts and murderers: it was full of bigots and degenerates of all kinds; and if Roland had been able to convince himself that Phelps were some southern bigot, aiming to bring him down as a *nigger*—or a closet homosexual angling for his next tryst—then everything would have been settled in his mind. But there was something too simplistic—and *hopeful*—in that. To say that a man was a bigot or a pervert, put the accuser and his society at ease, because it identified the accused as a socially condemned fool, soon to be done in by the force of public opinion. But to say that a man was *hungry*, was troubling, because there were none who haven't been moved by the pangs of an empty belly—or an empty soul.

—While on television, there were grainy images of a man fully engulfed in flames, running down the middle of the street, Roland meandered up the block, acutely aware that he was no match against the world. Something quintessentially sacred had been desecrated in him: his faith in the world and the sanity of men had been shaken; and in this light, not only was Phelps some new prototype of humanity, but what lay ahead was even clearer. He had knocked Phelps out; and the man, enlisting all the power at his disposal, would destroy him. It was as simple as that. Phelps would get him fired—invent some pretext and *ruin* him! Phelps's power was about to run him over, and Roland had to prepare himself for the blow. For a while, he felt as helpless as a newborn baby; but perhaps, just as a newborn has its parents to attend to it when it cries out in the night, Roland had the beast within—which was always ready to strike out when danger appeared on the horizon. And slowly, as the events of the night played in his mind, his shock and disillusionment were overcome by revulsion—and *hatred*. All of it—Phelps, the Mayor...—sickened him so violently that the hatred welled up inside of him and left him certain that the only option open to him was *fighting*. All of a sudden, the beast within, outraged not only by what Phelps had done, but by what the man *could* do, began to growl. Anger could either drive one insane or lead one back to one's sanity; but in Roland's case, he didn't care which it was: all he knew was that Phelps was his enemy and that he would have to fight fire with fire—*even if the battle was a losing one*! Methodically, he worked at trying to evoke thoughts of vengeance and destruction—just as he knew Phelps was doing! It suddenly occurred to him that he could sue the firm—take them for *millions* of dollars...! For entire minutes, his mind was entranced by images of him taking Phelps and all those other bastards to court—and *ruining* them, like they would ruin him. He went about it with the desperation—and in the end, the *futility*—of an impotent man trying to effect an erection; because in the final analysis, it was the dawning prospect of himself as some kind of trailblazer of homosexual sexual harassment suits, which put that out of his mind and, at the same time, put him in touch with his reason.

With the notoriety he had received lately, such a suit would be *headline* news. And the idea of him becoming one of those pathetic fools on those talk shows, who mumbled lachrymose tales about how he had been victimized, was a definite no-no. Yes, Phelps was his enemy, but it occurred to Roland that the most precious thing he had was not his job, but his *dignity*: his *manhood*. He would fight Phelps, but he would fight him as a *man*, not as some gossip on the street. *Yes*, unfolding slowly, like a flower opening its petals to the sun, was the renewed realization of Phelps's abysmal hunger. Such a life, juxtaposed to what Roland's life had been like for the last few years, was no comparison. Phelps's life was all so pointless, that

Roland, upon reflection, couldn't bring himself to believe that the man was anything but some sick rarity, soon to be culled by the forces of nature. And, on second thought, while he had knocked Phelps out, his reaction—his revulsion at the man's touch—had been justified. Roland had survived more than Phelps in his lifetime and would never let that depravity drag him down. All of a sudden, he was walking straighter: there was life and purposefulness in his steps again. Yes, what mattered, was his *essence*—the fact that he was Roland Micheaux, and that he had succeeded in this world on nothing but pure wit and determination. In fact, there was nothing that Phelps could do to him, short of taking his life, that could take that away from him. Scores of firms had expressed a desire to retain his services; following his last set of appearances on TV, even the *networks* had offered him positions as a legal analyst—

Roland laughed out, suddenly reassured and self-satisfied. As desperate as he had felt just moments ago, he was now relieved. There were still complications and hurdles ahead, but his essence was fortified again; and knowing who he was and what he had been able to accomplish, left him convinced that he would somehow make it through—conquer whatever foe life threw at him. And he had just won that huge case—he was going to be on television in the morning...*and he was a star*.

He was walking past a dance club now, and as he looked at the young "beautiful people" waiting on a line to enter, their joy and excitement seemed to be a sign that everything was right with the world. However, when Roland was about halfway down the block from the dance club, a white girl stepped out from the upcoming doorway. A gaudy neon sign was above the entrance, announcing that jewelry and electronic equipment could be pawned there for "Big $$$." As the girl stepped below the sign, Roland saw that she was no older than 14 years old. She was in a black miniskirt that clung tenaciously to her boyish figure. Her face seemed as though it had been *painted* with makeup, not simply that makeup had been applied; and her hair was "big," stiff with mousse. She stepped before Roland, a sordid imitation of sexiness flashing in her eyes as she chewed a huge wad of gum:

"You want a date, baby?" she drawled.

"What...?"

"Looking for some fun?"

"You're a *prostitute?*" Roland said in bewilderment.

"No, no...nothing like that," she said defensively, looking around as if fearful that someone had heard. And then, as though from some voice of shame within herself: "...I'm just trying to get something to eat..."

Those words struck a sensitive cord in him, and he looked at her with a heart that was suddenly sick—suddenly attuned to the devastating scope of hunger in the world. It was as though fate had produced this girl to tell him to keep his guard up. He had barely survived Phelps's hunger, and here was this girl again, trying to suck him in. He looked at her bony figure and her anemic eyes then. She was probably some runaway, either chasing big dreams or running away from irreconcilable nightmares. He took out his wallet and handed her a hundred dollar bill.

"Where you want to go?" she said, smiling again.

"I don't want to go anywhere—"

"I wasn't begging, you know," she said, as though hurt.

"I know you weren't," he said solemnly. "You were just hungry. Go get something to eat," he went on. "...Go home if you can: hunger's a dangerous thing to have in this city." He nodded vaguely then and went to walk off. But it was then that the pealing noise of a quickly braking car startled him. He whirled around, freezing as he saw two police officers step out of a cruiser!

"Don't move!" a pudgy, donut-eating one shouted, resting his hand on his gun as he rushed out. Roland's first thought was that Phelps had called the police on him! All his old fears came flooding back! He was trembling now, raising his hands in response to the officer's demand. His mind was so chaotic—so suddenly raging with fear—that everything seemed to be passing him in a blur—

"What's going on here?" the other cop, a lean, stern-looking white man, demanded. "You trying to buy sexual favors? We seen you exchange money!"

Roland's lips were trembling: "No—*no!*" he said as if just realizing what the words meant. "It wasn't like that. She said she was hungry. *Ask* her," he said, turning to the equally fidgety girl. "I was just helping her out—I didn't even want to go anywhere with her!" He was babbling on, sounding like one of those fools that he used to defend when he worked for the Public Defender's Office—

The lean one turned to the girl: "You a runaway?"

"...Yes," she whispered, bowing her head.

"He telling the truth?" he went on, gesturing to Roland.

"Yea," she said, "he was real nice to me—gave me a hundred dollars to get something to eat."

The donut-eating cop had been squinting at Roland, as if trying to place his face: "Ain't you Roland Micheaux?"

Roland's stomach convulsed. He felt terribly ashamed for some reason—as though he actually had tried to pick the girl up; but seeing no use in denying his identity, he nodded.

"What you doing out here?" the lean one inquired.

"I was just walking home," Roland pleaded again, sounding pathetic.

"Well," the lean one started in a conciliatory air, "these are dangerous streets, mister—especially with this heat. There's a riot going on in Brooklyn as we speak. Heat drives people mad, you know. [Roland nodded contritely.] They get like rats in a cage. All they want to do is strike out at the closest thing to them—don't care who or what it is."

"You better get on home," drawled the pudgy one, while he gestured for the girl to come with them.

Roland nodded to the officers, glanced uneasily at the girl, then walked briskly away. However, once around the corner, he began to run at full speed.

* * *

CHARLES MARENGA WAS thankfully thousands of kilometers away from New York City and its madness. He was in the third week of a five-month tour of Africa, and was presently in Ghana. He had left New York soon after the shouting match with Mayor Randolph—and the Kain debacle. Inwardly, he was sick of it all—and his place in it—but outwardly, he cursed Randolph and America as vehemently as ever. In truth, something had changed in him—and had perhaps *been* changing for some time now. Whatever the case, he emerged from the doorway of the beach cabin and stared out dreamily at the pre-dawn sea. He yawned at that moment, then smiled vapidly as he began to walk towards the ocean. A short, rotund man, he looked ridiculous in only his shorts, but there was no one to see him. The sand tickled his toes as he moseyed towards the ocean; and he again smiled contentedly to himself, as he looked down the Ghanaian coastline and saw the thin band of dawn. The morning sky was one of those dreamy mauves: it was dark and mysterious now, but as the light grew, it would become bright and spectacular. He was getting a knack for such things now—an ease of spirit that allowed him to see things that only weeks ago, would have been beyond his comprehension. Some of the stars were still visible: he stopped on the edge of the ocean and smiled at them as well. It was the sky that had given him his first dose of sanity after he decided to take a few months away from New York and America—and all of their contradictions and entanglements—to come to Africa. It had been the night sky—striking him as a place of infinite peace, with stars glittering so brilliantly that they seemed like sparkling diamonds—that had unlocked some hidden part of his soul. He remembered thinking, that first night in the desert of Morocco (there would be no five-star hotels and tourist resorts for him), that no one could be troubled—could be preoccupied with the entanglements of mankind—with such a sky at his disposal. To listen to all the far-off night sounds, lying on ones back in the middle of nowhere: to gaze at the infinite peace of the heavens, knowing that there were no demands being made and nothing to do but rest…how could the problems of the world exist in the face of that? The African guides whom he had hired, openly laughed at him—the funny black American who acted as though he had never seen stars, or plains or valleys—but Marenga didn't care.

—While in the Brooklyn slums, the side effects of rage and justice-taking rose into the air with the rest of the pollution and filth, Marenga let out a peaceful sigh, stepping into the ocean. The water chilled him at first, so that an inadvertent squeal escaped from him; but after plunging himself headlong into it, he found it warm and soothing. He waddled out farther then, enjoying the sensation of near weightlessness. When the water was to his neck, he began to swim, going out farther. He laughed for no good reason, then took a mouthful of the brine and spit it out playfully, like he had seen dolphins do off the coast of Mauritania. All at once, he had the feeling that here, for these few moments, the world was his and he could do whatever he wanted. It occurred to him that he could swim naked if he wanted; and as the thought passed through his mind, he wrenched off his shorts and threw them towards the shore. Then, giggling to himself, he swam out farther, giddy with the sudden, carefree joy. He felt as though he were drunk. *This is what it means to be alive*! he thought to himself. No more New York, filled with psychotic weirdoes like Jasper Kain; no more rallies; no more Mayor Randolph...no more protests to lead—no more senseless strife that was doomed to be forgotten after the initial media frenzy.

—While in America, the chaos of the night was being superseded by the systematic violence that was their culture, Marenga swam deeper into the ocean; and as the waves washed over him, he felt as though layers of his life—like dead, ugly skin—were being washed off. The feeling of peace and well being again seized him, and he laughed out for no good reason. However, as he hadn't exercised in decades, he was soon exhausted from his efforts. A vigorous sprinter in his youth, he was now a flabby man on the verge of old age. He floated on his back for a while as he panted for air and stared up at the dreamy sky. *Just enjoy the moment*! he thought to himself, just as he was about to unleash another laugh. But as soon as he opened his mouth to laugh, he realized that something strange was happening. He had stopped swimming, but he was still being brought out to sea. Looking over his shoulder, he saw that the shore was about 150 meters away—and that he was still being drawn out at an alarming rate! He was caught in a rip tide! *Don't panic*! he said to himself, trying to recall everything he had ever heard about rip tides. Yes: he should let it take him out, and not fight it. His mind went over everything, and the realization that he was reasoning it out filled him with joy and excitement. Suddenly, while the sea pulled him deeper into itself, he laughed almost insanely at his triumph over the ocean. It was trying to thwart his peace: steal him away from Africa. But he would outwit it, he thought with a scheming grin. He would let it think that it had him, then he would escape. He began swimming parallel to the shore, just like he had read in books. That was the way to outsmart it. He was so gripped by the game that he didn't realize how spent he was. When he finally freed himself from the pull of the ocean and looked back towards the shore, he saw that he was about 400 meters out!

The first pang of danger hit him: it wasn't a game anymore. He began swimming back—way too quickly. His weak heart began to protest and ache; his lungs felt as though they were already filled with water; and as for his limbs, as he hadn't exercised in years, they felt like lead bricks. The panic began to build in him. He had been paddling for two exhausting minutes, and yet the shore still seemed as far away as before. He panicked at the thought that he was still in the rip tide—was still being pulled out to sea! He began to swim harder: to expend energy that he didn't have. He was practically thrashing in the water now! All that he could manage was an ungainly doggie paddle. He misjudged a paddle stroke and went under, gulping down a mouthful of brine. He wanted to look up and see how far he was from the shore, but he couldn't bear the thought that he was still being drawn out. *Oh, God*, to die like this...after all that he had been through—all the protest marches...He had marched with Martin Luther King for God's sake, getting clubbed over the head by southern sheriffs during the 60s; he'd been shot at by rednecks, and attacked by dogs; and after all that, he would die like this—something as untheatrical as a drowning! A *drowning*, due to the fact that he was a fat slob...And then, all of a sudden, he remembered that he was naked—that they would find his naked, bloated body washed up on the beach, there to repulse the first hapless fool to come upon it. *God*, to die like this—like an *animal: senselessly*...! And his protesting heart suddenly felt as though it were being squeezed from within. He wanted to scream out at the sensation, but every time he opened his mouth, another gulp of the sickening brine went down into his belly.

The prospect of death sent his mind off violently. It wasn't that his life "flashed before his eyes," but that suddenly remembering all the dreams of his youth, and contrasting them to the reality of his recent life, he was left with an acute sense that his time had been wasted.

—While in the Brooklyn slums, the people that had torn their world apart began to come to grips with what they had done, Marenga drowned off the coast of Africa, seeing his wasted life. And how senseless it all seemed to him now! He had been at the vanguard of a direction-less procession, inciting crowds of his people to be angered by periodic police killings of unarmed black youths—and other such obvious transgressions by the white community. He had allied himself with Black nationalists, like the self-avowed Black Racist, Botswana Glade, and taken as his constituents those whom one might be tempted to call the rabble: the poor and marginalized residents of the slums. But all of that ostensible rabble-rousing had been a farce; his education at Princeton and Oxford, where he had been a Rhodes Scholar, had been a farce. Only now, as he was close to death, was he sufficiently free of that world to see all of this clearly. In fact, as he prepared for death, Marenga could have been some divine dreamer, unfolding the events of the Brooklyn slums. His wasted life was the personification of their self-destructiveness....But as a youth: as a *youth*, he had seemed to have everything and *be* capable of everything. He had set out to fight racism and inequality, presumptuously thinking that he could change the very nature of the world...but a horrible leap of faith had been made somewhere along the way—not only in him, but in the millions of people the world over who saw themselves as victims of the social order! How eager and jubilant the victims of racism and sexism, and all the newfound "isms", now seemed. Victimhood was now a badge of honor, like a monk's sufferings, so everyone was claiming to be victimized. Look at all the frivolous lawsuits, all the idiotic talk shows. And now, even white men were claiming to be victims of the social order. Bewitching them all was some new idea, which had the deceptive appeal of weight loss programs that demanded neither exercise nor *effort*. It was the contradiction of getting power *through* one's powerlessness. All those people, ready to consider themselves wronged. The only thing that was needed was that one spark in the wrong place and everything would go up in flames.

And as these thoughts passed through Marenga's mind, his exhausted limbs thrashed feebly in the water; as the pain in his chest coursed through him, the violence being done to his body seemed to match the violence that had been done to his soul—and the violence coming to fruition in New York City. He closed his eyes now, and the past and present became one swirling mess, with the urban riots and social eruptions of the '60s and '70s, and the media frenzies of the present day blurring together.

—And while in the America of the present, images of the riot and the equally brutal crackdown consumed the public, and leaders from all quarters rose up to explain the madness, Marenga continued his haphazard journey through his own history and that of America, suddenly realizing that this wouldn't be the first time that he had died. In fact, at the end of the 60s, a disillusioned Marenga had looked around at America, realizing not only that his kind was unwanted, but that he was a bastard son of the land that had nourished him and shaped his ideals. America was debilitating to those very individuals who believed in its jargon: who tried to pull themselves up by their bootstraps and put faith in justice and "the American way." For those individuals, America was a god: its ideals were edicts sent from above; and when those ideals showed themselves to be nothing but lies, all the bastard sons fell victim to that hatred that only the religious and the jilted knew—

And now, here he was in Africa, preparing for death. His leaden limbs flopped languidly in the water as he expended the last of his energy. His weak heart seemed to pump not blood, but rhythmic pulses of pain. His stomach was full of seawater by now; and with all the water that he had already inhaled, his nasal passages and throat burned. He glanced up, about to look at the shore one last time, when he miraculously saw that it was no more than 30 meters away!

How was it possible! New life filled him from nowhere. He was paddling again—as violently as before—but filled with hope this time. The shore was ahead! He could hardly believe it! He was paddling violently now. Sand! There was land beneath him: he touched it first with his flailing, unbelieving hands! He tried to stand up, but he was too exhausted for that, so he stumbled along, hunched over like some deformed beast, before collapsing onto the beach. He retched suddenly and violently then, vomiting up the brine that he had swallowed; but then, all of a sudden, he was laughing: giggling between gasps for air. He laughed at the pain in his chest, at his lightheadedness—at *everything*! Somehow, he had survived. *How*, he didn't know and didn't care. All that he knew was that he was alive, and that these moments were his. He lay there naked and carefree, dreamily watching the sunrise.

* * *

BACK AT CITY HALL, NEWS of the riot hadn't quite hit yet; and about everything, there was that proverbial calm before the storm. Randolph ambled down the luxurious corridors, towards his office. But now that he was safely within City Hall, even hiding didn't make too much sense anymore. All that he could think about was that new thing: the stripper and her demands. As odd as it seemed, he wasn't really horrified anymore. He had made his bed, and now he would sleep in it. In fact, he was so exhausted by the night that a side of him couldn't really be bothered. All about him was that sense of peace that came when one knew that everything was out of one's hands. It was as though he had just returned from a long, tiring journey: only after he had rested and regained his faculties, would he be able to put his house in order. The need for filth left him; his delusions about soul mates, all struggling against filth and the coming destruction, became brittle to his touch, and fell away as well; so that now, all that there was, was an enveloping emptiness.

The door of his office was open, and the light was on. He walked in, still in a daze. He would sleep on the couch in the corner. He went to the attached bathroom and washed out his cut. He would probably need a tetanus shot...He got a clean shirt from the adjoining closet—which was stocked with several shirts and suits—then he walked back into his office, buttoning up his shirt.

Randolph was at the window, staring out dreamily, when a man walked into the room. Randolph became aware of the man's presence because the man was whistling; and when he turned around, Randolph saw a short, fat Latino of middle age whom, by his uniform, and his cart of cleaning utensils, Randolph assumed to be the janitor. The man stopped abruptly when he saw the Mayor.

"Sorry," the janitor apologized quickly, "I didn't know you were here."

"No problem," Randolph said in an offhand manner, "finish your job." And at that, he turned back to the window, soon lost in his thoughts as he stared into the darkness—

But all of a sudden, a young white aide ran into the room, almost colliding with the janitor's cart. Randolph jumped and swung around at the commotion. It looked as if the aide had just woken up: his shirt was hanging out of his pants and his tie was crooked; he came running up, panting and wide-eyed: "Sir! Thank goodness you're here! They said I'd find you in here!"

"What is it, Radix?" Randolph whispered, a note of alarm already sounding in his voice. The janitor had stopped sweeping and was staring anxiously as well.

"It's *crazy*—there's a race riot going on in Brooklyn, sir! People have been *killed*—dozens wounded!"

"A riot?" Randolph whispered strangely, wondering why he wasn't surprised: why it all seemed so natural to him.

"*Crazy*," Radix repeated. "...First, this white man runs over a young Puerto Rican kid with his car, then speeds through a red light, hitting another car. Then, after the accident, the man gets out of the car and shoots the other driver; and then, as the mob runs up to him, he shoots several others before he finally runs out of bullets and they attack him....After beating him unconscious, the crowd began to riot. The police shot about 10 of them, sir!"

The janitor gasped!

"*God*," the young aide went on, nervously combing his fingers through his hair, "we're lucky Marenga's out of the country! And heaven only knows what Charlotte McPrice is going to say when she finds out!"

Randolph was a little annoyed by the mention of those two; and to get the aide's mind back to the matter at hand, he demanded, "When did this begin?"

"About three quarters of an hour ago, sir. The police are still containing the violence."

"But it *is* under control, right?"

"It's hard to know, sir...Still some trouble spots, but the police have broken up the larger groups...and then there are all the fires to put out."

"Is the shooter still alive?"

"We don't know, sir—the police haven't been able to get to him yet!"

Randolph groaned equivocally to himself; then, shaking his head, he signed loudly and said: "Okay, get me the police commissioner on the phone and contact the rest of the cabinet. As soon as the riot is under control, set up the usual press conference at the hospital where they take the worst victims." And when Randolph nodded to show that he was finished, the aide ran out of the room, leaving Randolph alone with the janitor.

Randolph went over to his desk to fetch something; the janitor's concerned eyes followed him.

"It's pretty bad," the man ventured.

Randolph looked up in surprise, having forgotten that the man was there. After a pause, he replied: "Not any worse than usual." He seemed distracted, but not in a standoffish manner. There was a side of him that watched his own actions and was surprised and relieved to find himself acting like the Mayor again. He felt *real* again; and having reacquainted himself with the sensations of a man of respect and power, he was desperate to forget about the bestial madness of the preceding weeks. He looked at the janitor, suddenly assured by the expression of respect and faith in the man's eyes. Buoyed by that faith, Randolph went on: "The thing to do, is to act quickly, before it spreads." He was silent for a moment, drifting on his thoughts; then he added, in a far-off voice: "New York—all the big cities in fact—...they're just accidents waiting to happen. A few incidents like this, back-to-back..." He shook his head ominously and left it at that. But that was all that needed to be said. They stood there, in the sudden silence, thinking it over. A short moment later, the young aide again ran into the room and broke the spell. The janitor unconsciously stepped aside when the man entered; and then, while plans were made and the screechy, defensive voice of the police commissioner came over the speakerphone, the janitor nodded his head and stepped outside.

* * *

ROLAND RAN THE remaining blocks and into his building, darting past old Sam, the startled doorman. He was panting when he locked his front door behind him—even though he had taken the elevator and his door was practically right across from the elevator. He felt as though his insides were turning to mush! The realization that he had babbled on to those policemen like...like a *criminal—like a scared nigger*—ate away at his soul. And what would have happened if that runaway had said that he tried to pick her up! He would have been *ruined*—if not legally, then definitely in the public eye. He felt as though he had just missed being hit by a truck. He could have easily ended up as one of those fools that appeared on the local news every night, going through that daily nigger dance: paraded before a media gauntlet while trying to hide their faces from the cameras. He often thought about things like that—it was perhaps inevitable, with all that he had been through. His father's ghost was always there; his father's genes were *in* him; and maybe, he would find himself thinking from time to time, so was his father's soul: his father's mindless lust, his senseless brutality…Perhaps those things had been passed on to him, like a disease lying dormant in the genes of his soul; and when the time was right—when the genetic trigger had been activated—he would revert to the demon state, surrendering to the madness that had gripped his father, killing like his father had killed—

The phone rang and Roland jumped! It was a cordless phone, and he had left it on the couch. After the panicky feeling subsided somewhat, he walked over feebly and picked up the phone.

"Hello?"

"Roland!" shouted a woman.

"Yes?" he said, still trying to place the voice.

"It's me," the woman said, "*Candice*!"

"*Candice*!" He felt suddenly hollow—*numb*.

"Dallas went crazy!" she shouted.

"*What*?"

"He came home drunk with his face all beat up and kicked me and Mindy out!"

"*What*!"

"I'm out on the street," she started crying. "I couldn't think of anyone else to call. He's mad when he's drunk!"

"He threw out his *three-year-old* daughter?"

"He came home with a big bottle of champagne, saying something about this was the time for celebration. [Roland shuddered.] He told me to grab Mindy and 'get the hell out!'"

"Maybe you should call the police!"

"The police!" she cried. "Can't we just come over," she pleaded, "—spend the night—until he cools off?"

Roland had forgotten that she was an illegal alien—she didn't want anything to do with the police. He still felt sick to his stomach—and alarm bells were raging in his mind; nevertheless, he sighed, seeing no other way. "…Yea, I guess you can come over," he said at last. "Can you get a cab?"

"Yea," she said, seeming relieved, "I'll be right over."

He stared into the darkness after she had put the phone down; he stood there listening to the dial tone, not quite able to believe that it had really happened. He felt *sick*! He put the phone down—tossed it back to the couch—and collapsed on top of it. Lying there, he wondered, like Andropov and Randolph and Marenga had wondered before him, how the hell he had come to this place. He tried to effect the magic that had freed him the last time, but he couldn't remember the spell. He felt as though he were on a yo-yo, spinning wildly between courage and craven despair—or maybe from one paranoid delusion to another. With all that had happened tonight, he was sure that he was going mad; and needing desperately to drown his thoughts, Roland grabbed the remote control from the coffee table and switched on the television. He began flipping through the channels…Something caught his attention—maybe it was the melodramatic tone of the reporter:

"…At least a dozen people shot—six now confirmed dead," Maria Santos ranted, "…dozens of others wounded by mob violence…and then there is the seven-year-old boy that this beast ran down with his car…!" The chaotic scene at her back, with the flashing lights of emergency vehicles and the darting urgency of police officers, firemen and medical technicians, was mesmerizing. As he watched those scenes, he found himself thinking about his father again, seeping back into the quagmire that always came with the reality of death and madness. He offered up no defense to those thoughts this time: they were something which he could no longer profess to fight….Every day, some little thing happened to show him that those formative experiences had warped his mind—were perhaps a cancer growing within him. A few months ago, he had been watching television just as the station announced that the FBI had finally captured some ax-wielding serial killer. Roland had sat there frozen as they prepared to show the captured man. The reporters had been talking about how brutal the man's murders were and how many lives were lost and ruined; and yet, Roland had been aware of an inexplicable sense of relief at the fact that the killer was white….

Roland emerged from his reverie and looked over at the television once again. After Maria Santos described the killer as a middle-aged white man, Roland sat back, lowered the volume and closed his eyes....

* * *

ANDROPOV DIDN'T REALLY HAVE A body anymore: he was just a conglomeration of throbbing nerve endings. His momentary emergence back into conscious was more alarming than the devastating extent of his injuries. A paramedic, he suddenly realized, was over him, yelling some gibberish that he had no time to decipher. Or maybe the man wasn't yelling at all—maybe it was only the echoing in his head. A bone was sticking out of his chest, which, upon reflection, he realized was a rib. The siren was drilling into his head, as though a jackhammer were opening his skull. Whispers reverberated in his ears; swallowing was like eating fire; breathing was like having a trunk falling on his chest. All of his front teeth had been knocked out, and his eyes were swollen to the point of almost closing. Everything looked red and blurry to him; and as he rode in the ambulance, he was only vaguely aware of what had just passed....The police had had to fight to get to him; the people, incensed, had almost rioted again when the paramedics tried to take him away before a boy with a broken leg—

But the stultifying darkness was coming over him again; everything was fading away—all light, all sensations...all thoughts and *awareness*. Therein lay bliss.

* * *

BOTSWANA GLADE, MARENGA'S second in command, was getting dressed in the darkness of his bedroom. He could have turned on the light, but he preferred the darkness somehow. He dressed himself in a dapper suit, and tied his bow tie with what seemed to be the practiced ease of a blind man. He did it slowly and deliberately, with a facial expression, which, if it could have been seen in the darkness, would have been inscrutable. When that was finished, he brushed his long, straightened hair before the mirror—even though, in the darkness, all that could be made out were the whites of his bulging eyes. His wife tossed in bed, but was sound asleep. Less than an hour ago, the phone had awakened them both. After picking up the phone and listening to the young aide's high-pitched ramblings about how the police had shot into the crowd, Botswana Glade had only said a single word into the receiver: "Yes." As he often got calls in the middle night, his wife of 20 years had thought nothing at it; but as he completed the finishing touches to his coiffure, Botswana Glade was possessed by the same tingly feeling he had had while the aide talked about death and destruction....

When he was confident of his preparations, he walked quietly towards the bedroom door. When he opened it and stepped into the light, a young, dreadlocked aide—actually the one that had called from Marenga's headquarters—stood at something resembling attention. Botswana Glade stepped out into the hall and closed the door behind him. Now that he was in the light, the equine characteristics of Botswana Glade's face could be seen. He had a hideous overbite—which he was known to bare when enraged. But as his mouth was closed, the bulge of his upper lip simply gave him an oafish appearance. His slim build and long, straightened hair, made him seem effeminate. And these characteristics—along with his radical political stances—were a godsend to political cartoonists, who exaggerated his appearance into a ghoulish caricature.

As Botswana Glade stepped farther into the hallway, the young aide, unable to gauge the expression on his face, thought it best to simply nod to the man. However, the man just walked past him, not even bothering to acknowledge him. The aide was dressed in a colorful dashiki, while Botswana Glade was in a dark suit that fitted elegantly over his slim figure. He walked down the hallway with the erect posture of a classical dancer, seeming to float on air. The aide stared after him for a while, then, coming to his senses, he caught up with him just as he reached the front door. After the youth ceremoniously opened the door, Botswana Glade stepped out onto the stoop, looking like a dictator greeting his brainwashed subjects from the balcony above the majestic square of the capital. But this was Harlem; and across the street, were cheap tenements; instead of subjects, before him were half a dozen camera crews and the handful of photographers and reporters who, in Marenga's absence, had come looking for a story. Botswana Glade looked out at them—generally, avoiding eye contact—contempt flashing in his eyes as a quivering grimace came over his face. They excitedly trained their cameras and lights on that face, their first indecipherable onslaught of questions littering the air. It was then that Botswana Glade's stentorian voice came out shrill, seeming too high for a man:

"Here we go again!" he screamed with a slight nasality, his horse teeth finally bared to the world. "Look at what the filthy bastards have done…!"

* * *

ROLAND BURST UPRIGHT in the darkness of his posh, midtown condominium. What his dream had been about, he had no idea: he only knew that he was terrified. He looked around warily, trying to get his bearings—and to make sure that there wasn't some monster hiding in the shadows. The television was still on—the same woman was on the air, screaming about death and madness—

Roland grabbed the remote control and switched the television off, suddenly desperate for silence. As he remembered Candice's call, he wondered how long he had been sleeping. He looked at his watch, which said that it was a little after one in the morning; but as he couldn't remember when he had come in—and seemed unable to gauge any other reference points—that information was useless to him. He now found himself thinking that perhaps Candice's call had been nothing but a dream; perhaps all that had happened with Phelps, and his confrontation with the police and that runaway, had been nothing but a dream within that dream. Ghost images of the Brooklyn riot, and Phelps and Kain still fluttered in his mind. It was all so bizarre—so *farfetched*—that from deep within him, came the impetus to laugh. He was caught in those first, strange moments of awakening, when everything seemed possible and impossible. The powerful and pitiful alike were all mad; the world was chaotic and churning, and all that he could think to do, was laugh. He remembered his own terrified babbling to the police, and wanted to laugh even louder. And yet, he didn't laugh at all. The impulse to laugh was like a blanket which covered most of his nakedness, but which left other parts out in the cold. No matter how he tried to contort his body, the blanket would never cover all of his nakedness.

He was exhausted—not merely overcome by tiredness, which

could be resolved with sleep, but *exhaustion*, which seemed as though it had been *programmed* into his soul. He sat on the edge of the couch and took another deep breath, wondering when it would end. However, remembering his court victory and his booking at the network morning show, he felt his panicky sense of relief building once again. The people loved him—were desperate to hear about his doings. At least, in his present state of mind, that was how it appeared to him. Maybe he was delusional—maybe just desperate beyond reason; but whatever the case, as his strange, panicky relief grew, sleep lost whatever grasp it had had on him. He practically jumped up from the couch then, suddenly wanting to exult at the triumph of being Roland Micheaux. He walked over to the French doors with what seemed to be a confident, athletic stride. Beyond the French doors, the city 20 stories below him suddenly seemed magical. Even the red, menacing sky didn't trouble him anymore. The skyscrapers in the distance were like towers of light and magic; and as he stood there, with his face pressed against the glass as if he were a child staring into a candy store, it was as though all of it could be his.

The sight of the city always triggered a sense of excitement in him. It was the urge to enter the great competition that was always going on. He wanted to be out there, proving himself. In fact, he wished that it were dawn already, so that he could go out and prove himself on the airwaves.

Still looking out on the inviting city, he slid open the French doors to go out on the terrace; but as soon as the doors were open a crack, a blast of the stiflingly hot city air made him shut them and retreat back into the air-conditioned room. He took another step back before he realized that he was shivering. *What the hell is happening to me*! he cursed himself. The heat wave was driving him crazy, too: putting him on edge like everyone else—

And just then, he whirled around in a panic as the phone rang from the couch, where he had tossed it. It was as though a killer had snuck up behind him! He stared at the phone in disbelief, having to somehow convince himself that it was only that. He took a deep breath to calm his racing heart, then walked over and picked up the phone:

"Hello?"

"Sir, it's Sam."

The doorman? Roland thought to himself, frowning. "Yes?"

"That woman you used to date is down here—she's got a kid…"

"*Candice,*" he whispered, seeming suddenly frail. He sat down heavily on the couch, staring blankly into the darkness. He felt trapped. He wanted to hide—to *flee*…anything to get away from the relentless specter of Phelps; but then, after the surge of panic subsided somewhat—at least enough for him to get a grip on himself—he remembered, suddenly and completely, that he had an enemy in Phelps. All the troubling images of the strip joint accosted him again; he remembered how he had wandered up Broadway in a daze, feeling fear and uncertainty that he hadn't felt since he was a youth. Phelps had done all that, and the man would enlist all his power to destroy Roland. Even in his drunkenness, the man was wreaking havoc on Roland's life: just imagine what would happen when the man was sober! Imagine tomorrow, when the man remembered what had happened, and realized that Roland now had knowledge about him—grounds for disbarment and ruination. The man would realize then, like Roland realized now, that it was "him or me." Slowly, as Roland sat there, there came the realization that if necessary, he would have to *destroy* Phelps and everything that the man represented. Just the scope of it left him in a daze, trembling slightly from the ruthless demands of the beast within him. He stared helplessly into the darkness, bewildered by the extremes of his mind; but then, as the doorman asked if he was still there, he whispered: "Send her up, Sam."

He sat there for about 20 seconds after he had put down the phone, his mind numb. He had felt charged with energy just *moments* ago, but now he felt…*drained*. He was sick of this strange yo-yoing—spinning wildly from euphoria to despair. He just wanted it all to stop—so that he could rest. And it was not only Candice's connection with Phelps that was weighing him down, but the queasy feeling he always had at the prospect of seeing old lovers. Candice was a beautiful woman, but she, like all the other women he had ever been with, had never really touched his soul—or been able to dwell there for long; and so, without that spiritual connection, all that there had ever been between them was the soulless act which he had shared with countless others. True, he had been intrigued by her seeming originality, but the reality of their sex life—of his desperation for the illusive peace that came with a woman—only shamed him. How joyless and meaningless all that sex seemed to him now—all his dealings with women, in fact. In a world of illusions and madness, he was desperate for something real—

The doorbell rang. He bolted to his feet, then walked over to the door warily, as though some killer were waiting on the other side. An internal voice kept reminding him that Phelps was his enemy, and that he had to get more evidence against the man—evidence that Candice, as the nanny, could provide. When he opened the door, Candice was standing there, looking haggard; Mindy was sleeping in her arms—

"I didn't know where else to go!" Candice cried. The way she looked now—like some pathetic welfare mother—in contrast to the glamorous woman that had intrigued and mesmerized him, made him feel uneasy. Phelps was bringing them all down....

"Come in," Roland said, gesturing for her to enter. He hastily turned on the light as they entered—only then realizing that they were in darkness—and led Candice deeper into the room.

"—He came home like a madman!" Candice went on. "He just burst into my bedroom and told me to take Mindy and leave—I guess so that he could have sex with Cindy."

"—*Cindy*!" he said anxiously, just then remembering her, "—you think he might do something to her?"

"*What?*" she said as though the idea were ludicrous. "...And if he does, it's their way, if you understand me. They do weird shit," she said, lowering her voice. "You know how crazy rich white people are. Sometimes I hear them screaming out in the middle of the night!"

Roland stared at her uneasily; but, despite himself—despite the fact that a man forcing his three-year-old daughter and her nanny out into the streets in the middle of the night, was heartless, if not *criminal*—he smiled and shook his head in wonderment at the extremes of lust. Or maybe it was just the expression of amused bewilderment in Candice's eyes that made him laugh; or maybe it was only that he was tired of thoughts of Phelps just now, and wanted to rest.

Just then, Mindy, probably roused by their voices, stirred from sleep. "Uncle Roland!" she screamed upon seeing him.

Roland caressed her cheek and smiled. There was something wondrous about the excitement of little children; and as Roland saw it, all his thoughts of hate and madness fell away. He was overcome by a feeling of protectiveness and *caring* for the little girl, which was as all-encompassing as the grace of God. He turned to Candice then, saying, "Take Mindy to the guest bedroom. You can sleep in my bedroom: I wasn't going to sleep anyway."

At that, Candice smiled in gratitude and walked out of the room; Mindy waved back at him as she and her nanny disappeared into the darkness; but now that he was alone, Roland stood there, wondering what the hell he had gotten himself into.

* * *

OUTSIDE, THE UNREST WAS ostensibly winding down. Although there were still sporadic pops of gunfire in the air, and a few buildings and cars continued to burn, the fire and police departments seemed to have everything in hand. But it was just as the last of the wounded were taken away in ambulances that the violence really began to flare up. Miraculously, just before Maria Santos and the rest of the media had gotten there, a bystander had videotaped it all from his bedroom window; and now, yet more dark, grainy images were being sent out to all the news organizations. The bystander had gotten the footage of Andropov emerging from his car just after the hit-and-run murder and the accident at the intersection. The bystander had zoomed in just as Andropov, his face pasty and inhuman in the footage, began firing at the charging mob. The footage would in time be playing as far away as Bangladesh, showing how the mob began mauling the man....The bystander had captured the first appearance of the policemen on the scene; he had captured the first people being shot down by police bullets...and the last corpse being carried away. It was all on videotape: irrefutable proof of madness. The video was like a vision from heaven—like an icon before which the faithful could genuflect and sing their praises to the heavens. But what video had made real, the viewers and broadcasters and politicians made unreal. A simple question of what had happened, was succumbing to the mysticism of the camera. Moralists and hand-wringers were already posing with those images as a backdrop, asking how it could have happened in America; and somewhere in Hollywood, a producer was already trembling with excitement at the prospect of a TV movie. It didn't matter what was real and what was fiction, because the fiction was their reality. The fiction was the lens through which they chose to see their lives and their problems. The preachers of fiction, who appeared on their screens in every fathomable guise, explained away the randomness of their lives, of success and failure, and of death; and in return, the people cried Amen and Hallelujah.... Ten people were now dead, and dozens wounded: that reality was nothing compared to the fiction that was coming.

* * *

COUNCILWOMAN CHARLOTTE MCPRICE, the Democratic challenger for Mayor, stepped out of the banquet hall with the purposeful, confident stride that had become her trademark; and in her wake followed scores of clapping well-wishers and photographers. It was that old reality again: the city was composed of millions of different universes, and even as the madness of the Brooklyn slums was being broadcasted internationally on satellite feeds, it seemed impossible a few kilometers away—a few *blocks* away, in fact.

Charlotte McPrice was tall, with an erect posture that exuded authority and ease. Her mane of red hair seemed to glow supernaturally in the night, or maybe it was the posh lighting beneath the awning of the banquet hall. Even while others faltered in the heat, and the chaos of the Brooklyn slums began to take its toll on the national consciousness, she stood there as though even the forces of nature—or the forces of nature corrupted by man—were no match for her. Behind her, the people were gathering in an attempt to get a final glimpse of her, looking like wives ceremoniously seeing their husbands off to war. She was that indefatigable one-woman war machine, inspiring, at the same time, patriotism, hatred of the enemy, and a strange reverence for God.

It had been her most successful fund-raiser yet—four thousand people at $5,000 a plate. Her keynote address—a boisterous speech on why the quailing incumbent Mayor, Alexander Randolph, was no match for her—had garnered her 10 minutes of standing ovation after the fact. It had taken her an hour just to reach the door: everyone had wanted to shake her hand—to touch her essence, as if the thing could be rubbed off. They had followed her out here: middle-aged women in glittery evening gowns and corporate CEO types who stared at her, transfixed, succumbing to the same spell that had bewitched the young West Virginia rednecks. The limousine was waiting on the curb; but seeing it, she suddenly remembered something. She turned around, looking for someone; and seeing her inquisitive expression, her campaign manager, a short, perpetually harried-looking old man named Ned Wisinski, rushed to her side.

"Have you seen my husband, Ned?" she asked, having to bend down to talk to him.

Wisinski shook his head, seeming heartbroken that he hadn't been able to answer her question and put her mind at ease. This desperation to please had always amused her, so that she smiled now, if only to console him.

"He probably left early," she said nonchalantly, again waving to her cheering supporters before heading for the limousine. That was the ease that they all knew and loved....

She had grown up in the mountains of West Virginia—a coal miner's daughter, just like the country song. It had been some backwater town, replete with the mandatory trailer parks: a virtual wasteland, where the cultural center had been a tavern on the interstate highway, where all the long distance truckers stopped to eat. It was a world where the men had been drunkards whose ultimate wish was to own a pick-up truck with a gun rack, and the women had either been brazen hussies who liked the abuse of their men, or saints who hated it, but endured it for the sake of the children. Growing up in those surroundings, the youngest of seven children, she had gotten a good view of it all—at least good enough so that by age five, she had known that she wanted no part of it. She hadn't wanted to see what America could be: a broken-down mother reaching middle age and the mandatory conversion to the flock of Born Again Christians; an alcoholic father who, in her first year at Yale, would freeze to death while stumbling back home from the interstate tavern...

It had been a world where hate, like the dampness of a swamp, seeped into everything. All around her, people that had hated their lives for generations, had surrendered to the three things that the desperate always reverted to in order to salve their pain: alcohol, sex and religion. Some had combined all three in ingenious but ultimately self-defeating ways, and called it a full life. In a sense, it had been a world of clichés—a maudlin country song brought to life—and she had seemed to be the only one to realize it. They hadn't so much seemed to be living, as carrying out badly written tragic roles to their inevitable conclusions. They had been satisfied, in effect, with their own dissatisfaction with their lives; and seeing it all, some incredible force had endowed the young Charlotte with energy and drive, so that she could, it seemed to her, outwit the entire lot of them and escape.

Her entire youth had been a colossal struggle not to become some trailer park damsel in distress, like all the other women around her. It had been a struggle not merely against people, but an ethic instilled in everyone around her. She had had to be a clandestine warrior, fighting against her very family—against everything she had ever known. She had had to figure out when to be strong, when to be soft, when to seem indifferent—and when, finally, to risk it all and stand up for what she really cared about. With the men, it had only been their laughable, teen-age lust that she had to outwit; but with the women, it had been the more complex—more *driven*—force of jealousy. As it was, the lusty were easily distracted in their pursuits; but the jealous, fed by their self-destructive dissatisfaction with their own lives, never lost sight of their quarry.

Needless to say, with those early dealings behind her, the most vital lessons of politics had been learned: make yourself self seem accessible, but from a distance; make them want you, but keep out of their reach, so that they can't spoil you....After graduating first in her law class, she had moved to New York City and joined one of those liberal, civil liberties/civil rights organizations. On that record, she had been elected to the City Council four years ago. And now, on to bigger and better things....

Reaching the limousine, and the chauffeur who was holding the door open for her, Charlotte McPrice waved to her supporters one last time. There was genuine love in her for those people, even though she couldn't help thinking that there was something exasperating about them, which was like a dog's too-eager, too-animated welcoming of its master. Whatever the case, it was upon entering the vehicle that she saw a figure slumped over in the darkness. After the initial surprise, she eventually recognized her husband. At first she thought that he was sleeping, but then she discerned, from his glossy eyes—and the stench of whisky—that he was drunk.

"I want a divorce!" he belted as soon as she sat down beside him.

She groaned noncommittally while he glared at her. She had met him at Yale: a rich kid from good South Hampton stock, now an insufferable bore, bored with his daddy's immense fortune.

"I could ruin you, you frigid bitch!" he went on. "All your beloved fans would hate you…if they only knew what a slut you are!"

She sat there staring at him with a bemused expression on her face; the silence unnerved him, so that he felt compelled to go on:

"There are things that I could say! They'd give me six figures for a book on you!"

But she only laughed, her voice still calm and gentle as she said: "You poor fool, I'm only a New York City Councilwoman. Don't you think that you could blackmail me better *after* I became Mayor?"

His eyes opened wide: "Yea…that's right!" he said in amazement, as if he had never given it thought before.

"Of course I am right," she cooed to him, resting his head tenderly on her breasts as the car started off. "Rest now," she whispered, "you'll be able to ruin me soon enough."

* * *

JUST BEFORE DAWN, while Roland lay on the couch, sleeping soundly, Candice came up to him and, caressing his face, awoke him. He was surprised, first that he had fallen asleep, and then that she was naked. She kissed him before he could say anything. She kissed him sloppily, shoving her extraordinarily long tongue down his throat, so that he almost retched.

"Candice," he said the first chance he got, but she put her index finger to his lips.

"No strings," she said. Not waiting for a response, she bent over him once again, and kissed him; he stared up at the ceiling in bewilderment—*numb*. He was in a pair of shorts and a T-shirt. She took off the T-shirt, practically flinging his arms over his head, so that she could wrench it off. And then, with equal alacrity, his shorts were off, and she was stroking his penis. His erection was due more to the pre-dawn accumulation of urine in his bladder than sexual arousal, but the sight of it made her smile, nonetheless. He stared at her, wondering what the hell was happening; and while he was still trying to make sense of it all, she straddled him—was on top of him, moaning sonorously, while he lay there in bewilderment. She was holding his hands above his head—he hadn't moved them since she flung them there to take off his shirt; her breasts, firm as there were, were nonetheless hitting him in the face as she rocked back and forth on him. In the early morning light, her face had a strange, demonic expression, which he assumed was pleasure. A few shrill cries escaped from her, making Roland cringe. She was one of those screamers, Roland remembered with a rising sense of discomfort. He winced every time she screamed—and every time her tits hit him in the face. She must have taken his wincing for pleasure as well, because she giggled suddenly as she began to ride him with more urgency. He hated being held down like this—being hemmed in by her thighs and hands. He had a sudden impulse to push her off: to fling her from him and cover her mouth with a cushion so that she would shut up. And as she screamed in his ears and ground herself against him, he suddenly remembered Mindy, who was sleeping in the other room. The thought of the little girl coming out and seeing them there was sickening....Was this the way Candice was with Phelps! Roland thought suddenly. Was this why she was such a "godsend," as Phelps had called her? The thought of being up in something that Phelps had...*he shuddered*! It occurred to him, suddenly and strangely, that Candice had been wrong: that women couldn't tell what men thought when they had sex, because his mind raced with panicky thoughts of hatred and disgust—of which she was obviously oblivious. And her screaming was maddening! She was still holding him down; and as she galloped her way to orgasm, she dug her fingernails into his arms. Roland was grinding his teeth to keep from screaming himself; having had enough, he tried to push her off, but gripped by the throes of ecstasy, her strength was twice that of his. He couldn't take it anymore! With a grunt, which she must have taken for an orgasm, he reared like a horse that, frightened by something in its path, threw its master. They both fell to the plush carpet. He was ready to fight her—to *strike* her if necessary, in order to free himself—but she was laughing now: giggling with that strange post-orgasmic joy that women always seemed to get.

"You're still great!" she purred as she sloppily kissed his neck and panted in his ear. The end of her screams had curtailed his madness, but now he felt suddenly inept—*bereft*. While he was lying there in confusion, she rolled him over, so that she was again on top; and before he could do or say anything, she kissed him, got up and ambled off to the bathroom.

Roland got up like an old man—like someone drained of life. His erection was still there, mocking him. He walked over to the French doors then; and without thought, he wrenched them open and stumbled out. The stifling heat blasted against his body, but he didn't care. He stumbled to the edge of the balcony like a drunkard, looking at the pale sun rising on the horizon. But he felt suddenly dizzy—and nauseous—so he stumbled back against the wall, already covered with sweat as he panted for oxygen in the filthy air. Crumbling into a patio chair, he sat there with his head resting heavily in his hands, wishing, for the slightest instant, that he were dead.

3.

Society of Strangers

Just before dawn, there was a soft glow in the heavens; and for those few moments, the smoggy skies were lit up in hues that were so spectacular that it proved, once again, that beauty could be found in anything, including filth. It was about half past five now. Mayor Randolph sat wearily in the back seat of the limousine as he and his chief aides zoomed towards the hospital news conference. There was a strange, anxious feeling in him, which, from time to time, peeked its ugly head out from beyond the wall of his exhaustion. After all, there had been a riot. People were dead—many from police bullets. Millions of dollars in property damage had occurred. Madness itself had infected the streets; and if not for the massive, uncompromisingly brutal response of the police, it could have been much worse. Randolph had just toured the blocks of the rampage, looking at burned-out husks of buildings, smoldering wrecks of cars and garbage-strewn streets that looked like they had been the focus of sustained mortar fire. The police presence along the blocks of the rampage was still massive. The rage that had consumed those blocks was the type that could flare up at any time, so things would be tense for a while. People were still standing on street corners, waiting around for something to come and make everything right. There had even been reports of them attacking the police when they were asked to disperse. Their neighbors and relatives were dead and maimed now, and those things were difficult to forget and reconcile.

In fact, in the dozens of TV interviews during the night, the people on the streets of the rampage had admitted it themselves: the maniac who plowed over that kid and shot into the crowd was still alive—holding tenaciously to life in the hospital Randolph was to visit—and none of them would rest until he was dead. A kind of death vigil was already going on in front of the hospital. Those who had lost—and *could* lose—loved ones were there now, mourning their losses. However, the vast majority were simply there to hear that the maniac was dead; indeed, the vast majority were waiting for their chance to go in and make everything right, themselves.

Later that morning, Botswana Glade was planning to hold a protest rally in front of the very same hospital that Randolph was to visit. The man was already appearing on TV, saying that it had in fact been the police who caused the riot—who had escalated the violence by their brutal response. He was saying that the police were no different from the maniac; and people in ghettos everywhere, who knew what it meant to lose everything—people for whom the police weren't a force for order, but *oppression*—agreed completely; in fact, thousands of them were on their way to the hospital now.

But everything was becoming myth now. Randolph had stayed up all night, planning and coordinating things that he could now barely remember. As Mayor, he was supposed to make sense of it all and work in the best interest of the city, but he felt like a man trying to move water from one bucket to another, with a sieve. It didn't seem as if anything he did would be enough. And with all that had happened last night—and the shadow of the stripper's threat hanging over anything—he was too wary of the world to act on its behalf. The events of last night at the strip joint combined with the footage of the riot and the senselessness of everything else; obsessive thoughts about soul mates that were either bent on saving the world, or destroying it, along with thoughts of Kain's religion, and happiness gone astray, combined into one swirling mess and he felt helpless against it.

However, that the world was on the verge of something horrible: Randolph could feel this in his bones—and see it in everything that was happening around him. As he drove along, he stared at his three aides—who were talking excitedly amongst themselves—and couldn't help smiling at their presumption of being able to influence the fate of the city. Everything was out of their hands now; and even while Randolph wanted to do the right thing, his heart honestly wasn't in it.

As for his three anxious aides, they suddenly seemed ridiculous to him. His chief of staff, Abraham Levin, was a balding, middle-aged white man with a perpetually unhealthy appearance. For some reason, Levin always reminded him of a vegetable. Today, it was a potato that had been left in the bag too long, and was now no longer firm, but instead characterized by a strangely repulsive squishiness. Chet Radix, the aide who had found him in his office last night, was a baby-faced man just out of college. Radix was like some demented acolyte to him, whose fragile innocence and faith were in his hands. And his speechwriter, Bill Dalton, was just a pencil-thin "stuffed suit," whose only redeeming quality was that his prattling speeches seemed to mirror the views of the voting public.

Randolph looked at the men with an intensity that they must have taken for gravity and consideration, but he was far away from them. In his heart of hearts, he knew that what had happened in the Brooklyn slums was beyond whatever statements and proclamations he could ever make. Alexander Randolph, the glib politician, who had risen like a star in this world because he had been able to convince people that he cared, now essentially didn't give a shit. And it wasn't that he was preoccupied with his own ruined life—he suddenly didn't give a shit about that either. He felt as if he were in a new skin: an *invulnerable* skin, totally disconnected from the goings on of the world. The sensation was so overwhelming that it was as though he had received a blunt blow to the head. He felt like his soul was being rewritten: that he was metamorphosing as he sat there, and that the new being that arose would either be a god, or a devil….

They were now about seven blocks from the hospital, driving through nondescript neighborhoods that were lined with the usual apartment buildings and storefronts. It was only half past five in the morning, but the great multitudes were already beginning to come out on the streets. The city that had never really been asleep was shrugging off the night. All of those people, either rushing off to work, or standing around burning with the rage of last night…He shook his head. Every once in a while, as he drove about the city, he would look out on those multitudes; and it would occur to him, suddenly and completely, that he, as Mayor, was somehow connected with all those restless millions. Looking out on people whom he had never seen before—and would never see again—he would find himself thinking that the city—the *world*, in fact—was just a conglomeration of intersecting points. All the sidewalks and subway platforms and bars and theaters were places where the great multitudes met at random; and all the interactions that arose in those places, were nothing but the products of bewildering chance. Millions of people, living in a random world...yet trying to make sense of it with gods and laws and whatever they deemed to be their culture. All those strangers, trying to make sense of one another in a world of *billions*...He had sat there once, grimacing unconsciously as he imagined the overload which would come if he knew everything about even 1% of the people he passed on the street or saw on television. Multiply that bewilderment by nine million, and that was the city; by 260 million, and that was the country; by six billion, and that was the world! But in their media-driven society, with its so-called information revolution, all that bewildering information was constantly about them, like an odorless, colorless, poisonous gas accumulating within the confines of a room.

...He definitely wasn't ready for this news conference. He tried to jumpstart his caring and sense of proportion, but it all seemed so very hopeless to him now. He needed rest and solitude more than ever; however, as he looked out of the window, he realized not only that they had reached the hospital, but that there were hundreds of agitated blacks and Latinos outside. For these protesters, there were at least a *thousand* policemen. And then there were the dozens of camera crews and reporters, who seemed to dart through the crowd like sharks in a feeding frenzy. If there had been some escape clause—some way to turn his back on it all and flee back to his sanity—then Randolph would have exercised it. But he was trapped. He tried reminding himself that he was the Mayor, and that this was his duty; but as he stared at the restless throng outside the window, a resurgent wave of wariness—even *panic*—gripped him. It was like a sudden feeling of nausea—of *sickness*—at the prospect of something vile yet unavoidable. He felt as though he had sold his soul, not so much to the devil, as devil-worshippers. The events of the night were that devil; and here they all were, paying homage to their master. For the first time in his life, the prospect of a media frenzy revolted him: seemed *evil*. He felt as though he were being sucked into a sinkhole—

He took another deep breath, trying to regain his focus; but before he could effect the magic, the car door opened and his aides ushered him out into the stifling heat of the world. The din of the crowd was like a declaration of war and madness. As he was pushed along, he felt like a student who had forgotten everything he had spent the night cramming. Failure was imminent! The massive crowd surged on either side of him, held back only by the vigilance of the police. The reporters were the first to come, all waving their microphones in his face; and then, beyond them, were the protesters, some of who were chanting for justice/revenge, some of who professed to be chanting for peace. He looked at everything—the media, the chanting crowds, his agitated aides...—feeling panic and revulsion welling up in him like vomit in his throat—

It was at that moment that Maria Santos managed to circumvent the police barrier and the rest of the reporter corps, stepping boldly into Randolph's path. Her decisiveness seemed to take everyone by surprise; Randolph instinctively recoiled as she stepped up with her cameraman, shoving a microphone in his face as she declared:

"*A stripper in Greenwich Village claims that you raped her last night*!"

A moment of silence seemed to grip the world. At first, Randolph didn't really hear: he was only able to make sense of the words after they echoed in his mind a few times. And then, as he stared at Santos in horror, he found himself thinking, *So this is it*! Everyone looked at him oddly. Santos stood before him with a smug smile on her face, reveling in his reaction. But soon, for some incomprehensible reason, Randolph found himself laughing. Along with the chaos of last night, the accumulated filth of the passing weeks was falling on his head, and all he could think to do, was laugh. *It's all over*! he thought; and, for the life of him, he laughed even louder. In the face of all this, Santos's smug smile became a frown. Randolph was far away from her now—far away from *everything*. These weeks of filth and madness were finally bearing fruit, and he didn't presume to offer any defense against whatever was coming. He stood there, laughing like a simpleton, while those around him looked on in confused silence. Levin, first reassured, then disturbed by Randolph's laughter, was the first to come to his senses. Scowling at Santos, he hauled his chuckling boss away.

* * *

LITTLE DID ROLAND Micheaux know that the seeds of his destruction were being sown in the events currently taking place in the city. But the life cycle of seeds can be anywhere from a few minutes, to decades—even centuries—

A pealing noise brought him out of his stupor. He had still been on the balcony, drenched in sweat from the heat as he stared at the clouds of smog. There had been some augury there, in that airborne filth. A part of him had been desperately trying to understand it, when something began ringing inside the condominium. As he looked around confusedly, the reality of his episode with Candice seized him, and he shuddered—

The phone was still ringing. He stood up and went to the threshold of the French doors, looking in uneasily—as though expecting some monster to attack him. Shaking his head anxiously, he entered the room. As he was drenched in sweat—and naked—the air-conditioned room chilled him. He walked over to the coffee table and picked up the phone. His hand was trembling slightly—as was his voice:

"Yes?"

"Sir, it's Sam."

"Sam..."

"You have visitors, sir."

"Who?" He instinctively looked at the wall clock, which said that it was 20 minutes to six.

"A couple," Sam went on. And then, holding the phone away from his mouth, he asked the people to repeat their names. "...Dallas and Cindy Phelps, sir."

Roland almost dropped the phone! He almost *collapsed*! He was trembling all over now, as though he were standing out in the middle of the arctic, freezing to death. Candice came out of the bedroom then. When she saw the distraught expression on his face, she stopped in the doorway with a mixture of curiosity and concern.

"Sir?" Sam said again. "Are you there?"

"Yea," Roland said in an uneven voice; he cleared his throat nervously. "...What do they want?"

"They came for their daughter."

Roland made some equivocal grunting sound. He suddenly felt

like a trapped animal, hearing the steps of the hunter in the distance—

"Should I send them up, sir?"

Roland was nibbling at his lower lip.

"*Sir?*"

"Yea," Roland blurted out, responding more to the insistence in the man's voice than anything else. It was only after Sam put the phone down, and Roland found himself listening to the dial tone, that the full extent of it hit him. *Phelps and his wife were on their way up here*! He suddenly realized that he was naked. He tossed the phone on the couch and dashed for the bedroom. Candice was still looking at him oddly—

"Phelps!" he explained, rushing past her to get a robe: to find some way to clothe and arm himself. He had to prepare! She was still looking at him oddly when he tied the robe around himself. And then: "I wonder how they knew you and Mindy were here?" he mused.

"Dallas called me this morning," she answered in an offhand manner. "I have a cellular phone"—and she took it out of the pocket of her robe and showed it to him. Then, frowning again: "You all right, Roland?"

But her nonchalant tone—and a flashback of what had happened an hour earlier—only unnerved him further. For some reason, it reminded him of the night of the banquet, and he definitely couldn't deal with that now. Phelps was coming...*God*, he didn't feel well at all! And then he remembered that he had that TV appearance this morning! He had to be in the studio in an hour! He felt as though the world were moving too quickly: as if he were standing out in some busy intersection, doomed to be run over by the next truck—

"You all right, Roland?" Candice asked again—

"*Yea*," he said tersely. She took a step towards him, but he couldn't be around her now. Like before, when she came to him on the couch, he had the urge to push her away: to strangle her—*anything*—so that she would shut up and get away from him! "I'm fine...I'm fine," he said; and as she continued to come to him, he was on the verge of screaming it for the third time. But just then, the doorbell rang. Roland flinched. Candice, seeing his reaction, was again about to ask him if everything was all right; and to get the hell away from her, he pushed past her and walked out of the bedroom.

How am I going to play this! he wondered as he walked to the door. He had no idea! The night before, the reality that Phelps was his enemy had given him clarity of purpose, but Phelps's coming here now was a grand outflanking maneuver that even Sun Tzu would have envied. The war was beginning and he had been caught without even his drawers on! Roland had to focus! He glanced over his shoulder nervously when he reached the door. Candice was still standing in the bedroom doorway with a combination of curiosity and concern on her face. He looked away from her uneasily, taking a deep breath as he reached for the door.

He opened the door the way people did in horror movies: brusquely, as though expecting some monster to leap out at him. But all that he saw was the comely tanned face of Phelps's wife. "Cindy?" Roland said confusedly, when he saw her and *only* her there. She was smiling at him, looking as though she didn't have a care in the world. Roland looked down the hall with a frown: "Where's Dallas?"

"Oh, he's just getting something from the car," she said, giggling suddenly. "We didn't wake you up, did we?"

Roland watched her smiling face, nonplused. She was wearing a white, frilly blouse and a kind of tennis skirt: something that seemed indelibly connected with the ease of well-to-do country clubs. Her long blond hair was arranged in a sophisticated manner around her shoulders. There was a youthful healthiness about her; and yet, with her ease—and ostensible clue-lessness as to what her husband was—she and her good cheer seemed unhealthy, if not unnatural.

"Thanks for keeping Mindy and Candice for us last night," she went on in her usual giggly, schoolgirl tone. "I hope we didn't put you out."

He had been staring at her confusedly, his mind anxiously going over what Phelps could possibly be planning for him; but seeing her imploring smile, and remembering that she had asked him a question—and that he had kept her standing out in the hall—he quickly brought her in, saying, "No problem at all."

Cindy and Candice waved to one another in greeting, both smiling. Roland unconsciously shook his head to keep from thinking about the bizarre sex triangle. Candice was leaning against the bedroom door now, still with her godforsaken calmness.

"Can I get you anything?" Roland said abruptly. He had needed to say something.

"Just Mindy," she laughed. "It's all Dallas's fault," she went on in her giggly way. "He's desperate to get out to our house in the Hamptons for the weekend. He's always acting on the spur of the moment. And with all that rioting stuff in the news, I can't really blame him. You know," she went on breathlessly, "Dallas was *mugged* last night!"

"Oh?" Roland said.

"Yea, he came home with his face all bruised. But you know Dallas: nothing can really get him down. Even with the mugging, he came home with a bottle of Champagne…such a romantic, that man."

"*Champagne?*" Roland said, dubious of Phelps's romanticism.

"Yea," she snickered coyly, "that's why he made Candice and Mindy spend the night with you….And sorry again to wake you up so early," Cindy went on, apologetically, "but Dallas wanted to get out of town right away."

"Yea, I know the feeling," Roland added under his breath; she frowned at him, then smiled vapidly—

At that moment, the doorbell rang again. Roland had left the door slightly ajar, and Phelps walked in before Roland could move. The left side of Phelps's face was swollen and discolored horribly. Roland grimaced at the sight of it; and then, there was a feeling of queasiness at the reality that the man was actually in his home—

"I know," Cindy responded to Roland's reaction, going up to her husband and caressing his shoulder, "that mugger really got him good."

"He sure did," Phelps laughed enigmatically. There was a gleam in the man's eyes that made Roland cringe. And just then, as if Roland were not confused enough, Phelps handed him the small, glossy paper bag in his hand.

"What's this?"

"It's your present. I almost forgot it in the car. Congratulations on winning that case!"

Roland looked at the package uneasily, part of him thinking that maybe there was a bomb in it. "What is it?"

"Open it and see!" the man said, smiling.

Candice came over then, and they all stood around eagerly as Roland looked in the bag and pulled out a small case. "It's a Rolex,"

Roland said in disbelief.

"Yes," laughed Phelps, "all our new partners get one."

"Partner?" Roland said, looking at the man in puzzlement. Was it all some trick to disarm him? Phelps was his enemy, he reminded himself; but instead of the necessary hatred, all that came was confusion and uneasiness. The realization that Phelps was more at ease than him, unnerved him. Phelps had already accounted for everything—even the man's wife didn't suspect that anything had happened! If the man could do all that, then think about what he could do to Roland! Phelps and the two women were cheering now, and Roland tried to smile and act graciously—even while his mind raced with thoughts of caution and self-defense. He was trying his best to smile and act at ease when a joyous cry came from the doorway of the guest bedroom.

"Mommy and Daddy!" Mindy screamed. The little girl, no doubt awoken by their cheers, ran out of the bedroom and leaped at her parents.

—While in Brooklyn, the forces of self-destruction gathered to hear Botswana Glade's words, Phelps caught her and held her up, so that the three of them stood there hugging and kissing. Everyone was laughing now, but as Roland looked at them, a wave of revulsion washed over him. *It was all fake*: Phelps's love for Cindy and his daughter…Phelps: a depraved man playing family man; Cindy, a good-natured, but essentially clue-less woman playing the perfect wife and mother. The only real one was Mindy, and only because she could at least be excused in her blindness because she didn't yet have the tools to see. As for Candice, who stood by the side, smiling, he had no patience with her either. He just wanted them all gone: out of his home, out of his *life*…!

"Candice," Phelps laughed at last, looking up from their saccharine love fest, "get dressed and we'll all head off."

Candice dutifully went to the bedroom.

"Daddy!" Mindy exclaimed, "what happened to your face!"

"Just a little accident."

"Do you want me to kiss it and make it better?"

"Of course! [Mindy kissed him with a loud smack.] Ah," he said in relief, "all better."

Roland felt as though he were going to throw up! Phelps

glanced at him then; and seeing Roland's expression, his tone changed immediately.

"Sweetheart," Phelps addressed his wife then, "take Mindy to the car: I want to talk to Roland for a moment."

Roland's stomach churned at the words; he felt the blood draining from his face! This was it: the battle was about to begin!

"Goodbye, Uncle Roland!" Mindy called, while Cindy giggled again, whisking the little girl into her arms and out of the door. Roland stared at their retreating forms, panicking inside. His reaction to Phelps was the reaction one would have towards a bear that one had come upon in the woods. He froze, wary of making eye contact with the beast, lest he provoke it into attacking. He was totally cowed by the man, and this realization drained even more of his ease and strength and *manhood*. At first, neither of them spoke. But when Roland glanced at Phelps, he was surprised to see the fear in the man's eyes. It was so unexpected, that it was startling. Phelps wasn't meeting his eyes either—as if he were even more terrified of Roland! Had he overestimated the man? he wondered. The prospect of Phelps's weakness reassured him somehow; but even then, he wondered if that weakness might just be an act....

Whatever the case, Roland forced himself to speak up. "What was last night about?" he said, finally broaching the subject. He was still holding the watch in his hand: "What is this?" he added, holding up the Rolex. "An attempt to buy me off?"

"Look," Phelps pleaded, looking sorrowful, "I was drunk...I don't know what came over me."

Roland was feeling better all the time! "Is that it?" he said with a smirk, "—the insanity defense?"

"Nobody has to know about this, right?" he said, uneasily.

Roland stared at him for a while; then smiling, he shook his head. "Look, I don't want anyone knowing about last night, any more than you do. I guess on that count, we can come to a truce between us. What you do with your life is your own business: I ask only that I not be involved in it."

Phelps nodded nervously.

Candice came out of the bedroom then, dressed in the clothes of the previous night. When she reached them, she smiled and caressed Roland's shoulder, and he had to summon all his will not to shudder at her touch: not to go into a rage and strangle them both. But he kept his head, and after Phelps nodded contritely to Roland one last time, the two of them left.

When the door closed, and Roland found himself standing there by himself, he stared at the door in disbelief. Either it was over, or it was just beginning; either Phelps was a pathetic fool, or the man was some maniacal genius, in whose web Roland was trapped. Roland felt even more depleted than ever; and just then, remembering the TV appearance, he groaned and rushed to the bedroom to get ready.

* * *

SOMEWHERE IN THE BUILDING, a man was screaming hysterically. Dr. Joel Fishman led his twelve students, and two burly orderlies, down the wide corridors of the New York Institute for the Criminally Insane. No one said a word as they walked; and all about them, there was reverence and hopefulness—as though they were on a religious pilgrimage. The outside world, with its polluted skies, oppressive heat and impending chaos, seemed like another universe. The air conditioner was on full blast here, and everything seemed almost preternaturally clean. As for their surroundings, everything was white: their lab coats, the wide, empty corridors, the orderlies' uniforms, the fluorescent lights above...It was like the arctic—a huge wall of whiteness, in which one could lose one's sight and sense of proportion. Someone was still screaming; but in this strange place, it seemed almost melodious, proving, once again, that beauty could be found in anything—including madness.

Dr. Fishman was a slender white man of moderate height and middle age. There was a certain smugness and self-satisfaction about his movements, which reminded one of a celebrated maestro about to conduct a masterpiece. Ready to begin the first movement, he stopped before one of the locked metal doors, then nodded to the two orderlies, who came to the front and opened the door.

It was a small room—about twelve meters by seven meters. The orderlies and Fishman's students entered first. A skinny black man was lying supine on a cot, staring at the ceiling. There were no windows in the room—just blank white plaster walls—so it was as though they were in a place beyond night and day. The two orderlies positioned themselves by the man's bed—one at the head and the other at the foot. There was something ghoulish about their expressions, which conveyed all the indifference of Frankenstein's monster. In the meanwhile, the students formed a semicircle around the supine man's cot. When that was completed, Fishman ceremoniously entered the cramped room and stepped into the semicircle. He paused then, and looked around the room dramatically, before declaring:

"Here, ladies and gentleman, is the famous Jasper Kain."

...Two months had passed since Kain's capture, but they had never let him speak. They hadn't even given him a proper trial. They had only hidden him away, as they were hiding him away now. Even Roland Micheaux had deserted him—running away like a scared child; so that now, Kain's years of work were all for nothing. Kain had lain there for weeks now, waiting for the chaos that was destined to come. He had been slowly locking himself away—not necessarily to save him self, but so that he would be conscious when that great explosion came.

For days on end, he would be unaware of what was going on around him. Orderlies would come around, forcing him to eat and change his clothes and take his medicine. Psychiatrists would come in and try to talk to him, but none of these things would really register in his mind. However, when Fishman walked into the room and pronounced his name, Kain looked across for the first time. There was something about the sound of Fishman's voice that wrenched him from his apocalyptic daydreams. Confused by his emergence back into the world of men, the pink, eager faces of those gathered around him made him recoil. But at last, his eyes came to rest on Fishman (who, in the cramped room, was no more than a meter from him); and frowning, he finally recognized the man.

Fishman had been the "psychological expert" at his court hearing. The man had come to Kain the morning after his capture, asking him pointless questions about his mother and childhood. Spouting his Freudian drivel, the man had then reappeared as the featured witness at the farce that found him "mentally unfit to stand trial." Kain's lawyer had been a sweaty 35-year-old who, in his five years as a public defender, had only managed to win two cases! And unfortunately for Kain, one of those victories had come at his expense. As it was, both the public defender and the district attorney had wanted to get

Kain declared incompetent. It had all been a farce.

And with the strangeness of time over the last few weeks, it was as though those events had happened years ago. Kain instinctively found himself looking at Fishman the way one looked at someone whom one hadn't seen in ages. He looked to see if the man had more wrinkles now, or had gotten fatter. The fact that there was no change at all, added to Kain's belief that Fishman was somehow immutable—some inert substance floating through the universe.

It was then that Fishman turned halfway to his students and began, in his precise monotone: "In Jasper Kain, we have the prototype of a new kind of mental illness—a uniquely *modern* illness. [He paused dramatically then, as though allowing his students to soak in the poetry of his words.] Jasper Kain is not merely a man misled by his delusions of grandeur—and his own dissatisfaction with his life—he sees himself as some kind of vengeful angel. And it is in this mindset which we see the truth behind not only his actions, but his psychological makeup. He is another in the long line of criminals who have been gripped by the sexual allure of violence."

Kain had been listening intently, but seeing where Fishman was going, he lay back on the cot, staring at the ceiling again. Fishman went on:

"Ironically, when we look at Kain's actions, we see that while he was pulled by the allure of being *known* for violence, he went out of his way to avoid *being* violent. This is the telling thing about him. He wanted the reputation of a Jack the Ripper, who brutalized women—sliced them up and *killed* them. He wanted the sexual release—and, indeed, the *notoriety*—which dismembering an innocent person entailed in his mind; and yet, he chose something that when severed, would cause no pain: cause no blood to be spilt. *He chose hair*!"

—While in Brooklyn, the forces of self-destruction gathered to hear Botswana Glade's words, Kain smiled to himself. Fishman continued:

"But the mere cutting of hair never satisfied him. Of course, how *could* it! He wanted to be violent, but his violence was never, so to speak, *consummated*. He remained unfulfilled—*impotent*, if you will. [Kain snickered to himself.] As it was," Fishman said with a frown, annoyed by Kain's interruption, "Kain eventually became a laughingstock. The terror which he wished to inspire in his victims, turned into gales of laughter; the hair grew back, leaving a strange kind of celebrity status for his supposed victims. They appeared on television by the dozens, somehow ascendant and jolly, despite his attempt at desecration and dismemberment. Indeed, towards the end, people even began to fake attacks upon themselves by giving themselves hackneyed haircuts, so that that they, too, could become celebrities. This further thwarted and marginalized Kain, who was now a secondary character in his own supposed reign of terror. He was never gratified by the act that was supposed to spur him to ecstasy.

"This," he added with a flourish of his hand, "explains the comical conclusion to this entire affair. It is obvious that Kain *wanted* to get caught. He wanted to once again become the focus of his own fiasco; and so, in an orgasmic, climactic farce, he effected the means by which he could be captured—and captured in the *spotlight*. He attacked the Mayor of New York City, in what amounts to *broad* daylight, knowing what it would mean. He made sure that it was an event where the cameras would be rolling. He didn't even *try* to escape! He just stood there, grinning. He wanted his great moment of martyrdom to have a grand cinematic appeal. That had been the moment of no return: the moment when he could have been violent—taken the plunge, so to speak—and slaughtered not only the Mayor, but socialites from the banquet. But even then," Fishman went on, raising his hand theatrically, "he remained a laughingstock. Instead of taking action, he remained impotent. It was then that people—even those who rushed to get a glimpse of him and afford him his ephemeral celebrity status—saw him for what he was: a small man who needs help. And," he concluded compassionately, "he *will be* helped, my young colleagues, through therapy and medication. Like I said before, he is *thoroughly* harmless. Once he is freed of his delusions—and acknowledges whatever sexual failings he has suffered through his entire life (I bet he is even a virgin!)—he will once again be a productive member of society."

Fishman had paused dramatically, ready for the reverent sighs and nods which were the psychiatric equivalent of a shower of applause, but all that there was, was Kain's sudden, howling laughter. Fishman first looked at him in surprise, then annoyance, as Kain, suddenly reassured that the seeds of self-destruction had been sown in their society, laughed out triumphantly.

"Orderlies," Fishman groaned to get the men to restrain Kain, but Kain was laughing even louder now, his voice supplanting that of the lunatic screaming down the corridor. Fishman had been around madness for 30 years now, but something about Kain's laughter took even him aback. This discomfort was rare for him, and he didn't like it. Desperate to restore order to the rarefied world of his institute, he turned halfway to his students, his face now wearing a crooked, twitching grin: "I see that we'll have to start that drug regimen right away!" But when Kain only laughed louder, Fishman, unnerved by it all, screamed, "Orderlies!" gesturing for the two men to restrain the cackling man.

* * *

RANDOLPH WAS INSIDE THE hospital now. The protesters and Maria Santos were behind him for the moment, but peace was nowhere in sight. Everything was falling apart! He kept seeing the smug, vengeful expression on Santos's face. The woman had been out for *blood*! In an hour, all the major news services would be carrying the story—and his end would be irrevocable. This was the calm before the storm, but even the calm was chaotic and churning....

He was walking down a corridor now, surrounded by an entourage that now included about 20 people. Most were reporters and camera crews, who had been handpicked to show Randolph visiting the wounded. It was all staged. Seven video cameras now faced him; the cameramen were walking backwards, suddenly striking him as crabs. In a few moments, when the frenzy of his scandal seized them, they would rip him apart...a photographer kept snapping his picture, and each time the flash went off, it was like an explosion in his mind—

Was his life really over? After his disgrace, he would be thrown out of office—probably *impeached*—and then he would be as good as dead. How the hell had it come to this...? But what was the use anymore?

He suddenly became aware that the police commissioner was walking by his side. The latter was a fat, ruddy-faced man who had a perpetually sorrowful expression on his face. The man looked like a dog that had done something that it knew was wrong, and now hid from its master. The commissioner's placement had also been planned in advance, to show that the Mayor supported him. But as Randolph walked along, he began wondering what good these machinations could do. People couldn't be *tricked* out of their madness; all those hundreds—soon to be *thousands*—gathered along the sidewalks to see that the maniac and the police paid for what they had done, didn't give a shit who walked by Randolph's side…!

They finally reached the first victim's room. A teenage Latino was lying comatose in a bed with myriad tubes and bandages and pieces of equipment attached to him. He had been the first one that the maniac shot down; afterwards, the boy had been trampled by the mob. Two women were by the side of the bed, crying and consoling one another. Randolph, surrounded by the commissioner and the rest of the entourage, took in the scene with reverent silence. But even as Randolph stared at the scene, he felt himself drifting away from them all.

In fact, even before Levin pulled him away from Santos, Randolph had felt himself withdrawing from the world. He saw everything that was happening around him, but he saw it all as though from a great distance. At that moment, he was overcome by the sensation of being pulled apart; he felt as if one hand were pulling him back into the light of past—which contained his old self and values—while another hand was pulling him into the abyss of the future. His safety and sanity were in the past; but the hand of fate, which wrenched him towards the future, was stronger. Still, even as he left the past and everything he had ever known, behind, he *knew* this feeling—could actually put a face to it—and that face was in his distant past as well, like everything he understood.

…Thirty-odd years ago, he had been like a god—a tall, muscular god, with blazing speed and the courage to take on anything. Indeed, the image of Randolph winning the national championship for his college football team was indelibly burned into the myth of America. The footage of Randolph first fighting off two tackles, faking out two others, then throwing that perfect pass to his on-running receiver, seemed to be the embodiment not only of what Randolph was—but of what America could be. He had always been a man of motion—a *star*—running confidently towards what he knew to be his destiny. That confidence had been there because even as a boy, growing up in Harlem, he had known that he was going to be great. And as a sense of confidence with one's own life tended to make one appear more attractive to others, Randolph had always been popular. Even as a boy, others had looked towards him for a nod or a smile, as if any small gesture from him were assurance that everything would be all right. There had always been what was tritely known as a gleam in his eyes. It had been as though he could see something that no one else could; and as the lost and confused were likely to put all of their trust in those who seemed to know where they were going, he had been a born leader.

As for the women, in those carefree days, he had been able to take his pick. Even before he reached puberty, the young girls had tried to get a piece of him: to *brand* him with their love; because even then, love had seemed to be all they had to give. Like their mothers before them, the less hope they had, the greater they had loved—and the more desperately they had tried to *prove* their love to him. For those quickly blossoming girls, like all the needful hordes, he had been their imagination, their hope, their will and purposefulness, in a world that had seemed like a raging river, pulling them inexorably towards the rocks. Their ultimate state of being had been fear; his hadn't so much been courage, as a type of cosmic ignorance, which insulated him from the realities of the ghetto streets.

With the help of this strange cosmic ignorance, his first year of college had been wondrous. It had all been his for the taking: athletic glory, academic excellence, social standing...His athletic scholarship had been to one of those Midwestern universities in a town whose population dropped by 80% when school wasn't in session. That had been his first glimpse of life beyond New York City. There had been farms all around the campus—so much open space! At first, the peacefulness of it had taken him aback. So much freedom to roam and *breathe*! It had been the way someone living next to a noisy highway, or railroad, would be startled by a peaceful night's sleep. He had walked around that rustic town like a country bumpkin gawking on his first visit to "the big city." And then, everything had happened so quickly…There had been the frantic rush to register for classes, and the first few grueling practices for the fall football season. But even then, Randolph had been at ease. He had shrugged off the strange antagonism of some of his white teammates and classmates, and gone confidently about his business....And then, a month later, everything had been further heightened when he was thrust into the starting quarterbacking role—a role usually reserved for whites. He had become a national figure overnight—especially after leading the team to two straight victories against national powerhouses. Still, even as 60 thousand fans cheered for him and his teammates carried him off the field on their shoulders, it had been just another natural happenstance to him—not some great milestone, as everyone was saying.

Whatever the case, the national press had hovered around him, constantly asking for interviews as he led his team to victory after victory. On campus, he had been a kind of god, insulated from everything by his athleticism on the field. Things had been so busy, that he didn't go back home until the next summer....So much had changed in a year—or maybe it was only that the gulf of time had allowed him to see things clearly. He had stepped from his sheltered, fairy tale existence, into reality. At first, he had had to readjust himself to the unsettling density of the population around him—and the constant noise. For a moment, walking down Lexington Avenue with his suitcase in one hand, he had wondered how it was that people managed to live like that: live stacked on top of one another, *like animals*. Everything had seemed new and suspect. When he finally got home, he had hardly recognized his little family—which he had always fantasized as being some pillar of strength and rectitude. He had found his mother sitting on the couch in a sleazy-looking feathery robe, watching a soap opera. Everything had seemed...*warped*, as if these were strangers that he was meeting. He had come home to find out not only that his younger brother was a junkie, doing a five-year stretch in jail for armed robbery, and that his 14-year-old sister was seven months pregnant, but that their mother seemed to care less. He had seen the filth of his home for the first time: the overflowing sink, the dusty corners, the peeling plaster...and the reality of his family...their very emptiness—and *neediness*—had repulsed him.

...And they had all seemed so needy to him. Need that could never be surfeited...For the first time, he had been ashamed, not only of his family, but of his *people*; because everyone, finding out that he was back in town, had come around, clumsily trying to ingratiate him- or herself with him. The young women had again renewed their assaults with their love; obscure childhood playmates had seemed desperate to convince him that they had been the best of friends. It had all repulsed him—as his mother's request for a little cash to buy some beer had repulsed him. For the first time, he had looked out of his window and seen a horrible, crumbling place. He had understood the constant shriek of sirens for what they were. He had turned on the television; and all of a sudden, everything had been there: reports of the Vietnam War, protests about the war, protests about racism and inequality, about *everything*, it seemed. Bewildered, he had gone for a walk, finding out that one of his closest childhood friends was now dead—and that many others were either in jail or hooked on drugs...or had been shipped off to Vietnam. Suddenly, his childhood—with all of its imagined peace—had seemed like a farce; and for the first time, all that he had wanted to do, was flee from the lies. It had been as if his house were burning wildly out of control, and that the choice before him was between escaping with his life and trying to save those within. And maybe in this, he had chosen the path that his people had always seemed to take. Black people—*his* people—who had run from the south to the north, foolishly thinking that they could escape racism; who had run from the supposed bigotry of the white man, and yet who seemed even more terrified of the desperate black man whose needs they could never get rid of...black people, who, in trying to escape the horrors of slavery, had found it impossible to escape the entanglements of freedom...how was he to feel about them?

He had stared at them, unsure—and terrified by the huge chasm of confusion before him. In the face of all of these new fears, Randolph had fled from the city after being back for only two days. He had fled back to Iowa without saying goodbye to a single person. As it was summer, the campus and the town had been practically deserted. He had been in the student union, watching the news and seeing the strife that he had just discovered. In some city, there had been some race riot or another, set off by frustrations and fears and outrage that had been out of proportion with everything he had ever felt before. He had watched it in a daze, thinking to himself that this was what came of needfulness. Just then, a flirtatious white woman had come up—one of those liberal types who was desperate to show

how open-minded she was. He couldn't recount the details of how it had happened, but a few minutes later, they had been in his room, having sex. There had been no real propositioning—no coquettish probings into one another's dating status. It had all been instinctual: *animalistic* maybe. Even attraction had hardly seemed to apply. They had both been attractive in the classical sense, but they had been far beyond that: beyond words, beyond definitions and categorization. It had happened in a whirlwind: he had found himself sucked under, unable to breathe and terrified of drowning. It had hardly even seemed like sex at all. Caught in the terror of the whirlwind, he had groped her body, and yet he had hardly seemed to be seeking pleasure. In fact, they had hardly seemed like partners at all, any more than two victims of an avalanche could call themselves partners. They had been whisked away, as powerless to stop the outcome as they were to stop gravity….An hour later, whatever had gripped them and dragged them away, relinquished its grasp. It had all been so strange to him. He had stared into her blue eyes as she lay there panting. He had had sex with her, yet it had not seemed to be about her, as much as it had been a grand struggle against his past: against all the needs of those around him. Somehow or another, he had been annealing himself with her shrieks of ecstasy. He had been, in a sense, losing his virginity—losing his *ignorance*—to get in return the hardened shell he knew that he would need in order to survive….

Back in the present, Randolph nodded thoughtfully to himself. He and the entourage were once again walking down the corridor, going to see another of the wounded. His aides watched him anxiously as they walked, suspecting that something horrible was growing within him, but nobody said anything. As for Randolph, with his childhood memories in mind, it was now clear to him that he had never really gotten over the horror he had felt upon returning to his mother's home: he had only postponed it all. He had been like a slovenly housekeeper, cramming all the refuse beneath the carpet and into the closet, in his desperation to create the illusion of order and cleanliness. All the filth was bound to burst forth eventually. In fact, the filth within him wasn't simply the product of a few weeks: it went back for *decades*; and before that, there hadn't simply been innocence, but *ignorance*—which was perhaps the filthiest thing of all….

The next room was the maniac's. That was what everyone was

calling the shooter—since even the FBI couldn't figure out his identity. And with the need for vengeance being so high in the city, four policemen were guarding the man's door. As for reporters and camera crews, they were of course excluded from the room—as the image of the man would only incite further violence. Randolph, the commissioner and a doctor were the only ones allowed to enter the room; and after they entered, the door was quickly closed behind them.

The maniac seemed to be covered in bandages from head to foot. His left leg and right arm were in casts; his neck was in a brace, and his face was bandaged, leaving only openings for his eyes and mouth. As expected, there was nobody here to mourn for the man. Randolph, who had been the last to enter the room, froze just beyond the threshold of the door. The window was open slightly, and Randolph could hear the mob gathered outside: it was like thunder rumbling in the distance. Randolph looked at the maniac then, thinking, Here is a man who is so vile to the senses, that he has to be hidden away. Out there, was a world that was desperate to rip the man apart; and with Randolph's scandal imminent, he felt some strange connection with the man. After his scandal broke and they all rose up to taunt him and take their vengeance, he would be no different from that man. And as these thoughts passed through his mind, he walked up to the side of the maniac's bed and looked down at the man's bandaged face—

Suddenly, the man's eyes opened. Randolph recoiled, the way one would recoil at the sight of a corpse coming to life. Randolph stared into the man's eyes in surprise. But discerning the man's moving lips, and realizing that the man was whispering something, Randolph instinctively bent down, putting his ear to the man's lips. In the meanwhile, seeing that the man was conscious, the doctor came up, and was about to ask Randolph to step to the side, when the Mayor recoiled. His face was suddenly drawn and haggard. He backed away from the maniac then, as though hoping that in putting distance between them, he would be able to block out what the man was saying.

"*—Kill me*!" the maniac was repeating, over and over again—

"What's he saying?" the doctor and the police commissioner asked in unison, but Randolph was too numb to hear. He felt dizzy and sick…and he had to get out of there. "Kill me!" the man had said; and for a strange moment, Randolph had found himself considering it—both for the man and himself. He had felt himself being soothed by the thought, drawn into it the way one was drawn into quicksand—

As Randolph burst into the corridor, a torrent of questions assaulted him; and seeing all the reporters and cameramen and aides, he instinctively cringed against the wall. He was trapped!

* * *

ROLAND WAS STARING AT his new Rolex watch when the cab stopped in front of the studio. It was a quarter to seven. Still bewildered by the events at his condo, Roland was lost, caught between the urge to celebrate and a frantic voice in his soul that was telling him that it was all a trick, and that he had to arm himself against Phelps. He had rushed to get here on time; but after getting out of the cab, he stopped and looked around confusedly. The chaotic scene in front of the warehouse-looking building, with hundreds of agitated, shouting people marching up and down the sidewalk, didn't seem real; with the oppressiveness of the heat, it seemed like a whole other world. It wasn't even seven o'clock in the morning, and yet waves of heat were already emanating from the sidewalk. The heat seemed not so much to be coming from the sun, as from within the earth—from *hell.* And as he looked around, the people marching up and down the sidewalk didn't so much strike him as human beings, but as tortured spirits, roasting in that hell.

At first, he thought that it was a strike, because the 100 or so sweat-drenched people—most of whom were blacks and Latinos—were holding signs and chanting, "No justice, no peace!" But on second thought, it seemed to be more than that. Four camera crews were busy videotaping everything; and against the wall of the building, hundreds of people, most of whom were white, were waiting on a queue, watching the protesters warily. And of course, there were dozens of policemen around, all watching the protesters with that gruff, enigmatic expression that always seemed to grace the faces of police officers.

No, it didn't exactly seem like a strike. Somehow, the energy was all wrong; and after Roland looked up and saw the bulletin board, he realized what was going on. The people on the queue, old codgers and tourists from the "heartland of America," were there to see the show; the protesters, angered by the events of the Brooklyn Massacre—as it was now being called in the media—were there to support the man who seemed to be the featured guest of the morning show, Botswana Glade. The bulletin board read:

Today:

Activist, Botswana Glade
Supermodels, Alana and Trudy
Bestselling Author, Armand Deville
Attorney, Roland Micheaux

Once again, Roland felt himself being drawn into something over which he was to have no control. He needed a respite from all the problems of the world, but the show was like a microcosm of that world. It had it all: boundless rage and the threat of violence with Botswana Glade and his protesters; sex, in the form of the anorexic supermodels. It even had the self-righteous search for justice, in the person of Roland Micheaux: famed lawyer and defender of the poor and defenseless.

As for Armand Deville, he was a ridiculously successful writer of what were commonly known as trashy novels; and as such, he was the coup de grâce of the burlesque. His novels were horrible; but better and more profitable than talent, Deville, one of those "tall, dark and handsome" white men whom white women were always professing to want, had a loyal following of love-starved female readers. His female protagonists fought crime—and *men*—and were so sexually aggressive that one sometimes got the impression that he was writing about the mythical caveman days, when our ancestors looked for prospective mates with clubs in hand. His last novel—*The Ashes of Lust*—had been a phenomenal Bestseller. Roland hadn't read it of course: the cover alone had made him laugh. As it was, the covers of most romance novels usually had a muscular man groping a voluptuous woman who was so gripped by passion that her breasts were practically bursting out of her blouse; but in a twist, Deville's book had had a "strong" woman practically disrobing a man who seemed either to be swooning or quailing in terror at the prospect of the woman's libido. For all of this, Deville was of course heralded as being a trailblazer of gender equality—or whatever they were calling it nowadays—and was therefore perfect for television and mass consumption.

—While in Brooklyn, the forces of self-destruction gathered to hear Botswana Glade's words, Roland shook his head at it all, willing himself to smile. The world was a grand farce; and for once, he was reassured by that fact. He saw the horror of life framed the way it was on television, in 10-second sound bites, soon to be followed by a "feel-good" public interest story and a commercial for "feminine protection." Everything could be forgotten in time and made light of, so what was the use? Why not get drunk and join the party—imbibe whatever narcotic they were selling today and go about your business? Roland again felt the urge to laugh. In fact, he chuckled to himself, already feeling a good buzz coming on. His relief couldn't possibly have been sane, but what was nowadays? He thought about his anxieties on the ride here, and suddenly wanted to laugh at those as well. To hell with Phelps and Candice and all of them: they were all laughable to this drunken Roland. The events of the last 24 hours were just more meaningless acts in a universe of meaningless acts. The only thing to do was laugh: have another drink and say to hell with it all. Yea, he would go into the studio and join the party—go with the flow, as they say. Tomorrow, it would all be forgotten, and there would be another tantalizing narcotic to soothe them—

His cellular phone was ringing. He took it out of his jacket pocket and looked at it oddly. "Yes?" he answered the phone.

"Micheaux, this is Mr. Rosencrantz!" the man announced in a gruff voice.

Rosencrantz was a senior partner at his firm, with whom Roland worked directly. "Mr. Rosencantz…" Roland repeated. For some reason, he was uneasy. "Is anything wrong, sir?"

"Report to my office this morning," the man said in a stern voice that was out of character for him.

"I'm about to appear on TV."

"I'm aware of that!" he said in annoyance. "Report to me after that's done. I'll expect you at 10 o'clock."

"Is anything wrong?" Roland said again.

"Something very serious has just been brought to our attention," Rosencrantz said in the same uncharacteristic tone. And then,

Roland was listening to the dial tone. He stood there for at least 10 seconds, still holding the phone to his ear. *This had to be Phelps's doing*! What to do now...! He was frozen in place, staring at the scene that had only a minute before left him laughing. What was happening to him—and his life! What to do...!

He looked around desperately, now more lost than ever. Happening to glance down the sidewalk, to his left, Roland noticed a side entrance, in front of which a nervous-looking man was waving at him, trying to get his attention. There were also two burly guards standing there....

"Mr. Micheaux!" the man—an intern by the looks of it—squealed as Roland approached. "Thank goodness you arrived on time!"

Roland could only look on, his face drained of life.

The intern was already sweating profusely—as was Roland—

"Just go straight down the hall," the intern said, shuffling through some dirty-looking papers, the sight of which unconsciously made Roland cringe. "There should be a dressing room there for you," the intern went on, already looking nervously out of the door for other guests. "Someone will come in and get you ready," he added as an afterthought....

Roland shuffled down the dimly-lit hallway, still hearing Rosencrantz's voice resounding in his mind. Damn Phelps! *What had the man said*...! And feeling the way he now did, the realization that his harried image would be on nationwide television within the hour, drained more of his poise. The obligatory numbness came over him then. It was one of his body's defense mechanisms: a natural narcotic that made everything insensible and inscrutable that his mind couldn't accept and reconcile....As Roland shuffled deeper into the building, he got glimpses of the set through an open section in the wall. It seemed suddenly fake: a living room floating in the darkness, surrounded by lights and cameras. Some stage workers rushed past him; and on the set, others were assiduously getting everything in order. In fact, everyone was in a hurry, suddenly striking him as fairy tale characters screaming that the sky was falling. *But maybe it was*! Rosencrantz had summoned him as though he were some worthless law clerk.

Roland's gait was now that of a tired old man...and he was lost.

He suddenly realized that he had merely been walking down the labyrinthine passages—and that he had no idea where he was. He was as confounded by the waking world, as he was by the world of horror that his mind framed for him. Desperate for something concrete, he tried the first door that he came up to. Opening the door cautiously, he peeped inside, seeing a luxurious dressing room, with a huge dressing table in one corner and a settee in the other. He nodded nervously to himself, stepping in. But just as he closed the door behind himself, a woman called from an adjoining room:

"Gwen? Is that you?"

Before Roland could say anything, the woman rushed out. Roland stood there frozen, because the woman—a tall, shapely red head whom he recognized immediately as the hostess of the show—came out dressed in nothing but an open robe. Her breasts were showing, as was her pubic hair. *I guess she actually* is *a red head*! Roland thought to himself. He glanced over her shapely body as he stood in the same frozen pose, waiting for her to scream. He stared at her face—her *eyes*—and it was then that he knew that he was undone; because, for the life of him, there was neither shock nor fear in her light green eyes: no concern, really. The way she looked at him, it was as though *he* were the naked one. He was more unnerved by the openness of her eyes, than he was by her open robe, because it was as though she might actually be seeing him: be *inside* of him, seeing his secrets. In fact, as she looked at him, there didn't seem to be any limit to what she might be seeing—or to what she might *be*. Behind those eyes was a place that both excited him and terrified him. And it was for this reason that she suddenly seemed beautiful to him—*wondrous* in fact. She presently smiled, saying:

"You're Roland Micheaux, aren't you?" Her voice was strangely resonant—*soothing*.

He paused before he spoke, not yet trusting his voice. He found his jaw muscles unusually tight when he opened his mouth. His mouth seemed too dry—he swallowed deeply, then answered: "Yes." He took another deep breath; then said, upon releasing it: "And you're Samantha Dearly."

As she nodded, he suddenly found himself smiling as well, relieved both at his words, and the fact that he had been able to speak. At that moment, she walked casually past Roland and over to the dressing table. She closed her robe as she walked—but in a way that made it seem as though it hadn't needed closing. It was as though they had always stood before one another like that, either both naked or both fully clothed. She picked up a tube of lipstick and began to apply it. Roland stood there, staring at her in that strange moment. She looked at him in the mirror again and smiled; then:

"Since you're here, would you mind helping me with my necklace?"

"Sure," Roland said, moving with too much alacrity. She handed him the necklace—which was made of flat marble-like plates and joined by three latches—then she turned back around so that he could put it on. They could see one another via the mirror. She hadn't tied her robe and Roland could see the smooth, firm outlines of her breasts. He had to loop his hand around her to put on the necklace. Her hair smelled incredible: the scent conjured images of some tropical grove, with a waterfall…kilometers away from anyone and anything. It was suddenly as though they were the only ones in the world. She pulled her hair to the side, so that he could have access to her neck…he felt as though his head were swimming. Somehow, he managed to attach the first latch of the necklace. He was moving slowly—fumbling actually. He didn't want it to end. He just wanted it to be them there, forever. While he fumbled with her necklace—and her neck—she inadvertently backed into him—and his erection. He couldn't help gasping at the sensation. What was happening…but he was tired of thinking. He could feel the soft, firm outline of her behind through the thin robe—certainly she could feel him. He looked in the mirror to see her face, but as she was still holding her hair out of the way, her face was averted. He managed to attach the second latch, but she was still there, pressed against his erection. He put his face closer to her hair and smelt her in—took a long deep breath that left him even giddier. God, he didn't want it to end—this strange respite from all the chaos and problems of the world. He would do anything to hold her in his arms. He attached the third latch, but not wanting it to end, he let his hands wander down the warm surface of her neck, to her shoulders, and then from her shoulders, to her back and hips; and she was still there, pressed against him as if they were the only ones in the world. She let her hair go at last; and for a moment, they stared at one another via the mirror. His eyes were clouded over with longing—and, beyond that, the deep bewilderment of his life. She turned to him then, staring up into his eyes, as if seeing it all; and for once, he didn't hide—*couldn't* hide. She was holding him now, and he pulled her softness to him. He had needed something soft—something *reassuring*. Instinctively, he bent down and kissed her. At first, it was soft...a universe of carefree pleasure; she put her arms around his neck, so that the scent of her perfume flared in his nostrils and made his head swoon. She was so soft, all of her...but then, all of a sudden, her tongue was wild in his mouth; her arms, still entangled around his neck, were like a noose, strangling him. A side of him, suddenly terrified—*suddenly remembering Candice*—wanted to push her away and run out of the room; but instead, he grabbed her behind. It wasn't a caress or a fondle, it was a grab. The force of her body against his put him off balance, so that he stumbled back into the wall. It was suddenly as if they were fighting one another—at *odds* with one another. She seemed to be biting at his tongue; her nails in his neck and back were like a beast's talons clawing into him. From her throat escaped a groan that was more like a growl: a declaration of war and madness. From his throat escaped a similar noise. It was guttural and horrible. And now that the battle lines had been drawn, it was his turn to push her back. There was the settee to the side: they both collapsed onto it, their struggle not ceasing for an instant. It was as if they would both rend one another to death. And yet, deep within him, he was aroused by the battle: by the internecine war that they had found themselves in. She was clawing at his back more savagely now; he was grabbing her ass with one hand, rubbing her brusquely between her thighs with the other. And then, he was sucking at her neck, tasting her salty sweat—

She pulled away, either the first to come to her senses, or the first to have burned off the fuel of her lust. She stared up at him; he stared at her, horrified by what he suddenly realized was the horror in her green eyes. The horror was definitely there, although it was clouded by a host of other emotions. In truth, her face wore one of those nebulous expressions that could have been anything from ecstasy to terror. Roland guiltily pulled his hand away from her crotch; he sat up on the settee, and she sat up with him. They were still staring deeply into on another's eyes, searching for the thing which would give meaning to the soupy mix of emotions that bubbled within them both—

All at once, she sucked in air sharply; and as she breathed deeply, Roland realized not only that she had been holding her breath, but that so had he. They were both breathing again. Their chests heaved for those first few breaths; but even after their breathing became relatively normal, they still stared at one another, trying to make sense of it all.

"Well then," she finally said with a laugh that was like a sigh of relief, "maybe we should have a date first."

* * *

CONSERVATIVE ESTIMATES SAID THAT there were now at least four thousand angry protesters in front of the hospital—and it wasn't even eight o'clock yet….Mayor Randolph was led to the lectern that had been set up in the cafeteria of the hospital. He had just spent about half an hour visiting with the wounded and their families, telling them insipid things like, "Hang in there," and, "We'll try to make sure this never happens again," while cameras captured the entire thing. But while he said those words and smiled in their faces, he had kept hearing the pained whisper of the maniac demanding, "Kill me, kill me…!" And of course, while he walked along, hearing and seeing those images, the specter of Maria Santos and the stripper had lain in wait.

During his weeks of filth, a side of him had always known that this moment of reckoning was the logical end of his actions. Even now, as he looked up and saw a crowd of about 200 people, with camera and sound crews, photographers, as well as the requisite policemen and curious onlookers, he was relatively free of panic and terror. He had no more to give, and was now willing to accept rest on any terms they chose—including death.

Maria Santos was standing ascendant before him—literally right in front of the lectern. Her fellow reporters had congregated around her, asking her what she had heard, and who her source was, but she only shrugged her shoulders coyly. Actually, the message from the stripper had been on her voice mail this morning. The stripper was actually a big fan of hers. And as soon as Santos heard the message, she had rushed over to the young woman's apartment, practically drooling as she heard how Randolph had supposedly lured the woman to the back and attacked her. Oh no, of course the woman wasn't a prostitute and didn't do that kind of thing. She was just a young woman, barely out of high school, who was trying to survive in New York. She had dreams of becoming a ballet dancer, and Randolph's attack had shaken her so badly that she didn't know if she could go on. There had been tears in her eyes at that moment, as she recounted how Randolph, that towering beast of a man, had attacked her. She had been no match for him. Of course she had given in and let him have his way....

Emerging from her idyll, Santos smiled and looked up at Randolph, who was about to begin his speech. He was to give the speech, but she was the focus of attention. This was her ticket to the big time—*no more scraps*! In the air, there was the expectation that something major was going to happen. Randolph, with a twinge in his belly and a lump in his throat, realized that this was the moment of truth, when he would shed his life like an unfertilized womb shed blood. He looked down at the audience and the reporter corps, seeing them all the way he had seen his aides in the limousine—as though from a great distance. He felt so empty just now; and all at once, while he stood there, fidgeting with the speech before him, he found himself wondering if what he had been thinking all these weeks was actually true: if there were actually others like himself out there: individuals taking the same steps that he was taking, thinking the same thoughts that confounded and bewildered him. He had once called such men and women soul mates; but such a group of people, all creeping towards the evil that seemed to lie at the end of the maze...He couldn't help but think of himself as the carrier of some devastating disease; he could feel the thing gestating within him, changing him, and it occurred to him that if a large enough group of people felt what he felt and had as much dormant hatred and resentment in their souls, then their society was doomed....

He began reading the speech that Dalton had prepared; but while the words rolled off his tongue, his thoughts were elsewhere. His mind went to things that he hadn't thought about in years: the first time he had made love to his wife; the first steps and words of his son; his first idealistic run for office...His entire life seemed to pass him in a blur, as though saying goodbye to him. His mind was still in a daze when he came to the conclusion—but that made no difference now. As for the speech, there had been nothing original in it. It had been so constructed as to sound both compassionate to the families of the victims, and express the outrage of those who had lost businesses and faith in society. He had done it all with the necessary grace. And perhaps the airy tone of his voice had added a certain poignancy to it. Whatever the case, when he was finished, and it was time for questions, he sought out Maria Santos and pointed to her and her alone.

At once, she demanded: "What do you have to say to the allegation that you raped a woman last night!"

Incomprehensibly, a glimmer of a smile came to his lips once again. Now that the moment of truth had come, a feeling of peace and calmness filled him. He would tell them everything now. But what was there to tell? What *was* the truth? *Rape*? he thought to himself for the first time. Is that how that hooker was going to play it? The reality of the Mayor of New York City going to a strip joint to ask for sexual favors wasn't bad enough: she had to invent lies...? It was while he looked down at all of their eager, expectant faces, that he withdrew his neck from the noose and stepped away from the gallows. They stood before him, self-righteously demanding honesty from him, and yet everything about them was dishonest.

"Anyone who thinks me guilty of something," he said in an even voice, "I urge to go to a court of law....You know what *really* offends me about this nonsense?" he went on in a new, more pained voice. "Right now, dozens of families are mourning their dead and wounded; but instead of working to mollify those losses, and find out the truth about the events of last night, the drive is on finding out if I'm getting laid or not."

Everyone laughed—except for Santos.

—While outside the hospital, the forces of self-destruction gathered to hear Botswana Glade's words, Randolph went on: "People have *died*! Businessmen and women have seen their livelihoods literally go up in smoke. The city, *at this very moment*, sits on the verge of mob violence, with men like Botswana Glade fanning the flames of hatred; and the first question I hear, is an allegation of sex. With all due respect, madam," he said, glaring down at the suddenly blanched

Maria Santos, "you aren't Judge Starr, and whatever young woman you've scraped up from the gutters, isn't Monica Lewinski! [More laughter!] Bring your witnesses, madam. Bring your semen-stained dress if you wish! [Even more laughter!] Bring all of it before a court of law and I'll answer your allegations there and submit to the will of its judgments. But right now, this city needs to heal. Botswana Glade is going to hold a rally in front of this building. The city needs me to deal with *those* concerns, not the rumor and innuendo that all public figures are now forced to submit to. We need to *heal*!" And at that he looked around earnestly and said with a sigh:

"Now, are there any *relevant* questions?" A torrent of hands went up, and Randolph began the press conference anew. Maria Santos, seeming suddenly haggard, walked off then. Like Marenga at the banquet, she was unable to understand where she had gone wrong and how Randolph had managed to thwart her; but unlike most others, who had been cowed by Randolph's power and *accepted* it, Santos left vowing that she would take revenge and bring him down—no matter what.

* * *

THE THREE MEMBERS OF the precinct's special drug unit cruised down the Harlem streets, headed for the slum that they had finally gotten permission to raid. All three men had on bulletproof vests and black, army-style fatigues. They were always quiet before they went on a drug raid; but today, instead of the usual pensiveness, there was a certain uneasiness that didn't necessarily come from the prospect of the work ahead. As they stared out of the window, at the ghetto streets, all three men seemed gripped by revulsion. Indeed, riots always had a strong effect on police officers: they were either cowed by the upheaval, or came to the conclusion that they would have to employ harsher methods in the future. Something new and *vile* was out there; and today, it wasn't only the crumbling tenements and the crime and the filthy streets. It seemed, strangely enough, *too* peaceful; and in that sudden peace, there was the promise of violence.

"—It's cooking us," Fred Holtzman said out of nowhere. He was a chubby, bald, slovenly-looking cop about 45, who was the philosopher/jokester of the three. He was sitting in the back seat of the unmarked sedan, staring out at the world with a strange intensity in his eyes. The driver, Michael Colina, a chiseled 40-year-old who had been in the marines for 12 years, glared at him via the rear view mirror, then went back to staring out of the windshield. The man in the passenger side seat, Louie Leonard, a bald, pencil-thin cop of 47, with a huge aquiline nose that made him look like a vulture, looked over his shoulder—not *at* Holtzman, just over his shoulder, actually up at the roof—and said:

"*What?*"

"This city is just a goddamn pressure cooker," Holtzman went on, "...some demon's stewing us. You smell that air—that's like roast meat...the way the upper class Brits cook it. You ever see how they cook the birds they hunt. They tie them up for a couple days—let them rot a little. Then they cook it...they like their meat a little putrid."

"Please," Leonard groaned, "I'm about to lose my lunch here."

But at that, Holtzman chuckled to himself with a self-satisfied air, sitting back in the seat. Leonard's revulsion had filled him with a kind of impudent, boyish pride; but looking over at Colina, and seeing the man's continued indifference, he felt the pleasure leave him. He hated silence—and something about Colina had always unnerved him—so he quickly went on: "So can you believe that Brooklyn wacko, asking the Mayor to kill him?"

"I say good riddance," Colina grumbled for the first time, "—just get it over with."

"Nah," Holtzman said with a strange glee, happy to have drawn Colina out, "that guy hasn't suffered enough for what he did."

—While in Brooklyn, the forces of self-destruction gathered to hear Botswana Glade's words, Colina chuckled mirthlessly, again looking at Holtzman via the rear view mirror: "And what did he *do*? [There was something strange gleaming in his eyes] Animals killing animals—that's all it was—"

"*Kids* died, Colina!" Holtzman ejaculated.

But Colina remained calm as he went on: "A rat's a rat—no matter how old it is."

"What the hell's gotten into you?" Leonard was saying now—he was always the diplomat of the three.

"This is bullshit," Colina cursed, his voice calm yet menacing,

"—*all* of it! Just *hours* after a riot, they got us out here, busting a drug dealer who's little more than a junkie himself. We're concentrating on the small fish and then we keep wondering why nothing ever changes. This entire system is set up for us to fail. What the fuck are the three of us supposed to do against all this shit. They got us stuck in the basement, with paperwork up to our asses; and they think because they call us the special drug unit—or whatever our title is this week—then we're going to do something."

"But what can we do, Colina?" Holtzman said to placate him, "—we're just street cops, we don't got power to change nothing."

"Damn right we don't got power!" Colina raged, the veneer of calmness leaving him. "The thieves and robbers and killers—all the scum—*they* got the power. They got it because we *give* it to them. You know what I seen on TV the other night? There was this story on that crazy fuck, Jasper Kain...turning criminals into folk heroes: that's what we're doing. Crazy scumbags are our heroes. Killers and robbers are role models. Ever listen to rap music? All it is, is glorified crime, with niggers talking about getting pussy and who they robbed. Those are the role models....All these assholes out there on the streets...creating a beast they can't control...and then they wonder why shit is fucked up—"

"Hey, Colina," said Leonard, in a tone which hinted that he really hadn't been listening, "you sure you don't want SWAT in on this bust? We don't want anything messy—especially with a riot last night—"

"*Fuck* SWAT!" Colina cursed him. "If you're too scared, you can wait in the car and play with your dick while I handle business—and that goes for you, too, Holtzman."

"Who said anything about being afraid?" Leonard said, defensively. "I'm just following orders. The last thing we need is to give Botswana Glade something to harp about. And operating procedure says—"

Colina glared at him, then shook his head: "Listen to you: 'following orders'... 'operating procedure.' You think the drug gangs let bureaucracy hold them back? Bureaucracy's the reason the country's falling apart. We got people more concerned with fitting into the system than getting shit done! Everyone knows what's happening out there: we don't need undercover cops and vice squads to figure out where the crime is. All that shit is going on right in front of our eyes, and we're frightened to move without filling out the proper paperwork—*in triplicate*. In the meantime, everything's going to hell! Desperate times call for desperate measures, not 'operating procedures!'"

"All right, already!" Holtzman laughed. "For a 'man of action,' you sure do talk a lot!" At that, he laughed again, tapping Leonard on the shoulder, so that the man felt obliged to chuckle along. Only Colina was silent, sitting there sullenly as he looked out at the streets that he hated so much....

When they finally drove up to the dilapidated slum, it was about eight o'clock. On the front stoop, a youth had been groping some young chick—who giggled coquettishly under his ministrations—but seeing the three white men alight from the car and get their guns and other equipment from the trunk, the youth stopped and watched them warily.

Colina was the first of the cops to step up. "Police," he said, casually gesturing to the badge on his bulletproof vest, "—you live here?"

"I ain't do nothing, man," the youth said combatively.

"Did I accuse you of anything?" Colina said in his low, strangely caustic voice. He stood there, waiting for an answer from the kid as the other two cops walked over. "—All right then!" he said in response to the youth's sullen silence. "You live here or not?"

"Yea," the youth groaned, "I live here—so what?"

Colina chuckled to himself, then: "Listen, junior," he said, moseying up to the top step so the kid could see how much bigger than him he was, "that is a *real* bad attitude you got there. I suggest you change it quick. [He placed his hand on his holster, conspicuously.] When I talk to you, you listen and keep your fucking mouth shut; when I tell you to answer, you tell me what the fuck I want to hear, you understand me?"

The youth stared at him sullenly, the fire gone from his eyes.

"All right, then," Colina started again. "Now, do you live here?"

"Yea," the youth whispered, glancing ashamedly at the girl he had been trying to impress.

"What? *Speak up*!" Colina demanded.

"Yes," the youth said sorrowfully, bowing his head.

"You have the keys?"

"Yea."

"All right then," Colina said, gesturing with his head for the youth to open the door.

The youth's hand was shaking when he put the key into the lock; Colina stood threateningly at his back, waiting impatiently. After the deed was done, Colina turned to him and said: "See how smoothly everything goes when you cooperate with the police?" He proffered a loaded smile then—the youth looked away....

The hallway was hot, dark and smelly, conjuring the feeling of being trapped within a rotting carcass. When they reached the fourth story apartment, they were about to bash open the door with the battering ram, when Holtzman tried the knob and realized that the door was open. They entered a small kitchen that was in utter disarray; two huge rats looked at them disinterestedly from the nasty-looking counter, then casually went about their business. Beyond the kitchen there was a small, equally disheveled living room. The three policemen filed stealthily through it and towards the open doorway at its end—from which came the sounds of a television. The three cops crept up with their guns drawn. A woman was screaming; after a moment of confusion, they recognized the disconnected—at times *chaotic*—sounds of sex. Colina crept up to the door and peeked inside: it was a filthy bedroom; on a bed next to the window, a scrawny black man was pumping savagely into a plump Latina who must have weighed about two and a half times his weight. Colina turned back to the other two, who were at his heels.

"On the count of three," he whispered. "One, two, *three*!" The men rushed in! The suspect screamed out when he saw the men. Colina and the other two charged the bed; but with lightning quick agility that no one could believe, the totally nude man leapt from between the Latina's legs and out of the window, onto the fire escape. For a few seconds, they all stared at the window in disbelief.

Colina was the first to come to his senses. "I'll get him!" he screamed, leaping up on the bed to get to the window. The Latina, also coming to her senses, pulled a sheet over her plump nakedness and began to squeal hysterically.

The fire escape looked out on a dreary alley. The suspect was climbing up to the roof. Colina looked up at the man's scrawny buttocks in disgust. "Stop or I'll shoot!" he screamed, but the man was already at the top of the fire escape, disappearing onto the roof. Colina cursed under his breath and began to make haste up the fire escape. He was breathing hard when he got to the top. At first, the man was nowhere to be seen, but then Colina saw him about two buildings over. He was leaping from roof to roof. Colina set out after him at full speed. There was a strangely euphoric feeling in him as he chased down his quarry. And ahead, the man was slowing, looking around in a panic. He had reached the corner building of the block, and had run out of roofs. He looked back at Colina in horror as Colina slowed and started walking up. There was self-satisfaction showing on Colina's face now. He even smiled. The man was still looking around like a trapped animal. Colina waited for him to come to the conclusion that there was nowhere for him to go; but:

"Get back, or I'll jump!" the man screamed suddenly, getting up on the ledge.

Colina stared at him in confusion for a moment, then chuckled at the ridiculousness of the demand. "So jump then!" he laughed, pointing his gun at the fool. The man, finally detecting the flaw in his logic, groaned and went to step back onto the roof—

"Get the fuck back up there!" Colina screamed, pointing his gun again.

The man was shaking, his eyes seeming on the verge of popping from their sockets—

"*Jump*, you stupid son of a bitch!" Colina cursed him again, while the man began blubbering like a scared toddler. "*Jump*!" he screamed, half jokingly, "—it'll save me the paperwork! *Jump*!" he raged, the harshness of his voice making the man begin to cry—

"*Colina*!" a voice called then; and looking over his shoulder, Colina saw Holtzman running towards him.

Having gotten that reprieve, the suspect leapt back onto the roof and ran past Colina, towards Holtzman. "He's *crazy*!" the man cried, tears dribbling down his cheeks. "Keep him away from me...he's *nuts*!"

As Holtzman took the babbling man away, Colina watched them in annoyance; but then, all of a sudden, for a reason that even he didn't know, he began to chuckle to himself—first low, then loud...*sick*. Holtzman looked back at him uneasily; the suspect cringed, begging Holtzman to take him away. In the meanwhile, Colina just stood there, his facial muscles still twitching as he looked up at the hazy abyss of the sky.

*   *   *

FOR ROLAND, LIKE ALL of them, the moment of truth was drawing close.

—While in Brooklyn, the forces of self-destruction gathered to hear Botswana Glade's words, Roland entered the smaller, less-luxurious dressing room, and sat before the mirror, watching himself in the silence. The face staring back held a combination of horror, disbelief, amusement and triumph. The last 24 hours were a stream of all of those things, full of too many contradictions to be real. What had just happened in Samantha Dearly's dressing room personified it all. It was too dream-like—too much like one of those dubious, boastful letters sent in to men's sex magazines—for him to believe it himself. But it was while he was staring at himself in the mirror, trying to make some sense of it, that everything went crazy.

First, the makeup woman burst into the room. It was a hideous, gypsy-looking crone, who came in mumbling something about how busy and late she was. She reminded him of some bizarre character from *Alice in Wonderland.* She had a figure reminiscent of an unkempt bed: there may have been a body under that rumpled cloth, but Roland couldn't tell, nor did he wish to know. She twirled Roland around in the swivel chair, soon attacking him with a powder puff. He coughed while she went about her ministrations; he tried to wave away the cloud of powder, but she slapped his hand out of the way. She was pressing her flabby breasts against him now. The odor of her perfume was pungent in his nostrils—it reminded him of a funeral parlor: it was too flowery, as though expressly to mask the decay. She kept rubbing up against him as she rushed around, this second combing his hair, that second straightening his tie—

The door burst open then; and, along with the noise of hundreds of people finding their seats, a lanky white man in his mid to late twenties invaded the room. By his walk, and the strange, perturbed expression on his face, Roland knew immediately that he was gay. The man walked up to Roland and the woman—who had ceased her ministrations, as if out of respect—and paused dramatically, one hand instinctively going to his hip, while the other brought the writing pad up to his eyes. Apparently, he was short-sighted, for he squinted at it for a moment, while Roland and the woman waited.

"All right, then!" he said in a raspy, stereotypically gay voice. "The super models are late!" he went on, looking at Roland condescendingly, "and you will be second, in their place."

Roland nodded uneasily. He liked to think of himself as a free thinker who couldn't care less about other people's sexuality; but with these flamboyantly gay men, the very act of pretending that one didn't notice (and as such, didn't care) was inherently farcical—especially since their every action screamed: "*I'm gay*!" Roland couldn't help thinking of the man as a crude caricature of a bitchy woman with PMS. But even as he thought this, there was an internal voice of censure; and with this internal censure came guilt and uneasiness. Nowadays, the difference between the queasiness that came with encountering that which was alien and incomprehensible, and *bigotry*, was narrow—if not inseparable; and the only way to escape the thought police, and the brand of bigotry, was to nod, smile disingenuously and go about your business.

"—Make sure you're ready on time!" the gay man declared—again seemingly out of nowhere—so that Roland jumped in his seat. Having made this declaration, the man exited the room like a prima donna leaving the stage. When they were alone, the old crone eyed Roland critically one last time, shrugged (as though he looked like hell, but there was nothing more she could do), then made for the door. As she was about to open the door, she mumbled for him to go to "the green room" and wait for his turn. He leapt to his feet and went to follow her, but she gave him the look that people gave to stray dogs that they suspected wanted to follow them home, so he slackened his pace enough for her to leave him.

When he opened the door himself, Roland saw how hectic the studio had become. Everyone was being let in now—all the restless ticket holders from outside. They were people from small towns all over America, for whom this was the highlight of their lives. They came equipped with cameras and autograph books, so that they could impress their neighbors when they got back to their little "in-the-middle-of-nowhere" towns. Roland wandered down the hallway once more—back the way he had come. His stomach twinged as he passed Samantha's dressing room....He walked on. Through an open section in the wall, he could see the audience. The ushers were showing them to their seats now. Roland stood there dreamily, while stage hands rushed about and the stage band tuned their instruments and played disconnected, cacophonous bits of music as they warmed up.

It was while he was standing there, that the intern who had greeted him at the entrance came up. The youth was sweating worse than ever. He looked like he was going to have a heart attack! "There you are!" he screamed. "We were looking everywhere for you!"

Roland looked at him with pity. A few years of this, and the kid would be a horrible, ulcerated wreck of a man.

"Wait in the green room," he announced. Then: "It's this way," he said, tugging on the sleeve of Roland's jacket. The man led Roland farther down the corridor and opened a door for him. Roland entered the spacious, square chamber, which, because of the dim lighting and the fact that it was windowless, nonetheless had a cramped quality to it. Right across from the door, there was a huge TV, before which a man in a dark suit was standing. Between the man and the door, there were two rather long burgundy couches, which faced one another. To the left, there was a huge dining table, with heaping trays of donuts and danishes; and against that wall, there was an entire kitchen, replete with coffee and cappuccino machines.

Roland stepped into the room; and as he did so, the nervous intern—who had been holding the door like a worried prison guard, making sure that his charge was locked up and accounted for—closed the door behind him. It was then that the man in front of the TV turned around, and Roland saw Botswana Glade. On the screen, were the images of the riot—the video that the bystander had taped. Roland and Botswana Glade stared at one another; and unaccountably, they both stared with a certain amount of antagonism.

"You're that playboy lawyer," Botswana Glade said at last, still scrutinizing Roland.

"My name is Roland Micheaux," Roland corrected him, stepping up. He had intended to shake the man's hand, but he stopped about halfway there, and they stared at one another once more. As Roland saw it, men like Marenga and Botswana Glade were nothing but laughable relics from the 1960s. Their existence was a kind of collective joke: either to annoy and reassure whites by their very ridiculousness, or, by that same uncompromising ridiculousness, to shame the black masses and spur them on to mainstream ideologies and aspirations.

Botswana Glade chuckled suddenly in the silence and began: "There are two kinds of successful men in this world, Mr. Micheaux. The first type is the man who will accept anything—who waits around for the alms thrown to him, like a beggar. Such men, if they can make themselves seem desperate enough, and can do a little song and dance for the passersby, can eventually become rich, collecting a dollar here and a quarter there. On the other hand, there are those who go out into the world and, instead of *collecting* change, *forge* change, demanding success on their own terms."

"Let me guess," Roland said with a smirk, "I'm the former and you're the latter."

Botswana Glade smiled a dead, menacing smile. "Men like you exist only to put people at ease—to make them laugh. You're a well-paid harlequin."

"And why do men like yourself exist?" he continued with a smile.

"I'm here to uncover and disseminate the truth."

"*Whose* truth?"

"My own of course!" he said with a laugh; and sobering quickly—almost *insanely*—he went on, "The truth must always be your own, Mr. Micheaux. Men like you and Randolph get rich by accepting other people's truths. You'll accept anything....There's a war coming, Mr. Micheaux, and men like you are going to be the first casualties. It's always the weak links that break first—"

But just then, the nervous intern again opened the door and poked his head inside, telling Botswana Glade to come with him and wait off-stage. As Botswana Glade walked past Roland, en route to the door and the waiting intern, the man smiled derisively, almost *pityingly*, at him. "Time for me to forge history," he said to Roland....

Finally alone, Roland walked over to the kitchen and got himself a donut and some coffee. He ate slowly and deliberately in the silence, willing his mind to be still. What else could possibly happen...*And what the hell could Rosencrantz possibly want from him...!*

There was always something waiting in the recesses of his mind; and no matter how many times he tried to bury it, it always managed to claw its way to the surface…!

The show began about five minutes later. Roland sat in the green room, which, for some reason, wasn't green, and watched everything on the huge screen. All the backstage workers had seemed like chickens with their heads cut off, so he couldn't believe the cheerful, easy tone of Samantha and her co-host when the show finally began. Of course, as he watched Samantha, he was enchanted. It was all so dream-like that a side of him still wondered if their encounter had really happened. As for the show, the first few minutes were taken up by meaningless banter and jokes, while Samantha and her co-host sat on the set and drank coffee. Her co-host, Bart Mitchell, was a perpetually grinning Texan of middle age, who acted way too silly for a man of his age, height and build. He looked like someone who had failed at doing the evening network news, and was now banished to this idiocy. Then there was a moment of suspect, TV outrage, with the requisite gasps, as Samantha related the story in the news that morning, about the man who had run over that kid, shot those people and then been beaten to the brink of death by the mob. They revealed that the man was now conscious and asking to be killed. They also revealed that doctors had found high levels of cocaine in the man's system. During this time, there was of course a little gossip about Randolph and Maria Santos; but returning to the "hot" news, they showed the bystander's video, which was showing everywhere by now; and Charlotte McPrice was all over the news as well, explaining how Randolph's incompetence was responsible for it all; and then, they showed a video feed from their own sidewalk and the front of the hospital, where Botswana Glade's supporters were still chanting their slogans. Thirty seconds into all of this, Roland had allowed his mind to drift off….

A commercial break later, Botswana Glade was introduced. He did not smile, and there was only scant applause for him. He talked softly and deliberately for 30 seconds or so. But then, at Bart Mitchell's urging, he went into a lengthy, high-pitched disquisition on the Brooklyn Massacre and the maniac, expounding on how the police were devils, and Mayor Randolph was a false prophet and a scared hypocrite. Roland groaned then, thinking to himself: *All these niggers, competing for scraps by stabbing one another in the back*! But as he sat there, listening to Botswana Glade insinuating that there was somehow a conspiracy in all of the random acts of violence that had happened the night before, something in Roland's gut—some creepy, anxious feeling—told him that the man was mad. Botswana Glade, it suddenly occurred to him, was Jasper Kain: but a Jasper Kain who wanted to destroy the world not by *shaving* heads, but by cutting them off. The realization that thousands of people were going to congregate to hear the man's words, suddenly made him shudder. The man's words were even now being broadcasted across the country. Botswana Glade was about to succeed where Kain had failed, and there didn't seem to be anything that any of them could do about it.

Then, it seemed as if in no time at all, it was Roland's turn to be on the air. The nervous-looking intern came running in, yelling that Roland's moment had come, and that Roland should just act naturally. Roland, numb from the roller coaster ride of the last 24 hours, was too preoccupied and anxious to be annoyed.

He walked backstage with the youth, fighting to pull himself together. He was to be on the air in *minutes*—but he wasn't ready! He needed a few minutes to himself—just like at the banquet two months ago! The strange parallels, along with the shadowy horrors surrounding Phelps and Rosencrantz's summons, ate away at whatever poise he had left. His image would be broadcasted across the country in a matter of *minutes*! He wanted to run away—anything to keep from making a fool of himself! He was overcome by a kind of stage fright that was so severe that he felt himself on the verge of throwing up! But somehow, he forced himself to be still....

Bart Mitchell was telling some joke in prelude to introducing Roland. With the Botswana Glade segment over, they all seemed relieved. The audience was boisterous, laughing at anything Mitchell said. Offstage, there seemed to be movement everywhere. Roland's eyes darted around, but his mind was too excited—too *chaotic*—to register most of it. And then, the next thing that he knew, Mitchell was calling his name and some stagehand was telling him to walk out, onto the set. He was in the light now, almost rocked by the wall of applause. He could barely see—it was so bright! But then, once again, his eyes focused, and he saw Samantha standing statuesquely in the same set that had looked so fake this morning. All of a sudden, it seemed like paradise to him, because she was there. He suddenly had a yearning for a woman—not *sex*, per se, even though that was undeniably part of it...The closeness of a woman—the trust and love of a woman—seemed either like some missing link to his joy or an aegis against all that might trouble him. He was grasping at straws now, trying to get through this any way he could. Watching her, as she smiled back at him, he was either overcome by hope, or by terror. Samantha was holding out her hand now, then kissing him on the cheek....Mitchell was shaking his hand....

Time seemed to be flying past, like the world outside a rushing car—or like the world beyond the giddying splendor of a merry-go-round. For some unaccountable reason, he felt at ease again. As the show continued, there was some initial banter about the Brooklyn Massacre, which Roland navigated by repeating the same platitudes he had been hearing all that morning. For the life of him, he was actually doing it! His natural poise came out of nowhere, and he watched it as if he were a member of the audience. He waxed poetic on justice and the state of modern society, before giving a few tidbits about his most recent legal victory to show that justice could in fact be achieved. The applause for him was *thunderous*—

But just then, the chaotic scene in front of the Brooklyn hospital appeared on an offstage monitor; and as Roland glanced at it, he had a sudden and violent flashback to his father and that day 20 years ago. He felt suddenly lost. Samantha was saying something; but ever so briefly, he was remembering Phelps's perverseness and the enervating strangeness of Candice's sex. He remembered Rosencrantz's terseness and the prospect of losing everything. He was close to the edge. He had made a wrong step, and all of a sudden he was staring into the abyss. Once more, a side of him wanted to rush off—to run away as quickly as he could—but he beat it back with all the savagery that he could muster—

"How has your life changed since you were declared one of the city's 10 most eligible bachelors?" Bart Mitchell was asking him now. Mitchell had a smile on his face, and members of the audience began to laugh as well. Roland, still lost in his fears and uncertainties, took a deep breath—which everyone must have taken for coyness. He glanced at Samantha then, and was once again overcome by how exquisite she was. Maybe it was that which saved him. She was sitting there with her legs crossed seductively, smiling back at him, and he nodded his head dreamily before looking back at Bart. Then, suddenly remembering the latter's question about how his life had changed, he smiled and said:

"My life's the same, but the women have gotten more beautiful." The audience burst into applause and laughter then—as did Samantha and Bart. Roland's words hadn't been that witty, but faced with the specter of his father and Phelps and Rosencrantz, he found himself laughing with the rest of them, suddenly desperate to believe in their laughter.

* * *

THE LIGHTS HAD been turned off by the time Jasper Kain emerged from his drug-induced nightmare. His mind was groggy from what Fishman had given him, and it took a few minutes before he was able to retrace the events of the day, or night, or whatever it was outside. He lay unmovingly on his cot, now unable to fall asleep. Locked in his cell—which, to his disappointment, wasn't padded, as he'd always heard—the hatred began to bubble within him again. It was hatred like he had never felt before: irrational, *seething* hatred. He had spent his time philosophizing about the difference between chaos and madness, but those differences, if they existed, were meaningless to him now. The entire world had laughed at him, but they would all be brought to pay for what they had done to him. Micheaux, Randolph…all of them.

As he lay in the darkness of his cell, there was no way that Kain could have known what was happening to the city; but in his soul, there was all the self-destructive chaos that was coming fast on the horizon. In fact, it was almost as though Kain were conjuring their lives; because in his mind's eye, he saw the myriad triggers to "all hell breaking loose": some innocent black kid getting gunned down by the police, for instance; some proto-Rodney King beating, captured on tape—so that the rage would flare up and consume the world like it had Los Angeles. And there, in that orgy of self-destruction, was the horror of Columbine and the sleazy underbelly of some public sex scandal. *All* that filth and madness combined into one swirling mess, so that Kain laughed out in the darkness at the irony that *he* was the one in the madhouse. He had tried to talk to them, but they had refused to listen. He had been their only chance at peace, and yet they had destroyed him—*crucified* him—hiding him away in this madhouse like a nightmare thought too terrifying to acknowledge…They presumed to contain him with locked doors and prison walls—the ridiculousness of it made him laugh out in the darkness. In fact, Kain had allowed them to capture him. He had stayed behind these walls not because he was imprisoned, but because he had been formulating his next move. Now, refreshed by his hatred of the world, he knew that his place was out there in the chaos, manipulating the ever-malleable souls of men; and having already resolved the means of his escape and seen the perfection of it, Kain laughed out again. In a short while, he was destined to step out before them, like a stern father; and when that time came, he would be the only one laughing, cheering them on as, step-in-step with the demands of his will, all his misbegotten children rose up to take their revenge.

* * *

ROLAND'S APPEARANCE ON THE morning show had been a grand success. He headed out of the studio, feeling good—until he remembered that it was time to see Rosencrantz….

When Roland got outside and hailed a cab, the world was not only getting hotter, but darker. The heat was like nothing he had ever felt before. And he was so tired of this yo-yoing—careening wildly from euphoria to horror…As soon as he was in the cab, headed towards the office, and *Rosencrantz*, he wrenched off his jacket and lay back in a daze. His shirt and undershirt were already soaked through with sweat. He glanced out at the world as it passed him by, wondering how much more he would have to take. The moment of reckoning was at hand, but exhausted by all that had passed, the only thing he could do was wait for whatever fate had in store. He was so very tired…This was the time to plan and pool his strength, but his mind was like an overworked beast of burden, unable to move—even under the whip of its master.

The dark, smoggy world beyond the cab seemed to be nothing but a projection of his soul. All the confusion and lethargy and violence and suffering he saw out on those streets, was simply an incarnation of himself and his dreams. And the thing that had just happened with Samantha…there was no sense to be made of it. In the wake of everything that had happened in the last 24 hours, his encounter with her both terrified him and left him in the same euphoric trance that had gripped him while he was in her presence. He had never done anything like that before: had never treated any woman the way he had treated Samantha. And yet, he had never enjoyed being with a woman as much. There was a reckless streak in him: the events of the last 24 hours attested to it. He was trapped in a minefield: common sense told him to be still; and yet, something was forcing him to walk. In fact, he was darting through that field at full speed. He was going be blown to bits eventually—and yet he couldn't stop himself! The danger was everywhere: in Samantha, in Rosencrantz, in Phelps, Kain, Candice…*all of them*! And yet he couldn't stop….

The cab came to a jarring halt; and looking out of the window in a daze, Roland realized that he had arrived. The world seemed even darker now. It was as though the poisons they had vented into the sky were coming back to them. Out on the sidewalk, the people moved like exhausted slaves being whipped by some invisible brute. Even the traffic was crawling along—as though the entire world were grinding to a halt. There was a hideous bronze modernistic statue of a man in front of the building; and as Roland watched it, he felt as though the statue were he. The man in the statue seemed deformed—or as if he were melting. His mouth was held open, like that of a man screaming in agony; his hands were clutching at the air, like those of a man beseeching his attacker for mercy. The man seemed like some casualty of war—an innocent bystander who had never gotten a chance to take a stand—and was immolated by his indecision….

* * *

IT WAS ABOUT 10 o'clock in New York City now; but the later it got, the more the strange dark clouds overhung the city; and the darker it got, the hotter it got. It was well over 37 degrees Celsius now.

Cars with steaming radiators stalled in the middle of the street, snarling traffic all over the city. The air, filthy with the exhaust from this stalled traffic, and the pollution and haze of the passing weeks, was barely breathable. One could *taste* the air—see it wafting by. People couldn't breathe; with the smog, they could barely see; and down the city streets, all the drivers of the stalled cars seemed to be honking their horns, cursing the incompetence and stupidity of the drivers in front of them—and the fools who were honking behind them.

It was in this context that the rally for the victims of the Brooklyn Massacre began. At least five thousand people were now in front of the hospital, conducting their death vigil. Botswana Glade had been stuck in traffic for an hour, cursing impatiently, along with everyone else, but that only meant that the people, whom had been chanting their slogans all along, were more riled up. As Botswana Glade neared the scene of what was going to be his triumph, a smile came to his face. Sitting in the back seat of Marenga's Benz, Botswana Glade felt a surge of energy that made him want to laugh out. He was ready for war! There was a thunderous sound raging in him, and even before he looked out of the window and saw all of those animated thousands, he knew that that thunder came from their souls. According to his logic, only by devolving into bestiality, could one rise with the angels; and as he looked out of his window at the enraged masses, he wanted not only to be the implement of their insurrection, but *resurrection*....

A dais had been set up on the front stairs of the hospital. When Botswana Glade alighted from the vehicle and began making his way through the crowd, the people let out a resounding cheer; and the man, pulled along by his bodyguards, put his head back and laughed.

* * *

UPON EXITING THE elevator, and entering the floor occupied by his firm, Roland stopped uneasily. The reception area was uncommonly still and dark. The old receptionist looked up at him slyly—he was certain of it! He nodded to the woman and walked on. His gait was unusually stiff and uncoordinated. His mind was blank when he entered the office area; but looking around confusedly, he saw that there was no one there! The dozens of cubicles of the associates were all empty; and the glass-enclosed rooms along the wall, where the partners had their offices, were empty as well! Even the lights were turned off!

"What the hell…!" Roland whispered. But then—

"*SURPRISE!*"

The lights suddenly came on; balloons fell from the ceiling; jaunty party music began playing; and from behind the cubicles immediately in front of Roland, about 50 people jumped out!

—While in Brooklyn, the forces of self-destruction cheered for Botswana Glade, Roland stood there gaping as the people rushed up to congratulate and hug him! Someone put a silly party hat on his head and he stood there like a simpleton, still trying to make sense of it all. He was looking around confusedly when Rosencrantz, a gaunt, totally bald, middle-aged white man with an impeccably groomed appearance, came up with a big smile on his face.

"Congratulations, Roland!" the man laughed. "You did us proud again!" He patted Roland on the shoulder then, and everyone applauded once more. Roland was still in shock; it was at least twenty seconds after they had burst from behind the cubicles that he realized what was going on around him. With the vestiges of a stupefied grin on his face, he realized that Rosencrantz's tone during the phone call had only been a ruse to get him to come to the office for this party. And if that was so, then he had nothing to worry about with Phelps! He laughed out then, overcome by relief. In fact, they were all laughing now, and that laughter rose up in the world, drowning out all else. He was soaring high! And at someone's urging, Roland began recounting his experiences—sans his encounter with Samantha Dearly—chuckling to himself as he saw their amazed faces. He was acutely aware of the power that he had. And it *was* power: the ability to hold and move people for no other reason than he was who he was. Roland forgot everything about moments of reckoning and yo-yoing chaotically between euphoria and horror. He was tired, and all he wanted to do was revel in the present: hold onto it like he had held Samantha….

Finally, Mr. Rosencrantz told him to come into his office. "Did Dallas tell you that the partnership is yours?"

"Yes," Roland said, slightly unnerved by the intrusion of the man's name.

"Dallas's was one of the loudest voices for you."

Phelps? Roland mused in disbelief; he wondered if that was some trick on the man's part, but no: it was obvious even to him that he had overestimated the man; and besides, he was just tired of it all.

Rosencrantz smiled coyly at him, then: "How do you feel about handling the Cranston case?" he said, scrutinizing Roland closely. The case, as Roland remembered it, involved a class action suit against a huge conglomerate called Cranston International, which was being sued because its baby food exceeded the allowable limit of pesticide residues—and because it used experimental, "unapproved" preservatives. Ten babies had supposedly died from severe reactions to these preservatives. It was an open and shut case, with a potential settlement in the hundreds of millions. (There was nothing like death to start the money rolling in.)

When Roland nodded his head, Rosencrantz smiled and shook Roland's hand.

They both laughed then, like two conspirators. Yes, Roland thought out of nowhere, he definitely wasn't that scared 13-year-old anymore! He was moving up in the world now: moving up faster than he had ever thought possible. For an instant, he was overcome by the feeling that nothing could possibly go wrong; but then, just as suddenly and overwhelmingly, came a feeling of panic at the thought that he was tempting fate; and at that moment, something exploded in the air. Both he and Rosencrantz recoiled violently, turning to the window.

* * *

NICOLI PETROVICH ANDROPOV WAS SLOW to emerge back into consciousness. For obvious reasons, he was confused as he looked around. He was like someone slowly emerging from a dream, trying to differentiate what was real from what wasn't. He tried to look around, but immediately became aware that he couldn't move. It was as though he were packed in lead. Making do, his eyes scanned the small, darkened room. The lights were turned off; and with the blinds drawn, it seemed like nighttime outside. Still, the illumination provided by the EKG monitor and other pieces of equipment, was enough—perhaps *more* than enough—for him to see. There were tubes and sensors everywhere. He tried to move his head, then immediately put the thought out of his mind as the sharp pain went down his spine. He winced, realizing, among other things, that there was a tube in his nose. And there were others in his arms, and wires of some kind connected to sensors on his chest. It seemed as though he were attached to some octopus...!

The budding realization of how he had come to be there—and of what he had done—was vague at first. Initially, there were only disconnected images and sounds: ghosts streaking across oblivion. But then, as he saw the mangled body of some kid, and the bullet-riddled bodies of others—and began to glean his own part in all of these horrific events—the realization of what he had done became like some blunt object, clubbing him in the head. He had *killed* people...He had leapt off a precipice, into some strange dimension devoid of conscience and meaning...and now, having been regurgitated, half-digested, back into the real world, there was a necessary disconnect between him and his actions. Here he was, lying lacerated and broken in the hospital, being patched up by the people who would in time come to deliver their justice onto him. Whatever place he had had in humanity was lost forever. He felt like some deformed creature—some repulsive troll—forced to inhabit the shadows.

Everything was still jumbled in his mind, but there was one certainty: he had to get out of there—flee before anyone came back and saw him. And with the realization of what he had done becoming clearer to him all the time, the thought of being *seen* brought with it its own horrors. He wasn't a man anymore—a human being. And he would never again be regarded as one. Anyone coming in contact with him would either run away in disgust or turn on him the way someone turned on a rat trying to enter the sanctity of his home. The thought of being patched up—of *living*, and having to account for those fleeting moments of madness and bestiality—left him quivering. It wasn't that he wanted to *escape*—he only wanted to escape their eyes. Death was inevitable: in fact, he craved it, the way a greedy man craved food and wealth.

Indeed, he had been dreaming of death for a long time now. He had dreamt of death as he pumped his penis into that whore and cruised down those Brooklyn streets. There had been death everywhere. His life, his dreams...everything had been circumscribed by death....And he had killed....What did those words even mean? People were dead now—because of him. They were dead as he was dead, or, at least, as he *would* be, when the authorities finally got their hands on him. He had taken some unfathomable step, and there was no going back. He couldn't even make his own life right, how could he possibly begin to rectify the damage irrevocably done to theirs. Death had brought him to this strange place, and the only option was to again turn to death: it was the great cycle, to which all things had to submit.

As thoughts of flight and death filled his mind, he tried to get up and realized, once again, the terrible extent of his injuries. He lay back down, panting and wincing from his efforts. A kind of claustrophobic terror gripped him. What if he *couldn't* move: was paralyzed, and forced to live out the rest of his life in some hospital bed/prison! The thought was worse than the throbbing pain coursing through his body. To be trapped here, unable to move—or to *flee*...his only hope was that he would never recover: that he would fall back into unconsciousness and never again look upon this sickening world. But damn it, as extensive as his injuries were, he was acutely aware of some demonic strength in him, keeping him conscious! He had to get out of there! He had to do *something*! He just couldn't lie there, waiting for the people whose laws and taboos he had broken, to come and deliver their justice onto him.

But *how* he would get away, and what he would do, were questions too theoretical in nature to guide him. He only knew that he had to move: first, he had to get out of this bed...he would think about the rest later. He steeled himself again. It seemed to take forever, taxing every iota of his strength and will, but groaning and grimacing, he managed to sit up. He was beyond pain. His broken ribs were like knives stabbing him; the pain down his spine was like nothing he had ever conceived! He could literally feel sutures in his abdomen bursting! He felt as though any second now, the final one would pop, and his guts would spill out. And now that he was sitting up, the tube in his nose—which he realized descended down his throat and into his stomach—made him suddenly want to retch...! And he had to rest again; like a climber ascending Mt. Everest, each step was an exhausting agony, requiring a period of recuperation before taking another step into oblivion....

It seemed to take forever before he managed to get his feet to the ground. One of his feet was in a cast; the knee on his other leg was swollen horribly, so that it could hardly bend. The thought that he would never be able to escape with such injuries, confronted him while he sat there, so that he pushed himself on purpose, as to not leave a free moment for thought. The ghosts were still hovering above his head; the mangled corpses of his dreams and aspirations were lying at his feet...He began to pull the tube from his nose. The sensation was...*sickening.* There was a cast on his right arm; his shoulders and back throbbed mercilessly...But he had to keep going; and in a way, the pain was guiding him, insulating him from thought and the world of men. He began pulling the intravenous tubes from of his arms....While he was disconnecting the sensors, the EKG went flat.

It was now or never: he had to get the hell out of there! His first attempt to stand up was futile: the pain was beyond conception! He had to suck in his breath sharply to keep from screaming—but even doing that was like having a bomb exploding in his chest. He was forced, by mere self-preservation, to sit down again. The thought of being trapped came again! And if the people came in and found him like this, they would tie him down, so that there would never be another chance! It was as this thought fired his will and gave him the energy to attempt to stand, that the door burst open and the emergency medical team—along with the officers posted outside—rushed into the room. The EKG, seeming to flat-line, had set off an alarm. The sight of them was horrible. They turned on the light, and the brilliance stunned him, making his head swoon. They were coming at him—yelling nonsense that he couldn't decipher at the moment. As weak as he was, he had to fight them off! Some old doctor, trying to push him back into bed, was yelling at a frail young nurse to administer a sedative. There were more arms on him now: how he was fighting them off was anyone's guess! It was probably that demonic power again. He kneed the doctor in the testicles, then somehow managed to hold off a cursing orderly. And all the while, he had his eye on the young nurse, who was fumbling with the syringe, trying to fill it with the sedative. It was then that that old thought hit him again: if he couldn't escape, then he had to find some way to end this quickly. In a millisecond, he grabbed the empty syringe from the nurse and pulled the plunger back, sucking it full of air. Then, in the same motion, he jabbed it into his neck, injecting the huge air bubble into himself. He gasped at the sensation—at the horrible pain that left him shuddering and frothing at the mouth—while the medical team looked on in stunned horror. He felt as if his insides were being pulled apart. And then...the pain in his chest, like a beast clawing at his heart...he couldn't scream anymore...he couldn't *move*. All that there was, was pain and then a mild sense of triumph as he watched their fading faces, knowing that the world—and their justice—was now beyond him—

It was while the horrified medical team was staring down at him, that something exploded in the air. At first, they all recoiled violently, but then someone went to the window and pulled up the Venetian blinds.

Andropov's window looked out on the front of the hospital, where Botswana Glade's dais had been set up. Botswana Glade had been making his way up to the dais when the noise resounded in the air. The very foundations of the city seemed to shake. Everyone looked around in horror; and just as the members of the emergency team looked out of the window at all those startled thousands, the invisible thing again exploded in the air. People began screaming that it was a bomb; Botswana Glade's bodyguards had knocked him to the ground and flung themselves on him. People were ready for the world to blow apart—for everything to come to a crashing end—but just then, the heavens opened up and the rain began to fall.

The first raindrops battered the windowpanes and the tops of people's heads like gunshots. Those who were inside, all rushed to their windows then, and looked out at the rain they had spent the last month hoping for. But for those who were outside—*even those at Botswana Glade's rally*—their first impulse was to run to safety. The raindrops were strangely heavy; in fact, it seemed more like hail than rain. It was only after the people found shelter that they joined those who were already inside and looked out on the world in amazement. The rain was coming down in sheets now—a kind of catharsis for all the madness, all the grief, all the filth...everything that had come with the sweltering heat. The world was purging itself; and for those wonderful moments, everyone was still and no one said a word.

Book Two

4.

The Fetish Spirits

Benjamin Thomas was going to be shot to death today, but such was life in the ghetto. It was autumn now (the end of October), but there was a physical autumn, which was a function of the earth's rotation around the sun, and there was a spiritual autumn, which was not so much a change in season, as a state of mind. Autumn was nature's way of dealing with extremes. It was constructive destruction—personified by the trees shedding their leaves and going into dormancy, in order to escape the harshness ahead. It was a time of contradictions, sandwiched between the hope and excitement of summer and the cold inevitability of winter.

But in the ghetto, autumn wasn't a passing season, but a way of life. An entire lifetime spent in a world were everyone was preparing for the worst—and desperate to get what he or she could, before it was too late...Why bother remembering what had passed, when it could all come crashing down at any moment? Why plan for things—why have hopes and dreams—when none of it was going to last?

Still, maybe, in this context, the forgetfulness of the ghetto was a survival instinct. The heat, and the Brooklyn Massacre, and all the things that had gripped them, were killing them slowly; and the only way to survive—and postpone the inevitable coming of winter—was to forget....

Benjamin Thomas smiled to himself and walked across the street. It was just after five o'clock in the afternoon, but the sun had already set. This was yet another change that had come with the season. Still, youth was beyond the changing of seasons; and as 16-

year-old Thomas walked confidently up the ghetto streets, he was insensitive to the cold wind and the creeping darkness. In fact, as he walked along, with the graceful, athletic stride that often made people stop and take notice, he was his own universe. He was still possessed by the callow belief that he could do anything and that nothing was beyond his purview. He was the kind of youth whom men wanted for their armies, and women wanted for their beds. That tall, athletic frame regularly motivated dozens of girls—who otherwise had no athletic interests—to come to all of his varsity basketball games. His movements seemed like controlled chaos, where the brutality held within might burst forth at any second; and as such, the generals and lovers both wanted to tame that brutality, and to channel it off into destruction and pleasure, respectively.

Just then, he spied two remarkable specimens of womanhood across the street. They were standing by a payphone, as though waiting for a call. When they happened to look his way, he waved to them: one waved back; the other, disapproving of such a straightforward show of interest, snatched her friend's hand down and scowled at her. What a joke it all was! he thought with a confident smile. But what else was there to think at 16 years old? To him, getting these young chicks was like pulling a con on a fool who seemed set on giving up her money; rather, the fool didn't just want to *give* it away, she wanted to be *cheated* out of it. They practically *wanted* to be lied to—to be *mystified*. They wanted to be told the most outrageous stories—"chatted up" until their heads were on the verge of bursting from the convoluted fantasy—as though the reward for such patent dishonesty was the clumsy, coquettish sex that the young women all seemed to have for barter. This strange mindset had confounded him for a while, but it was all part of the game now; and to him, life, in the final analysis, was just a game.

As Thomas saw it, everything was reducible to terms of sexual victory and defeat. He had seen it on public television nature shows, of all places. He had seen peacocks doing their mating struts, and bucks clashing heads and antlers to become the alpha male; and walruses—huge beasts—goring one another with their tusks for weeks on end, wasting away and left scarred and deformed, all in an insane drive for a few paltry seconds of sex. That titanic struggle, he had realized at an early age, was going on all about him. At first, as a seven-year-old, watching the show, *Nature*, on PBS, it had only mystified him—even *bewildered* him; but then, like all the beasts in the world, at the onset of puberty, with the hormones coursing through his veins, it had *excited* him. To him, the women lamenting that men were dogs, were only half-correct. The whole truth was not only that men *were* dogs, but that women were, similarly, bitches....Yes: he was crude and sexist, but he was unapologetically so, because even the most precursory glance at the world—and at what women, themselves, seemed to want—told him that there was nothing so *sexy*, as unabashed *sexism*. Women, for all their cries of wanting a sensitive, feminized man, dreamed of *him* when their eyes were closed. It was he who was on the cover of their romance novels: the ever-malleable lie of human sexuality.

Looking at the two women across the street again, he was like a peacock, flashing his plumage to the peahens, who feigned indifference while all the while taking stock of him. As he waved again, the *other* woman, who had before seemed so dubious about his charms, smiled back—to the outrage of her friend. While the two women argued, he laughed to himself, then continued up the block. Yes, it was all a joke after all....Later tonight, he had a "rendezvous" with a young woman from his social studies class. Her mother worked nights—just like his mother—and it would be so very easy...And then, tomorrow night, there was the Halloween party on 130th Street. He could hardly wait for that! Yes, it was all about the competition—the *game*—so the entire house of lies was still exciting. He was like a young lion, still practicing at hunting, not yet having to face the realities of the hunt—the life and death implications of survival....

When he reached his tenement, he jumped up onto the stoop and, like a playful antelope testing his muscles, bounded into the building. The graffiti-coated front door was off its hinges again...Entering the hallway, and beginning to ascend the steps, his expression suddenly soured. That old Dominican woman on the first floor was always cooking some pungent stew. Today, it smelled like dirty socks and garlic. He held his breath and hastened his steps, hoping to reach his fourth-story apartment before he lost consciousness. Between the second and third stories, the burning in his lungs became too much for him and he exhaled forcefully. He attempted to inhale, found that the stench was even more nauseating, and held his breath again. As such, he was a little dizzy when he reached the fourth story. He rushed to get his keys ready, so that he could dart inside the apartment and take his first untainted breath. However, when he turned to his door, he saw not only that the entrance was open, but that the door, itself, was lying on the floor. He froze, still standing there with his keys at the ready. Inside, it seemed as though a hurricane had been unleashed. The kitchen cupboards were all open, their contents spilt like animal entrails. The furniture was all either overturned or heaved into some unlikely position in the room. His mother, he realized after a few seconds of shock, was bent over, searching through the rubble. She stood up and stared at him numbly, dressed only in a housecoat. She was a short, plump woman of middle age, who had worked hard all her life had either been left wiser or beaten and morose by the entire struggle. Benjamin was her only child—and the only remnant she had of his father, who had been killed 16 _ years ago, in a financial transaction involving crack. As she stood up and stared at her son, she seemed as if she were ten years older—as though something so terrible had happened, that it had drained the life from her. Thomas unconsciously flinched at the sight of her. She seemed suddenly haggard, *decrepit*. He rushed over to her, clasping her by the shoulders:

"Mama!"—he looked around with wide, unbelieving eyes—"We get robbed?" His darting eyes eventually came back to her. "You all right?"

But she shook her head, as though still in shock. "The police," she managed to say.

"*Police*!" The word made a wave of anxiety surge over him.

"They were here..."—she looked up at him ominously—"looking for you."

"For *me*!" he said with a nervous laugh.

But his mother's face was still grave. "Some special drug unit...said somebody called Benjamin Thomas was some kind of drug lord—you're wanted for 12 counts of murder."

"*Me*!" More hysterical laughter escaped from him.

"Of course it *ain't* you!" she shouted in annoyance, life finally seeming to creep back into her. "I told them that!" she said angrily. "It's an obvious mix-up. They said you were 5'8" and 280 pounds, with a bushy beard and a scar on your forehead! You have to go down to the police station and clear this up."

"*Now?*" he whined, "I was gonna go out—"

"*Fool*!" his mother cursed him, gripping him by the lapel of his jacket with one hand, while waving the other threateningly. "Didn't you just hear what I said to you? Don't you see that broken down door lying there? That's because the police threw it there when they came rushing in with their SWAT team! You see all this shit on the floor! That's there because they emptied out all the draws, cupboards and closets, looking for your drug stash! You see these goddamn welts on my wrist!"—and she shoved them in his face—"That's from wearing handcuffs for three hours while they asked me where the drugs and money were! This is *serious*, and you worried about getting some goddamn pussy!"

"—I'll go, mama," he said quickly, suddenly ashamed.

"*Damn* right you'll go!" she cursed him again. "All you young fools," she started in disgust, "...as soon as you grow two hairs on your balls, you loose all your goddamn sense!" She looked up at him with a snarled lip then, going on, "I'm going to tell you *one* thing son, and I hope it serves you the rest of your days." She paused then, staring ominously into his quailing eyes before declaring: "Pussy ain't *shit* to get!"

* * *

CHARLES MARENGA WAS DYING, and he knew it. He was a middle-aged man who couldn't walk up a flight of stairs without becoming dizzy. He had a paunch and plump, stubby limbs; and he was dying, as he knew that they were all dying. The feeling was vague yet unrelenting as he emerged from sleep and looked out of the plane's window, seeing the glittering spectacle of New York City's nighttime skyline below him. His ears were still stuffed up from the air pressure, and his body was cramped from the irregular position in which he had fallen asleep; and these things, combined with the drowsiness of his mind, left him wondering if he was still dreaming: still locked away in some fantasy world. He stared out of the window for perhaps a good two minutes before he realized what it was that he was seeing. Below him, the intricate network of streetlights, the head and taillights from the ceaseless flow of rush hour traffic, as well as the glittering illumination from buildings, seemed to make up remarkably vivid constellations. It was like an inconceivably huge Christmas decoration, at once gaudy and peacefully mesmerizing. He felt suddenly small—or maybe it was only the realization of New York City's size and power and restlessness. The scope of possibility within that place seemed as limitless as the number of stars in the sky; and for a moment, as he stared dreamily out of the window, it reminded him of the sky of African nights, in which the stars had stood out with a magical boldness and clarity that made them seem like jewels hanging from the sky. His mind went back to the tent in the middle of the Sahara, where, for the first time in a long while, he had had solitude. Besides his guides, there had been no other humans around for 200 kilometers: no noisy cities, no traffic-clogged streets...and for a little while, there had been an extraordinary feeling of peace within him as he looked around the landscape and managed to convince himself that this was all that there was of the world—and all that he would ever have to be concerned with.

But he was back in New York City again, and there was an energy here—a *power*—that was daunting. Entire countries could be lighted for *months* on the power that New York used in one night. That place below him literally glowed in the night; and as he watched the spectacular show of lights, he grew wary at the thought that that boundless energy was being drained from the people, themselves—from their *souls*. It was as if the place below him were not merely a city, but some huge spiritual siphon; and that having died—having been annihilated by the realities of Africa—he was making his final descent into hell....

Yes, his five-month exploration of what he and his constituents had idealistically referred to as "The Motherland," was over. He had been like a pilgrim, hoping to renew his faith in a place that had been writ large in his imagination as holy. But Africa, in the end, had been a farce—just as he and everything he had ever believed in, was a farce. Towards the end, the Africans, discovering that "The Great Charles Marenga" was touring their countries, had rushed to meet the man that had once marched with Martin Luther King. But that man had been destroyed a long time ago, just as Martin Luther King had been destroyed.

Still, in the beginning, it had been wondrous. In Tanzania and Zimbabwe, he had addressed the Parliaments and cheering crowds of *thousands*. In South Africa, government officials had met him at the border and driven him to meet Nelson Mandela. That euphoric greeting had been even more overpowering and intoxicating, when contrasted with the reality in his own country, where the city's black Mayor refused to even use his name in public....But over the passing months, Africa became like a cloying whore who, through her ministrations, had once carried out the task of propping up his ego; but who, in her insistence at staying by his side, was now only a reminder of his debasement. After 30 years of telling the wretched inhabitants of backwater southern towns and urban ghettoes that they had descended from kings, and that Africa had been the cradle of civilization and humanity, itself, he had awoken one morning, shivering in some makeshift hut in the middle of the Kalahari Desert, acutely aware that he had no home, no past...no foundations at all, save for the insecurities he had brought from America.

He had gone to Africa in search of life, but Africa had destroyed him—just as it had destroyed generations of would-be adventurers and missionaries. In a sense, his five-month tour of Africa had been nothing but an impromptu study in world philosophy, where the wreckage of Capitalism and Socialism, of Colonialism and Revolution, of Dictatorship and Democracy...*of every hackneyed idea and dichotomy that the world had ever conceived*, was lying half-buried and rusting in a huge garbage heap. He had driven across Africa, seeing the beautiful mixed with the ugly; the strong with the weak; the old and traditional, sprinkled haphazardly with that which professed to be new and modern. He had seen things that he had never even conceptualized before, along with scenes that he could have seen from his stoop in Brooklyn. He had seen *everything* in Africa, because this, as everyone was saying nowadays, was a *global* world: a world where a blip on the Malaysian stock market had last week caused the New York Stock Exchange to drop 150 points. There was an interconnectedness about everything that was unfathomable—and yet more real and telling than all of their whiny movements and philosophies combined. A disastrous devaluation of the Philippine Peso meant that a factory in Portland, Oregon was going to be moved to Mexico: it didn't make sense, but it was going on all around them. In a second-rate hotel in Brazzaville, he had not only been able to view that story on CNN, but the latest details of the sex scandal involving Mayor Randolph. In the face of all of these new realities, and hundreds more that he couldn't even conceptualize as yet, the foundation of everything he had ever believed in, was being eroded away. While lives and lifestyles were constantly being destroyed by the startling interconnectedness of the world, he and his constituents, like women's groups and every other group which professed to be oppressed, had spent their time romanticizing the power and selfishness of some universal cult of evil (white) men. But that startling interconnectedness had no face—no soul, no *motives*. It was incapable of caring if its victims were black, if they were women, if they were Jews, or homosexuals, or *whatever*. Job seekers were moving from state to state on the whims of investors in foreign lands, who decided to consolidate factory production in China. These realities were beyond race, beyond gender, beyond culture—*beyond even class*! It was beyond the whiny, bourgeois pettiness of *all* of their movements; and knowing this, the realization that it was meaningless to think of that immolating interconnectedness as either good or evil, left him nonplused. For the first time, he, who had always prided himself on being an activist, looked around and felt that it was meaningless to fight. He was acutely aware that he was old: that he had lost the youthful single-mindedness and enthusiasm that had once made him think he could fight against 400 years of American racism—

And he was afraid—not only of the world, but *himself*. He felt suddenly soul-less: not simply that his soul had been drained, but that there was something evil within him; and while he had gone to Africa in search of hope and renewal, as he looked out of the window, he couldn't help thinking that he was bringing this newfound evil with him. He didn't feel like a man anymore. He wasn't merely an exhausted traveler: he was an instrument of evil, shaped either by the will of some devil or the presumptuousness of men—which was just as destructive. And all the people in the city below him, who didn't have the spiritual antibodies necessary to resist his evil, would be like lambs to the slaughter....

Shaking his head, Marenga chanced to look towards the floor, where he saw something that resembled a ball sticking out of his carry-on bag. Distracted, he bent down and pulled on it, so that the rest of it emerged. It was a hideous, snarling fetish doll that some official in Namibia—or was it Swaziland—had given him. It was only about 20 centimeters long, but its head was two-thirds of its body. He frowned at the hideous, snarling face, his mind blank; but in time, he was amazed to find himself relaxing. As contradictory as the notion seemed, the fetish was somehow a testament to the end of superstition. It was now a kind of tourist souvenir, making fun of the beliefs that still held millions. The official that handed it to him had worn an Armani suit and driven a Mercedes Benz. Maybe one day, thought Marenga, their society would hold up the items associated with Western beliefs in a similar manner, with a good-natured wink at that which had once been set in stone, but which was now rightly seen as so much drivel.

* * *

THOMAS WALKED BROODINGLY OUTSIDE, still somewhat numb, but left with an acute awareness that his pride—or whatever passed for his manhood—had been seriously breached. Then, as his mind cleared, the idea of the police—images of them breaking the door down and storming into his home, handcuffing his mother and screaming threats and demands at the half-dressed woman—tore at something more vital in him. What good was manhood when such things could happen? He felt suddenly bereft—*demolished.* His usual confidence was gone, replaced by a feeling of vulnerability and helplessness that almost made him want to cry.

He *hated* the police! They had frisked him a couple of times, jumping out of their cruisers and ambushing him, claiming, when they found nothing incriminating on him, that he had "fit the description" of some miscreant in the neighborhood: some villain that they, as forces of justice, were in the act of apprehending....Nothing brought on hatred like a feeling of helplessness: the knowledge that you had been wronged, and that there was nothing that you could do to rectify it....

He walked down Malcolm X Boulevard with these thoughts and uncertainties fluttering in his mind. Or maybe it was only a presentiment that his life was about to end....It was about half past six now, but it seemed like the darkest night. The wind seemed suddenly biting, as though winter had come and entrenched itself while he wasn't paying attention. He zipped up his Knicks jacket and walked on, a little hunched over against the wind. On the corner of

125th Street, a crowd had gathered. He was so preoccupied that he would have passed them and gone on his way, except for the fact that the crowd was so big that he couldn't pass without going into the street. For some reason, the people were laughing hysterically; and it was as this laughter pierced the air that he looked up and saw a bum with a shaggy beard standing on a crate—the proverbial soapbox—seeming to preach to the people.

"...We got churches out here saying that if we do wrong we'll go to hell," the shabbily dressed man said in a preacher's intonation. "*Fools*," he went on, "where the fuck they think we are now! [The crowd, composed mostly of young black men, howled appreciatively.] They say if we endure this hell without causing a fuss we'll go to heaven. *Crazy*!" the man screamed, waving his hands violently. "There ain't no way out of here! And no matter how much you bend over for the Devil, all you'll get in return is a worn out asshole!" Even Thomas snickered at that one. He stepped in closer, suddenly forgetting about his errand. The man on the crate was scrawny and disheveled, but there was just something hysterical in his eyes and his intonation. No one would have guessed it, but behind that bushy beard, was Jasper Kain! Without his huge, ridiculous Afro, which he had shaved entirely off, he looked altogether different; and after the media frenzy, everyone had forgotten about him. Even his escape had received only minor attention (probably because the media had been obsessed with Randolph's sex scandal).

Whatever the case, while the homily continued, Thomas realized that the man seemed to have helpers: two other black, middle-aged bums, and a white kid of college age, were handing out pamphlets. When the white kid came around, Thomas took a pamphlet. It read: Manifesto of the Sons of Kain. Thomas chuckled to himself and put the pamphlet in his pocket for later amusement—

"What the hell do you want peace for!" the man boomed. "This is no time to be pacified! This is *hell* that we're in, so burn, baby, burn! Feel that hot brimstone on your flesh, and know that you're in the presence of the last true nigger! [The people again howled approvingly.] I'm not here to put you at ease, to enlighten you, to show you the way to peace and understanding!"

"—Tell them brother!" screamed one of the toothless bums, to everyone's delight.

"No, I'm here to fuck your head up!" the man screamed, to more gales of laughter. "If you're at ease, I want to scare the *shit* out of you!"—Some people were laughing so hard that they were crying—"I don't got the spirit of *God* coursing through my veins, I got pure evil in me. I'm not here asking for donations…to get you to repent your sins…*none* of that shit! I'm here to scream in your goddamn ears till your eardrums burst! I ain't looking for converts; I'm here so that you'll walk away saying: 'Fuck you, nigger!' Yea, yea…!" he said, while half the crowd doubled over with delight. "I want to infect whatever goodness you have left: to put you on that cosmic plane of pure evil. I ain't one of those preachers you see on TV every Sunday morning, got God on their tongue, but the Devil in their soul. I'm *pure* evil! Yes, brothers and sisters, evil is the last pure thing left on this earth! Evil is the last thing that God has deigned to let our corrupted minds understand. Ha, hey!" he laughed, an insane gleam in his eyes. "This ain't the Church of the Immaculate Conception; I ain't one of those Gherri-Curl-wearing, Cadillac-driving, store-front preachers who tells you to give up your cash. This is the Church of Shit and Stale Piss, and I'm here to burn in you like a bad case of gonorrhea—"

But at those words, the annoying boop-boop of New York City police sirens sounded at the curb. Everyone turned to see two white officers step out of a police cruiser. For some reason, Benjamin Thomas froze; but everyone else was soon laughing as the strange preacher and his disciples darted down the street, laughing insanely.

"All right, break it up!" The policemen were yelling now. The crowd of young black men looked at them sullenly—with *hatred* even. Grumbling, they went on their way, as the two policemen stood before them like overseers. Remembering his errand, Thomas thought about going up to the two officers and telling them what had happened, but that would have required too much personal interaction.

Sighing, Thomas set off for the police station with a wary step. He just wanted it all to be over, so that he could go about his life—the great game—and find solace in its simplistic rules. He smiled wistfully as he walked, thinking that after he was through setting the police straight, he would stop by that young chick's house and, to use the jargon, "hit the skins."

* * *

THE THEME MUSIC FOR Maria Santos's new network show was being played; the director was counting down from five to one, as Santos stood on the set triumphantly. When the theme music ended and she was given her cue, she smiled cordially and began:

"Welcome, America. It is through your will that we have been granted this vehicle to bring the stories of America to you, *the people*. You are the soil from which we draw nutrients, and in which we are anchored. In other words, America, this is your show. This is the vessel of your thoughts and hopes and ambitions. We are here to get back to that old adage which made America what it is today: The customer is always right. We are your servants, more susceptible to your will than your congressman, your mayor, the *president*, even! You have to wait years to cast your vote and show them how you feel; but you only have to wait milliseconds to show us your will, by simply changing the channel. We are your means of empowerment. We are your voice! As such, we don't think ourselves presumptuous in calling this show, simply, *America*. It is about all that makes us great, and all that keeps us from greatness.

"This being so, who better to have on the inaugural show, than one of America's suddenly rising lights: Ms Charlotte McPrice. Through her famous line, 'We're Americans, damn it!' we have all been reminded of our place in the world. Suddenly, people are putting those words on bumper stickers; those words now regularly appear in television shows and movies. People all over this country are using those words in their daily conversations! In those few simple words, she has tapped the vital courage that is America, and we are all grateful.

"Let us not waste any more time," Santos went on, beginning to walk over to the couches on the set. "Here she is, America: Ms Charlotte McPrice!"

The theme music began again. There wasn't a studio audience; nevertheless, there was suddenly the sound of applause. McPrice walked out in a red business suit with her usual statuesque self-possession. She was made for television: made for *America*. She and Santos laughed and hugged one another as the piped-in applause waxed in the air.

* * *

THE POLICE PRECINCT was a grim place, which looked dirty and dilapidated from the outside, and even more so from within. It looked like one of those asbestos-polluted old places, with crumbling walls that forever looked as though they needed to be painted. The special drug task force, one of Mayor Randolph's new programs to "get tough on crime," had its office in the basement. The place, to put it succinctly, seemed like a rat hole. It was dimly lit, and the furniture was old and rickety—actually discarded relics that had been stored down there when the officers upstairs got new things. The rat hole had been busy an hour before, when the unit returned from an unsuccessful bust. The SWAT team and forensic specialists, whom they had dragged along, had shouted recriminations against the members of the unit, saying how they had wasted their time just to frisk an old woman. Only the three members of the unit were left now—mostly to finish the paperwork. Detectives Holtzman and Leonard sat morosely at their desks. Colina stood in the corner of the basement, by the small window near the ceiling, looking up at the dark world. All three cops were silent until Holtzman looked across at Leonard and said:

"Hey, Louie, you think Randolph really fucked that stripper chick?"

The bone-thin Leonard looked up from his paperwork with pursed lips, apparently giving it thought. "Of course," he said with a grin, "wouldn't you? Why else would he refuse to deny it?"

"I don't know: she seems like a gold digger to me. Notice how she ain't go to the police yet? She just keeps appearing on the air, crying on cue, talking about how innocent she was."

Louie thought about it for a while, then shrugged his shoulders. "Hey, Colina," he called across the room, "what you think?"

But the man only stood there with his back turned.

"You still got your panties in a bunch about that bust?" Holtzman laughed uneasily.

"I'm telling you," Colina started, turning around threateningly, "that was the place! That cunt mother of his was hiding him—saying all that bullshit about how he didn't come home from school yet!"

"You *sure* that was the place?" Leonard put in.

"Of course I'm sure!" Colina shouted at them. "Didn't you see it in that bitch's eyes. I don't trust *none* of those fuckers. The police force was meant to keep order among people who want it—not *these* people…Stab you in the back the first chance they get…Fuckin' rats, all of 'em—"

"What the hell is eating you?" Holtzman laughed, even while there was a note of alarm in his voice; he looked nervously at Leonard, seeing the same bewildered expression.

"What's with *me*?" Colina went on. "We just gonna turn our backs and try to forget that a murderer's out there?"

"Calm the fuck down, Colina," Holtzman laughed nervously again.

"Don't tell me to calm down! I ain't some goddamn rookie!" he raged, his face turning deep red. "I've seen too much on these streets to not know what's going on!"

"All right, damn," Holtzman said with even more forced laughter. "You seriously need to get laid, pal," he said, shaking his head.

"Fuck you!"

"Well, I never said I was offering!" he joked, at which Leonard—who usually tried to stay out of these arguments—laughed as well.

While the two men laughed, and Colina glared at them, the phone on Colina's desk rang. Scowling at the other two, he walked over and picked it up. "Colina!" he belted into the phone. But then his eyes grew wide as he listened. A moment later, he banged down the phone and ran towards the stairs. The other two stared expectantly at him—

"It's Thomas!" Colina said, rushing past them, "—he's waiting upstairs!" The other two first looked at one another in disbelief, then leaped up and rushed after him. What could it mean? They were all running up the stairs now, as though Thomas might escape their clutches again.

"Where is he?" Colina yelled to the desk sergeant when he reached the waiting room. He had a look of madness in his eyes, exacerbated by the fact that he was panting and flustered from his run. The sergeant looked at Colina warily before gesturing towards the kid in the corner of the empty waiting room, who was reading a magazine. Colina rushed over to the kid, just as the other two cops arrived. As Colina approached, Thomas stood up.

"Look, I didn't do nothing," Thomas barely managed to say, before he was shoved back into the seat.

"Shut the fuck up!" Colina belted, towering over him. "Where'd you hide it?"

"Hide *what*?" For some reason, he laughed—

Colina hauled him up by the lapels then heaved him against the wall, putting his forearm to Thomas's chest. "You son of a bitch," he cursed the kid, "stop fucking with me!"

"Colina!" the desk sergeant screamed, while Holtzman and Leonard looked on in shock.

"Look, man…!" Thomas started, but Colina punched him in the ribs then, so that he fell to the ground, wincing in pain.

"He don't even match the description, Colina!" Holtzman yelled from where he stood.

"*Fuck* the description!" Colina cursed. "This is him!"

"Yo," Thomas started, finally getting his wind back, "I didn't do *shit*, man!"

"Shut up!" Colina barked; and at that, he kicked him—

"I *knew* it!" a woman suddenly screamed. They all turned to see a plump black woman come in dressed in an all-white nursing aide uniform.

"Mama…" Thomas moaned from the ground.

"Something told me you bastards would do this!" she screamed at Colina. She ran up to them then, and pushed Colina aside, so that she could get to her son; but Colina, incensed, and in no mood, slapped her in the face, so that she fell heavily to the ground—

And then, as though some animal instinct had been unleashed in him, Thomas leaped up and punched Colina squarely in the jaw. As Colina crumbled to the ground, Thomas jumped on him, raining wild blows on the man. But Colina, remembering his old marine days, grabbed Thomas's arm; and, twisting it, he flung the kid to the side. Colina leapt to his feet a millisecond before the enraged Thomas. Thomas, like a bull, went to charge; but all of a sudden, something exploded in the air. At least, it seemed like an explosion in the closed quarters of the waiting room. But then, just as suddenly and inexplicably, Thomas fell to the ground with a loud thud. Only Thomas's mother seemed to have understood what happened, because she screamed out. Leaping up, she, too, charged the gun-toting Colina with all the hatred and madness of her son. But after another explosion, her unmoving body fell on top of her son's. In the horrible silence, they all started down at the bodies; but it was obvious, from the way that those sightless eyes stared off into the distance, that they were dead. Colina stood triumphantly then, the wild look of battle still in his eyes as he replaced the gun in his holster. The others stared on in disbelief—in *horror*, in fact. Colina looked over at them nonchalantly; then, suddenly annoyed by their expressions, he screamed:

"Well, you saw them! They came at me like *animals*! I *had* to shoot them: it was self-defense!"

* * *

FINALLY ON THE GROUND, Marenga and the hundreds of other passengers hurried down the passageway that led to Immigration. The process went smoothly enough: the middle-aged white man behind the desk looked at Marenga's passport, peered at his face with dawning recognition, then stamped his passport. At that, the man grunted equivocally and waved Marenga on.

—While in Harlem, the Thomases lay lifeless in their own blood, and the seeds of hatred and madness began to sprout from that blood, Marenga followed another passageway, which led to the Customs Department. Just before Customs, there was the moving belt that brought out their luggage. He waited for his baggage with a mind that was still numb from his trip and the scope of the conclusions that he had reached at its end. He moved listlessly towards the Customs Officer after he had grabbed his bags, hardly even bothering to look up. The officer was a tall black man in his late twenties. There was a military precision about the man as he simultaneously searched through Marenga's bags and interrogated him.

"How long were you out of the country?" the man demanded.

"Five months," Marenga answered distractedly.

The man glanced at Marenga's passport, double-checked the name and picture, then went on: "Visiting Africa, Mr. Marenga?"

"Yes, sir," Marenga answered, suddenly annoyed with the entire process.

The man grunted and went back to unloading Marenga's clothes. As the man stacked Marenga's folded underwear on the metal table, Marenga grimaced—not in shame, but in further annoyance.

"Anything to declare?" the man inquired.

"No, sir."

Just then, the man took out the fetish and shook it, hearing something rattling within. "What is this?" he demanded.

"It's a fetish," he said curtly, in a tone that suggested that only a fool wouldn't know what it was. For some reason, a scowl came over the officer's face as he watched it; and unaccountably, that expression pleased Marenga.

"What's in here?" asked the Customs Officer, shaking it again.

"I don't know," he said, testily.

"I have to open it."

"There's no way to open it," Marenga said, his annoyance growing. "It's glued on."

"I'll have to break it, then."

"You *can't* break it!" Marenga said, outraged. "A dignitary gave it to me in Namibia"—or was it Swaziland, he thought.

But the Customs Officer only chuckled, a wry smile coming over his face. "I *can't* open it?" he laughed. And then: "Maybe you should step this way, sir."

"*What*!" Marenga exploded.

"Gather your things and step this way."

"What the hell is this about?"

"You have given me sufficient cause to suspect that you're smuggling something—"

"Don't be ridiculous! I'm—"

"I don't care who or *what* you are! Here, *I* give the orders. Get your things and follow me, or we can do it the hard way." Having said that, he nodded to two armed officers.

Marenga groaned in frustration, then grunted for the man to get it over with. The man loaded Marenga's things onto a cart, then wheeled them down an adjacent corridor, while Marenga followed testily behind. He was taken to a moderately sized room with a huge metal table in the middle of it. Besides that, there was nothing else in the room, save for one of those huge mirrors that no doubt had an observation room on the other side of it. Two young white officers came in; Marenga stepped to the side. One of the officers started unloading Marenga's bags, while the other officer busied himself trying to crack the fetish open.

The original black officer stepped up to Marenga and said: "Take off your clothes, sir."

"*What*!"

"Take off your clothes!"

Marenga was in a dream—a *nightmare*, in fact. He disrobed in a daze, mesmerized as he watched the two other officers ravaging his things. Marenga, now shirtless, was loosening his belt now. He looked up at the black officer as he unzipped his pants: *You worthless young nigger*! he thought to himself. The man stood above him with the same military precision. He noticed the hatred in Marenga's eyes, but that recognition only produced a grunt of pleasure from him.

Marenga looked on as the last of his things were thrown in a heap on the steel table. He was standing there in his underwear and socks now; the black officer stared at him, his face like stone. With a gesture, the man told Marenga to remove his underpants. Marenga stared back at the man with the same harsh intensity. He pulled down his shorts: *Is this what you wanted to see, faggot*! he thought. The man's gaze hadn't moved from Marenga's eyes. They stared at one another, the hatred exchanged between them. The officer smiled, then said, in a voice that only he and Marenga could hear: "It's niggers like you who make things hard for all of us."

Marenga couldn't move! The extent of his rage made his breath get caught in his throat. He felt suddenly weak, grimacing at the arrhythmic thumping in his chest. All of a sudden, it was as if an icy finger were clawing at him; he gasped at the first touch, then bit his lower lip to keep from screaming, as the ice turned to fire. *You piece of shit*! he went to curse the smug officer, but he had to suck in his breath when the pain in his chest gripped him like nothing he had ever felt before. The sensation was twofold: first, there was the sensation of an explosion within himself, then there was the even more debilitating feeling that the world was being sucked into him. All its pain and sorrow and violence and destruction, was being sucked into him, so that he almost collapsed from the weight of it. He wasn't merely having a heart attack—he was the conduit for a world on the verge of blowing itself apart. He felt it all within him at that moment: the Thomases, Kain's madness, the self-destructive anger of *millions*...it went on and on, filling him up until he felt that he was going to burst. He panicked then, but not at the thought of death, itself, but at the thought of dying like *this*, before this grinning fool—

With a final blow of his baton, one of the white officers broke the fetish in two and the contents within were allowed to fall onto the table. All three officers gathered around the object and its contents as Marenga stood to the side, with his drawers around his ankles, willing himself to live. The officers stared at the sandy substance on the table for a while; the black officer bent over and put his finger to it. First he sniffed it, then he dabbed it on the tip of his tongue. His face soured. Another officer repeated the procedure, a frown coming to his face:

"It's sand," he said.

The black officer looked back at Marenga, still smug. "Well, I guess everything's fine here, sir," he said, unapologetically. "You may leave now," he went on, but there was biting condescension in his phrasing. The two white officers left; the black officer stood by the door, watching Marenga. The old man looked around at all that had been undone, and then finally at his flabby body in the reflective glass. He felt so...*unreal*. He stood there naked, wounded, *raped*, able to think of nothing but vengeance. He looked over at the black face of the officer at that moment, hating not only it, but the entire country and ethic that had spawned it. It seemed as though his entire life had come down to this moment. It was no longer even a matter of him having wasted his life, but of life, as he had known it, having wasted *him*.

—While in Harlem, the stunned police officers gathered around Colina and his victims, asking what was to be done, Marenga was enveloped by a kind of boundless, rampaging hatred. He looked at his bloated, sagging, middle-aged body, again feeling something new and horrible growing within him. The sensation was almost orgasmic in its intensity, leaving him shuddering and light-headed. Africa had been a five-month orgy; his life before that had been foreplay; and now, at last, with this final spasmodic thrust, he had reached the fulfillment of his lust: hatred—pure, maddening, *insatiable* hatred. The cry for vengeance was unrelenting...But he wasn't strong enough yet. Within him, was the will to rip all of their heads off—to perform inconceivably brutal acts of violence—but he had to bide his time. First things first, some palliating demon kept whispering in his ears. Yes, they would all come to feel the hell he was carrying around in his soul, but he had to get out of here first—escape to fight and kill another day. He took a deep breath to steady himself, then he began to put on his clothes.

The black officer still stood at the door, watching his every movement with a look of amusement. Marenga took his time, fighting not to betray the depths of his weakness....At last, he gathered up his things, saving the fetish for last. Very meticulously, he scooped up the grains of sand, pouring them back into the crack in the skull, as if the sand were blood. It was then that he turned around to look at the officer. The man stared back at him indifferently; then, as he saw that Marenga was ready to leave, he exited the room and went about his business.

Alone, Marenga put his bags back on the cart, holding the broken fetish tenderly, as though it were a baby. Then he pushed the cart outside, and past the black officer. The horrible new feeling was still growing within Marenga as he walked through the terminal tentatively. In his arms, the hideous face of the broken fetish seemed even more grotesque, now that it was cracked in two. But all of a sudden, that very repulsiveness was his only hope. He had once thought of the fetish as a testament to the end of superstition; but as he walked through the bustling terminal, and towards the exit, he was suddenly desperate to believe in all the magic that it had once professed to embody. He gripped it, willing whatever heathen spirits it had once channeled to return and serve him. It was as he stepped out into the chilly New York night air, and saw one of his young aides waiting with his car, that Marenga knew, with a horrible certainty that brought a quivering grin to his lips, that justice would be delivered onto this place, and that they would all pay for what they had done to him.

* * *

LITTLE DID Roland Micheaux know that the seeds of his destruction were being sown in the events currently taking place in the city. But the life cycle of seeds can be anywhere from a few minutes, to decades—even centuries....

Roland now stood ascendant in the grand ballroom of the New York Hilton. He was waving to the hundreds of people that had come to the press conference. Dozens of flashbulbs exploded in front of him as he stood on the podium. At his back, were Rosencrantz and some of the petitioners of the class action suit. Roland, as the head of the legal team that had gotten Cranston International to quickly settle out of court for a landmark eight-figure sum, was at the center of the excitement.

"We have achieved a great victory for America today!" Roland declared. "It is a long-overdue victory for the consumer; and in this case, it is the most innocent and susceptible of consumers: the baby!"

—While in Harlem, other officers came running to investigate the gunshots, only to see Colina standing proudly before the corpses of the Thomases (like a game hunter), the applause for Roland was resounding. Roland's boss patted him on the back then, and unconsciously licked his lips at the $50 million fee that was coming to the firm. Roland was unquestionably a star now—there was no denying it! When the question and answer period began, even the reporters—as jaded as they were—looked up at him with sudden awe. And then, after the press conference, scores of people came up, wanting to shake his hand and ask him further questions; but finally finding a use for the rest of the legal team, Roland deflected those questions onto them. Rosencrantz, seeing him sneaking away, smiled and laughed:

"Where you off to again!"

"Another appointment, sir," he laughed, cheekily.

"Who is this mystery woman you're always running off to?"

"Mystery is the spice of life!" Roland laughed obliquely, bowing to them all and taking his leave.

* * *

—WHILE IN HARLEM, the fidgety policemen decided that the first thing they had to do was take Colina into custody, and Colina took out his gun and told them all to back away, Kain and his men—who were actually only a few blocks away from the police precinct—trudged down the dark side streets of the ghetto, towards their hideout. Kain had met these men—with the exception of Maury Feingold, the Jewish kid who fancied himself an anarchist—at a homeless shelter. There had been hundreds of them, languishing either in chaotic madness or the debilitating kind of freedom that came with having nothing. Hordes of scatterbrained imbeciles, all denied psychiatric care and housing because of state cutbacks: Kain could have built an army, if he had been so inclined. As for himself, as insane as he obviously was—or "mentally ill" to use the modern, politically correct phraseology—the idiocy of state psychiatric bureaucracy, not to mention severe cutbacks in funding, had made his escape a breeze. Perhaps, also, the extent of his madness had given him the strength to appear sane. Some voice had constantly been in the back of his mind, telling him when to smile and what to say and how to allow himself to be treated by the condescending psychiatrists and attendants—who had been easily manipulated, because their ultimate fantasy was that they had the ability to cure madness. A few teary, heartrending episodes by Kain, in which he regurgitated his doctor's theory about his mother not loving him and asked the doctors if they thought that the society would ever forgive him, had been more than enough to get himself transferred to the minimum security wing of the facility. There had been three group sessions a day, in which several other blubbering idiots spouted drivel about their lives. Kain had invented similar stories, sometimes barely able to keep from laughing at the convoluted nonsense that came out of his mouth. All the while, the philosophy of blessed self-destruction had been working itself out in his mind. After a week of these teary sessions, Kain had made his escape by posing as an orderly.

—While back at police headquarters, Colina cursed them all, accusing them of having surrendered the streets to scum, Kain and his men continued their trek down the cold, dark, tenement-lined streets. Just then, one of the old black men, known as Crazy Eddie, exulted: "The people like us!" flashing one of his infamous toothless grins.

But as Kain, who was in the lead, turned into an alley, he casually declared, "*Fuck* the people."

"Yea," Feingold added, "fuck 'em all…!" He had been a freshman philosophy student only two weeks before, doing a report on homelessness. But he had interviewed Kain and had never been quite right since. Of course, he had left school and turned his back on his parents' comfortable home in the suburbs of Connecticut, in order to overthrow the world and bourgeois society.

Whatever the case, it was about a second or so after turning into the alley that they saw a heavyset white man in a trench coat. The man's smile was smug, especially seeing the momentary shock on the faces of the men before him. Kain and his men instinctively leaped back, but the white man before them only smiled and shook his head.

"Maury," sighed the sleazy-looking private investigator that Feingold's parents had sent to bring him back, "you forced me to do this!" he lamented; and at that, he took a .45 out of his coat and pointed it in Kain's direction. "This man," he said, gesturing derisively at Kain, just escaped from the goddamn looney bin! He was the *Hair Jacker*, for God's sake!" When that seemed to have no influence on Feingold, he exploded: "Your parents are worried about you, kid! This isn't normal!" he said, looking over Kain's followers. "Goddamn, couldn't you have joined a *frat* like everyone else—have a couple of orgies, do some drugs...! Shit, *whatever*! This is crazy! Look...okay, the pressure of school was too much for you. Perhaps you can take a year off, then go back to the university—"

"Get the hell out of here!" Kain screamed, finally coming to his senses.

"I'm holding the gun!" the private investigator pointed out, "—*I* give the orders."

"—I'm not going anywhere with you!" Feingold screamed at the man.

"You're coming with me kid," the PI informed him with a sardonic laugh. "We can either do this the hard way, or the easy way. Either way, I'm bringing you back home."

But Kain laughed softly then, at which time his followers joined in.

"What the hell is so funny!" the PI demanded.

"Do you really think that you are in charge of this situation?" Kain said.

"Let me see," the PI said sarcastically, "I'm holding the gun. That seems to put me in charge."

"You put too much faith in the threat of violence, Mr. Weiss."

"—How the hell did you know my name!"

"That's of no consequence. The matter at hand is that you would like to take young Feingold back to his parents. I know how you can do that with the least possible trouble."

"What are you talking about?" Weiss said, suspiciously.

"How would you like to bargain for this boy's soul?"

"His *what?*"

"You heard me correctly, Mr. Weiss. I'm offering you the means to win his soul."

Weiss couldn't help laughing. "Who are you supposed to be, the Devil?"

"As far as you and you clients are concerned, I am. All you have to do is come with me and we can get this over with."

"To where?"

"Are you afraid, Mr. Weiss? We are unarmed, frail and insane: you are sane, relatively healthy and armed."

Weiss continued to look at him suspiciously. He knew that he should just take Feingold and go, but something about Kain intrigued him. His curiosity had been piqued. "—You still haven't told me where."

"The place you've tried to follow us to for the last few days—without success. [The brows of Weiss's eyes rose.] This is a chance both to solve a mystery and win young Feingold's soul."

"And how do I win his soul?" Weiss said with another sardonic smile.

"You win simply by matching your sanity against my madness. You have faith in sanity, don't you? You believe in a rational world, don't you, Mr. Weiss?"

"And what if I do?" Weiss said in the same joking manner.

"Well, I believe in chaos and madness—and the malleability of the human soul. I believe that given a chance, most people will choose madness over reason. This is your chance to prove me wrong."

Weiss laughed heartily then. "You're *good*, Kain," he said, nodding his head. "I can see how young Feingold got his head fucked up by you. But see, I don't give a shit about philosophy—and I don't let *nobody* fuck my head up. The only thing I really care about is getting paid—and that happens when I bring back this kid here. See, as you noted before, I'm armed, and unless you've *totally* fucked up this kid's head, I think that if I point this gun at him, he'll come with me."

But Kain only laughed again. "Either you're already mad, or you're a fool, Mr. Weiss. Certainly you don't propose to shoot young Feingold, here. That would preclude you from getting paid—which you stated before was your only motivation. So, obviously, the threat of violence is not going to suffice here. [Weiss looked unsure for the first time.] Moreover, even if you managed to get him away from me, you'd be taking back an enemy, Mr. Weiss. Are you going to handcuff him in the trunk while you drive? Obviously you haven't given thought to everything. I'm offering you the chance for his *soul*: the opportunity to bring back a pacified mound of putty, ready either for your hand or the hands of his parents. I'm sure his parents would compensate you *double* if you managed to complete such a feat."

Weiss was still looking at him suspiciously—and now with confusion and a certain amount of alarm. "And what do I have to do?"

"All you have to do is come with me—prove to me that reason is more powerful than madness."

But Weiss's instincts began to exert their force; and shaking his head, he blurted out: "You must be *mad* if you think I'm going anywhere with you!"

"I *am* mad," Kain said, matter-of-factly. "I've never denied that. Come on, Mr. Weiss: the night is getting cold. And you still have the gun, don't you. Certainly you still trust violence."

"*Damn* right—and I trust getting paid even more!"

Kain smiled. "...I am understanding you better, Mr. Weiss" he went on, in the same calm manner. He reached for his pockets then—

"Don't move!"

"Relax, Mr. Weiss. I am unarmed." And at that, he brought out a huge wad of $100 bills.

Weiss's eyes bulged! The man stared, *entranced*: he had to shake his head to break the spell. "Where'd you get that money!"

"That's of no consequence, Mr. Weiss. All that matters is that you want it. So, let's sweeten the pot, as they say. You said before that you only care about getting paid. I have, here in my hand, $10,000, Mr. Weiss. [Weiss looked at it again.] Feingold's parents are only paying you $2,250—"

"How the hell did you know that!"

"That, too, is of no consequence, Mr. Weiss. Let us stick with the matter at hand. Prove to me that your reason is superior to my madness, and I'll hand over not only Feingold, but this wad of cash."

"I could just take them from you!" he said, uneasily.

"Could you?" Kain laughed. "If you thought you could, you would already have done so. The fact of the matter is that you relied on the threat of violence alone. [He gestured to his followers then.] Do you really think that these men care about life and death? They are the dregs of society, Mr. Weiss. They have slept on sidewalks on the coldest winter nights; they have eaten out of garbage cans. Do you really think that your pointing a gun at them is going to make a difference? Now," he said to the suddenly fidgety Weiss, "you may be able to shoot one of us, but the rest of us would be on you.

"No, Mr. Weiss," Kain said with a sigh, "you didn't think about this at all. Indeed, the only reasonable thing to do, is come with us. [He waved the money again; Weiss looked away from it uneasily.] If you have any faith in yourself—and your reason—then you'll come with me." Not even waiting for a response, Kain calmly walked past Weiss, who still stood there with his gun drawn—but with a trembling hand. Kain's followers walked past next; and after they were all about five paces away, Weiss began to follow them, looking increasingly uneasy.

* * *

—WHILE IN HARLEM, Colina finished up his tirade and fired his gun above the heads of his fellow officers, so that they ducked and scattered, Maria Santos smiled at her guest and said: "...So, are you looking forward to your big debate with Mayor Randolph tomorrow night?"

"Of course," McPrice laughed, "I always look forward to a chance to prove myself the better man!"

While Santos and her guest chuckled at the witticism, the piped-in audience clapped uproariously....A commercial break later, the woman accusing Mayor Randolph of rape was greeted by Santos. After they sat down, Santos held the woman's hand compassionately in order to give her the courage to tell the story that everyone had already heard dozens of times.

* * *

—While in Harlem, Colina declared that they would never take him alive, darting from the precinct house, and into the night, Roland walked into his dark condominium and shut the door quietly behind himself. There was a candle burning in his bedroom. Roland tossed his briefcase on the couch and walked towards the light with a smile on his face. He began to undress now, tugging at his tie and throwing off his jacket. When he reached his room, he saw Samantha lying on his bed seductively, in only a teddy. There was something exotic about her as she lay there, under the flickering wick of the candle. Soon, he was in her arms; her mouth was on his, her tongue searching wildly. He needed her desperately—it was beyond desire: it was *need.* Being with her was like a narcotic. He craved it: felt, in moments of forced depravation, that he could kill for it if necessary.

—While in Harlem, the corpses of Benjamin Thomas and his mother lay almost forgotten on the floor as 15 police officers chased after Colina, Samantha let out a moan. Roland moaned as well....Soon, he was inside of her, and she was clawing at his back. They seemed like two beast thrashing—*fighting* one another. She liked to be choked and slapped and cursed, and all kinds of improbable things; and during those subsequent moments of discomfort, he would think, with a gnawing unease, of his father raping a white woman, and Phelps's perverseness...But the next time that he saw her, everything would be forgotten, and he would again delve into the wonderfully thoughtless bestiality of their sex.

*   *   *

—While in Harlem, Colina jumped into a police cruiser and zoomed off, Kain led his men and the private investigator into a virtual wasteland. The buildings had been razed, as though in preparation for new construction, and everything was in huge piles of rubble. Weiss was still following at a distance, with his gun kept at his side and his finger on the trigger. As there were very few streetlights here, Kain and his men were only dull silhouettes against the darkness. Weiss had gotten so used to following them, that he had probably surrendered his immediate fears and concerns to this act. But when the men opened a manhole cover and began to file in, something in Weiss's gut churned. He walked up warily, watching as the men descended into the dark hole. The only one who remained outside, was Kain, and he presently gestured for Weiss to come closer.

Weiss walked up uneasily. "What is this?"

Kain smiled then, saying, "If you've characterized me correctly, then this is the gateway to hell, Mr. Weiss."

Weiss looked down into the darkness—

"Don't tell me you're afraid, Mr. Weiss."

"I ain't afraid!" he said defensively. "—I just ain't stupid, that's all."

"That's right, you aren't. Therefore, if you don't come now, then you lose everything: Feingold, the $10,000. These sewers go on forever: you'll never see us again."

"I could still take the money from you!" Weiss informed him, but Kain only laughed again, still with that disconcerting calmness.

"If you search me, you'll find that I have no money on me, Mr. Weiss. It's on young Feingold's person. So, you see, you really have no choice. Do you want to go first, or should I?"

Weiss's mind was working furiously! "I could tell the police where you are! Those people in the looney bin would love to know where you are!"

"Right you are, Mr. Weiss," Kain laughed again, "but if you were going to do that, you would have done it days ago. The fact of the matter is that you want to get Feingold on your own—without help. That way, you not only get the credit, but all the money. There's a reward for me, but you're not the kind of man who gets his collar like that: like a frightened kitten. You want to be the one in control: the one to subdue his victim, not the one who hides behind a bush and then goes in to collect the reward after the police have done the work—"

"I could just take you in now!" Weiss continued, his voice rising unsettlingly.

"Of course you could," Kain conceded, "but then you wouldn't succeed in your goal. I would be in jail and you would get the $500 they are offering for my return, but you would never see Feingold again—and there is the $10,000, which you would never see again either.

"So," Kain continued, "are you coming or not?"

Weiss looked totally distraught. His every instinct told him to be that scared kitten Kain had mentioned, but something about Kain's words had struck him to the quick; and seeming to come to the conclusion that there was no choice, he blurted out, "*You* first!" pointing his gun again. Kain shrugged his shoulders and complied. Weiss followed a few seconds later; when he put his hands on the rungs to descend into the dark, cramped smelliness, he was alarmed by how much they shook. Looking down, he couldn't see anything! His gut was telling him that it was a trap, but for the life of him, he couldn't stop—couldn't *think*! He was more than three-quarters of the way down the rungs, when the trembling in his limbs became so severe that he lost his grip and slipped. He had been holding the gun in his hand, but it fell along with the rest of him; and before he even knew it, he was lying in the sludge, groaning and disoriented. There was a dull light down the corridor, and from that dim illumination, he realized that Kain and his men were standing above him; a millisecond later, he realized that he had lost the gun! He went to grope around in the filth for it, but Kain turned on a lantern then, saying:

"Get up, Mr. Weiss: I have your gun here." Kain's face looked horrible in the lighting—as did Weiss's! But Kain calmly handed the gun to Weiss then. "Come on, Mr. Weiss." And he laughed then, going on: "See, I put no faith in your kind of violence. Put that gun in your pocket and follow me."

—While on the Harlem streets above, Colina fled into the night, able to think of nothing but taking revenge on the world that had betrayed him, Weiss did as told. He didn't so much comply as surrender—and he was still shaking. They walked for another five or so minutes, down labyrinthine passages that Weiss, with a deepening sense of alarm, realized that he would never be able to navigate on his own.

In time, Kain and his men entered a little nook in the sewer—followed by the fidgety Weiss. Actually, it was the basement of an abandoned, sealed-off building, which could only be reached through the sewer. Kain switched on a light then, and Weiss flinched at the brightness—and everything else around him. The place was replete with everything from electric lighting and heating, to full living and dining room sets, a television (which had been left on) *and* a refrigerator—all of which Kain had had his men procure using certain disreputable means.

"What the hell is this place!" Weiss demanded, feeling more and more that he was out of his element, in some twilight zone.

"Have you already forgotten why we're here?" Kain laughed, to which his men instinctively chuckled along. "This is where you will match your sanity against my madness, Mr. Weiss—and win $10,000." Kain nodded to Feingold then, and the youth took out the wad of bills and held it up for Weiss to see.

Weiss again looked away nervously; and with the light, he could see his clothes at last: he was totally covered with sewer sludge. The realization that he had no idea where he was, confronted him again—as well as the realization that nobody knew where he was either! How the hell could he have been so stupid!

And then, at that moment, a sound came from the corner of the chamber, where there was a closed door. Someone or something was banging on the other side of it!

"What's in there!" Weiss demanded.

Kain smiled enigmatically then, saying: "One of your colleagues, Mr. Weiss: someone else who professes that reason is superior to madness." Before Weiss could respond, Kain and his band walked over to the door and fought to open it (it was locked with a huge bolt). Weiss followed numbly behind; and when the door was finally open, a bone-thin, disheveled white man stood in the doorway. But at the sight of Kain, the man retreated. There was a dim light inside the small, windowless room, and a small cot, on which the disheveled man now sat, looking up at Kain warily. The walls were unpainted bricks and the entire thing reminded Weiss of a dungeon. There was a pungent toilet in the corner—or at least a commode. Kain entered the room and stepped up to the man calmly; Kain's men made space in the doorway, and Weiss stood there with them, staring inside in disbelief.

—While on the Harlem streets above, Colina ran red lights and zoomed down crowded city streets at 80 kilometers an hour, Weiss looked into the room, seeing that the elderly man—the *prisoner*, by the looks of it—was covered in nothing but rags and muck. The man had a bushy, disheveled beard, scraggly hair and a wild look in his eyes—all of which spoke to long captivity and madness—

"How long are you going to keep me here, Kain!" the man suddenly demanded.

"What?" Kain laughed, "—don't like the accommodations? They're the same ones you kept me in when I was in the Institute."

—Yes, believe it or not, that man was Dr. Fishman, Kain's erstwhile psychiatrist. Three weeks ago, learning that Fishman was to go to a psychiatric conference—and receive an award—Kain had gotten a limousine and posed as the driver, saying that the service was all part of the award. Fishman, inwardly seeing the luxury as his due, had stepped into the vehicle without thinking it odd or taking time to take stock of whom his driver was. While they drove along comfortably, Fishman had taken a drink in the bar of the limousine; and 12 hours later, he had awoken in this small, windowless room.

"Kain," Fishman pleaded, "this has gone on long enough. What do you intend to prove?"

"That madness is superior to reason. All you have to do is realize this, and I'll let you go."

"Okay," he said, "madness is superior to reason."

"Nice try," Kain laughed, "but you're still acting rationally."

Fishman swore then! "I know what you're trying to do!" he screamed then, "but it's not going to work."

"Of course," Kain laughed, "you know everything."

Fishman groaned, raking his hand through his filthy hair in frustration. And then, in the calmest voice he could muster: "As I've been telling you, Kain, this isn't about me, but about you—and your delusions: your failure to see the problems of your life as your own doing. You're trying to punish me now—like you tried to punish all those people whose heads you shaved—"

"I'm doing to you exactly what you did to me!" Kain returned. "You kept me in a room no bigger than this, claiming that you were trying to make me sane—to *cure* me. Now," he laughed, "I claim to want to drive you insane!"

"Kain," Fishman tried to reason with him again, "this is *kidnapping*!"

"It's exactly what you did to me! You think I *wanted* to be in that room!"

"You weren't well Kain—*you still aren't*! The law said—"

"Don't try to use that cop-out on me!" Kain raged. "You claimed to be an expert on madness—now let's see if you know what madness is! I'm keeping you exactly as you kept me. If you had intended to cure me of madness, then you don't have anything to worry about!"

"I didn't keep you in filth!" Fishman couldn't help but scream. "This is all about *revenge*, Kain!" But catching himself, Fishman sighed and took a deep breath. "...Look Kain, you shaved those heads to get revenge on the world. It was nothing but acting out, because you felt so impotent to change the world. You're *harmless* Kain—but bewildered by your harmlessness: the fact that no one fears you; no one rushes out to carry out your will—besides these homeless bums," he said, pointing at Kain's men. "I've said it before, and I'll say it again—no matter how long you keep me here. We both know that you don't have a violent bone in your body, Kain—"

"Then why did you back away when I entered the doorway?" Kain laughed mordantly. "What is that I see in your eyes, if not fear?"

"..*Kain*," Fishman said from the depths of his frustration and exhaustion, "if you were violent, you would have *killed* all those people, instead of simply shaving their heads. You need *help*, Kain. Come back to the Institute with me now. In your heart, you know you're not well."

—While in the outside world, members of the media heard the first reports of Colina's shooting spree over the police scanner and rushed to investigate the story, Kain shook his head resolutely. "I've told you already, Fishman: there is only one way out of here, and that is for you to understand madness: to be *cured* of sanity! To get out of here, you have to understand what madness is—"

"*Stop saying that*!" Fishman couldn't help himself; and then, in a lower voice: "How long are you going to keep me here?"

"I'm not keeping you here: you're keeping yourself here."

Fishman raked his fingers through his hair again. It was at that moment that Weiss, who had been looking on with a blank, uncomprehending expression, suddenly realized that he was seeing in Fishman's squalor and desperation, his own fate. He was snapped back into consciousness then, acutely aware that he had to defend himself. He grabbed for his gun, but then frowned and looked down at his pocket in horror—it wasn't there!

Kain laughed out then; and at that moment, Weiss looked

around to see Feingold holding the gun on him. Weiss had been so engrossed in the goings on of the room that he hadn't realized that he'd been pick-pocketed! Feingold gestured with his head and Weiss was pushed into the room, seeming drained of life. He sat down on the cot, next to Fishman, looking up at Kain in horror.

"I'll be back in a day or so, gentlemen," Kain said as he made his way for the door. But then, remembering something, he nodded to one of his men, and the latter handed over the shopping bag he had been carrying. "Here are enough groceries to last you a couple of days, gentlemen. Maybe during that time, you'll have an epiphany and come to understand madness." The two men looked on in horror, unable to move; and then, the door was closed on them, and they were alone in the putrid darkness, and Kain was gone.

* * *

—WHILE IN HARLEM, six police cruisers chased after Colina, and backup from helicopters and the surrounding precincts was called for, Charles Marenga sat in the back seat of his Mercedes Benz, staring out of the window pensively. His aide was driving him home now; but still gripped by thoughts of vengeance, Marenga's mind coursed with myriad chaotic images. They were presently driving past a public housing development; and as Marenga watched the decaying buildings that he, himself had once campaigned for, his upper lip unconsciously curled in disgust. Inside those buildings, he imagined the graffiti-covered corridors, with their pungent smell of stale urine and feces. There were some young black men on the corner—who, in his state of mind, he assumed to be drug dealers; and as he watched them, his mind suddenly flared up with images of the requisite gun fights and turf battles that arose within that place, with the young and innocent every day losing their lives and souls.

—While in Harlem, news helicopters rushed to capture the police chase for the TV audience, Marenga looked at the world, seeing it as an open wound that needed to be cauterized. He had spent his life trying to amass those whom he and the entire world had conceptualized as powerless, in a misguided attempt to empower them. But true power wasn't about numbers: it couldn't be amassed, like coins in a purse. True power wasn't about the *getting* of things, or even the *doing* of things. Power couldn't be *garnered*. It wasn't an end, to be attained. The more one worked towards it, the more diffuse it became. There was no *reason* to power, any more than there was reason to a thunderstorm. It was what it was; and as such, he, who had spent his life campaigning and protesting, all in some misguided attempt to "empower" the powerless, had wasted his life. He hated everything at that moment: his life, his society…*everything*. He wanted to see it all destroyed: all the bourgeois pettiness; all the people—black, white, male, female...fighting over scraps like *animals*.

—While in Harlem, TV helicopters broadcasted the images of the police chase on network feeds, cutting into time that had been set aside for "feel good" situation comedies, Marenga sat in the darkness, thinking of the vengeance to come. An entire nation of whiners, marching from one media frenzy to another.

—While in Harlem, Colina's car ran through an intersection, running over a half-deaf old woman, who hadn't heard the sirens and helicopters, and those images were broadcasted to millions of homes—*now nationwide*!—Marenga sat there broodingly, conjuring his hatred. There was evil out there, and evil within him; but like a diver's body against the pressure of the ocean, it was only the force within him that was keeping him from being crushed flat. An entire world of self-destructiveness and madness…It occurred to him that what he was up against, was a vast religion, spreading with the historical brutality of Islam and Christianity, combined; and like those religions, it shared the refrain: Prostrate yourself before our God, or perish! Now that he thought about it, all those whiny, scandal-obsessed, self-serving people were only so because they were jealous worshipers, who looked out at the world and saw their mighty god bestowing others with the felicity that they thought was their due. Blacks looked at whites and were jealous and resentful—but the opposite was also true! Women looked at men and were jealous—*and vice versa*! And it wasn't confined to America: this god was beyond America—was in fact the global economy! It was a brutal, insatiable god, which bestowed its graces haphazardly and wreaked its vengeance with equal heedlessness; and the people, even in their moments of greatest joy and prosperity, were frightened out of their wits by its works.

—While in Harlem, reporters responding to anonymous tips

arrived at the police precinct, frantically piecing together what had happened (and broadcasting those findings to a horrified public!), Marenga looked out at the slums beyond the car, knowing that he was seeing the true incarnation of the American ethic—*of god's will.* The suburbs and the slums were simply arbitrary settings on a twirling roulette wheel, where everywhere, there was fear and insecurity; because in the final analysis, the very fear and paranoia which wreaked havoc on the psyches of slum dwellers, were also present in the suburbs—where the middle-class always had to be on the lookout for threats to its gains. All that any of them could do to fight off the insecurity, was to prostate himself before his god—the economy—and spend! spend! spend! That was their amen and hallelujah. Their soothing narcotic was purchase power—not money, which was real, but purchase power, which was a function of credit and financial voodoo. They were "happy" so long as they kept on consuming: kept buying houses and cars...paid for junior's college expenses and went on a yearly vacation. So they went into *more* debt—and therefore had to fight off more insecurity—but they were happy, and the economy, their great god in the heavens, was happy...at least for a little while. And what were recessions and depressions, but low points in their collective religion, when the people were too doubtful to spend? What priests called faith, economists called consumer confidence; and it was both of their jobs to keep it going, so that their religion could prosper and draw more converts. And emerging markets were being discovered every day: vast, fertile plains of new converts to their religion—new *buyers*! Just look at the soaring national debts of the developing countries: yes, they had caught the spirit too! And just like Americans, they were all whiners—worshippers who were caught in some sick paradox between showing their strengths and their weaknesses, with the sickest of them realizing, in time, that their greatest strength *was* their weakness. This was how one got aid: be like Russia and claim that if aid weren't given, then the fragile edifice of market capitalism would crumble, and some reactionary extremist, *some infidel*, would seize power—

Marenga had to get some fresh air!

—While in Harlem, 20 cars and three helicopters chased after Colina, and the order went out that Colina had to be stopped at all costs, Marenga bellowed:

"Stop here!"

The aide looked around confusedly. "Sir?"

"Stop here: I'm going to walk home!" He was only about two kilometers away from his brownstone…and he had to get outside.

"But, sir," the youth pleaded, even as he pulled over, "the streets aren't safe."

"Listen to yourself!" Marenga said in disgust. "Are you afraid of your own community now!" As soon as the car stopped, Marenga practically jumped out, onto the dark, tenement-lined streets that held his people. The aide looked back at him anxiously, but: "I'll see you at home!" Marenga bellowed, with a violent expression that made the youth drive off in frightened haste.

However, as soon as the youth was gone, and Marenga was alone in the cold night air, he felt the pain in his chest return. He felt dizzy, too, so that he retreated to a stoop that was almost totally blocked by pungent bags of rotting garbage.

—While in Harlem, Colina came to the conclusion that he wasn't going to get away, and, like Andropov months earlier, looked around for a means of ending his life, Marenga sat down heavily on the stoop, clutching his chest as the pain consumed him. It was the same feeling: there were both the sensation of an explosion emanating from within him and the feeling that all the pain and madness of the world was being drawn into him. As he looked out on the filthy street, he found himself thinking that if he were to die tonight, he would have no legacy. He had no children…no *power*—either as how he had once defined it, or as it now seemed to be. Surrendering to his emptiness, he leaned against the dilapidated door of the tenement, breathing in the nauseating stench from the garbage bags. He looked out on the world then, as the moon rose above the eroded gray bricks of the tenements; and for an instant, there was the fantasy that he was the city: that he was the *world*, and that if he died, the world would die with him. For a moment, it wasn't simply that he was an out-of-shape, middle-aged man, but that he was the city; and that his deterioration—as sudden and inexplicable as it now seemed to him—had been part of God's grand design.

—While in Harlem, Colina took out his gun and put it to his sweaty temple, Marenga sat in the gutter, somehow drawing strength from the surrounding filth. He looked out on the surrounding slums with the same appreciation with which a monk watched his meager surroundings and his daily sufferings. The pain in his chest was a sign from the heavens, and all he could do was tremble with joy as he received those blessings. The will of God was in the surrounding bricks and concrete and *filth*: these were the proofs of divine felicity. Indeed, everything around him was a testament to their god: the vast economic system. These were the products of men's hands and souls. Mountains had been torn asunder for cement; forests had been felled for wood; the bowels of the earth had been scoured to supply the metals and minerals and fossil fuels that were necessary for it all. All around him, there was filth; but that filth was the product of toil—of *civilization*—and therein, if *anywhere*, was the power that defined everything.

—While in Harlem, a police car tried to ram Colina, and millions of engrossed TV viewers across the country saw Colina's car dart through another crowded intersection, almost losing control, Marenga let the contradictory, self-destructive peace consume him. Humanity had tamed the natural world—*pillaged* it, in fact—and that was how it should be, because he knew that that brutality was the nature of his kind. There was nothing pristine—nothing *untamed*—about humanity, and survival *demanded* brutality. Humanity was *filthy*—and irredeemably so. It was that filth which was responsible for humanity's ascension over the other beasts.

—While in Harlem, Colina finally pulled the trigger, and, a second later, his car flipped three times, eventually ending up on the sidewalk (where a few hapless spectators had gathered to watch the chase), Marenga settled into his contradictory peace, suddenly finding himself in a place beyond pain and pleasure and regret. His mind was a chaotic jumble, seeming to match the arrhythmic thumping in his chest; and he sat back, peacefully aware that he was dying, just as the city was dying. But at the same time, he felt the filth of the city upon himself—*within* himself. It was there, infusing him with the strength of humanity's self-destructive brutality. The sensation was somehow superseding the pain in his chest. It was as if a current were coursing through his body, rending his insides. Self-preservation told him to flee—to detach himself from the current—but he was incapable of independent movement: of independent *thought*, even. He looked up with blurred vision, seeing the city again; and it was so repugnant to his senses, that he knew, all at once, that the city would be his legacy: that the city had been his lover and his progeny, and that he would survive in it after his corporeal form was gone from the world. It was being rended as he was being rended; and if, after the metamorphosis which was attuning him to his true brutality, he managed to survive, then the city would live on as well. Something was guiding him: imbuing him with so much power that he wanted to cry out to the thing that could only be God. He had to hold on: he *would* hold on, because God had willed it.

—And, while in Harlem dozens of police officers surrounded the wrecked, overturned cruiser, seeing, on Colina's bloody, brain-splattered face, the triumphant grin that had followed him into death—and over those images, the high-pitched voices of the reporters rose in the air like some testament to madness—Marenga sat there with the assurance that they would all pay for what they had done to him. There was power in filth and all the pillaged things of the earth; and finding himself imbued with it, he got gingerly to his feet and began to stumble home, drunk with the madness of God's will.

* * *

KAIN HAD TAKEN HIS men upstairs, to the abandoned lot that still held the rubble of the buildings that had been demolished. To keep themselves warm, the four of them stood around a huge fire. They had put pieces of wood—broken beams from the building and old furniture that had been discarded with the rubble—into a drum and set the contents on fire. They stood there, holding their hands up to those flames in silence, suddenly melancholy. Or maybe it was only Kain.

"Let's all get drunk," he began, taking a bottle of cheap whiskey from his coat, "for tomorrow, we'll be sane again." He took a swig, and passed the bottle to Feingold, who was to his right. "God created narcotics for a reason, my sons," Kain went on. "He clouds our minds, so that we can see clearly; he drives us insane, so that we can know what logic and reason are. He puts us in the darkness, so that we can know the light. Seize the darkness within, and you'll see; embrace insanity and the road ahead will be made clear; seep into confusion and senselessness, and you will discover the meaning of the universe. Yes, get drunk, my sons. God loves drunkards and lunatics—they are the last true followers of His will—"

But just then, by which time the bottle had come back to Kain, a figure emerged from the darkness at Kain's right. They all turned to look; but before anyone could say or do anything, the man—a disheveled old bum in an army jacket—raised his sledgehammer into the air and brought it down squarely on Feingold's head. The sound was sickening—like a watermelon hitting the ground. Feingold fell heavily to the earth, right next to Kain. The other bums, seeing the kid die, ran away screaming. But Kain only stared on casually while the army-jacket-clad bum placed his sledgehammer down nonchalantly and stepped up to the drum to warm himself.

Kain looked at the man with pursed lips. "I say, sir, why did you do that?"

The man looked up as though only now noticing him. "I was cold," he answered tersely.

"I see....Care for a drink?" he said, handing over the bottle.

* * *

IT WAS APPROACHING ten o'clock now. The events surrounding Colina's flight were quickly becoming myth—as were the actors involved. However, for some reason, the news hadn't reached City Hall as yet. Mayor Randolph sat at his desk, staring unseeingly at a chart of financial figures. A precursory glance at the scene would lead the viewer to believe that he was hard at work, but the fact of the matter was that he was daydreaming—dawdling, in fact. He could have gone home hours ago, but he stayed here, somehow wary of the lonely emptiness of Gracie Mansion—and the outside world, in which his sex scandal seemed omnipresent. Every magazine seemed to have an article on him; every news broadcast had some tidbit about his depravity; even situation comedies couldn't resist getting a few jokes about him into their plots. But strangely enough, he was almost bored with the entire thing now. The stripper had lied to him: there weren't any cameras in the strip joint, so it had all come down to her word against his. She didn't even have any stray semen to blackmail him with. She seemed to realize that Randolph wasn't going to give her anything, but this only made her more bitter and self-destructive. She had gone so far, that she was trapped in her own media frenzy. When Randolph watched her on TV, crying like a baby, he almost felt sorry for her. Feminists were lining up behind her now, congratulating her for refusing to accept victimization, but it was all a farce.

As for the rest of his life, his divorce had been finalized a month ago—he had put up no fight. His marriage was behind him, as was his strange mid-life crisis...and his political career. The election was only days away and he was trailing Charlotte McPrice by 40 points.

He had given his bodyguards the night off once again, and settled himself in his office, somehow finding solace in the silence. In fact, for the last few nights, he had slept in his office. After the violent upheaval of the summer, everything was settling back—not the way it used to be: just settling. All the matter was there—for matter was indestructible—but everything was dust.

Just then, the phone on his desk rang. He first looked at it with indifference; then, as it continued to ring, he looked at it with annoyance. There was a hideous jack-o-lantern next to the phone—he looked at the snarling face strangely for a moment; but coming to his senses, he picked up the telephone receiver gruffly: "Yes?" He listened for a while, then a dumbfounded expression came to his face: "*Who?*" He listened again, but still seemed not to believe what he heard. At last, he said: "Okay, escort him in." He sat back in his chair then, still somewhat confused. He looked at the clock on his desk and thought to himself: I wonder how he knew I was still here? It was while he was thinking this, that he got up and began to pace the room. Happening to look up, he noticed the huge abstract painting on the far wall. It had been a gift from a rich constituent. He walked over to it distractedly and stood before it, his face creasing. He had had it for a month now; and every time he watched it, it conjured the conviction in him that it had been created when the artist, walking up to the canvass with paints in hand, slipped and splattered the entire mess against the canvass. Somehow, it was worth well over five million dollars. That meaningless conglomeration of colors—

"It's a piece of crap isn't it?" a voice ventured from the doorway.

Randolph turned around abruptly, only to see Marenga standing in the doorway with a guard. Marenga looked strangely aged since the last time he had seen the man. The sight of the man triggered recollections of how Marenga had laughed at him that day, and Randolph's face unconsciously creased. But despite all that, there was something about Marenga that wasn't quite right—which disarmed him somehow. Marenga, known for his dapper suits, now wore a disheveled black suit that looked like it had been worn thin by use. The man's collar seemed not simply undone, but as though it had been torn open. His entire shirt was damp and discolored with sweat; and his tie was pulled to the side—as though he had wrenched it loose in a fit of suffocation. There was something insalubrious about him: his face was wet with perspiration even though it was five degrees Celsius outside; and on that face, the distress was plain for anyone to see....

Forty-five minutes ago, Marenga had set off for home, wanting only to leap into the madness; but two blocks later, whether it was a pang of conscience, or his last iota of humanity, he had rebelled at the thing which lay before him—which was *growing* within him: actually *sustaining* him. He had looked about desperately for something with which to fight off the madness; and his mind, finding nothing else, had proffered Randolph. His coming here had been yet another last-ditch effort. He had hailed an oncoming cab and jumped in, sensing vaguely that Randolph, with whom he had quarreled for years, had the tools to best him, and thwart the incomprehensible stream of logic that he now found coursing through his mind.

"You an art lover?" Marenga ventured then. He sounded winded—as though he were laboring for each breath.

"I like beautiful things," Randolph answered him suspiciously; nevertheless, seeming to put the bulk of his apprehensions aside, he nodded to the guard, so that the two men were left alone.

"—So, I take it that you didn't come here for the art," Randolph said, curtly.

"No, I came to talk to you."

Randolph gestured for Marenga to take a seat in front of his desk. "What about?" he asked, sitting down; but at the same time, he frowned as he watched Marenga's rickety gait, and the feeble way in which the man took his seat.

"Don't worry, Randolph," Marenga laughed, seeing Randolph's apprehension. "I'm not here on business—or at least, not business as you know it. I have no recriminations to make—no ultimatums—I simply want to revive that long-forgotten art: conversation."

Randolph frowned: not so much at Marenga's words, as *Marenga.* The man still sounded winded—and he was sweating profusely. Randolph went to ask the man if he were all right, but the sudden thought that that would be a sign of weakness, made him put the idea out of his mind. "Conversation?" he said with a bemused smile.

"Yes, *talking*: not repeating slogans, or stating positions, but genuine conversation. You know what I mean, don't you?"

Randolph pursed his lips, staring critically at the distress written all over Marenga's face. But then, "Yes," he said with a wry smile, "I know what conversation is."

"I want to start," began Marenga, "by apologizing to you—for all the arguments I started with you: all the strife I nurtured…for all of it."

"What's this about?" Randolph said, suspiciously.

"I have no agenda, Randolph," Marenga said, solemnly. "Nobody is ever going to know that this conversation happened.…No, wait," he started in a new voice, "I lied: I *do* have an agenda…to hell with it," he said as though exasperated with the stupidity of it all. "I'm giving you one chance," he said with more urgency, "—you…the city. I'm giving you this chance to stop me."

"Stop you from doing what?" Randolph said in bewilderment.

Marenga looked at him then—looked up with eyes that had been attuned to the brutal will of the city—and it was all there. On some level, he knew about the Thomases; he saw the feverish reports on the 24-hour news channels; he saw the great mobs all congregating to the scene of the crime, their outraged voices at first demanding answers, then only blood. He saw it all in a flash of light that was so brutal to his senses, that none of the individual images stayed with him. The only thing that was left was a heightened sense of urgency, which combined with all of his fears and uncertainties. For a moment, he was lost in time, drifting on the chaos of the city's consciousness. He looked around confusedly, realizing that Randolph was his last link to the world of men. He stared into the bewildered contours of the man's face, desperate to get his bearings. All of this probably took place in a millisecond, but it seemed like hours before Marenga finally felt himself being anchored to the world of the present. He sighed in relief, but seemed even more feeble now. At last, he swallowed with effort and looked up at Randolph once again:

"I'm giving you a chance to save yourself," he whispered at last.

"*What?*" Randolph said, suddenly wondering if Marenga was mad.

"The city's about to tear itself apart!"

—Randolph got up nervously and went over to the wet bar to mix a drink. He thought about calling the guard; but for some reason, a sense of morbid curiosity got the better of him. When he looked up, Marenga was staring at him intently; Randolph gestured towards the bottles of liquor, but Marenga shook his head. After pouring himself a drink and taking his first sip, Randolph ventured: "So, what's this all about?"

Marenga, who had been waiting patiently, nodded before going on: "Something's coming, Randolph, and if you don't stop me, I'm going to be at the head of it. [Randolph looked on, utterly lost.] Right now," Marenga continued, "it's gathering strength…—I can *feel* it," he said, gasping for air after every few words. "We're at a strange place in history, Randolph. It's make-or-break time for all of us….I left five months ago because I felt it then—I felt my own place in it. I'm tired of it all, Randolph: all the preordained, senseless struggles—all the meaningless political wrangling. This is the calm before the storm. I've *seen* things—"

"What are you talking about?" Randolph said with an admixture of alarm and curiosity.

"Like I said," Marenga continued, desperately needing to make Randolph understand, "we all have our role to play. I have a role, you have a role…we're all taking part in it. The world's *connected*, Randolph, but connected by *meaninglessness*. [Randolph's face creased even more.] Now is the time to question it all, Randolph—to stop it, if it *can* be stopped. This is our *last* chance," he said, looking as though he were going to collapse at any moment. "We can't just sit around anymore: it's complacency that's killing us—"

"What the *hell* are you talking about, Marenga?" he said at last, losing all patience.

"It's our *last* chance!" Marenga said, on the verge of hysteria.

The words echoed horribly in the chamber; Marenga was looking at him imploringly, but Randolph only sighed to himself, thinking: Marenga *is* mad! Strangely enough, his first impulse was to laugh vindictively—like Marenga had laughed at him—but he was suddenly weary of the entire thing. "Look, Marenga," he said with another tired sigh, "maybe you should leave—"

But Marenga was laughing now. He shook his head and chuckled softly to himself, while Randolph stared at him, frowning. "You think I'm mad, don't you?" Marenga said then.

"Yes," Randolph answered, simply.

Marenga laughed even harder, his entire body jiggling. Something about it was contagious, so that Randolph, despite everything, began to laugh as well. Suddenly, he just felt silly—and even Marenga's madness didn't matter anymore. While he shook his head and chuckled to himself, he walked back over to his desk and sat down heavily. "Okay, Marenga: you're mad, I'm mad…we're all mad. Why are you really here?"

Marenga was still chuckling softly to himself. He seemed totally drained now. "I guess the madness drove me here," he said, to which they both began to chuckle once again. "Misery loves company: I guess madness loves company as well," he snickered.

But as Marenga's laughter sounded in the closed quarters of the room, something within Randolph broke, and he found himself remembering the thought he had had during his weeks of filth: that there were other warriors like him out there, fighting the same battles that he fought—soul mates of a sort, all beaten back by the realities of the world. He remembered his own madness; he remembered how, at the announcement of the Brooklyn Massacre, a part of him had been certain that he had sensed it: had been at *one* with it. He sobered suddenly:

"…What are you feeling, Marenga?" he started in an anxious tone. "What's got you so upset?"

After a final chuckle, Marenga shrugged his shoulders, then began with a sigh: "I hate the world, Randolph. It's as simple as that." Having said that, he paused and looked at the man earnestly. "I hate everyone and everything in it…I'm *tired*, Randolph. I'm tired of everything. I'm an old man, looking back on my life and hating it all. You said I was mad—and maybe I am—but I've never been so sure in my life that something's out there—something *evil*. I can feel it. I may even be the source of it," he said quickly, "…and I came here to warn you—"

But all of a sudden, Marenga looked up sharply, his eyes narrowing: "Now I see what's going on here!" he laughed. "You've sensed it, too, haven't you! [Randolph shook his head feebly.] You're the Mayor—you've *lived* through it all. You've *seen* it all—and *felt* it!"

Randolph just sighed to himself, unable to see the use of denying it—or confirming it. He just sat there with a blank expression on his face, seeming suddenly drained—just like Marenga had seemed at first. "Why'd you come to me, Marenga? Why me?"

"I needed another lunatic to talk to," Marenga said with a smirk, but neither of them laughed this time. The joke was suddenly stale; and beyond the ease that had been built up between them, they sensed the harsh, sobering realities of the world.

"What happens now?" Randolph asked then, but Marenga only looked towards the windows—and the dark world of chaos beyond them—wondering the same thing himself.

* * *

THE MEDIA HAD somehow gotten access to the surveillance video from the police precinct's waiting room. In the morning, those images of death and madness would adorn all the papers and news broadcasts. Multi-page spreads were already being coordinated; network specials documenting Colina's insanity were already being considered. Heads were going to have to roll for this, or so the media were saying. Now that those images were before them, there were yet more icons before which the people could genuflect and sing their insane praises to the heavens.

* * *

FEINGOLD WAS DEAD as well. The kid lay amongst the rubble at Kain's feet, his blood still seeping out from the crack in his skull. "…The only way to get rid of all evil, is to kill everyone," Kain said, desultorily. He had been talking nonstop for the last half hour or so. He and the murderous bum were the only ones there. The latter was still drinking Kain's bottle of whiskey, ignoring him. Actually, when Kain handed over the bottle, the man had considered it his, and had never passed it back; and Kain, engrossed in his disquisition, had forgotten about getting drunk.

"The search for purity in a profane world can only lead to madness," Kain went on, while the bum stared unseeingly into the flames. The latter had put a turned-over garbage can next to the fire and was sitting on it, while he held the bottle of whiskey in his arms like a newborn baby. Kain had remained standing, like a professor before a student. He continued: "I was just telling my men that we were all going to be sane in the morning. I believe that each one of us has a choice if he wants to be sane or not. Sanity is socially prescribed, you know. So it's possible for the society to be insane and the madman to be the most logical thinker….

"The doctor at the madhouse I was in said that I was harmless—said I would never kill. Now, as I see it, if the only surefire way to get rid of evil and live in a pure world, is to kill everyone, then I would have to be a killer, wouldn't I? I would have to seep into chaos and *kill*. So the big question is if I have it in me or not—a killer, I mean….I know what *they* say sanity is: I've got to figure out if I'm willing to live with that—or to *die* with it. Those are my choices….

"You drunk yet? [The bum took another swig, still staring into the flame as though mesmerized.] No?" Kain went on. "That's good. It ain't right to kill a man when he don't know what's coming. You ain't really killed until you can look into the eyes of your victim and tell him what you're going to do. That's *real* killing. Now, when you think about it, you didn't kill my disciple like a man. You snuck up behind him—did it like a coward…I'm gonna kill you to your face—tell you all about it before you die. ….We should all kill the cowardly killers among us. Even in the Old West, they understood that you don't shoot a man in the back. You 'call him out' as they said—shoot him out in the open, like a man. We've got an entire world of cowardly killers. They kill you behind your back; and after you drop dead, they act like they had nothing to do with it. They'll drain your soul—*everything*—like a parasite. Suck you dry…! Kill you like cancer—from within…Attack the vital organs: entrench themselves in everything you need to survive, until the only way to get rid of them, is to cut out your cancerous liver, kidneys—all the things you need to survive. Horrible way to die—even worse way to live. That's what they do today—underhanded killing….

"But I'm gonna help you out; 'cause you see, *this* kid here"—and he pointed at Feingold—"he's trouble. He's two things a poor black man should never deal with: he's rich and he's white. They already sent a detective after me. When this kid ends up dead, they're gonna come looking for *me*, not for you. They're gonna try to kill me in their old, underhanded ways. They'll bring me out before their cameras; first, they'll suck out my guts, maybe chop off my tongue—*figuratively*, I mean—...let me starve—waste away. After all that, they'll probably sentence me to the death penalty: kill me twice. That's all the death penalty is—killing dead men...*superfluous*. So, the way I see it, I have days, probably *hours*, before they begin that slow, painful death on me. Now *you*...you've already set it all in motion. Time's ticking...and there doesn't seem to be any way out of it. The only thing to do, as I see it, is to find out the truth about the world before I go. I've figured out most of it by now, but I'm not sure about some vital things. Somehow or another, it all rests with what that psychiatrist said. Either I'm a killer or I'm not. Either I'm able to do what it takes, or I'm just a joker, like everyone says....

"Put down that bottle now," he said with a deep sigh, while the bum, still ignoring him, took another deep swig and blinked drowsily at the flames. Kain picked up the sledgehammer then. At the motion, the bum watched him indifferently; then, as Kain raised the sledgehammer above his head and began his swing, the man screamed out, his face highlighted horribly by the flames.

5.

The Music Box

These were the last moments of Roland Micheaux's life. He sprung up from sleep, searching the darkness for the source of the shrill noise that had awoken him. He awoke so abruptly that it was as though he were still dreaming: still 13 years old, running away from his father. Those images projected themselves onto the darkness around him, so that for a moment, he was lost. The waking world took shape slowly; the images of his dream faded with equal reluctance. And the shrill noise was still in the air; like an anchor, it kept him locked in place, besieged by all that that 13-year-old felt. He searched the darkness frantically, caught in some bizarre fight or flight impulse—

An arm appeared out of the darkness! In a deft movement, the shrill noise was cut off; and as Roland stared into the darkness, the world finally began to make sense. He checked the hands on his luminescent wrist watch (which said that it was just after three-thirty in the morning), then he stared into the darkness as Samantha got out of the bed, yawned, checked the pager that she had just turned off, and headed for the bathroom. He was suddenly overcome by a feeling of relief; but exhausted by the strange early-morning struggle, he fell back onto his pillow.

—While outside, the story of the Thomases began to take on a life of its own, Roland sighed and lay peacefully in the darkness. Turning his head, he watched his girlfriend's retreating silhouette. In the bathroom, she turned on the light, and he took in the entire length of her smooth, creamy nakedness. He liked the idea of their sordid lovemaking contrasted with the sweet, "all-American-girl" image which was seen every morning on network television; and at that moment, he was madly in love with her—or at least the *thought* of her. She was there with him, like some aegis against his nightmares. It felt so good to lie there, knowing that there was love in him and that he didn't have to work at it. In fact, his love, and his life in times of happiness, was like the exhaustion that came after a hard day of work, when everything was complete and all that lay ahead was rest. This new peace was like a wonderful dream, so that he felt like laughing out in the darkness. He remembered the Cranston International case then—and his ascension into the stratosphere….

The sound of his girlfriend starting her shower brought him out of his reverie. He smiled unconsciously, remembering their first chance encounter. But two months later, theirs was still a relationship of trysts. They met at cabins for weekend rendezvous; they left coded voice mail messages for lunch time sessions and after work meetings. There was something thrilling about the secrecy—and the silence. They made it a point to talk only sparingly. They didn't know what the other's favorite color was, or their favorite food. A touch was all that they needed; entire conversations were to be had with a facial expression, a gesture or a kiss. Sometimes they didn't even have sex at all, but instead lay for hours in one another's arms, saying nothing with words, but exploring vast universes of possibility with touch. With their busy lives and their high profiles, there was something wonderful about the silence and secrecy and, at times, *bestiality*. And it wasn't even that anything would happen to either of them if their, for lack of a better word, affair, were ever discovered. It was just that they couldn't stop the fantasy of danger; and that after all this time, they were loath to change the comfortable syntax of their relationship.

After a few minutes, Samantha came out of the bathroom, turning off the bathroom light as she came. She was dressed in a pair of jeans and a blouse (both of which she would change at the network). She came over to him and straddled him playfully, kissing him on the forehead. They stared at one another for a while, both of them smiling. Outside, the wind was howling softly. It was so perfect: so *peaceful*. His feeling of love for her waxed high again; but this time, he needed it to be real: needed it to be more than some panic-stricken impulse. She kissed him on the lips this time, then got up to leave. He turned his head and watched her disappear into the darkness. He wanted to call her back and tell her of his feelings, but there was no rush: there was always time....

Still smiling, he closed his eyes and went back to sleep....However, a few minutes later, just as the dream world was about to envelop him, the phone rang. He sat up and stared at it: at first with annoyance, then with alarm, because rarely did anyone get good news at four in the morning. He picked it up:

"Yes?"

"Mr. Micheaux?"

"Sam?" Roland said with a frown. It was the doorman.

"It's that woman again," he said ominously, "—and that kid."

Roland lay there for a good three seconds before it hit him. "...*Candice?*" he said, more to himself than the doorman. The doorman groaned to give his assent. *What the hell...!* Roland thought, warily. He hadn't seen Candice since the last time Phelps went on his sex binge. The thought of Phelps repulsed him; and the mere thought of the meaningless, self-destructive sex he had had with Candice—not to mention the sex that Phelps was probably still having with her—was *nauseating*. Some more seconds passed; a side of him considered telling the doorman to say that he wasn't there—but that wouldn't work, as she was no doubt standing right in front of the doorman. Seeing no other way, and suddenly remembering Mindy, he sighed. "...Send her up, Sam."

He got up in a daze, put on a robe, then went to the living room, where he turned on the light and sat down on the couch. Has Phelps been drinking again? he wondered. Probably. He and Phelps hadn't exchanged anything beyond the standard salutations since they had had that talk all those months ago. Now the man's weirdness was impinging on his life again. He had neither the time nor the patience to enter that again. As such, by the time Candice rang the bell, he had worked himself into a fit of self-righteous anger. He walked to the door in four brisk strides, his face stern and his jaw tight. But when he opened the door, his jaw dropped open. Candice was crying: she was a mess! She looked as though she had just been in a fight; her left eye was swollen and her hair looked like a disheveled bird's nest. Little Mindy seemed exhausted and dazed. The little girl was in pink, fluffy bunny pajamas, replete with huge floppy ears and bunny slippers. She smiled vaguely at him when he opened the door, but otherwise seemed ready to fall asleep.

Roland quickly brought them in and sat them on the couch. Mindy looked tired beyond reason. "Come on sweetheart," he said, taking her from Candice. "You can sleep in here." And at that, he rushed her off to the guest bedroom. The little girl lay like a sack of potatoes in his arms. In the room, he took off her slippers and placed her underneath the covers. She closed her eyes soon thereafter and went to sleep. The feeling of anxiety was still growing within him when he went back outside. Candice was balled up on the couch, rocking herself. Roland was going to ask her if she wanted something to drink—some hot chocolate maybe—but the sight of her made him put all that off.

"What happened!" he demanded. Still, she seemed not to hear. He went up and touched her; she recoiled, looking as though she were going to scream; then, seeing that it was only he, she seemed to come to her senses. He repeated the question in a softer voice. She stared at him for a while, then burst into tears.

"He's gone crazy!" she cried.

"Phelps?"

She nodded, like a child forced to admit some horror.

"What did he do?" Roland asked, uneasily.

"God!" she cried. "You don't know what he's like!"

Don't be so sure! he thought to himself.

"He said if I told, he would report me to Immigration..."

"He make you have sex with him?"

"*No*!" she said in frustration, as though that were too trivial a thing. She seemed to be fighting to find a way to make him understand. Then: "He makes me watch—"

"*Watch*?" Roland said with a frown.

"He puts me in the closet, then...he brings in Cindy...and then they..." She looked up into his eyes, unable to say the rest.

Roland nodded his head, looking away. Still up to your old tricks, he thought. "How long has this been going on?"

"A couple of weeks. It's not normal, the things they do...! Sometimes he ties her up! Sometimes I think he's going to strangle her...! [Roland, remembering the things that Samantha cried out for, winced.] And his back is all scratched up. He liked her to do it!

[Roland groaned, feeling slightly ill.] But *tonight*..." She stopped short, wringing her hands anxiously.

"What happened?" Roland managed to whisper.

"Tonight...he had me watch as usual. They were doing it, and then, all of a sudden...[She started biting her fingernails; Roland pulled her hand from her mouth.]...All of a sudden," she went on, "he tells Cindy to go get something from the closet, where he had placed me! I couldn't move! Cindy came walking up to me—that stupid, trusting woman!" she cursed her. "She does anything he wants...! She walks up, opens the closet and sees me standing there! I still couldn't move! I was just in shock! As soon as she sees me, she screams! I scream too! And then, all of a sudden, she starts punching me, calling me all these names. At first, I was so much in shock, I couldn't move. But in the background, I hear Dallas laughing—that son of a bitch! I hear him laughing, and I knock her back—that skinny woman, she couldn't do me nothing! I slapped her back and went for him! I was gonna *kill* him!"

Roland groaned.

"I leaped at him...and he still laughing, as though it's all a joke. But that bastard soon had me held down, like he always held down Cindy. The way he was laughing, I thought he was gonna take me right there, but I saw Cindy then. She was still standing by the closet, kind of in shock like. Things were working in her mind, you see! Hearing Dallas laughing, and seeing him over me like that, she realized that it was him who had me in there! All of a sudden, she grabbed a lamp and hit him in the head with it. It would have knocked out a normal man, but it only weakened him enough for me to push him off. Next thing I know, he springs at Cindy, blood gushing down his face...*God*!" she cried.

"What happened!" Roland demanded.

"I just ran—ran for my life. Somehow, I remembered that little girl, Mindy. I just grabbed her from her bed and ran with her...ran for my life. And all the while, I still hear those two fighting!"

"You should have called the police!"

"*Police*!" she said, outraged. "And tell them what! I ain't even legal here since I stopped going to school! They wouldn't listen to me. And besides, *those* two freaks...it's all a game to them! If you had seen some of the things I've seen them do...!"

"What about *Cindy*?" Roland asked anxiously.

"What about her!"

"You don't think she's in danger?"

"Not any more than usual."

But Roland was still concerned: "You must have felt there was *some* danger—you took Mindy."

"I took Mindy because I have some decency!" she said, hotly. "One day that child is going to grow up and realize what her parents are. If they haven't corrupted her by then, then God help her!"

Roland sighed to himself, still deep in thought. "So what's going to happen now—since you won't go to the police?"

"That's why I came here," she said, looking up at him.

"*Me*?" Roland laughed nervously. "What do you expect me to do?"

"Do whatever you want," she said in an offhand manner. "I'm not going back. I just needed someplace to leave Mindy—I'm leaving town."

"*What*? Where are you going?"

"I have a cousin in Boston. I've had enough."

Roland sighed again. "Well, I guess you're right…" And she *has* been through a lot, he thought to himself—and most of that because he had introduced her to Phelps. He couldn't help feeling somewhat responsible. "Look, Candice," he said in a new voice, "I'm sorry…if I had known how Phelps was—the *full* extent of it—…I never thought it would go this far."

But she only shook her head, as though it were too late for any of that now. He looked at her, trapped between ineffectual guilt and the urge to push everything to its natural conclusion—whatever that was—and get the entire thing over with. Whatever the case, there was something about this that was not right, and it spurred him towards the latter state of mind. "You *sure* Cindy is okay," he said again.

But Candice only laughed, shaking her head as she said, "If you had only seen half the things I seen…"

"Well, all right," he conceded, uneasily. And then: "You can sleep in my bed—we'll figure everything out in the morning."

She nodded and left him. But as he looked at her retreating form, a quiver of uneasiness more powerful than anything he had felt in years, went up his spine; and just then, it occurred to him that today was Halloween; and that the day, and the coming night, were set aside for the celebration of death and mischief.

* * *

MARENGA DIDN'T LOOK well as he sat in the back seat of the cab, but he was strangely at peace...maybe not peace yet, but at least he was contented with the moment, which was perhaps all that one could ask for. Thinking about Randolph again, he didn't know if anything had been accomplished; even now, what had been said between the men blurred into one long tirade, free of conclusions and prescriptions. They had talked for five hours in all, discussing the nature of the world, the 1960s, the nature of "the struggle," even the chances of the Knicks winning the title this year...But no matter what happened, at least he had talked to someone: let out the proverbial steam. He felt like a man again....

The cab stopped and Marenga paid the turbaned driver before getting out gingerly. He was exhausted, and the knowledge that he was going to sleep well filled him with simple joy. But just then, he looked up and noticed that there were four news vans in front of his house: all the major networks were there! Seeing him, the news crews rushed out to greet him, at first seeming like attackers. He unconsciously took a step back, but they were already upon him, yelling, "Have you heard!"

"...Heard what?" Marenga said, looking at them as though they might still attack him. It was then that several of them began talking at once, telling the story of Colina and the Thomases with the fits and spurts of a drunk vomiting up his guts. And then, they all shoved their microphones into his face, waiting eagerly for him to return the favor and vomit up his guts as well.

But Marenga only stared at them for a moment—stared *blankly*—while they trained their cameras on him and waited anxiously. He felt as though he were going to faint: not from the news, itself, but from the wave of revulsion that went over him. Whatever peace he had had, left him decidedly, so that he felt suddenly empty. "Let me just have a few moments to collect myself," he managed to say at last. They begrudgingly made room for him and he walked up to the house, still in a daze. But once he was free of them, he shuddered, remembering his evocation of the fetish spirits.

* * *

ROLAND HAD INTENDED to stay up for the rest of the night; in fact, something about the entire situation with Phelps and his wife was so unsettling, that he had been sure that he *couldn't* sleep. He had turned on the television and lain on the couch, watching the chaotic images surrounding Colina's murder of the Thomases. And there had been images of the growing mob in front of the police station where the Thomases had been killed….Nothing had seemed real anymore; as such, the violence on his TV screen hadn't really registered in his mind. It had been nothing but background noise, meaningless in the face of his inner anxieties.

But somehow, he did fall off to sleep; and just like the last time Candice came over, he opened his eyes to see her standing before him in the darkness. At first he thought that it was a dream—some recollection—because it seemed exactly the same as the last time. The only thing was that she wasn't totally naked this time: she had her underwear on. Also, the television was still on; and highlighted by those scenes of violence, Candice looked like a ghost. She bent over him and caressed his face. Her hand was warm and soft—almost soothing—but the thought of her next to him was suddenly revolting. She bent lower to kiss him and he pulled away quickly, sitting up. He was panting for air, seeming terrified as he stared at her. She frowned, looking at him confusedly; and against the backdrop of the chaotic images still showing on television, she looked like some mournful spirit. He had an impulse to turn on another light, so that she could again seem like a human being, but—

"Don't you find me attractive anymore?" she said, staring at him in confusion.

He hated that question. "…I just don't want to, Candice…" He didn't know what else to say.

"It's Dallas, isn't it?" she said suddenly.

"What?"

"It's because I let him…touch me."

"I don't care about that—"

"But you always wanted me before."

"Candice…"

"You don't think that I'm good enough for you, do you?" she said, hysterically.

"What are you talking about?"

"You just wanted something cheap and meaningless—"

"*What?*"

"You're like all men: a *user*!"

He had a sudden impulse to laugh; but seeing the tears in her eyes, he was unable to move a muscle. She ran off then, back into his bedroom. He stared at her in disbelief, wondering what the hell had happened to her. Where was the poised, confident woman he knew from the night of the banquet? What had Phelps done to her! She didn't even talk like a human being anymore, but like some cliché romance novel character….Still, he was guilty as well—and maybe he *had* used her: not with calculation, as wronged people liked to think in retrospect, but, perhaps worse, as a convenience. And yet, she had used him as well; and before she had bitten off more than she could chew, she had no doubt tried to use Phelps. Thus, there they all were, in a world of misogyny and misanthropy, where need and desire often countermanded common sense and left them wounded shells of themselves, with nothing to comfort them, but the self-righteous delusion that they had been wronged.

* * *

BY THE TIME Marenga arrived at the Harlem police precinct where the Thomases had been murdered, it was a little past five in the morning. He had been chauffeured over to Manhattan by the same aide that had picked him up from the airport. He had sat in the back numbly, while six news vans followed his car and the young aide talked about outrage and justice.

Botswana Glade was already on the scene, with about two hundred of the more diehard protesters. Things were clearly getting out of hand. The mob had congregated in front of the police precinct's entrance—which had been locked and barred with a steel partition. People were standing on top of cars, yelling a hundred different hateful things at once. Some were holding makeshift signs; some had baseball bats and machetes. In the meanwhile, police reinforcements could be seen congregating down the block, getting on their riot gear.

When Marenga's car stopped at the curb—followed by all the news vans—Marenga didn't really have any intention of venturing out. In fact, he had found himself wondering what he was even doing there. But the invisible hand of fate drew him out of the vehicle and onto the pavement; and as he did so, there was an almost horrific cheer from the mob. Or at least it seemed horrific to Marenga's ears. It was as though those cheers were eroding something inside of him, acting as a kind of acid on his soul. Botswana Glade came up to him then, patting him on the back. The man's eyes seemed to gleam with excitement that had escalated to the level of madness. Marenga instinctively wanted to flee, but he was suddenly surrounded, engulfed by the mob. Botswana Glade said something to him then, but with all the chanting and chaos, the words were lost. People were chanting Marenga's name now; and as he looked at their excited faces, where the self-destructive yearning for vengeance was so clearly visible, he realized that he was now, somehow the epicenter of their madness.

It was then that the police announced a warning over a loud speaker, to the effect that the protesters were having an illegal gathering and that this was their last chance to disperse. As expected, this was met with defiant screams. The uproar rose in the air like nothing Marenga had ever heard before. He again felt it eroding something in him, *changing* him. And at that moment, he sucked in his breath sharply, feeling the terrible pain return to his chest. It felt as though someone had just stabbed him in the heart. In fact, there weren't words to describe the pain, which left him screaming out and disoriented. And yet, within the screaming, agitated mob, his pain and screams—and *madness*—were easily overlooked.

And soon, there were pops in the air, as the police reinforcements gathered down the block released teargas canisters. Yet, even as the acrid gas burned Marenga's eyes and made him choke, the pain in his chest rose up to shield him from the goings-on of the world. He stood there stiffly, jostled by the mob as people began running for cover and fresh air. He was lost in the chaos, waiting for the pain to encompass him fully and end his life. But presently, he felt an arm on him, pulling him through the mob; and when he looked up, he saw the same young aide. All Marenga could do, was follow. In fact, he wondered how it was that he was still standing. A side of him had been waiting for death, not with horror, but with the expectation of the peace to come; and when the aide put him in the back seat of the car, Marenga was disappointed as he realized that the pain was subsiding somewhat, and that he would live a little longer.

Presently, the aide took the driver's seat and asked Marenga if he wanted to go home, but the man only shook his head, saying, "No, the media will be wanting a statement."

* * *

MAYOR RANDOLPH SAT in the semi-darkness of his office, staring blankly into the nothingness. While outside, the chaos, like a boulder tumbling down a mountain, began setting off chain reactions, Randolph sat there, trying to figure out what Marenga had done to him. All that he knew was that something was gestating within him, opening his mind to new possibilities. Things were clearer to him now. There was something out there—just as Marenga had said; something was coming, and he and Marenga—and heaven only knew how many others—were soul mates, whose destinies were to be defined by the upheaval.

Randolph didn't even try to fight these thoughts anymore. Recalling his weeks of filth and his fear of Jasper Kain, he unconsciously nodded to himself. While he no longer believed that Kain was some ruthless spirit, the truths of Kain's religion couldn't be denied. The madness had come *with* Kain (not *from* him)—the way that a seagull blown in from the sea was not a harbinger of a hurricane, but a victim of it. There was something else out there—something larger, from which none of them would be able to escape….

Strangely enough, he had been finding some measure of peace in the darkness, but now that a new day was at hand, everything seemed to be coming to an end. The sun was fighting its way through the Venetian blinds now, seeming to impinge upon everything. Horizontal lines of light were cutting across his face. A normal man would be squinting by now, but Randolph just stared ahead, oblivious. Beyond the Venetian blinds, there were the muffled sounds of traffic—and *life*. It was almost as if those blinds were a stage curtain; and that beyond them, the production company was busily getting everything ready for the show—

The door to the chamber opened suddenly; the entrant took several quick steps into the room before stopping abruptly—

"There you are! We've been looking *everywhere* for you—the guards thought you had left!"

As though just waking up, Randolph looked away from the window and turned towards the door. While he was doing so, he again noticed the hideous jack-o'-lantern on his desk. The snarling, fanged face was facing him; his eyes passed warily over it before coming to rest on the young aide.

"How long have you been here, sir!" Radix demanded.

"Radix?" he said, squinting at the man. "...Since last night—"

"You know about the Thomas thing? It's all over the news!"

Randolph grunted noncommittally.

"You *have* to know about it!" he said in disbelief. "A policeman killed an unarmed, innocent black kid and his *mother* last night—*in* the police station...you haven't heard?" he said again. "The cop went on a rampage, running over three other people...!"

But Randolph only chuckled to himself, going back to staring at the window as though the aide's revelation had been a trifle. This strange reaction unnerved Radix, so that he declared:

"It's a *major* crisis, sir! It's all over the news! We have to act quickly on this! We tried to reach you...! Everyone thinks you're hiding. Worse than that, not only is that bastard Marenga organizing a march, but McPrice is milking this for all it's worth. With the election just *days* away, you can't appear ineffectual on this...! And then, there's the debate tonight...!"

Randolph was still staring unseeingly at the window.

Radix stepped a little closer to the desk, his voice lowered as he asked: "You all right, sir?"

Randolph chuckled softly: "I *felt* it, you know," he said with a strange kind of pride, "—just like the last time."

Radix was utterly confused—a little scared, too. This incursion into the private realm had unnerved him. He retreated back to business, his voice cracking slightly: "We tried to reach you," he repeated. "Is your pager working...? Even your bodyguards didn't know where you were. [Randolph was still staring unseeingly; the aide's voice grew more unsteady and panicky.] You have to act quickly, sir!" And then, when all else had failed: "You're the Mayor of *New York City*!"

—Randolph chuckled a strange, sardonic laugh: it was horrible in the silence.

The aide stepped in a little closer to the desk, but cautiously, the way someone approached a strange dog. "You all right, sir?" he repeated, almost whispering it this time.

Randolph laughed again, but there didn't seem to be any mirth in it. "...Just tired." He shook his head then, again noticing the hideous jack-o'-lantern. Some well-meaning constituent had no doubt provided that monstrosity as a Halloween gift: people were always giving him useless things....There was still a barely perceptible smile on Randolph's face, but it didn't seem peaceful—nor was it sarcastic, or even affected. It seemed to be many things and nothing at the same time. Randolph sat there, with his strange, far-off smile; and then, from nowhere, it seemed, he looked away from the snarling face and up at the aide, saying: "You spend so much time trying to keep the monsters at bay—"

"Sir?"

"That's all I've been for the last four years: a dragon slayer, hired to keep the city safe from the monsters...Marenga was right—"

"Marenga!" Radix ejaculated, the way a true believer mentioned an infidel.

"You just get tired, that's all," Randolph went on; and at that, he went back to staring at the window.

"...Sir, I'm..." He was shaking.

The smile was still on Randolph's face: it looked like an etching left by a sharp knife in a mound of putty. It didn't seem to convey anything at all; if anything, it demonstrated a horrible emptiness within. He suddenly seemed like one of those hollow porcelain dolls, which at first glance was enchanting; but which, over time, showed itself to be soul-less, with that expression of vapid peace, which would never change.

"*Monsters*, Radix," he started desultorily, as if finishing off some dialogue that had been going on within himself. He turned from the window and faced the young aide: "You can't stop them—not in this place. Maybe it's better to let a couple through, so that people remember what monsters are: what *evil* is."

"...Sir?" He was really getting nervous. His mind shot to something, and he went to it desperately: "Can I get you a drink, perhaps?" He rushed over to the wet bar in the corner of the room. "...You've been up all night you say?" he squeaked as he poured out a drink.

"Monsters, Radix..."

"...Sir..." He was so unnerved that he gulped down the contents of the glass himself. The biting whiskey in his throat steeled his courage: "Sir!" he belted; the loudness of his voice took him aback, so that he made a conscious effort to lower his tone as he continued: "You have to get it together! We're in the midst of a *reelection* campaign!" He stepped up to the desk again, forgetting about the drink he was to bring: "Sir, your big debate with McPrice is *tonight:* this could be it for us—our *last* chance. And, on top of that, there's this Thomas murder and the public relations nightmare with the police department—not to mention the rally that Marenga is planning to protest it. He's planning to march right down here in a matter of *hours*! He'll be outside your window,"—he pointed to it with a trembling finger—"calling you a *coward*! We have to plan for all this. This is *D*-Day, sir...!"

But the urgency sounded feeble in the silence. Neither of them moved nor said a word for a good five seconds. At last, Randolph, who had gone back to staring at the window, sighed, saying, "Do what you must, Radix." At that, Radix, somehow managing to convince himself that things would be fine, nodded and rushed out. But the Mayor still sat there with the light cutting across his face, thinking about monsters and the upheaval to come.

* * *

ROLAND'S DREAM OPENED up like a sinkhole beneath him, and then he screamed out as he was tossed back into consciousness. It was again as if he were bringing all the horrors of his nightmare with him. The last time, there had been a pealing noise in the air; now, it was laughter: an entire *world* of it. He burst upright, but the morning sun was so brilliant that he almost immediately had to close his eyes. That millisecond, however, was enough for him to get his bearings. The television, he remembered, had been left on. He was lying on the couch: the television was on a console against the wall; and as the French doors were at an oblique angle to it, the glare was blinding. It was his girlfriend's show that was on. Some general morning perkiness was in progress, with his girlfriend's high-pitched adolescent giggles drowning out her co-host's pompous, coughing laughter.

Candice and Mindy! He remembered them suddenly. His dream had been about them—and Dallas and Cindy…He realized, with a feeling of frustration, that he couldn't recall exactly what the dream had been about. All that he was certain of was the lingering feeling that something horrible had happened. He shook his head, trying to figure everything out…That Candice and Mindy had come the night before seemed like a dream, itself. In fact, needing proof that it had actually happened, he got up and jogged over to the guest bedroom. He opened the door cautiously, grimacing slightly when he saw Mindy sleeping peacefully on the huge bed. The things Candice had said came back to him. *Shit*! Maybe something actually *had* happened to Cindy! Had that been what his dream was about—or were those simply his lingering doubts from last night? Trembling slightly, he closed the door softly and returned to the living room. He had to get in touch with Phelps to make sure that everything was all right. He flipped through his address book and was about to pick up the phone and call Phelps, when he looked over and saw that the door to the master bedroom was open. From where he was standing, he saw that the bed had been made, and that there was nobody there. He put down the receiver and walked over to the door, suddenly numb.

"Candice?" he called, but there was no answer. He went hopefully to the bathroom, but there was nobody there either. On his way back out, he noticed a note lying on the pillow. He snatched it up, then read it through twice. It said:

> *I left to get the early morning train to Boston. There was no need to wake you—you've done enough already.* [Her sarcasm made him queasy.] *Deal with the Mindy situation any way you wish. I've had it. Good luck, Roland. Tell Mindy goodbye for me. It always amazed me how something so pure and sweet could have come from something so polluted. Goodbye.*
>
> *Candice*

As he stood there with the note in his hands, a sensation of inner panic again seized him. It was the same sensation that he had felt last night, when he watched Candice retreating into the darkness. He was being entangled in something horrible—he was almost certain of it! Returning to the living room, he picked up the phone and dialed Phelps's number, but the line was busy. *Shit*! The feeling of being trapped picked up momentum within him, so that it quickly and inexplicably metamorphosed into some rampaging dread: a need to flee, like a criminal from the scene of a crime. He had always prided himself on his reason; but all of a sudden, he felt like a leaf in the wind: like a pawn of some dark, laughing force. He walked stiffly over to the French doors, needing desperately to clear his mind. On the television, Samantha and her co-host were laughing again. He ignored them....The view from the French doors always calmed him, and he needed that desperately at the moment. There was something enlivening about being 20 stories up, able to look out on vast sections of the city. As his view faced lower Manhattan, he could see the Empire State Building and the World Trade Center; and, off to his left, were the Manhattan and Brooklyn Bridges and, of course, Brooklyn. The view was magnificent! The sky was bright, making even the New York air seem inviting; and in a brisk motion, he opened the door and stepped out onto the balcony. It was the end of October and there was a definite chill in the air; but as he stood on the balcony, he found it refreshingly crisp.

Twenty stories below him, the cars moved fitfully along the streets. The muffled sounds of the city—honking horns and far-off police sirens—wafted up at him, sounding like whispers in the silence. The view usually enlivened him, but as he watched the people making their way down the sidewalks, they suddenly seemed like ants. It wasn't even the illusion of size that came with his great height—they just all seemed so locked away: so *insular*. The entire thing reminded him of being a child again: of visiting his grandmother on the bayou and looking down at the ants as they wound their way through the world in, as it had seemed to him, oblivious intentness. All of those people, rushing off to work...For some reason, he shuddered—or maybe it was only a cold breeze....He shook his head again: he just couldn't get over this sudden malaise—this *weird* feeling that something was very wrong—

And then, for some reason, he remembered the night of the banquet, and that strange story Candice had told him, about killing her uncle over sex! All at once, new, horrible possibilities flooded into his mind; and to free himself, he started pacing the balcony to burn off his nervous energy. In three strides, he was from one end to the other. He was like a lion pacing within a cage. The cage was everything around him—the entire city, in fact! And what was it about this place—about this *city*? It had always seemed like a great experiment that was still unfolding: like the ultimate test of human potential and frailties. Once, that had excited him; but lately—in stolen moments, between all his rushing about and success—it had begun to strike him as somewhat barbaric. Just last week, walking down Broadway, it had suddenly occurred to him that if one were to go for a kilometer in any direction, one would inevitably go from heaven to hell and back again: from luxury condominiums to slums decaying in the face of decades of neglect and abuse. Go for a kilometer in any direction, and one went from stories of triumph, to stories of inconsolable despair. But that seemed to be the trade-off in a place with so much possibility. It seemed that there could be no great highs unless there were abysmal lows. It was the way a good painter knew that it was the application of dark pigments that brought out the bright colors in a canvass—and vice versa. Maybe there were such highs in this city *only* because there were so many people willing to risk the depths. The high rollers could be found in the penthouses and slums alike. But more troublesomely, at least to Roland, the cautious and indolent were also tenanted in those places. There they all were: players in a game where the only tangible rule, seemed to be chance—

A cold breeze made him shudder—or maybe it was only a cold realization. Whatever the case, he suddenly felt timid before the world; and at that moment, he didn't care why: he just wanted to flee, as he had fled from his father and Candice's touch. Pulling in his lapels, he made a hasty retreat, back into the warmth and comfort of the condominium.

The television was still playing; and disillusioned by the increasing strangeness of his morning, he plopped himself down on the couch, staring unseeingly at the screen. It was probably a minute or so before he even became aware of what he was seeing. The news segment of the show had come on. The anchorwoman, Wendy Wu, an Asian American, was talking about how Thomas and his mother had been shot for nothing. A case of mistaken identity and the madness of one policeman had resulted in the deaths of six people. On the screen appeared images of the police chase the previous night and from the surveillance camera at the police precinct. Colina was shown gunning down Thomas and his mother, then his speeding car was shown darting down the street, hitting pedestrians and eventually flipping over, into a crowd. While those images played, Ms Wu talked about the unrest that had already been spawned by these events; and then, on the screen was a video recording of the hundreds of angry people who had congregated in front of the Harlem precinct house, yelling for justice and revenge. They were shown yelling their demands, then being driven off by tear gas.

All these scenes passed Roland in a blur. He watched them numbly, wondering, as he had wondered 20 years ago, what death could possibly mean to him—to *any* of them. And then Wu came back on again, talking about how minority leaders were calling for a shake-up at the Police Department; and then, Marenga appeared. It was a tape from the riot, right after the police dispersed the mob with tear gas. Marenga had set up an impromptu press conference down the block from the precinct, standing there like a waif in his rumpled suit. His eyes had still been red and teary; and he had been so weak that he had to lean against a parked car to support himself. It had been as though he were in shock; he had talked in a slow, rambling whisper that was haunting; and Roland, despite his urge to get away and block it all out, suddenly felt himself being drawn into the depths of the man's soul—

"Some say that I'm a rabble rouser," Marenga said, "but some things are so egregious that no man—no *person*—of conscience can stand idly by and do nothing. I call on all people of conscience to march on this city, demanding justice! There will be a rally today at City Hall!" he went on. "Some say that I am inciting violence, but the violence has always been there—it is only that we have been fooled by the illusion of peace and justice...."

Roland felt as though his head were going to explode! Everything was passing him by so quickly; and, along with the images from the television, he saw Cindy and Phelps and Candice. He felt as though he were being pulled apart in every direction. Wu was back on the screen again, talking about how the Mayor couldn't be found, and about the upcoming debate…and Randolph lagging badly in the polls; and then, McPrice was on the screen, her face florid as she declared that Randolph was missing in action and a coward—

And then Wu came back on again, then other commentators, then images of angry blacks and policemen… Roland didn't know how much more he could take! Somehow, it wasn't simply that he was watching a news report, but that they were invading his mind—his *soul*—and he was powerless against them. There, before him on the screen, was the omniscience of God: the ability to be everywhere at once, sweeping down into the souls of millions of people, this moment bringing felicity and joy, that moment bringing down inescapable wrath. And the next news item was coming on now. It was a report on Mayor Randolph's sex scandal. Roland couldn't take it anymore! All the churning madness was ripping him apart. Seeing the remote control on the coffee table, he practically leaped at it and switched off the television.

But then, when he was sitting on the floor, still panting as he stared at the blank screen that had before seemed like some supernatural gateway, he was lost again. He felt empty—*drained.* So many things on his mind…All at once, he was desperate for his girlfriend. It was the same feeling he had felt last night: that she was some aegis against all the madness; but suddenly wary of the world to which she, as a media personality, belonged, he found himself wondering if he even knew her. She belonged to that sensationalized world of gossip and scandal and violence and ruined lives. She was like some high priestess; and with uncertainties about Phelps and Cindy and Candice still raging in his mind, he was both terrified of the power of this priestess and desperate for it. It was Samantha's job to make light of it all—laugh it all away over a cup of coffee. However, the strange thing was that he had never really taken time to find out if she actually was like her on-screen persona. It had never seemed to matter before. Besides, part of him had probably always been a little terrified of knowing. Last night, he had been overcome by a feeling of love for her; now, he found himself wondering if theirs was even a relationship where love was applicable. It occurred to him that everything left unsaid was unreal; and maybe he had wanted that unreality once, but those times seemed at an end. It had been building over the weeks; but this strange new feeling in him, with increasingly troubling thoughts about his father's crimes and the Phelpses of the world—not to mention his growing *dread* of the world—had settled it. Everything seemed different. As for his girlfriend, maybe he had never wanted to know her before because he had never wanted to risk hope or fear or *rejection*. Their relationship, it suddenly seemed to him, had been like the city, itself. It had been everything and nothing, presenting both the possibility of self-fulfillment and self-destruction. And with this at least implicitly in mind, perhaps neither of them had wanted to gamble and find out which it was. All this time, they had been standing on a narrow perch, bordered on either side by a deep crevasse. For months, they had stood in that no-man's-land; now, it seemed inevitable that they gamble and choose one. As daunting as the prospect seemed, for the moment, the feeling of hope was preeminent in him: it was all that he had. He would tell Samantha that he loved her that evening. And then, he would sit down and talk with her. He wanted that more than anything at the moment—

"Uncle Roland?" an uncertain little voice called at his back.

Roland whirled around and stood up, seeing Mindy looking out confusedly from the doorway of the guest bedroom. She smiled when she saw him, seeming relieved; and seeing that relief and trust, something in Roland was reassured as well. The trust of children: how wondrous it was! He got up and went over to her; she came up to him as well, leaping up into his arms as she always did. She was still in her bunny pajamas, and the huge ears poked him in his eye. Still, he laughed along with her, suddenly relieved.

"Where's Candice?" she asked as he twirled her playfully in the air.

"Candice had to go away," Roland answered. And then: "Are you hungry?" Before she could even say anything, he was carrying her over to the kitchen, holding her above his head as if she were an eagle. She giggled with delight at the sensation. But after he placed her at his hip, so that he could open the refrigerator, they both saw, at once, that it was empty of everything save some ice cubes.

"Wow," said the little girl, "you must not eat a lot!" And as the little girl began to laugh, he found himself laughing along with her.

"How about we drop by a deli on the way back to your parents' house. We can't let you go home hungry, can we?"

"No!" said the little girl, raising her fist triumphantly at the declaration.

But it was while they were laughing, that a knock sounded at the door. Instantaneously, Roland stopped laughing. It wasn't necessarily uneasiness—just the strangeness of it. He put down Mindy and walked over to the door, wondering whom it could be. It occurred to him that it could be Phelps—just like the last time—but then he realized that if that were the case, the doorman would have called him. More likely than not, it was one of his neighbors, coming to announce some tenants' meeting. He was so sure of this, that he didn't bother to check before opening the door.

However, when he opened the door, instead of seeing one of his neighbors, he saw a middle-aged black man in an odd, mismatched outfit that was too big for him. The man had a clean-shaven head, and a bushy beard that nonetheless allowed Roland to see the man's huge grin.

"...Yes?" Roland said.

"Breakfast delivery, sir," the man said in a singsong voice, suddenly producing a huge picnic basket. Mindy came up then, looking at the man in awe. The aroma of freshly baked pastry filled the doorway, and the demands of Roland's belly left him confused for a moment, but he shook his head to free himself of it.

"Breakfast?" he inquired. "I think you must have the wrong apartment."

"You *are* Roland Micheaux, aren't you?"

"Yes, but I didn't order anything."

"You sure? You're quite a busy man—maybe you forgot."

And the strange thing was the gleam in the man's eyes. It suddenly occurred to Roland that the doorman wouldn't let a deliveryman upstairs without calling—especially one who looked like this man. "How'd you get up here?" he demanded.

"I took the elevator."

"Did you pass the doorman?"

"Of course," the man laughed in the same singsong voice. "How else would I be able to get up here?" Then, bypassing Roland, the man opened the picnic basket and bent down to Mindy, showing her the heaping pile of freshly baked pastry. And there were containers of eggs and bacon, and coffee and juice. The man was like some fairy tale character tempting a woodland child, and the little girl couldn't resist. She squealed out and grabbed a huge danish, sinking her teeth into it. It was so big that she couldn't open her mouth wide enough—

"Mindy!" Roland cried out in alarm; but at the man's urging, she grabbed the picnic basket—which must have weighed half her weight—and made haste to the couch, where she sat down to devour her breakfast. Roland watched it all in disbelief; when he looked back at the man, he was somewhat disconcerted by the pleased look on his face. "Well," Roland began, not quite knowing what to say, "what do I owe you?"

"What do you owe me?" the man laughed. "Now that's an interesting question."

"—Just let me get my wallet," Roland said, suddenly flustered. He turned and went into the room to get his wallet; but halfway into the room, he realized that the man had entered behind him, and was closing the door!

"I didn't say you could come in!" Roland said with rising alarm.

"There's no need to fear me, Micheaux," the man returned, still calm and carefree.

Something about the way the man had said that triggered something in Roland. "...Do I know you?"

But the man laughed with a strange twinkle in his eyes, saying: "Who can say? This is New York City—who knows who you pass on the street?"

Roland stared at him with a frown. "...Do I *know* you?" But as he said it, Roland's eyes widened and his jaw dropped. "*Oh my God!*" It was Jasper Kain!

* * *

THEY HAD BEGUN to arrive in front of City Hall by six o'clock in the morning: a mere handful of the more diehard elements. They had carried their banners, which decried the injustice of the Thomas murders and the ineptitude—if not collusion—of the

Mayor. They had even chanted their trademark, "No justice, no peace!" But as they were few in number, their voices had seemed feeble, if not comical, against the din of rushing traffic and the apathy of busy passersby. What had also made it comical was the fact that for this handful, there were a thousand policemen in full riot gear, and half a dozen huge police coordinating vans. Reporters and camera crews had also arrived on the scene, standing around like kids impatiently waiting for the matinee to start. Like children, there had been a perverse side to them, which hoped that the show, when finally viewed, would be as gruesome and spectacular as salaciously advertised....

By eight o'clock, however, that handful had grown considerably. At first, a steady stream had made that handful grow to a respectable 200 or so. Their chants, once feeble, had become genuinely raucous—if not fearsome. The policemen had seemed somewhat more ill at ease. They had been given orders to avoid all conflict—especially with the election near and so many people watching. The media, which had been warning of potential violence all that morning, had started darting around like a swarm of bees collecting nectar. By then, passersby had stopped and looked at the spectacle, or made a point to walk to the other block for safety's sake. The crowd, growing rapidly, had soon spilled out into the streets. Traffic, slowed to a crawl, had had to be diverted; cabbies had been screaming and banging their horns in frustration, adding a kind of insane symphony to the deafening chants for justice.

By nine in the morning, it was beyond anybody's expectations. There were at least five thousand people there now, and there weren't any signs of the tide being in abeyance. There were reports of local subway stations being packed with people coming to protest—on top of the usual rush hour traffic. There were at least half-hour delays on all trains; there were even reports of fights breaking out in the overcrowded trains and buses. Something was going to happen: everyone seemed to know it. Some came only for the show, and could care less about the Thomases. School kids—many of whom had already planned to be truant for Halloween mischief—showed up to watch; the unemployed and homeless gathered around, their life's frustration somehow encompassing the injustice of the Thomas murders. A good percentage of white people had also showed up: old-time socialist sects, idealistic college students and marginalized homosexual groups, who saw any action against "the system" as a step in the right direction. And there were some who came out in their Halloween costumes, dressed as Count Dracula and other such noted historical figures. Who knew why the hell they were there?

Whatever the case, the police, wary of direct confrontation, were placed between City Hall and the crowd. The field stations were frantically calling for backup. Maybe a good 10 or 15 thousand people would come when it was all said and done—maybe even *twice* that. As for that growing crowd, their chants were now not only deafening, but *maddening*. Drums had been brought out, adding a rhythmic urgency to the chants. People danced as they chanted. It would have seemed like a party, were it not for the fact that their voices were so angry—so *vitriolic*. Their hands were waving violently in the air as they stood in front of City Hall, packed in like sardines. Many of them were covered with sweat and half hoarse from screaming. They didn't seem so much as protesters, as a tribe of African bush warriors. One could imagine them with spears in hand; with the drumming and the chanting, it all seemed like some pagan ritual: a prelude not to words, but to *war*.

From the window of Randolph's office, one of his aides had shivered and turned away, saying, "God help us all when Marenga gets here and *really* stirs them up…!"

…But Randolph was alone now. There was to be a press conference in a matter of minutes, and his aides were giving him a few moments to clear his head. Everyone was worried about violence, but as Randolph stood at his office window and looked at the growing crowd, he didn't so much feel anxiety as a strange sense of excitement. Maybe there would be another riot, but he wasn't worried in the least. It was all out of his hands now. This feeling went against every political impulse that was left in him, and it was perhaps this realization that gave him the impetus to laugh—and to laugh with genuine mirth….

The door to his chamber opened after a soft knock and Radix appeared in the doorway. "It's time, sir."

Randolph nodded his head and followed the aide out. Other aides, and members of his cabinet, were in the hallway waiting for him. They all seemed agitated. As they began to walk along with him, they asked him questions about how he was feeling, and if he had memorized the statement: things that suddenly seemed like trifles to him. The men and women around him all seemed like gadflies now: he had an impulse to swat them away, which brought a slight smile to his face.

The press center was packed—and noisy. He still didn't know how he felt….When he entered, the room became as still and as quiet as a cemetery at midnight. The only noise seemed to be the shutters of cameras. He sighed imperceptibly, stepping up to the podium. The chanting from the crowd outside could be heard if one listened carefully….He saw no one; he stared down at the speech that his aides had written, his voice too soft and uninspired as he read:

The NYPD is the finest police department in this nation. Crime has been in a freefall over the past few years. Rapes and robberies are down; people are beginning to feel safe on the streets again. Still, the police department, like all bureaucracies, has always had its rogue element: has always had those whose only interest has been self-interest. There have always been those who have wanted to take justice into their own hands; and, perhaps worse, those who have wanted to take <u>*injustice*</u> *into their own hands. But in our eagerness to apprehend these rogue elements, we must not become guilty of their crimes. We must not usurp the very justice that we claim is our goal. Right now, the forces of chaos are amassing outside this very office, demanding that we rush ahead blindly. We must be deliberative and stoic, as all proceedings of justice must be. This is the way that we have survived as a nation so long: not through the mob instinct, but through the careful pursuit of justice. Lest anyone misunderstand me, let me be clear here: justice, when it finally comes, will be as harsh and uncompromising, as is necessary, but it will be justice.*

He stood there, staring at the paper, not quite sure what to do next. Then he remembered, in a strangely off-hand manner, that this was supposed to be a press conference. He looked up, seeing the torrent of raised hands and realizing that he was to be asked questions now.

"—Do you feel responsible for the Thomas shootings, Mr. Mayor?" yelled one reporter.

Randolph just stared: not necessarily at the reporter, but out, generally, into space. "*Responsibility*? Is that what all this is about?" But there was an earnestness to his voice that was close to bewilderment. He thought it over for a while, and then he sighed. "I guess so," he mused. "...Someone to explain why the monsters come: to explain away the fears. [His aides were suddenly whispering furiously behind him.] *Responsibility*?" he laughed out horribly, the way an old drunk laughed, oblivious of what was being said and who was listening—

But the next thing he knew, his aides were coaxing him away by the shoulders, while his press chief stepped to the forefront, saying: "The press conference is over."

* * *

ROLAND BACKED away in horror!

"Don't look so alarmed, Micheaux," Kain chuckled. "I'm not here to do you any harm—not yet, anyway," he laughed again.

"*How...?*" Roland whispered. He felt suddenly faint. He studied Kain's face closely: the beard had thrown him off; and without that ridiculous Afro, Kain looked totally different. The voice was the same, though. He should have realized it at once—

"I'm sane now!" Kain laughed. "Well, at least, I'm sane *enough*!" he chuckled. He took a step into the room and Roland instinctively retreated a step—

"How'd you get past the doorman?" Roland demanded again.

"Where there's a will, there's a way," Kain laughed. "Don't look so worried, Micheaux," Kain chuckled as he sat down beside Mindy—who had spooned out some of the bacon and eggs onto a Styrofoam plate and was wolfing that down as well. Kain took a donut from the basket then, still smiling as he said: "I'm only here to talk, Micheaux."

"—About what?" he said anxiously, still trying to recover his poise: to get over the fact that Jasper Kain was in his house!

"I came to tell you that I can do anything now," he said with a strange, euphoric voice. And then: "Sit down, Micheaux," he said in his usual calm tone, "—you're acting as though I'm a stranger. Sit down: we're all friends here. Why don't you have a croissant," he said, putting it on a Styrofoam plate and handing it over to Roland.

Roland took it cautiously, a side of him wondering if the man had poisoned it; then, feeling overburdened by the weight of it all, he sat down on the easy chair, which was at a right angle to Kain and Mindy. He felt a little uneasy about the little girl's proximity to Kain, but she was like a dog chewing its bone: perfectly heedless and carefree. In the meanwhile, Kain was watching him calmly, waiting patiently for him to get settled. When the man nodded in encouragement, Roland, despite himself, took a bite of the croissant.

"See, good, isn't it," Kain laughed.

—While at City Hall, the angry crowd continued to grow, Roland grunted noncommittally, still not quite able to believe what was happening.

"Here's a cup of coffee to wash it down," Kain added, fishing it out of the picnic basket. "It's just the way you like it: cream, no sugar." Roland stared in awe, wondering, as always, how Kain could possibly know that. The man stood up then, and handed the cup to Roland, who took it in a daze. "Here, young lady," Kain said to Mindy, handing her a container of orange juice. Roland watched it all, acutely aware that the world was mad....

"How did you get out?" Roland managed to say.

"Bah," Kain laughed, shaking his head, "you concern yourself with too many trivialities, Micheaux. The matter at hand is that I've come to tell you something wonderful."

"What?" he whispered, still holding the croissant timidly in one hand and the cup of coffee in the other.

"I have looked within myself and feel neither fear nor regret," Kain said with the strange enthusiasm that had unnerved Roland from the onset. "In fact, today is a great day, Micheaux. Remember that when they ask you about me."

Not this again! he thought to himself. Still, despite himself, he ventured: "Who's going to ask?"

"The media, of course. I'm sure you'll be a witness at my trial—"

"*What* trial?"

"All in due time," he laughed. "As for representing me at the trial," Kain nonchalantly went on, "I've learned from the last time I counted on you. I'm not presumptuous enough to believe that a man like you, who has achieved so much success, will deal with the likes of me. I'm sure your firm won't even let you do pro bono work anymore. You're too valuable—winning $200 million suits. Nah," he laughed strangely, "you're too much of a success now."

What the hell is that supposed to mean? Roland thought to himself. It was again as if the man *knew* him—had seen into his deepest dreams and fears. Roland frowned: had the man been studying him, *stalking* him, perhaps!

But there was now a look of serenity in Kain's eyes—even as the man looked over at Roland and the hatred and madness made themselves clear for the slightest moment—

"There is no such thing as evil, Micheaux," Kain said, out of nowhere, as if reading Roland's thoughts. "That's what I discovered last night, Micheaux," Kain continued. "That's what I've come to tell you. There's no good, and no evil: those are just arbitrary things created by society. All that there is, is action and reaction; and one day, when the universe exhausts itself, there'll be nothing left."

"Kain," Roland said from the depths of his exhaustion—mental and otherwise—"what does any of this have to do with me?"

"Because you're the center of it all."

Despite his best efforts, Roland couldn't help smiling.

"—How can you still doubt it?" Kain said in surprise. "Haven't you seen the news?"

"Kain…" Roland started, trying to ignore the sudden uneasiness that came at Kain's mention of the news, "why did you come here?"

"I came to tell you about last night."

"Then tell me already," he said impatiently.

"I did something that restored my faith in myself. Now, all the illusions have been washed away, and I have been made pure. I have infinite faith in myself now."

"Faith to do what?"

"Faith to bring sanity back to the world," he laughed. "Now that's a commendable plan of action, isn't it?"

"I suppose."

"Good, so I have your blessing then?" he said, cheekily.

"Do you really require my blessing, Kain?"

"Right you are, Micheaux!" he laughed. "Maybe 'blessing' is the wrong word. 'Acknowledgment' seems better."

"So, you want acknowledgment?"

"Of course, isn't that what the psychiatrist said at the trial: I was desperate for attention because my mother hated me and my father wouldn't play baseball with me....But everybody wants attention, don't they? Everyone wants to do something that nobody will ever forget. We all want that, don't we?"

"I suppose."

"But most of us are afraid of the consequences—afraid to act: to take the steps that are necessary."

"But you're not afraid?" he said, trying to gauge Kain's intentions.

"Not anymore."

"Not after last night?" he asked, pointedly.

"Right."

"And what *did* happen, Kain?" Roland said again.

"...I *killed* someone, Micheaux."

"*What*!"

"I took the final plunge...I just wanted to tell you—so that you'd know."

"...Get out," Roland whispered.

"What?"

"Get out...*please*. Just leave me alone, Kain....I never did anything to you," he said in a desperate voice that he barely recognized as his own. "Why are you doing this to me? I never did anything to you," he said again, looking as though he were going to cry. "Leave...*please*."

"...Very well," Kain said with a sigh, getting up. "I'll leave Micheaux, but that changes nothing. You won't be able to run forever."

"Just leave, *please*..."

Kain nodded, then he left. Roland didn't look up: he merely listened for the sound of the closing door. Only after the man was gone, did he look up. He needed it all to be over. He couldn't take it anymore—not Kain, not his worries about Phelps and the chaos of the world...He needed it all to be over.

"Mindy," he called to the little girl then.

"Yes, Uncle Roland," she said with a mouth full of food.

"Get your things together—it's time to go home."

* * *

NESTLED IN HIS Brooklyn brownstone, Marenga was getting dressed for the rally. A television was playing in the corner of his room, showing the entire Thomas controversy and his tirade on the injustice of it. There was also a scene from City Hall, showing the massive crowd that was gathering to hear his words. He looked at all the churning chaos and chuckled to himself, not with pride, but with an acute awareness of how ludicrous his place in it was.

There was something sinister growing in him, and he had no defense against it—he didn't *want* a defense against it, in fact: he only wanted to surrender. It was the urge to destroy that which one could not fix—which one could not make whole through one's machinations. It was, quite simply, the urge to be a man and hasten whatever evolutionary dead end was their collective destiny. Now, it was no longer even a matter of him hating them because of what they had done to him—but worse: what they had done to themselves. He had lost his faith in humanity—and irretrievably so. He had gone to see Randolph, hoping desperately that the man could point out some error in his reasoning. He had gone, in short, hoping to be *bested* by the man, but had instead found someone who had long been disarmed. The only thing left to him, was surrender.

Just then, there was a deferential knock on the door. Still staring at the television and buttoning up his shirt, Marenga bellowed: "Come!"

A youth about 22 years old, with dreads and a colorful dashiki, entered the room. He was technically an assistant, but Marenga considered him and the five or so others, who lurked around in support of "organizing the people," apprentices at best, and sycophants at worst. Marenga used to scour the ghettoes assiduously, trying to court such youths; but as of late, he had begun to think most of them hopelessly naïve. *Everything had changed*! Youths whom he had once praised for their diligence, he now found either unimaginative, in that they spent their time trying to recreate the mythical activism that had existed during the 1960s, or "slaves of the past," who did all that they could to assert their "African Heritage" when they, who had spent their entire lives in New York City, couldn't even conceptualize what such a term meant. The youth standing before him was of the latter sort. Marenga glanced at him with a certain amount of derision, then looked away.

"We're ready to leave for the rally, sir."

Marenga grunted equivocally and went back to staring at the television as he put on his tie.

The apprentice didn't know whether he had been dismissed or not; he decided to risk the latter and start a conversation. He ventured: "We're going to make history today, sir."

Marenga looked up at once, slight annoyance showing on his face. "No one *makes* History. It is not a contrivance." He went back to getting dressed.

Abashed, the sprig went to leave.

"Always know your terms, sir," Marenga called after him. The youth stopped and looked back sorrowfully; Marenga, perhaps just in a "mood," went on: "'History' is a serious term: use it wisely."

"Yes, sir." Bowing his head, the youth once again went to leave.

But Marenga, perhaps a little ashamed by the youth's obeisance, called him back. "Look, there are two notions of history: one as something that people write in books, and another as something that writes *people*. Both are, in their way, correct, but only one is not corrupted by human idiocy. Some say that History is made by the victors of wars, but that is foolishness. History—*real* History—can never be controlled, or even *steered*. History is pure violence. It is a *killer*! It does not care about right or wrong: about victor or vanquished. History is a *beast*! It is beyond the need for maintenance; it needs no nutrients to survive. It does not *plan*; it does not launch attacks. It has no conscience—no hesitation…*brutal*. Even to say that it destroys is foolishness when you think of it. To it, destruction *is* construction. It effaces with the same uncompromising violence as it gives birth. It is what gave us life and what will kill us. History, my friend, is *God*. You and I, Mayor Randolph, the *Thomases*, even: we're all irrelevant to it. Some pray to God for deliverance and hope; but God—*History*—is incapable of answering prayers. Those that History today showers with benevolence and felicity, it will tomorrow torture. [He chuckled to himself.] Now, that's some fucked up shit!" The youth laughed along and nodded, even though he had perhaps understood about two percent of what Marenga had just said.

Marenga was strangely cordial now as he tapped the dumbfounded youth on the shoulder and said: "We're all victims here. But I'm thinking about a time that must inevitably come. Martin Luther King talked about the Promised Land and Mountaintops and all kinds of wonderful things. I know: I was a young man listening to him—*hoping* with him. As a man, I realized that History was beyond hope. For a while, I became a revolutionary. I listened to Malcolm X and read Lenin, but even they were misled. Those who waited and hoped, saw a benevolent God; implicit in the message of the others was a vengeful, just God or *no* God. There *is* a God, but it does not care about hopes or justice. Yes, like King said, one day we will climb to that final Mountaintop and find peace. Like him, I cannot even begin to conceptualize how it will be done, but there will have to be a war: a *revolution*, in fact! [He chuckled sardonically at the word; the dumbfounded apprentice affected a simpering grin.] It will be a revolution like no other. I'm not talking about fighting against *people* or *regimes*, but *History*. I'm not here saying *love* God. I'm saying *hate* it! That's our enemy: *History*. I'm standing here, as powerless against it as everyone else. But there must inevitably come that time of *change*. And as nothing is as violent as History, we will have to fight it with equal violence and brutality. We will have to forget that we are human beings! We will have to *kill* History: to *murder* it, with neither conscience nor hesitation; without *ideology* or hopes of justice or *victory*. The revolution, my friend, will be against *our very existence*!" He stopped and narrowed his eyes at the quailing youth, then he lowered his voice to a whisper: "Find a way to do that *and* survive, and you will necessarily be in paradise, possessing the power of God, Himself!"

* * *

CHARLOTTE MCPRICE HAD been busy all that morning, coordinating a campaign that now seemed unstoppable. With Colina's rampage headlining the news—and social unrest breaking out on the streets—she had given a press conference earlier, repeating the charge she had been stating for months now: Randolph's incompetence was dangerous for the city—if not criminal. She now stood before the window of her private office, staring out on the Hudson River with a sense of quiet triumph. Through the open door at her back, her volunteers were busily answering phones and carrying out all the little tasks that would guarantee her ascension.

At that moment, Wisinski, her short, desiccated campaign manager, entered the doorway, but stopped short, just to stare at her. He did that often, always with a gleam of awe in his eyes. Her back was still to him; and something about the way the rays of the morning sun reflected off her shiny hair, gave the momentary illusion that she had a halo. *And maybe she is an angel,* he thought, only half-wistfully. His was the kind of objectification that the feminist streak in women wanted to castigate as demeaning, while the feminine streak craved and took pride from.

As for McPrice, beyond those who liked her for her policies, there was undeniably a segment whose primary draw to her was sexual—but not so much in terms of wanting to have sex with her (though there were many who did), but wanting to be clocked and protected by her. Hers was the sexuality of a god; and in just the same way that it was impossible—if not sinful—to think of Jesus Christ having sex, there was a similar disconnect about her. She was flesh, and yet seemed beyond the needs of flesh; and for some, this contradiction was a marker of perfection.

Still smiling, Wisinski stepped into the room, announcing: "We're up to a 45-point lead in the polls!" Barely looking away from the window, she nodded, a faint smile gracing her lips. Wisinski was just about to make a joke about Randolph self-destructing (and that stripper crying about how he had raped her), when the phone on her desk rang. Wisinski stopped in front of her desk, while McPrice walked over to the desk as well and answered the phone. Wisinski stood there smiling, thinking that he would tell his joke when she was finished, but he could tell by the cloud that came over her face, that her husband was on the other end of the line. McPrice wasn't saying anything: she just listened and stared blankly at her desk with a troubled expression. Wisinski could almost hear the husband spewing one of his post-binge excuses, replete with many blubbering exclamations of love and sorrow. Wisinski's face wrinkled then, and he felt something unmistakably dark coming over him. Maybe it was the violence of the city that possessed him, because he suddenly found himself thinking, in that presumptuous way of men, that he would do whatever it took to protect his god—and that the will of heaven could be furthered by thoughts and deeds that were unquestionably evil.

* * *

ROLAND TOOK A CAB to Brooklyn Heights. He could have driven his Benz—which he usually kept in a parking garage—but the thing about driving in New York City, was that the benefits and convenience of the vehicle were countermanded by the inconvenience of traffic and finding parking (and, of course, the reality of driving in New York City)....

These were the last moments of Roland Micheaux's life. But death was not like in the war movies, with the dying hero mumbling some courageous drivel into the ears of a heartbroken comrade. There was no way to die courageously; because the courageous, numbed by duty, never really saw death. To them, death was a triumph. They went into it with their eyes closed and their minds numb, like coma victims. Even fear, when it was strong enough, brought on this sudden blindness; so that to a certain extent, the fearful never truly saw death either. Death, when it was seen and felt, came slowly. Just like Kain had said, it greeted its victim cordially and whispered all of its secrets in its victim's ear. It made everything clear and plain; and in that final moment, when everything was seen, there was death—and only death.

—While at City Hall the outraged masses chanted their slogans, Roland sat in the back of the cab with Mindy. They were entering the block of Phelps's brownstone now. During the ride, the little girl had prattled on the whole time. Among other things, she had informed Roland about a girl from her preschool called Melissa, whom she thought selfish and rude. Apparently, Melissa wanted all the toys for herself; and for this reason, none of the other kids would play with her. In addition to this, Mindy also informed Roland of her acquisition of a new doll, which could soil its panties, burp and spit up the green, disgusting goop that was spooned down its gaping mouth. To Roland's alarm, she even produced the said abomination and made him kiss it!

But they were alighting from the cab now. Phelps's million-dollar brownstone was on one of those strange, pristine New York blocks, with oak trees and the veneer of suburbia; and five blocks over, there were slums. It was the same old thought: the city was everything and nothing....

Roland paid the Ukrainian cab driver and the latter rushed back to Manhattan, his mind aflutter with thoughts of that unsuspecting tourist whom he could bilk out of hundreds of dollars. Roland watched the cab disappear in a cloud of exhaust, then he looked up at the three-story brownstone, feeling uneasy again. Even Mindy seemed ill at ease.

Whatever the case, the block was just too quiet. He took Mindy in his arms again, then walked up the stairs to the entrance. Why was he feeling so strange...? There were cardboard Halloween decorations on the door, with glossy cartoon monsters, and a huge sign which read, "Trick or Treat." It all seemed eerie in the silence. His hand lingered over the doorbell before he pressed it. He laughed at himself nervously...He waited about 15 seconds, straining his ears to hear the hoped-for sound of approaching footsteps within—but there was nothing. He rang the bell again. *Shit*! Where the hell could they possibly be? Now what? He could bring Mindy home with him until her parents showed up...and call the police. Those were possibilities...But while his mind went over the irksome complications, he instinctively put his free hand on the doorknob and turned it. It was open! He stared unbelievingly. He called in a tentative voice: "Cindy? Dallas?" There was no answer. He felt really...*strange*; for some reason, his heart was beating violently in his chest—

Just then, he thought he heard something inside. He strained his ears to confirm it. "Cindy? Dallas?" Still, there was no answer. He was sure that he had heard *something* inside. He pushed open the door and stepped in, calling their names again. Part of him was praying that they would answer him, so that he could laugh out in relief and go home to fantasize about making love to his girlfriend. But something wasn't right here. Instinctively, he put the little girl down and told her to wait there. He crept deeper into the house: through the living room, with all of the Phelps's glittery trinkets and baubles, and through the luxurious dining room. He was coming upon the main bedroom. The door was slightly ajar. He stopped abruptly: someone was definitely crying within! *God*! He stood there indecisively, listening to the quiet sobs on the other side of the door. He fortified his courage—or whatever was needed to go on—then pushed open the door.

As the thick drapes had been drawn, the room was dark. The only illumination came from a light in the bathroom—which was directly across the room from where Roland was standing. The huge bed was placed perpendicular to Roland and the bathroom door. It was because of this placement, and the scant lighting, that Roland didn't immediately see Cindy. She was sitting on the floor, next to the bathroom door. She looked...*wretched*. It had been her sobs that he heard! He rushed over to her. Her hair was a mess; her nightgown was ripped, exposing her breasts—

"Cindy!" He touched her skin—she was cold! She was in shock! She was staring ahead...and, as though in slow motion, he followed her eyes. She was staring unseeingly at something on the floor; Roland looked down—a *body*! And *blood*! *It was Phelps*! Roland rushed over to see; but when he did, it was as if years of his life were pulled into some abyss. There was a gaping hole in Phelps's forehead! The man was lying there naked and bloody, his sightless eyes staring into space. *Shit*! *Phelps was dead*! There was no doubt about it. Roland recoiled as the realization hit him, scurrying back to Cindy. The sickly sweet smell of blood was nauseating. With the sight of Phelps, and the smell, he was sure that he was going to throw up. But just then, he chanced to look down, noticing the gun in Cindy's hand; and as the full realization of what had happened came to him, he shuddered. Maybe she had been sitting like that for hours—*since last night!*

He looked at her, his mouth gaping. "Cindy," he called, but she was still catatonic. "Cindy!" he yelled. "*Cindy*!" Finally, he shook her violently; and as though suddenly seeing him, she screamed out. It was the most bloodcurdling scream that he had ever heard! He scurried away, almost to the foot of the bed, by Phelps. Her eyes were wild—full of madness. To his horror, she was pointing the gun at him! *She fired*...! After the explosion, he sat frozen for a moment, trembling. Somehow, it had missed—actually going out of the bedroom window. For a moment, neither of them moved; there were no sounds. But then, footsteps could be heard coming down the hall. They turned their heads and looked towards the door. Hearing the shot, Mindy came running into the room, where she stopped, unsure. But seeing her daughter, Cindy started crying uncontrollably. There was something horrible in the woman's eyes now.

Roland, only then coming to his senses, realized that she was raising the gun again! Mindy had taken a couple of steps into the room, but stopped abruptly again. Cindy was aiming the gun at her daughter! Roland grabbed Mindy and darted for the exit. The thundering report from the gun came, hurtling past his ear. He didn't stop—he *couldn't* stop. Another report came…! All that he knew was running. The inside of the house passed him by in a flash. Outside, the neighbors, who had no doubt heard the scream—*if not the shots*—were staring. He darted past them as well. He was numb—*terrified*…thinking only of her coming to get him. Even when he got outside, he couldn't stop. He was running not only from Cindy, but everything he had ever fled. He was on automatic pilot, totally disconnected from what was passing before him. The little girl was crying at his shoulder—*screaming* in fact—but as he fled, he was only peripherally aware of her as well.

* * *

MARENGA AND HIS aides were driving to the rally in a rented limousine. They were going in style. About seven of them were sitting in the back, on two long seats that faced one another. Sitting across from Marenga was his second in command—Botswana Glade. Apparently, the latter had started up some bizarre Unitarian church in Harlem while Marenga was away. As they rode along, the man expounded a disquisition on why God was vengeful but just. He was holding a copy of the Koran in one hand and a copy of the Bible in the other. In conjunction to this, he wore a big golden cross around his neck and had a crescent moon pinned to his lapel. Rumor had it that in his younger days, he had been thrown out of the Nation of Islam for his weirdness; subsequent attempts to become a Baptist minister had been equally unsuccessful. Marenga watched the equine features of the man face askance; then, with equal dismay, he looked around at the other aides.

In addition to the dreadlocked, dashiki-clad youth, whose name was Clarence, there was a short, gaunt youth that they called "Bright Eyes." The latter's sight was so bad, that his thick glasses made him look like one of those "bug-eyed" aliens. Another aide, an ex-convict called "Bush Dog," was a huge, muscle-bound man with a scar over his left eye. He never smiled and rarely talked, which gave Marenga the creeps. Yet another one was brilliant, but had a nervous tic, and sometimes squealed out various expletives when excited. Marenga frowned at them all: what freak show was this! A side of him wanted to laugh—for they were all part of the cosmic farce; but another side of him, tired beyond reason, just wanted his eyes to close and his mind to cease its ramblings.

Marenga had run the entire gamut of emotions. As a child, growing up in segregated Kentucky, he had felt pity for the wretched around him; as a young man, coming to the city, he had looked upon those wretched people and been outraged. Now, as a middle-aged man, passing into old age, he looked upon the wretched around him and felt an inexplicable kind of contempt. All that was left was revenge. It was no longer a rampaging, seething impulse, but something that closely resembled peace. There was no need to plot and scheme on his part, because the cosmic farce was already in motion: all he had to do was bide his time and get ready to laugh—

But it was then that Marenga winced as the pain in his chest returned. A dizzy spell gripped him as well, so that he felt disoriented and nauseous. All at once, he realized that he was sweating profusely...*Just a little further*, he said to himself. He wanted to make sure that everything was in place, then he would gladly die....They were coming upon City Hall and the crowd. *Thousands* of people were chanting their hate-filled slogans; policemen were standing their distance, looking ominous. There were even vendors, selling hot dogs. Looking out on it all, Marenga was somehow reassured. He suddenly wanted to laugh again: giggle at the cosmic farce that had been had set in motion. It was all so senseless! They had come convinced that they wanted justice; they would listen to his tirade, leave angry...maybe riot—

But then, in a panic, he suddenly realized that that might be the extent of it—until the next black person was killed. For a moment he was stupefied by his oversight, realizing that this event alone might not be enough: that there was still more to do, more hatred to spread, more cattle to prod into stampeding. *Shit*, when would it end...!

It all rested on him. But what could he possibly do to ignite the flames of hatred and madness within them. Words weren't enough. With words alone, it would all die out in a week or so. After some patronizing remarks from "the powers that be," and the necessary passage of time, the blacks would lose their outrage; and the whites, who, like us all, were always eager to forget that which was troubling to them, would soon tire of this story; so that in a matter of time, it would all be forgotten. The fire that had brought them from their homes would be quenched; and now, as he looked out of the window, it occurred to him that he didn't even have faith that humanity would eventually destroy itself. To sane people, self-destruction was a fear; but as he looked out on that crowd, knowing what 30 years of ineffectuality had produced, he was suddenly terrified that it would *never* end: that God would laugh in his face one more time and keep the farce going forever, like a stale joke that everyone was compelled to laugh at.

The intensity of the crowd's chants grew as the limousine approached its epicenter. Having gotten word that Marenga was arriving in the limousine, the crowd began chanting his name. They had assembled to hear his words, but as he stared out on them, he wondered what there was to say that hadn't been said before…Oh *God*, he felt sick! It wouldn't be enough—nothing he had planned! It would just keep going on! He felt horribly weak all of a sudden; and in conjunction to this, parts of his body seemed to alternate between numbness and biting pain. He needed to lie down, but his aides were excitedly getting ready to disembark. The car was stopping now; the door was opening, and his aides were helping him out. People were cheering even more loudly now. *Oh, God, he felt horrible*! How was he even standing! People were patting him on the shoulder. He wanted to run from them, repulsed by their closeness, their smiles…their *numbers*! For a moment, he feared that they would kill him: lynch him like some escaped slave….It was over: the struggle…*everything*!….Oh, God, he felt *horrible*. He felt old and tired and *sick*! He wished that he were dead; and just then, the pain in his chest seemed to explode in every direction, encompassing his being. It was at that moment that he collapsed and the world went black.

They all watched Marenga collapse. A hush came over everything. It was Botswana Glade who yelled: "Get an ambulance!" A cascade of voices went through the crowd, with people asking what had happened. Someone somewhere—or maybe there were several people at once—yelled out that "they" had "gotten" Marenga. At this, a cry of outrage like nothing they had ever heard before, sounded in the air. Like a current through a wire, that cry coursed through the crowd. They had *killed* Marenga! This wasn't the time for shock or mourning: this was the time for outrage! Someone threw a bottle at a policeman; a police car got its windows smashed. Tear gas canisters were released. People seemed to be running in every direction at once. People were getting *trampled*! Screams of panic and agony joined the screams of outrage that had been in the air all that morning. There was madness everywhere. Luckily, someone had the presence of mind to pick up Marenga and toss him into the limousine. It was Bush Dog. Coming to their senses, the other aides filed in; and as the world went crazy around them, they drove away as quickly as they could without running anyone over.

* * *

OFFICERS FLANDERS AND Mucelli were driving down Atlantic Avenue in Brooklyn. Officer Sheldon Flanders, the older and fatter of the two, was proud of the fact that there had been a Flanders walking the beat in New York City since 1899. Of course, few policemen in New York walked beats anymore, and Officer Flanders certainly didn't do much walking at all. A 20-year veteran, his pendulous gut and multiple chins attested to a lifestyle of sitting in a police cruiser all day and making frequent stops at the local donut shops, delis and pizzerias. Something about him was redolent of a huge hog basking in the filth of its sty. It was either self-contentment or insouciance. He was fond of saying that after twenty years on "the force" he had seen everything and was surprised by nothing, which was to say that he was dense. At the moment, he had a young charge: a rookie, into whom he was to instill the essential mindset of the New York City Police Department. Unfortunately, young Officer Mucelli was not only in awe of his mentor, but eager to learn. Flanders was driving, his huge gut brushing against the steering wheel. Mucelli, after only a few weeks, was already well on his way to mastering that "I don't give a shit" expression and attitude of hardened veterans. He was sitting back in the seat, chewing a wad of gum with the slothful indifference of a cow chewing its cud. Every once in a while, he blew a gigantic bubble and nonchalantly looked out on the world with a kind of Clint Eastwood squint. Needless to say, he was in heaven.

"Pizza?" ventured Flanders.

"What? Pizza Hut? Sicilian? What?"

"C'*mon*, pizza's pizza," the veteran groaned.

"I mean you got your different varieties. You got your thin crust, your deep dish, your—"

"All right, already: we'll go to Geno's."

"What? *Again*? He don't cook the crust long enough."

"What do ya mean!"

"His crust is raw—"

"I been eating there 30 years! I been eating pizza before you were even sucking your mama's tits!"

"—All right, all right, we'll eat at Geno's. I'll just ask him to leave mine in a little longer."

Flanders watched him askance; he was about to unleash a string of expletives when the radio came on:

"This is a general alert! The rally in front of City Hall has escalated into a riot!"

"What the fuck did I tell you!" Flanders yelled, his face turning purple. "Didn't I tell you this was gonna happen!"

The report went on: "Marenga is reported to have collapsed before the riot ensued. An assassination attempt hasn't been ruled out! ["Oh shit!" cursed Mucelli.] Be advised that flare-ups are possible, given the emotional nature of the event. Do not, under any circumstances, have any unnecessary engagements with the minority community...!"

"That asshole, Marenga!" cursed Flanders. "A goddamn troublemaker. I bet he faked it!"

"You think so!" the rookie ejaculated, still awed by the veteran.

"Sure," he said with confidence, "I bet they faked *all* that shit, trying to prop themselves up. And that fucker Thomas wasn't even as innocent as they was saying. Them guys is always made out to be choirboys afterwards—no matter what the fuck they done. *Bullshit!* Marenga's to blame for all of it; and that bastard Randolph is gonna let him do whatever he wants—'cause he scared of losing the election. *Politics*!" he said in disgust. "As a cop, you're just a victim of it. They don't care about you. It's you against everyone!"

Mucelli nodded nervously, his eyes wide. But just then, the radio went off again:

"Attention, all cars in the vicinity of Brooklyn Heights and western Brooklyn, be on the look out for a young black male who just fled from a murder scene with a hostage. He was last seen running down Atlantic Avenue with a young white girl. It looks like a burglary that went wrong. He entered the house and shot the couple, taking their daughter as a hostage. The suspect is a young black male between six feet and six feet three inches tall, dressed in jeans and a leather jacket. His hostage is a white three-year-old girl, dressed in what was described as a pink Halloween costume. Officers are advised to exercise *extreme* caution: the suspect is assumed to be armed and dangerous!"

"*Shit*!" both men yelled in unison.

* * *

THE ONLY THING that made sense to Roland now, was running, and even that was more of an impulse than a thought. Driving that impulse was a suffuse kind of terror, which darkened the world and obscured everything around him. It was like a cold, fine mist. Instinct told him to flee from it; but as he was already in its midst, the only way to flee from it, was to run *through* it. There was madness in it: no matter where he went, it was covering him—becoming *one* with him. There was no escape—no relief. And every few moments, residual images of the scene he had just fled from, wafted back into his mind. Phelps's unseeing eyes…! Cindy's dementia…! People made way for him as he ran down the blocks: they could see the madness in his eyes….

Someone was crying! He had been hearing crying for a while now, but it had seemed so far away. All of a sudden, it seemed loud—*piercing*! He grabbed for his ears. He stopped. Mindy? Somehow, he had forgotten that he was carrying her. She was crying—practically *screaming*! He hugged her, only then coming to his senses. He instinctively patted Mindy softly on her back, telling her that everything would be all right. But the words didn't even register in his own mind. Looking around, he saw that he was on Atlantic Avenue: a wide, busy, four-laned boulevard, lined mostly with greasy-looking auto repair business; and on the second and third floors of these places, apartments of the low-rent variety. He had only gone about a kilometer and a half, and yet everything had changed—it was the same thought again! On his side of the street, there were tenements of the type he had left in Louisiana. In one of the tenements, an old woman watched him warily from a window; when he made eye contact with her, she quickly closed the blinds and disappeared. He felt suddenly weak. He must have run at least ten blocks—and those at full speed. Images of the scene again confronted him and he saw them with new horror and understanding. Phelps was *dead*! Cindy, in her dementia, had killed the man. *God*! His legs felt weak beneath him. The repercussions and implications of all that had happened almost made him collapse. He remembered how the neighbors had seen him running out of the house—and with *Mindy* in his arms for that matter! Somehow, he had become embroiled in…a *murder*! He leaned against a telephone pole, his eyes wide. His mouth was so desiccated that he couldn't swallow—he gave up even trying. His mind, so long in a daze, was alive with new terrors. First, he had to call the police and tell them what had happened. He was trembling. Mindy was still sobbing—he patted her back nervously….

He was looking around for a pay phone, when he saw a police cruiser driving down the block! What luck! He ran to the curb and started waving for the car to stop. There was a feeling of desperation in him that was so acute that he felt as though he were going to cry. He had to clear this up: it was all a misunderstanding. The police were stopping; the police were getting out—practically *running* out. He opened his mouth to explain—

"Put the girl *down*!" an old, fat cop yelled. Roland, in his preoccupation, didn't notice that the man had drawn his gun from his holster. Roland put Mindy down—though she began to cry again and clambered to be held. The cops were coming over; Roland again opened his mouth to explain—

"Keep your hands in the air!" yelled Officer Flanders.

Roland did as told: did it without thought, falling deeper and deeper into the abyss. And then Officer Flanders grabbed him and threw him against the police car. Roland was beyond shock!

"We got you, you bastard!" the old cop hissed, while his partner stood to the side with his gun drawn.

What the hell...! was all Roland could think as the cop put his baton to the back of his neck and began frisking him.

"You shot that couple and took their kid!"

"—*What*!" Roland managed to squeak.

"Thought you'd ransom the little girl off!"

"—No!...Wait...*What!* I can explain!" But he couldn't. He was shaking...stammering, just like any other scared nigger.

Not finding any weapon, the enraged cop hit him in the back with the baton. Roland didn't feel the first couple of blows—he had already been in shock. Presently, images of the Thomases flew through his mind. And then, there was the whole Rodney King thing, framed against a black, unreal backdrop. Some dark impetus made Roland whirl and jab his elbow forcefully into Flanders's jaw. The old cop grunted and took a step back, but he recovered quickly, letting his baton swing again. Roland ducked and it rattled against the top of the car. Undaunted, the old cop rushed Roland, heaving his bulk against the man. But Roland let his fists fly, hitting the man with a solid right to the temple. The man grunted and relented a little; and seeing his chance, Roland brought a vicious knee up into the man's mid section, then unleashed a well-timed left cross that caught the man in his jaw.

Now, the young cop, alarmed by the changing fortunes of the battle, raised his gun with a trembling hand, waiting for a clear shot. But no sooner did he think this, than he heard something explode. Everything stopped. The battle between his partner and the suspect ceased. Flanders, whose back was to him, froze, his spine arching. And then, for some reason that the young cop did not initially understand, his partner dropped heavily to he ground. But death in reality was not like death in the movies—where everything was quick and clean. The old cop began squealing out, flopping about like a fish tossed into a basket. His mouth was now frothing with a combination of saliva, mucus and blood. In fact, there was blood everywhere. And with the screams, it was all as sickening as it was maddening.

But at last, seemingly after minutes of watching the sick dance on the sidewalk, Roland and the young officer stared at the supine body with an acute sense in horror, because they realized that it was dead. At that moment, they looked up at one another with the same expression in their eyes. They stared for perhaps two or three seconds, neither of them able even to breathe. The young officer looked down at his gun, realizing, perhaps for the first time, that it had gone off—*and that he had killed his partner!* Roland was the first to come to his senses. He bolted. The young officer, seeing him run off, nervously fired his gun at him, but he was trembling so badly that his aim was way off. Once again, Roland ran without seeing and without thought. He felt like screaming: something was blaring so loudly in his ears that maybe he was. Or maybe the entire world was screaming—

Only running seemed right. He darted across the wide, busy boulevard—almost getting hit twice—then ran down the cross street. This mindless fleeing made him feel as though he were caught in a loop in time. He ran for about another block, and then darted into an alley, huddling behind a dumpster. He was beyond shock. How much time had passed, he had no idea. What had happened was still too vague and menacing for him to name it. All that he could grasp was the horror. Everything was spiraling wildly out of control and there seemed to be no way of stopping it—

There was someone over him! Looking up, he saw Mindy standing before him. She was crying as she stood there, still holding that repulsive little doll; but for a moment, he was possessed by an impulse to *kill* her: to rip her to shreds! He wanted to grab her and crush her head against the concrete, and, in so doing, take his revenge against the world…! But she was crying again; and as he saw the scared innocence in her eyes, the mad impulse receded, leaving only terror. *What had come over him*! He had only felt the impulse for an instant, but it had been there. He felt sick and drained. Seeing Mindy's tears, he grabbed her, hugging her tightly. Thankfully, the numbness soon came over him again.

* * *

—WHILE IN LOWER Manhattan, crowds were still being dispersed with tear gas and rubber bullets, Botswana Glade walked out of the hospital, looking drained. It was around noon, but it seemed much later. The sun seemed to be fleeing, darting towards the horizon as though it were terrified of shedding light on the world. The wind picked up, and the slight chill that had been there before, became more biting. Lapels were pulled closed; people bent their frames to the wind and squinted their eyes. This was Botswana Glade's posture when he and the other aides stepped out of hospital door and down the steps—

The reporters seemed to leap out of nowhere. He inadvertently took a step back, as though a band of muggers had just leapt out from behind a bush. He stood there, incredulous, while the 25 or so members of the media yelled questions at him.

—While on television, at that very moment, all the major stations had helicopter views of scenes from the riot, with people running in every direction and clouds of tear gas in the air—not to mention people looting businesses and firing guns at one another—Botswana Glade stood before the reporters, trying to make sense of what they were saying. At last, he took a deep breath, his voice faint and flat as he said:

"Marenga is in surgery now—the doctors think it was a heart attack—possibly a stroke as well." He went to leave—

"Do you feel any responsibility for the riot?" one of the reporters yelled. Botswana Glade stopped in his tracks, looking back with the same uncomprehending expression. The reporter went on: "So far, at least five people have been trampled to death; dozens of others have been taken to the hospital with various injuries. And there were reports of several stabbings and shootings, not to mention property damage and police officers—"

As though regaining consciousness, Botswana Glade reeled, his horse teeth becoming prominent as he lashed out: "You going to blame this on *us*! The only thing that this nation seems to understand is *violence!* This nation was *built* on barbarism: on the notion that the strong take it all, and that you *fight* for everything. There is no peace in this place: only submission to power....I'm almost sure they did something to Marenga—"

"What are you implying?" A reporter demanded.

Botswana Glade was fired up now: "I'm not *implying* anything! A black man—a man that this nation has always hated—has conveniently fallen just before he was about to make a crucial speech to a crowd of angry black people. What does that say to you!" At that, he walked off with his aides. But as he took his leave, it occurred to him, for the first time, that they *were* his aides—that it was all *his*.

* * *

REPORTS OF THE riot were everywhere—on every channel. All the chaos and madness was rising up again. It was a drug, and they were all addicted. And then:

We have a breaking story from an exclusive Brooklyn Heights neighborhood. A little girl has been kidnapped—and her parents shot…one killed. [There was a camera crew at the scene, showing the half a dozen police cars and vans in front of the house.] *The husband is confirmed dead, with multiple gunshot wounds to the head and chest. The wife was raped and shot in the head, and is now in critical condition at a local hospital. Neighbors heard screams and gunshots; when they came out to investigate, they saw the assailant running from the house with the couple's three-year-old daughter in his hands. The assailant is described as a black male about 6' to 6'3" tall, with jeans and a leather jacket. The little girl was white with blond hair, wearing a pink bunny…* [Someone handed her something; she looked a little confused.]

And we have yet another update. A few blocks away from the house, the same assailant shot and killed a police officer. [She paused for a moment after reading this, as though unable to believe it.] *Details are sketchy, but apparently two police officers, who had just heard an advisory on the shooting of the couple, came upon the assailant as he was fleeing with the little girl. After confronting him, a scuffle ensued, and somehow the assailant got one officer's gun and shot the officer's partner. That partner has been…confirmed dead.* [Her voice was a little shaky.] *The police are advising people in that area to lock their windows and doors and avoid all confrontation with this man. If spotted, the police should be contacted as soon as possible, as he is obviously armed and dangerous….*

* * *

"WHY DID THIS HAVE to happen *now* of all times!" yelled Mayor Randolph's chief aide, Abraham Levin. About a dozen voices were now raised in panicky conversation. Randolph and his entire cabinet were now in a fortified sub-basement of City Hall: the site that had been set up in the event of a terrorist bombing. They were sitting around a huge conference table—with the exception of Levin, who was pacing at Randolph's right. Also to the right, there was a huge television, on which the events of the outside world were being shown. The volume had been turned off, but that only made the scenes more unreal.

"First the Thomas thing," Levin began again, "and now a *riot*! What do you suggest we do about this, Alex?" Levin asked as he stood above Randolph, panting. As always, Levin reminded Randolph of a vegetable; today, it was a squash. The man always looked unkempt and suspect: his beard always looked shaggy; his eyes always looked beady behind his thick glasses. Moreover, Levin was one of those balding white men who insisted on combing his few remaining hairs over his scalp. Levin's were slicked down with grease that made his entire scalp seem to be oozing. Randolph unconsciously grimaced. Levin was still panting—and now sweating. Everything about him was insalubrious. Levin would never have made a good political candidate, Randolph thought: no presentation.

"*—And we have that debate tonight*!" Levin suddenly realized, to which all the other aides and cabinet members shuffled in their seats and looked nervously at Randolph.

Still, despite everything, Randolph's only reaction was an equivocal groan as he shrugged his shoulders.

"*Come on, Alex*!" Levin raged at Randolph's reaction. "Get it together, man!"

All the other aides and cabinet members were looking on in the uneasy silence; but totally indifferent to Levin's tirade, Randolph looked past the man—towards the television, where hundreds of people were having a standoff with a column of policemen in riot gear. The mob was throwing bottles, and whatever else they could find, at the police. It reminded Randolph of Palestinian boys throwing stones at Israeli troops. Somehow, it struck him as a joke, so that when he looked back at Levin, his face wore a strange smile.

"What the hell has happened to you, Alex!" Levin said, taking a step closer to the table, his face turning an oily mauve. "Get it together, man! This is *politics*, not the goddamn rosary society! We get shit done. [Randolph stared at the man with blank eyes.] That's why people put us here. We get shit done that they don't want to do for themselves or are too lazy or stupid to do for themselves! That's all politics is! We keep people content—by making them think their problems are taken care of—"

Randolph's eyes lit up: "Maybe they should do for themselves for a while."

Levin retreated a step, looking as though Randolph had just declared himself the Antichrist. "What the hell are you talking about…!" He was so enraged, that he shook. But then he sighed and took a deep breath to calm himself. "Look, the pressure's got us all a little crazy. After you're reelected, you'll go on a vacation and get everything cleared up. You'll see: it'll be like the old days. And I know you don't want to give all this up," he said, flashing a toothy grin that showed his crooked, coffee-stained teeth and swollen, purple gums. It was supposed to be ingratiating, but it was repulsive. He was now talking in that annoying, singsong voice that people used with their disagreeable toddlers, now declaring: "You get to meet foreign dignitaries and movie stars…you're the Mayor of New York City for God's sake! Wake up, man! There are people who would sell their *souls* to be where you are—"

Randolph chuckled then; on the screen, there were now scenes of people breaking the windows of a department store and rushing inside—

Levin's smile evaporated. He seemed uncertain for the first time. "Look," he said in a more anxious tone, stepping in front of the television so that Randolph would acknowledge him, "just rest, okay. Your big debate is tonight…*God*!" he whispered as the immediacy of it confronted him. "Look, just clear your head for a couple of hours—go in the back and get some sleep or something. We'll deal with the spin on the riot. Later on, when your head's clear, we'll come back and coach you for the debate…Or maybe," he started with a hopeful voice, "with the riot, we can cancel the debate."

But at that, Randolph spoke up. His expression was inscrutable as he shook his head and said: "No, there's no reason to put it off."

Levin looked at him oddly, nodded his head with a certain amount of uncertainty, then went over to talk to Radix.

* * *

AN HOUR HAD PASSED with Roland crouched behind the dumpster in that alleyway, trying to think of what to do next—and retrace how he had reached that place to begin with. It was amazing how quickly time passed when every road led to death….What remained of his reason, had told him to make some plan of action; but as he hid there, his jumbled, panicky thoughts had only added fuel to his fears. In fact, he had started walking again, just so that he could have some respite from those thoughts….

There was a side of him that instinctively wanted to go to the police. Logic told him to do it. But every time he tried to consider it, his mind went to the dead cop. Roland was convinced that the man would have beaten him to death if given the chance. And then there were the Thomases. The kid had been killed when he turned himself in—*the police had even shot the kid's goddamn mother*! And they had been innocent, too! Suddenly, it was as though things had gone so far that nothing could ever be made right again. A strange feeling of hopelessness was growing within him, mocking his every precaution—his every *thought*.

Now, as Roland walked along, the world didn't even seem real to him anymore; and just like 20 years ago, when the pale morning sun had been an augur of all that the day would bring, he now saw, in the cold, overcast day and shedding fall trees, not only an augur of future events but a reflection of his soul. He went anywhere he could hide: down alleyways and up the relatively deserted industrial district along the East River. It was getting colder; but even though he had taken off his coat and balled Mindy up in it in order to hide her, he couldn't really feel it. The little girl lay in his arms quietly, possessed by the same shock as himself. Twice, her doll had fallen from her fingers as she stared off in a daze. He had had to go back and pick it up for her….As for himself, he didn't even know what he was thinking. All that he knew—like Andropov and Randolph had known before him—was that he had to hide. Everyone seemed like a potential attacker. The paranoia was deep in his veins: everything was suspect—

His mind drifted, for the hundredth time, to thoughts of to Phelps's corpse and Cindy's dementia. Explanations eluded him—

reason eluded him. He felt as if he were some monster concocted in a madman's laboratory. The villagers were after him now—*tormenting* him....But he patted Mindy's soft, little body then; and at least for the moment, it calmed him. How unreal it all was: he was an accused murderer on the loose, and yet this little girl was in his arms, somehow keeping him within *sight* of his sanity. Feeling her little body was a reminder that things *could*, in time, be all right. It was proof that he was still a human being: that if she could find comfort in his touch and in his words, then he wasn't yet a beast—a *nigger*. He needed her desperately at the moment, and there was something unspeakably shameful about that....

There was a pay phone ahead; seeing it, his mind suddenly went to his girlfriend. He quickly picked up the receiver; and after he put in some coins from his pocket, he called Samantha's cellular phone number.

"Sammy?"

"Roland!"—she seemed relieved—"I was trying to reach you. Is your cell phone working? I thought you were caught up in the riot! You want to get together later?"

"Sammy...where are you?"

"I'm still at the studio." She sensed something in his voice. "Roland?" she said, suddenly uncertain.

"Sammy..." But he didn't know how to begin. Everything seemed to want to burst from him at once. He almost cried in the face of it all; he bit his lower lip, trying to hold the tide back. "Sammy," he blurted out, "something's happened."

"Roland?" It didn't sound like him at all—it sounded pathetic.

"*God*," he whispered. He didn't know where to begin. And then: "I'm sure it's been on the news—"

"What? The *riot*?" She lowered her voice. "Were you in *that*?"

"What riot...? No...there was a murder—"

"Rol..." she seemed to run out of breath; she took a deep breath, and then: "What is it Roland? You're scaring me. Tell me what happened!"

"*God*," he whispered again. "I'm sure it's been on the news: a couple in Brooklyn Heights—"

"*What!*...How were *you* involved?"

"The police think I did it. [She gasped!] They're *after* me. They think I *did* it!" he repeated.

"Turn yourself in!" she said quickly. "*Explain* everything...."

"They want to *kill* me!" he pleaded, his voice sounding pathetic again.

"Roland..." but then her voice trailed off, as though the full extent of it were just reaching her. "You have to give yourself up—they won't hurt you if you're innocent...."

He listened to her voice, desperate to believe. But just then, while she continued talking, not only did he remember the Thomases: he had an image of himself in handcuffs. He saw his mug shot all over the news—*just like his father*! He saw himself being led away in manacles, past the media—joining the nightly parade of jailed niggers on television! That was worse than death: worse than what they had done to the Thomases! Presently, he thought about the people at work seeing it. His innocence was irrelevant: it was their *seeing* it...and he would never get a major case again—

"No," he breathed into the phone. (She had been talking at the time.)

"...What?"

"No," he repeated. "...I can't." Again, he couldn't explain it all to her: there was just too much. "I want to clear this up...but without...*handcuffs*." That was the closest he could come to explaining it to her. "I want them to know that it was all a mistake...and then, I'll turn myself in."

There was silence on the other end, as though she were thinking something over. At last, she said: "Do you really have that couple's little girl?"

"*Yes*!" he said in exasperation. "...She's here with me, but it's all a misunderstanding. I didn't *kidnap* her...I didn't *kill* anyone...It's so...*silly*." He couldn't think of a stronger word, and this was suddenly frustrating to him.

There was another long silence. "What about the police officer you shot?"

"*What*! I didn't *shoot* anybody!" he squealed.

"Where are you now?" she demanded.

He looked around, seeing the 59th Street Bridge about two kilometers away. I'm in Queens—by the 59th Street Bridge.

She was still thinking. "Look, we have a sound stage in the city, on 47th Street—you met me there once, remember?"

"Yes, but…"—he grew suddenly timid—"people will *see* me—"

"No one will see you!" she snapped, her voice suddenly on edge. "It's small—rarely used. I can leave the door open and get the guard to take a break."

Silence: he couldn't think straight.

"Look," she went on, "I can get your side of the story on the air…and then you can turn yourself in like you said."

He thought it over for a while. "Yea," he said, suddenly brightening. "Yea, that's all I wanted—just to explain."

"Then I'll see you," she said, her voice all business. "I'll get everything ready." She went to hang up—

"Sammy," he said before she put down.

"…Yes?"

"I love you….[There was silence on the other end; he went on quickly.] I was going to tell you this morning…I know it's a weird thing to say—with all that's going on…I wanted to tell you this morning, like I said….I want us to talk, Sammy: to *know* one another…there's so much—"

"Just come over," she said, curtly. "I'll get everything ready."

After she put down the phone—that is, while he stood there, listening to the dial tone—he didn't want to admit it to himself, but there had been a horrible coldness to her voice. In the face of everything that had just passed, maybe he *couldn't* admit it.

* * *

THE CITY WASN'T yet on fire, but it seethed; and in that wild churning, there was the possibility of combustion. Botswana Glade had gotten about five blocks away from the hospital before making the driver turn around; besides, with the riot, traffic wasn't going anywhere. Many of the reporters had stayed at the hospital, waiting restlessly for news on the cause of Marenga's collapse. Reporters hated waiting, but they hoped that their waiting would be worthwhile. Many of them would have to make live reports for the five and six o'clock news broadcasts, and they hoped that they would have something new to say. Still, they knew all the tricks. News didn't have to be *new*—it didn't even have to be *news* for that matter—

only newly packaged. It was like adding seasoning to meat that was going rancid. If all else failed, one could always make hot dogs. Whatever the case, the atmosphere among the reporter corps, as they milled about their microwave vans, was upbeat. It once again became orgiastic when Botswana Glade's car pulled up. They were like a pack of dogs that ran to their master upon his return from a long journey. They jumped about him, seeming desperate to put their paws on his chest and lick his face.

Botswana Glade looked resplendent as he stood on the curb, surrounded by his aides. His bony chest was puffed out as he heroically looked from side to side, ignoring the reporters' questions. Now, *this* was news! Fifteen reporters had their microphones shoved into his face; ten cameramen clambered for the best positions, and just as many sound crews maneuvered huge microphones above his head. Finally, at the height of the tension, Botswana Glade's voice suddenly boomed:

"A war has begun, and there is no turning back! This is obvious from what is going on in the streets, but it is in the air as well—in our *souls*. A vigil is going to be held on this very spot"—and he stamped the pavement with his size 14 shoes—"until Marenga recovers! And you had all better *pray* that he does. We can no longer sit back as this country kills our prophets and leaders. My supporters and I are here so that none of this will be forgotten: not Thomas and his dear mother—not any of the people whom that insane cop ran over—and not *Marenga*!

"We will not be coaxed into forgetfulness about what has happened here today....And it's funny how a story about a murderous black man breaking into a white couple's home, has emerged just when people were about to see this nation for what it is—"

"What are you saying?" demanded a reporter.

"I am very clear in what I am saying," Botswana Glade continued, annoyed by the interruption. "I am declaring war against this country!"

"How do you respond to those who say you are only fanning the flames of racial conflict for your own ends?"

Botswana Glade chuckled through a scowl, and then: "I didn't start this fire!" he hissed. "This fire has been raging for *centuries*. [He laughed, as if some joke had just occurred to him.] If I fan it towards your house, it is only because I am tired of seeing my own community being burned. You alone have the means of putting out this fire. You seemed reluctant to do so when I was the only one being burned. Maybe you will be more willing to act when your own house is ablaze!"

* * *

ROLAND HAD RUSHED across the 59th Street Bridge; with the cold wind blowing off the East River, his body had been as numb as his mind. Once again, he had been fleeing desperately to Samantha, but what was left to him…? The view of the Manhattan skyline, at most times spectacular, had been like a hurried charcoal sketch against an already darkening sky. That was what he had always hated about the coming of winter: the creeping death of light—and *energy*. To him, the coming of winter had always been like a coffin's lid slowly closing about him. And as he walked along, he had kept seeing himself lying bound and motionless in total darkness, suffocating…! And the temperature had dropped precipitously in the last few hours. The icy wind howling past his ears had at times threatened to push him over the banister of the bridge's walkway, and into the churning waters of the East River. Once, for just an instant, he had found himself wondering if that would be so bad….

As he walked, ghost images of murder and madness had kept leaping out at him; and as his pace was brisk, it had been as if he were running from those ghosts. He had held Mindy close to his chest, trying to keep her warm as the biting wind dug into him. A side of him had just wanted to wander about—to *flee*, in fact; but as he knew that he couldn't keep the little girl out in this weather much longer, her needs had given drive and purpose to his steps. As for Mindy, she had been in her own daze, seeming content as long as he held her. She had still grasped her little doll in her hand….Meanwhile, Roland had gone on hastily, losing himself in the act of putting one foot in front of the other. Once, a man had passed him on the bridge; Roland had stopped, his mouth gaping as he stared back. He had been sure that it was Phelps! But then, with a shudder, he had shaken his head at all the things that haunted him, and continued on his way….

When he reached Manhattan, he sensed immediately that something was very wrong. With all the people now around him, he was definitely more on-edge. He knew nothing about the riot—besides Samantha's vague exclamations—but he *sensed* that something huge and horrible had happened: something greater than even himself. There were police officers everywhere! At first, he couldn't help thinking that the entire world had been mobilized to bring him down, but it was clear even to him that they were after something else. The people moved with a nervousness that was extreme even for New Yorkers. As for traffic, it was all hopelessly snarled. Drivers were cursing and honking their horns....There was a horrible kind of violence in the air, marked not so much by what people were doing to one another, but by what they were forced to carry inside of themselves. Life was the process of carrying one's burdens; and living in a complex, densely packed society meant not only carrying one's own burdens, but protecting oneself from the burdens of others; and on this day of random violence and madness, Roland sensed in their gaits, the exhaustion that came before one bucked under the weight. Still, like so many of his thoughts—especially on this day—it existed on a level that was so vague that it was more like a feeling than a realization. These were the people who were going to bring him down—who were even now taking his life apart—and yet, there was something pitiful about them as, in their desperation to escape the burden that the day's violence had placed on them, they rushed to find safety in their homes. Indeed, it was in this flight to safety that there was the worst kind of violence. The violence that brought down societies, was not so much evident in those willing to rush out and act on it, but in those who retreated to their places of safety and comfort before turning to look at the spectacle; because through this subsequent, passive openness to the images and realities of violence, they allowed it bypass societal barriers and seep into their souls.

As Roland looked around at the anxious crowds, it was as though the city were an intricate music box, with millions of dancing figurines. The music that they danced to was a combination of their fears and hopes, and honking horns, and shouting voices and the incomprehensible droning that always seemed to be in the background. Someday, the music would stop, and all the figurines would be frozen in place; and there would be a horrible stillness while God decided whether to crank up the box again or close the lid over all of their heads....

For some reason, he was thinking about his grandmother and the summers that he used to spend on the bayou. No, he knew *exactly* why he was thinking about her: she had been a woman of strength, into whose care he had fled in desperation—just like Samantha. The old woman, with her wizened skin and missing teeth, had been his respite from the world. She had lived in some darkened corner of the Louisiana swamp, like some voodoo queen; and he had fled into her power every summer, desperate for the protection of her magic. She hadn't even seemed like a woman at all—like a *person*—but like a protective spirit, there just for him. He remembered how she used to wander out into the swamp at night by herself, without fear of snakes and crocodiles, and all the other things that had terrified his childish sensibilities. In fact, she had been beyond concerns, sitting on that jaded rocking chair on her porch, telling him, in her mysterious ways, about the nature of the world. As Roland walked, he could almost hear her pigs squealing in the background and feel the warmth of the Louisiana sun on his skin; all around him, he saw oak and mangrove trees, with their lavish, fur-like covering of Spanish moss....What was strange, too, was that she had had an ancient music box and that he used to spend many hours watching the figurines inside dance....

The policemen—primarily traffic cops—were at many of the intersections, diverting traffic from downtown (which had received the brunt of the damage from the riot). Roland kept his head low and held Mindy tighter, not knowing whether that was for her or for him. But rationalizations were of no use to him anymore. His girlfriend was off in the distance: his only hope. She was once again that high priestess, conferring grace and delivering him from his sorrows. He would get all of this craziness cleared up, and then he would talk to his woman about love and the future. A fairy tale world was taking shape in his mind now; an entire kingdom rose up before him, with a beautiful princess and a courageous prince. There were hardships in the way, but the conclusion was clear: was preordained by heaven and the rules of fairy tales.

And as he walked along, his yearning for Samantha grew exponentially, so that it became a kind of madness within itself. All that he wanted—all that he could *think* about—was grasping her body close to his. He was almost running now. Some phantom energy fed his muscles and he found himself jogging down the streets....

The studio was a huge, nondescript building in the middle of one of those strangely peaceful side streets. Now that he was finally here, he lost his drive. He stood outside for a moment, looking up and down the block uneasily. There were hoards of people at the intersections, but none down the block. He looked up at the building again. It was a single coat of dark green paint—even the windows had been painted over. He just felt uneasy—*unsure*. It occurred to him that he still had his wallet—and that he could flee. All at once, getting to Samantha seemed wrought with too many perils—even for a courageous prince such as himself. He could go to the ATM, get some money and flee down to Louisiana—or wherever. His grandmother was dead now, as was his mother; still, there had to be places of ease and freedom out there, into which he could flee. Only flight seemed to make sense now. Yes, there were thoughts—*fantasies*, in fact—of rectifying it all; Samantha still shimmered in his imagination as the high priestess, but the events of the day had turned him into a coward. Rectifying it all counted too much on the beneficence others; and suddenly mistrustful of the promises and intentions of the world, he didn't know if he could go through with it.

But in the end, the fantasy of Samantha was the only thing that he had. In a contradictory sense, the fantasy was the only *concrete* thing that he had. The realization that she was waiting inside of the building, bridged the gap between fact and fantasy—or just clouded it to such an extent, that all he could do was surrender. Still, looking at the building, and realizing that he would have to leave the streets—where at least there was openness and the illusion of freedom—he had recollections of how he had crept down the corridors of Phelps's house. And there would be other people there—not just Samantha. The feeling of wariness persisted, even while he opened the huge door and saw that the guard post was unoccupied—just as she had promised. And the place was warm: this at least was inviting. At the little desk in the corner, where the guard was supposed to be, a note was written out to him in huge block letters. It read: "ROLAND, WALK UP TO THE 2ND FLOOR." He stared at it for a moment; even Mindy, as he held her, stared at it—even though she couldn't read. A weird feeling of déjà vu coursed through him. The building seemed too quiet as well: just like Phelps's. The impulse to run again seized him, but it was countermanded by the palliating image of his girlfriend—and the realization that he was spent. He needed this to end. He needed to rest and put this all behind him; and now, the fantasy of settling everything once again swelled up in his mind, so that there again seemed to be no choice. *I've come this far*! he chastised himself. Nevertheless, a side of him was numb as he walked up the dark, dusty staircase. He didn't want to think anymore.

His steps sounded horrible in the silence....The staircase led up to a huge sound stage. The door was open, and he stood in the doorway, in awe of all that he saw. He took Mindy out of his jacket now, and placed her on the ground, holding her hand. The room before him was *cavernous*. The ceiling was perhaps two stories above him. They used to shoot soap operas here, and the sets were still up: a living room scene, several bedroom scenes, a kitchen scene, a business scene...He watched it all dubiously: these pieces of life that seemed to float in the darkness. A side of him was alarmed when he saw all the people moving about inside. But then, deep into the room, he saw his girlfriend! She and a few others were standing next to a living room set. Roland's heart soared. All the cameras were being put in place and checked. There were also flickering video screens.

Roland took a few steps towards them; and as he did so, everyone stopped and stared at him. He felt numb...*unreal*. Mindy clambered to be held again, so he put on his jacket and took her in his arms. He began walking towards Samantha then. Everything was so strange...Somehow, he was now standing with his girlfriend and the rest of her crew. He was aware that there were several people around him, saying things to him, but he wasn't entirely aware of what was happening. Somehow, Mindy had been coaxed out of his arms. They had given her something sweet to eat. He felt arms on him, leading him towards the set they had prepared. He went to panic at this, but then he saw his girlfriend ahead—always just out of his reach, like a carrot dangling before a donkey's lips. They made him sit down on one of the sofas. It was too soft and he felt as though he would become stuck in its cushions. He forced himself to sit up on the edge of the sofa....His girlfriend was still just beyond his reach, staring at him with an expression that he could not gauge. They hadn't touched, nor had they spoken. They just stared. He couldn't read whatever was in her eyes, and this made him feel horribly lonely....The lights were blinding; the technicians were making the final adjustments now. His image appeared on one of the video screens, and he was aware, suddenly, of how wretched he looked. He hadn't shaved that day; there were lines under his eyes, and his lips were quivering slightly. He felt like a scared rat in a cage. He looked at his girlfriend, but she just seemed so far away—*so very far*.

A Latina, whom he recognized vaguely as Maria Santos, was going to do the interview—or so Roland guessed when the woman came up and shook his hand. She had a strange gleam in her eyes, which unnerved him. He glanced at his girlfriend, but she was staring at the floor and hugging herself—as if she were cold. Mindy was sitting on a chair not too far away from his girlfriend, staring ahead in a daze as she gnawed on a chunk of cake. They had covered her in a blanket—

Roland was suddenly aware that Santos was talking to him. He looked up nervously, realizing that the interview had begun. "—What?"

"What is your name?" Santos asked again.

"Roland: Roland Micheaux," he said in an unsteady voice. He cleared his throat.

"And why are you here?"

"I'm here...[He looked over at his girlfriend; she looked away when he met her eyes.] I'm here"—he lost his train of thought; he looked back at Santos, who was staring back with an encouraging but ultimately patronizing smile—"I'm here because I'm innocent."

"Innocent of what?" she chimed.

Roland had a sudden impulse to punch the woman in her stupid, smiling face. He stared at her, frowning. It was then that she sighed loudly—somewhat *dramatically*—before going on:

"You are in fact here, are you not, to claim that you weren't responsible for murdering Dallas Phelps in his house and then raping and shooting his wife, Cindy Phelps. *And*," she added for theatrical emphasis, "the murder of a police officer—not to mention, the kidnapping of Mindy Phelps, the couple's daughter."

Roland felt sick; he was suddenly aware that sweat was pouring down his face. He opened his mouth to say something, but nothing came out.

"Do you have any violence in your past?" Santos asked him, her eyes narrowing, as if she were laying a carefully placed trap.

Roland shook his head, and then: "No, I'm a lawyer"—some of the stage hands laughed; Santos smiled, and then:

"Do you think that your father's life has affected you?"

It took a while for him to digest what the woman had just said. "*What*...!" Roland was trembling. He looked around in dismay, perhaps searching for his girlfriend; but just then, his eyes landed on the video screens off camera. On one of them, was that scene from his recurring dream: him as a scared 13-year-old, being escorted through the sea of reporters. They were showing his father's mug shot now and running a piece from all those years ago, telling what his father had done. First, he was aware only of the numbness. Movement became sluggish; words sounded as though they were being slurred by an alcoholic. But then, building in him, was a fire that he knew to be rage. It expanded within him so quickly that he burst upright. The feeling of betrayal hit him. He looked over at his girlfriend, but she only stared back, her eyes blank. Either implicitly or explicitly, she was one of them.

"What is this!" he demanded, looking around desperately. "Stop this! Stop this *now*!" It was then that he realized that Santos had fled—disappeared into the darkness. Off camera, everyone seemed to be inching away. He frowned, just then noticing some figures creeping up in the darkness. *Policemen*! His eyes darted to his girlfriend, the rage bubbling to the surface.

"It's for the best!" she yelled out, already retreating into the shadows.

But he couldn't deal with that now. The dozens of figures were still advancing. He was backing away now. "No!" he kept repeating. He tripped over the coffee table of the set and landed on the ground. A phalanx of police officers emerged at his back. Their faces were hard and set. On the video monitors, the documentary on his father's wasted life was still going on. He didn't know where he got the strength or will, but Roland whirled and darted at the policemen who were coming at him from behind. He was so quick that he was upon them before they could react. He leapt at two policemen's feet and threw them to the ground. However, as soon as he was to his feet, a policeman grabbed him from behind—and two more approached from the front. But using the policeman who had grabbed him for leverage, Roland kicked both of the approaching policemen in their heads and sent them with the two that he had knocked to the ground previously. His was the strength of the Devil. The cop was still trying to hold him, but with a vicious elbow to the temple, the man was on the ground and Roland was free. One of the policemen he had just knocked down was trying to get to his feet: Roland kicked him viciously in the face and sent him to the ground. He then leapt over the entire pile and darted into the darkness beyond the blinding lights of the set. The policemen were still trying to corner him; but leaping over a luxurious bathroom set, he outflanked them all and was in the clear. Mindy, who had been roused from her daze by all the commotion, started running towards Roland; but instantaneously, Samantha grabbed her and held her. The little girl was screaming out for him, but Roland was running now. He leaped over two sets and outdistanced the confused police by a good deal. He was running back towards the entrance; but after a few strides, he saw that policemen were emerging from it as well! It was strange, but he didn't panic. Some dark avenging angel must have been whispering in his ear, because as soon as he saw the policemen, he went into action. He grabbed a stool from the kitchen set that he was currently in, then ran towards the wall, perpendicular to both groups of advancing policemen. They thought that they had him cornered against the wall, but when he was close enough, he threw the stool.

For an instant, the illusion took them all aback. It was as though he had broken the wall with his throw; but in fact, he had thrown the stool into one of the huge, painted-over windows. It shattered, letting in the dwindling daylight. In two steps, Roland was in the window, looking down. It seemed as if he were going to commit suicide; the policemen slowed, telling him to come back inside of the building. But Roland had spotted his goal. He was at the back of the building, looking down on an alleyway. The huge dumpster, piled high with garbage bags and empty boxes was two stories below. Before he could even think, the avenging angel told him to jump. He was in the air and there was a gasp from everyone inside the building. For a moment, there was an unbearable silence, in which the only sound was the pained cry of the little girl as she screamed: "Uncle Roland!" And then, there was the loud crash of Roland's body as it hit. Some policemen rushed to the window, expecting to see his body splattered against the ground, but they only stared on in disbelief—then *rage*—as they saw Roland scrambling out of the dumpster and darting down the darkening alleyway.

Roland ran, but it wasn't as before. He darted down the alleyways and side streets, but he wasn't running from anything anymore. He had a sudden impulse to laugh out triumphantly, remembering how he had eluded all of those policemen. But then, just as quickly, he remembered his girlfriend—and her treachery—feeling everything unraveling….

He had been running for several minutes, but now he slowed and began walking. Just around the corner, was 42nd Street. There were hoards of people—all walking along with that strange uneasiness. That was the thing about New York: no matter what happened, a block or two away, it was always as though nothing had happened. The world was constantly negating itself; lives were constantly being destroyed and disappearing into the nothingness…At first, watching the people around him, he was overcome by the urge to flee; but, at the same time, he knew that the best place to hide, was in a crowd. He joined the throng that was headed west, towards Broadway. The feeling of loneliness and isolation hit him hard then. He had nowhere to go and no friends to turn to. It was cold out now and he shivered in his jacket. The reality of what had just happened hit him again, and a little of the numbness that had been over him earlier, came back. They really believed that he *could* have done it! His girlfriend…*all* of them: they had *believed* it! It was not even a matter of if he had done it or not: it was that they thought him *capable* of it. He was desperate for the avenging angel again, but it was gone, leaving him stranded in this wasteland. The numbness was enveloping him now: maybe he was freezing to death and didn't know it….

He was passing by an electronics store, which had several television sets in its display window—among other things. He thought that he had imagined it at first, but there it was: his father's mug shot! And then, in the next instant, there was a picture of him—he recognized it from his news conference the day before. He stopped before the display window, unable to move. He couldn't hear the television, but he didn't need to hear, because he was watching Maria Santos' interview at the sound stage! They had already aired it! He looked like a lunatic on the screen, and then he was running from the police like a scared nigger, toppling over furniture...He saw himself wrestling with the policemen and fighting with them like an animal in a cage....It was as though he had blacked out while standing there, because when he came to his senses, he was watching scenes from the riot today. However, he didn't know that: it just seemed like his childhood memories were being projected onto the screen. He swallowed deeply and with effort. It was over: the story on the news, his life...*everything*. Roland walked on....

Kain had said that the world was going to end; and as Roland looked up to find himself in Times Square, with its flashing billboards and giant-screen TV, he couldn't deny it anymore. On that giant screen, nightmare images of the day's riot played. In fact, all around him was that world of chaos and madness, in which, on top of everything, he was a wanted criminal—a *murderer*, like his father before him. Still, unaccountably, a smile now came to his lips. It was with pride that he recalled how he had struggled with and outmaneuvered all those policemen; and as he revisited the image of the bullet-riddled corpse lying at his feet that morning, the madness seized him completely and he laughed out loud—

Presently, as his gaze returned to the giant-screen TV, he saw his image looking back at him from on high, like some sinister god. They were running that special report again, describing him as the latest version of evil incarnate—a murderer, cop killer, rapist...There was definitely no going back now—no way to reclaim his fairytale existence of wealth and fame; and as the bridges to his humanity had been burned, he found himself freed in a way that was at once wonderful and horrible. Like Adam of the Bible, the power behind the universe had turned him away from Paradise; but unlike Adam, he left not with sorrow and the hope of redemption, but with a newfound hatred for the power of God—which he saw flickering on the giant screen before him. All these years, he had fought the inevitable. He had fled from his father's murderous act—from everything he had ever known and feared. He had fought his way to the upper crust of society, and yet he still found himself in the same place he would have been had he stayed in the ghetto. *He was a nigger*....

6.

Surrender

For the most part, by eight o'clock that night, the riot had been subdued; but the violence remained in the souls of the people, gestating into something else as the hours went by. And it wasn't even like the last time, when they had Andropov to embody their rage. Colina was dead, and Marenga was comatose, and the Thomases rose up as martyrs to all the injustice and oppression in the world. The violence seeped into the hearts and minds of those watching it on TV; and by now, images of the riot were being broadcasted all over the world: scenes of people breaking into stores; people fighting with the police and one another; people lying around dazed and bloody, or dead...and then, there was the image of an old white woman being kicked and punched by a mob of black youths...It was all sickening to watch, but they couldn't help but surrender their souls to it.

*   *   *

"SMILE AND WAVE your hands, Mr. Mayor," an aide said, and Randolph stretched his lips taut over dry teeth. He was being hustled through the crowd now—towards the studio building where the debate was to be held. He had just given a statement to the press, back at City Hall, uttering empty phrases about peace, order and justice. And now, with images of the day's violence seeming to cloak and distort everything, the crowd around him seemed to be nothing but ghosts from the riot. Cameramen and reporters cluttered around him, yelling what seemed to be gibberish. They were asking him questions about the riot: about all the broken things....Beyond the media, the hundreds of bystanders and protesters seemed to surge towards him. Some were cheering and stretching out their hands to be shaken; others were booing, holding up banners that he couldn't read without his glasses.

Finally, he was pushed through a side door, which was hastily shut behind them—him, four aides and two bodyguards. The crowd was gone now. The crowd's cheers and boos faded away, as did its images. It was warmer and darker inside the studio building. He felt an urge to remove his trench coat, but he was quickly being hustled up some stairs now, swept along by the men that propped him up by the armpits. He let them lead him. It was all out of his hands anyway. Everything passed him by like the crowd, hardly even registering in his mind. The realization that he was to have a debate in a matter of minutes was first met with alarm, then, a millisecond later, with the same apathy as everything else.

This was what his life had been like for the last few years: this almost mindless running around. It seemed so much like a tiresome game to him now. Where once there had been excitement and hope, there was now just...he didn't even know what. The first Mayoral election seemed like a lifetime away. He had somehow been able to lose himself in the thrill of competition and the fallacy that all that the city needed—all that the *world* needed, in fact—was the right man. The people who had gathered in droves to hear his speeches had believed it as well. Bewitching them all had been the myth that one man could manifest bravery and thoughtfulness and moral uprightness in a population lacking in all three; and that such a man could not only embody the society, but also be a kind of crutch for the masses. It had been the myth of rugged American individualism: the fantasy of some hired gun being able to "clean up a town." It all seemed like so much shit to him now; but four years ago, buoyed by the cheers of the hopeful masses, he had fought his way into office, believing that he could "make a difference." He had stepped into the office of his predecessor—whom he had lampooned as being corrupt and indifferent to the needs of the city—only to look up and find himself speaking like the man, doing the same things that he, himself, had campaigned against. He had done to his opponent what McPrice was doing to him; and in time, someone else, basking in McPrice's ignominious defeat at the hands of the city, would be doing it to her as well. From the vantage point of his newfound apathy, he could see it all clearly now. It had truly been him against the world. For months, maybe *years* now, it had been a simple matter of survival.

His marathon conversation with Marenga came back to him then. When Marenga was leaving, the man had turned to Randolph and said: "I respect you, Randolph. You are an honest man, even though you have dishonest ideals."

"Isn't that a contradiction?" Randolph had replied with a smirk.

"Not at all. You *want* to have integrity when you deal with others, but you lie to yourself all the time. You lie to yourself, so that you can keep on lying to them."

"And what do I lie about?" he had said, trying to sound flippant, even while a sense of alarm began to build in him.

"You're an easy man to read, Randolph," Marenga had chuckled. "You have everyone else fooled, but not me—not anymore, anyway. You're not that easygoing, glib character that everyone thinks you are. The only reason there is hope for you yet, is that you aren't at peace: you aren't *complacent*. You and I aren't men of peace," he had laughed. "We're men of *violence*—of *war*. We're *killers*, Randolph: soldiers in a kill or be killed world...."

They hustled Randolph into a crowded dressing room, where he was again the focus of attention. Levin was there, looking insecure, but nonetheless smiling his crooked, repulsive smile to give Randolph confidence. They sat Randolph in a chair that faced a large mirror with bright light bulbs around its perimeter. He squinted...The lights were hot...He wrenched off his coat...There were aides everywhere, yelling instructions. He heard none of what they said. A stoic-faced white woman applied make-up to his face....He stared at his face in the mirror: it looked grim and old. He was only 48 years old, and yet he seemed haggard....

Someone poked her head in the doorway: "Only a minute until air time." It was a young black woman, just out of college, but Randolph couldn't remember her name at the moment. She had worked hard; but as Randolph got up, he had already forgotten her face...No matter...

"All right, it's show time!" the perpetually sweaty Levin yelled.

Everyone made way for Randolph, now shouting his or her support...White faces, black faces, Latino faces, all smiling and clapping—but he suddenly detested them!

"Try to smile more, Mr. Mayor," Levin yelled, but Randolph could do nothing but walk along, feeling the strange revulsion rising in him.

He made his way out to the dark studio, where the spotlights always blazed in his eyes, making him squint—and look deceitful. Three objects seemed to float on islands created by the spotlights. There were two lecterns and a desk. Everything else was cast in black; and he could only see silhouettes moving in the darkness, where he guessed that the cameras and studio technicians might be. He squinted and saw that his opponent and the moderator were already at their places. The moderator was sitting at the desk, which faced the two lecterns. His opponent was at her lectern.

Everyone had been on time, but Randolph.

They acknowledged one another's presence with dignified nods of their heads. Ed Muskie, the moderator, was a gaunt, desiccated white man about 60, with a completely bald head that shined in the bright lights. Charlotte McPrice looked incredibly young and vibrant. Everyone called her the progressive poster woman. During the last election, they had had a nickname for him, too. It had been something ludicrous like: The trailblazer. All of that was yet another part of the farce—it didn't matter at all....

As he stepped to the stage, everything about him—his every action, his every thought—seemed futile and self-destructive. The feeling of panic again tried to exert itself, only to be beaten back by the feeling that everything was beyond his control. His opponent's victory was imminent, and yet that didn't bother him in the least. He knew it as he looked at her. McPrice had a 45-point lead in the polls...she would be the first female Mayor of New York City, but that was yet another ultimately meaningless milestone of humanity. She seemed strong, and was certainly glib and optimistic—just as he had been. And yet, a side of him couldn't help but pity her. It was indeed time for change, but Randolph knew that if she won—*when* she won—she, too, would be riding the beast, holding on for dear life.

He stood behind the lectern, his face grim. The television crew was now whipped up into a frenzy, with a voice, whose face he could not see in the bright light, yelling that there were only 10 seconds until air time....

"Welcome everyone," Ed Muskie said when it was time, "to the final Mayoral debate between incumbent Mayor Alexander Randolph, and Councilwoman Charlotte McPrice—or is it Council*person*?" he asked McPrice with a smile.

"Councilwoman's fine," she answered. "I'm not afraid of being called a woman." To this, there was applause from off stage, where her supporters and aides looked on eagerly. McPrice and the moderator chuckled with one another for a while; Randolph, who stood there stiffly, felt as though he were a contestant on a game show.

After formerly greeting them both—a presentation for the television audience—Muskie went over the rules of the debate. McPrice looked on eagerly while Randolph only stared ahead. Muskie was now telling Charlotte that she had three minutes to make an opening statement, and she put on her business face, beginning:

"We live in a city that is facing many problems from many sides. The most poignant example I can give is the fact that there was a *riot* in front of City Hall today, ladies and gentlemen! There is disorder and panic on the streets as I speak. Today alone, two police officers were killed because of this social unrest—not to mention dozens of innocent bystanders. What we need is stability and order and prosperity, not sex scandals and riots!

"Four years ago, we were promised an end to many of our social and economic problems. We were promised *more* jobs; we were promised *better* education; we were promised *safer* streets; but what have we gotten? Look around you, people of New York: we have scandal after scandal; crime is worse, education is stagnant or in decline: the very buildings in which our children go to school are decaying; and for this, your taxes and mine have been increased to outlandish levels by the present administration. Faced with these facts, the action ahead seems clear.

"We have to get away from the laughable bungling of the present administration. We need a Mayor who will be *tough* on crime, who will *lower* taxes...! We need a Mayor who will bring back the standards of education that we grew up with, and which made America the greatest nation on earth! We cannot pussyfoot around the issues—or go missing in action! *We must attack*! And I am the woman who will do the attacking…!

"Tonight is Halloween," she continued in a lower, more pained voice, "and all around our great nation, innocent children are going out to play make-believe—to *pretend* to scare one another; but in this city, our children are *already* scared! They don't need make-believe to be afraid; because for them, there are real demons out there. It is time that we make it safe for our children to play make-believe again; and I tell you, people of New York City, I am the woman to do it, and now is the time to start!"

There was wild applause to this. Randolph had been staring at his lectern blankly, lost in all the contradictory feelings. He looked over at McPrice now, a side of him wondering if she believed all that nonsense. He nodded his head unconsciously: she believed it; she was beyond all doubt—just as he had been. Her shrill words were still with him, so that he shook his head to drive them away.

There was a long silence after the cheers subsided, and everyone stared expectantly at Randolph. He had memorized his statement, but it all seemed like so much drivel to him now.

"Mr. Mayor?" the moderator was saying, over and over again; as though coming to some decision, Randolph nodded to himself and looked up from the lectern.

"Yes, okay, Ed," he said, something strange glittering in his eyes. "Everything's fine," he went on to reassure them all, but a hush came over everything nonetheless. There was something horrible in his voice, which took them aback. And suddenly tired of fighting with whatever was rising within him, he sighed deeply and shrugged his shoulders, letting it all go. For some reason, he smiled as he looked over at McPrice again. "She's right: she's absolutely right," he said with a shallow nod of his head. It was said in a voice that he almost didn't recognize as his own. It was calm and peaceful—the voice of his very distant past—and he was both overjoyed and shocked to find it again. "I've done absolutely nothing during my tenure," he continued, as a collective gasp went through the audience. He was staring ahead blankly, nodding to himself as he heard the words reverberating from his lips. "Crime *is* rampant, good jobs *are* scarce, schools *do* graduate illiterates and delinquents...I'll go *further* than Ms McPrice," he went on, his voice coming quicker. "I deceived everyone last election,"—the studio was buzzing with voices; his own voice instinctively rose to counter them—"but only because you wanted me to: only because you *wanted* to be deceived!"

"—Mr. Mayor!" the moderator ejaculated.

"No, I'm fine, Ed. I'm only now becoming sane again." He looked at his opponent; she stared back with disbelieving blue eyes. "Yes, all of that was very true. I wish you well, madam."

"—Mr. Mayor!" Muskie burst out again, but an euphoric smile came to Randolph's face as he felt the burden being lifted.

"No, Ed, everything's fine. I'm not so much concerned with her winning, as with our losing...and we're all losing! [He almost had to shout over the audience now.] 'Get tough on crime?'" he said with a frown, "'Lower taxes?'" he chuckled. "...Yes, we're all losers..."

"W-We're going to go to a-a commercial now," Muskie was saying, but Randolph was already walking away, ignoring all of the staring faces and questioning voices. He walked away from it all, chuckling all the while.

* * *

IT WAS ABOUT eight-thirty when Roland Micheaux looked up from his daze to find himself stumbling down some nondescript city block. It was unbearably cold, but locked away from the physical world, he felt nothing. In contrast to everyone else, who walked hunched over, as though *they* were the ones who had something to hide, he walked with a careless stride, baring his chest to the wind. The streets were unusually empty—at least for New York. Most of the businesses—the eateries and delis and grocery stores—were closed. The upheaval of the riot was in the air, and everyone was desperate to be safely locked up in his or her home. As for the people who passed him on the street, they all seemed to be possessed by the uncharacteristic unease that he had noted earlier. There was now something about them that made him hate them even more. All those people, rushing back to the safety of their homes...Watching them, he couldn't help but be reminded of all that was lost to him. He had no home to return to now: no friends...The police—the *world*, in fact—knew all about him now, and would be waiting for him if he tried to go back to the condo.

Everything that he was—or was *supposed* to be—was even now being dissected by the media; and soon, there would be nothing left. In fact, everything was returning to the nothingness now—his life, his love...—and the ease with which he accepted this realization, told him that none of it could have been real in the first place.

Samantha...she had tried to kill him: had *betrayed* him! That mocking reality kept coming back to him as he somnambulated across town; but with his growing numbness, he couldn't really care anymore. All about him, there was the freedom of the damned. There was nothing that he couldn't do now, because there was nothing to go back to. He felt the same freedom that Kain, who had bashed in a man's head with a sledgehammer, now felt. What could they possibly do to him that they hadn't already done? The future opened up with new possibilities that only existed because of all that was now impossible and unattainable. For those few moments, walking along the cold city streets, all fear, all hope...everything that had shaped and guided him, was short-circuited, and he was *free*. Still, at the same time, he looked out on the world, knowing that there was a god out there, manipulating all of their lives—just as Kain had said—and it was a synthesized, man-made god. Out there, there was an all-knowing, all-powerful entity, incarnated in the form of scandal and public opinion; and Roland Micheaux, the one-time media star, was merely incurring its wrath.

As Roland walked along, he all at once remembered how, in the aftermath of Princess Diana's death (with millions of people over the world finding out that the paparazzi had literally chased her to her death), there had been a great hue and cry about the aggressiveness of the media. But at the time, watching it all, Roland had only laughed and shaken his head; because to him, it had been all too obvious that the actions of those millions, themselves—their *yearning for scandal*, in fact—had been what was driving the paparazzi! And just as the primitives had organized entire societies around the need to make sacrificial offerings to their gods, the high priests and priestesses of the modern age heard their master rumbling in the distance; and terrified of the works of their god, they slaughtered the hapless fools that had been picked to appease its hunger. But where there was terror, there was power to be had; and as they threw people to the rumor mill, all those high priests and priestesses out there were becoming gods themselves. Everywhere, there were gods *made* by scandal, gods *demanding* scandal and gods *done in* by scandal: a global orgy of self-destruction and backstabbing.

His strange feeling of peace persisted, but it was a peace nourished by hatred and the realization that his life was over. Even if he could find some mystical way to return to his former life, he no longer had faith in the world. He was like Dorothy in "The Wizard of OZ." He had looked behind the curtain and seen the true power behind the workings of the world; and now, all the illusions were torn away. Where there had been magic, he now only saw the crude manipulations of men; where there had been order and justice, he now saw random acts of violence….

He was on the eastern side of Manhattan now. He saw a police car and abruptly stopped, staring at it intently. But even then, he stared not with fear, but with a kind of morbid curiosity, wondering what was going to happen next. When the car passed him by and disappeared down the block, he only shrugged his shoulders and continued walking. It all seemed like a game to him now, with his only concern being how long he could hold off the inevitable. But the prospect of death brought with it its own kind of madness; and right then and there, on the cold, dark street, he resolved that when his time came, he would stand before the world with the defiance that his father *should* have had, and be that unbroken, unrepentant nigger….

In time, he reached Lexington Avenue and randomly set off towards the north. His hands were like ice, and his jacket seemed porous; and yet, he wasn't shivering. All his reflexes seemed to have been switched off….There were slightly more people walking the streets here—notwithstanding the fact that there had been a riot downtown just hours ago. But as he had thought before, in the space of a few blocks, the city went from heaven to hell and back again, contradicting itself; and as strangers darted blindly past him in the darkness, he thought to himself: These are the ones who are going to kill me. Out on the streets they were all locked away within themselves, avoiding eye contact and conversation—as though fearful of what they might do to one another. In their homes and offices and meeting places: that was where they cast their spells and looked about for sacrificial victims. How he would love to grab one of them right now, while he or she was defenseless on the street, and yell: "I am Roland Micheaux!" He smiled to himself as he thought of the shock and panic that would be in his victim's eyes when he listed his supposed crimes. He was suddenly gripped by the fantasy that he was some kind of suicide bomber, strapped not with sticks of dynamite, but with hatred; and that when he pushed the button, it would set off some cosmic explosion within himself, which would take them all with him. He kept thinking that his voice, energized by his realizations about the world, would shatter all their eardrums and bring their entire society crashing down around him (just as Kain had said). He was giddy with this fantasy now, telling himself that the next person he came up to, he would grab, screaming his revelations into his or her ears. The adolescent joy of it waxed in him for a moment, so that he was drunk with the thought of it. However, the next person to approach him was a white woman with a little girl who instantly reminded him of Mindy. He froze in the middle of the sidewalk. The woman, seeing him standing there, staring at her, sped up, clutching her daughter close as she darted past him.

He suddenly felt cold—and alone. He walked on, now bending like everyone else to protect himself from the wind. He was trembling at last...He shuffled down the street; a few passersby, taking him to be a drunkard, gave him wide berth. What did it matter...? Seeing a subway station, the prospect of warmth and protection from the wind was like a beacon to him. It was only when he was halfway down the stairs that he realized that there was a commotion ahead. Two teenagers were beating up a scrawny man, who was lying on the ground. The man was cursing and screaming, and the youths laughed while they kicked and punched him. Without thought, Roland walked down the stairs—again with that disconcerting calmness—and nonchalantly pushed the youths away from the man. The two boys, unfazed by Roland's interruption, laughed out merrily and ran towards the street.

Roland was just going with the flow now. He was free at last, and if the two boys had stabbed him, or blown his brains out, it would not have made a difference. The boys' victim, a bum with a shaggy beard, was still moaning on the stairs. Roland bent down to help him up, but when the man turned his face to the light, Roland gasped!

"What took you so long!" Kain laughed as he stood up.

* * *

OFFICER MUCELLI STARED at the interrogating lieutenant blankly. Self-preservation and self-destruction seemed to have the same end. Either way, he was done for, and there was no going back. The young officer was sitting in the interrogation room of the police precinct, facing a one-way observation mirror. As he took a glance at it, the face staring back at him was sallow and craven. Standing above him, was Lieutenant Craig Ericsson, whom everyone called Eric the Red, because of his red hair and Viking-like ruthlessness against his enemies. At the moment, however, the interrogation had a conversational, affable tone; several times, Ericsson, like most of the other officers in the precinct, had expressed his sympathy that Mucelli's partner, a beloved veteran of the force, had been killed. Everyone was rallying around Mucelli; their questions didn't so much seem accusatory, as tools to understand what had happened; but young Mucelli, looking into those sympathetic faces, had no choice but to be ill at ease—especially after what he had done….

"Okay," the lieutenant said for about the fifth time that hour, "tell me the entire story again."

Mucelli picked up the glass of water before him and took a long swallow. His hand was shaking, and this alarmed him. Keep it short and simple, he said to himself: add nothing; take away nothing that you've already given. He cleared his throat and began:

"Flanders and I were driving in the cruiser. First, we heard about the riot at City Hall, then we got the all-points bulletin on a man seen fleeing from a crime scene with a hostage—"

"You mean," said Ericsson, "Roland Micheaux."

"Yes, sir. But then, nobody knew who he was. All they knew was that a black man was seen fleeing from the house with a little blond girl, just before the police found her parents shot."

"Okay, what happened next?"

"Well, we were shocked of course…and since we were in that area anyway, we were on edge."

"So you were expecting something to happen."

"We're cops—we always expect something to happen."

Ericsson smiled; Mucelli felt a little relieved, so that he smiled as well before going on:

"We recognized Micheaux right away: he was carrying the victims' daughter."

"Did you call for backup?"

"No, sir. Everything happened so quickly. We looked up, and there Micheaux was. We got out of the car and told him to freeze and put the girl down."

"And then what happened?"

"Officer Flanders went up and started frisking him."

"Then?"

"Then, all of a sudden, Micheaux just attacked Flanders. It was like he went crazy or something. He smashed Flanders against the car—"

"And where were you at that moment?"

The panic surged in him! "I came up and tried to restrain Micheaux."

"Was your gun drawn?"

He swallowed. "Yes, sir."

"So, this is when Micheaux got the gun from you and shot Flanders?"

"That's about the time, sir. Everything was happening so quickly."

"Did Micheaux hit you?"

"He knocked the gun from my hand—"

"So, while he was fighting with Flanders, he reached over and knocked the gun from your hand—"

"He knocked me down, sir!" he said suddenly. *Shit*, he had forgotten that from the last recital. Micheaux *had* to knock him down—how else could he explain being out of commission when the shooting occurred.

"So," Ericsson started in an unconvinced tone, "Micheaux knocked you to the ground, beat off Flanders long enough to reach down and get your gun, then shot Flanders?"

"Yes, sir."

Ericsson stood before him in the same dubious air. Mucelli forced himself to look at the man—to not avoid eye contact like criminals always did. "Wait here," the lieutenant said then, walking out of the room.

Mucelli made it a point not to look up: not to stare at the mirror, behind which he knew the investigators were looking at his every motion. He felt sick to his stomach as he waited. He wanted another drink of water, but he was afraid of how much his hand would shake when he held the glass. He sat with his hands in his lap, waiting in the silence of the room.

When Ericsson entered the observation room, his captain and a lieutenant from the internal affairs department were sitting there. The captain had a grandfatherly face, but the internal affairs officer always reminded him of a Gestapo agent. The man had a pale, attenuated face and he always had the stench of cheap cigarettes about him.

"What do you think?" Ericsson said after closing the door. He addressed himself to the captain.

"What do you mean?" Captain Miller, a chubby 50-year-old, answered with slight annoyance sounding in his voice. "The kid just saw his partner shot by some kidnapping, raping psycho. How am I supposed to think about that?"

"But is that *all* that happened?" he said, glancing over at the agent, who stared back with indifferent bloodshot eyes.

"What the hell are you implying?" Miller demanded.

"I don't know," Ericsson started, the discomfort showing on his face. "Something's wrong here—*very* wrong. I just came from the room where they are holding the little girl that Micheaux supposedly kidnapped. She's not asking for her mommy or daddy. Who is she asking for? 'Uncle Roland.'"

"So fucking what!" the captain exploded. "So he had a bond with her—big deal! Most of the kids that are abducted are taken by someone they know—Micheaux worked at the same firm with the girl's father; half the kids that are raped, are raped by someone they know!"

"Stop that!" Ericsson couldn't help himself. "There was no sexual abuse of this child—"

"Only because that fucker didn't have time—"

"I don't know," Ericsson said uneasily. "Something's stinks about this. Who was Micheaux going to ransom the girl to—he supposedly shot both her parents. Besides that, we just got an anonymous report that it was *Mucelli* who shot Flanders—"

"*What the fuck*...! You gonna believe an anonymous report! Mucelli is a goddamn hero!"

"Now wait a minute—"

"*You* wait a minute!" Captain Miller began, turning a deep red. "His partner was gunned down right in front of him…You know, that's the sick thing about this country: it's getting so that people don't respect cops no more—don't respect *authority*. That's why there was that riot today; that's why two fine cops got killed and dozens wounded! This is the goddamn mindset of these people! They believe a criminal before they believe a cop! You said something's wrong? *Damn right something's wrong*! There's a lunatic wandering the streets and we're in here accusing a fine young officer! That's who we should be questioning: that scumbag who shot two upstanding members of the community. On top of that, he had the nerve to kidnap their kid and kill a police officer. This case is shut as tight as a constipated ass hole!"

Ericsson sighed then, glancing through the observation mirror at Mucelli: "I hope so—for all our sakes."

* * *

NO MORE SCRAPS for Maria Santos! What a wonderful day this had been: a riot, an exclusive interview with a murdering, raping celebrity, and now the Mayor's strange resignation. She took a certain amount of pride from the thought that she had helped to bring Randolph down—whether or not that was true. She was being cued for broadcast now, hardly able to restrain her excitement as she stood on the set of her show and stared into the cameras that would broadcast her image to millions. Her interview with Roland Micheaux, put on the air just minutes after the fact, was already a national story. It had been there just in time for the local and network evening news broadcasts. A rising star was now a murderous, raping lunatic on the run: it was perfect for mass consumption. More so than watching others rise, Americans loved to see those same others fall from grace. It was the national pastime. Even as the madness of the riot died down—at least ostensibly so—Roland Micheaux rose up to take its place. Everything was in place for her ascension. She had introduced the murderous Roland Micheaux to the world, and she was bent on being there when they hauled Micheaux in—or gunned him down. She was going to milk this for all it was worth. She had men tracking Micheaux in Manhattan now; crews were on standby, like SWAT teams ready for the fight of their lives….

And then she was on the air, waxing poetic about the horror of the riot, and Mayor Randolph's cowardice, and the fact that Roland Micheaux was a kind of metaphor for the city and everything that had happened: a glittering star who was poisoned by evil.

"Roland Micheaux was on a long spiral down into crime," she said. "The evil was *bred* within him—nourished by the same madness that gripped his father over 25 years earlier. On the outside, he was a successful lawyer: an upstanding member of society—gregarious and handsome. *He was even rated one of the ten most eligible bachelors in the city*! That was the illusion that he showed us all, while within him, the evil was stirring. That murderer is out there now," she continued, "—still on the loose; and just as we have to put this city and country back on the track of justice and order, so too we have to bring in Roland Micheaux: *by any means necessary*!"

* * *

ROLAND'S FACE WAS blank and pale.

"So," Jasper Kain exulted the moment they were on the crowded uptown four train, "the great Roland Micheaux is a nigger too, just like the rest of us!" The man then proceeded to laugh insanely for the next few minutes—while the express train made its way from 59th Street to 86th Street. The crowded Harlem-bound train was filled mostly with blacks and Latinos. And with Kain's loud cackling, Roland realized that everyone was looking in their direction! Even those who were trying to ignore Kain, took glances to see what was going on. There was not even one empty seat in the car; and this density, combined with Kain's disconcerting laughter—not to mention the man's apparent inability to be discreet—began to eat away at whatever resolve and peace Roland had been able to scrounge together.

At the first stop, 86th Street, Roland wanted to dash outside and run from them all; but Kain, gripping him by the arm as though he were a prized possession, pulled him to the middle of the car. They bumped several people, who turned and looked at them with annoyance. Roland tried to keep his face averted...He felt sick to his stomach!

"—Well, welcome to the nigger brotherhood!" Kain laughed as

he held the pole in the middle of the aisle and stood facing Roland's panic-stricken face. "The madness has come at last—just as I said it would!" Kain exulted, as practically everyone in the car again looked to see why the hell the man was making all that noise. Roland felt as though he were going to throw up! And the speeding express train, rocking back and forth as it zoomed uptown, was like a truck barreling towards a telephone pole. Roland was overcome by an insane impulse to escape—to pull open the doors and hurl himself out onto the electrified tracks! Just then, the express train zoomed past 96th Street in a blur. Roland felt as though they were going too fast: that the world was going by too quickly, and that they were all running out of time. And just then, Kain once again laughed out, saying:

"Now we can stand together, my brother, stripped of hopes of belonging and delusions of success. In fact," he went on, "we weren't made for this world, my brother. Like Sons of God, we emerged fully formed, with that sacred knowledge within us—but without the power and magic that made men follow Jesus. Still, being dutiful Sons, we craved Our Father's love and were desperate to prove ourselves worthy, thinking that with proof of worth, the power and magic would come. But Our Father disowned us—refusing to give us His name, His love, His trust...and we were left to fight for ourselves in a world dedicated to our destruction...*God's Bastard Sons*!

"But the madness has come at last!" Kain yelled euphorically. "And beyond this seeming chaos, Paradise awaits. [Roland nervously put his index finger to his lips, futilely gesturing for Kain to be quiet.] Everything is coming to fruition: all the hatred, all the chaos—all the seeds sown by this society!

"Didn't I predict it all, Micheaux!" he said, tapping Roland on the shoulder; but not only did Roland flinch at the man's touch: he shuddered when he realized that Kain had used his name! "Yes, Micheaux," Kain continued, as Roland looked on in stunned horror, "all the great men are seizing their madness today—you, Randolph, Marenga...and where the great lead, the rest must follow. Only in madness can there be peace and unity!

—Roland felt the first stream of nervous sweat run down his face. When he glanced up, several people seemed to be scrutinizing him closely—*as if they recognized him*! He had the feeling that he was falling through space: that solid ground was miles below him, and that when this hurtling journey finally came to an end, he would be splattered against the ground. Like the last time Kain cornered him, he had reached the point where he realized that he couldn't listen to anymore: that survival demanded violence. He felt himself on the verge of strangling the man—doing whatever it took—to keep the man at bay.

But seeing that murderous will building up in Roland, Kain only laughed out: "Yes, my brother, let that nigger hate set you free!" Kain began to laugh then; and as that horrible laughter sounded in the cramped space of the car, something in Roland fell away and he realized—as he had realized months earlier—that he was no match for Kain. He only had one chance left: he had to get the hell out of there! He looked around for a means of escape, but the express train zoomed past 116th Street, going nonstop to 125th Street.

Roland's mind was a convoluted mess. All he could think was that he had to get away: not only from Kain, but the world and its inhabitants. The train was finally slowing down as 125th Street approached. Kain was still chuckling to himself. Roland knew that as soon as the train stopped, he would rush out—get away from Kain: from *all* of them. He needed to be out in the open: away from all these people. Someone had just opened the door between cars—Roland could tell because the noise of the wheels hitting the tracks waxed in the air. He happened to glance in that direction just as two black transit cops entered the car. He felt as though his intestines were knotting themselves! Kain laughed suddenly—*defiantly*—just as the train entered the station and began its rapid deceleration. The cops were looking in their direction; Kain was laughing even louder: laughing like a *madman*! The cops were walking over; Roland looked in horror from them to the cackling Kain. He had a sudden urge to knock the man senseless. But then, the train came to a jarring halt and the doors burst open. Roland bolted for the door, knocking over an old woman; Kain, still laughing, ran after him—

"It's Roland Micheaux!" Roland heard someone scream—one of the policemen. Roland was darting through the crowd now: he ran up the steps with Kain hot on his heels. The cops were yelling now, but Roland couldn't hear—couldn't *think*. All that there was, was running. He jumped over the turnstiles and ran outside, numb to everything. Kain, still giggling insanely, was right behind him; the cops, though farther back, were still hot on their trail. But once outside, Roland looked about the Harlem streets indecisively, not knowing which way to go—

"Run, nigger!" Kain laughed. "I'm not ready for you to get caught yet!" The man tugged at Roland's arm then, and they ran down some street or another. Roland couldn't see anymore; Kain was in the lead and Roland let himself be led by the man's madness....A police car was coming down the street, going in the opposite direction from them. But when the cops spied them, they made a hasty U turn and began pursuit, their siren blaring. Kain, as though by instinct, turned down a relatively narrow one-way street. A truck had taken up half the street, and the rest was backed up with cars waiting for the light to change. The police car had to slam on its brakes to keep from hitting the truck. However, with its velocity, it slid, blocking the street as it ended up sideways.

As for Roland, all that there was, was running. He had been running all his life, and it seemed as though it would never end. They ran for perhaps another five or so minutes, but it seemed like an eternity. They were now running along the wide expanse of Malcolm X Boulevard, seeing blocks lined with the usual tenements. Loud music was coming from one of the buildings—a party. There were people in Halloween costumes standing outside, on the stoop. Kain darted into the building; Roland followed the man, numb to the world. Outside, he heard the sirens coming—

"Run, nigger!" Kain cackled again. They ran into the hallway. The party was on the first floor, and the door to that apartment was ajar. Kain pulled Roland towards the door, while outside, the sirens stopped in front of the building....The party was dark and packed, with dozens of costumed shapes moving erotically in the darkness. There was the heat and stuffiness that came when too many people were in too confined a space. Kain led them through the party. The partygoers were just kids, most of them. However, they were drinking beer, and a few joints were being passed around. Everyone stared at Roland and Kain—they were obviously out of place: both were panting for air and sweating. They looked like killers. Kain held Roland's arm and pulled him hastily towards the back of the apartment. People made way. At the back, Kain pulled the window open and hopped outside—into the back alley; Roland followed him, and the two disappeared into the darkness.

Everyone was staring quizzically at the scene, when, all of a sudden, the front door burst open again. Four policemen ran into the dark room with their guns drawn, they too looking like killers. Several people screamed; the kids holding the joints tossed them to the floor—

"Where'd they go!" a ruddy-faced policeman roared. He entered threateningly; everyone made way, but remained mute. The policeman grabbed a quailing kid by his costume—a toga—practically ripping it off. The kid was in shock, standing there with only his drawers on; the cop flung him to the side, going farther into the room with his gun still drawn. The other cops followed suit, screaming questions and demands that nobody seemed able to decipher....Who did it, nobody could later say for sure; but somehow or another, a beer bottle was thrown in the dark room, hitting the ruddy-faced cop in the jaw. In that dark chamber, a gun shot suddenly rang out: an involuntary reaction to being hit, perhaps. And then, all of a sudden, people were running and screaming; there was another gunshot, and then another as the panicky screams pealed in the air; and everywhere, there was madness.

* * *

FOR A WHILE, after Randolph walked out of the television studio and into the cold night air, there had seemed to be no more worries about struggling to hold on; no more worries about what he *should* have done, but didn't; no more worries about what he *wanted* to do, but couldn't. The future had seemed to be filled with boundless possibilities. He had walked on at a brisk pace, letting his legs and instincts guide him; but in the end, his mind, in its desperation to pursue those possibilities, had only led him deeper into the horror that he was fleeing. A cold, biting wind had been blowing through his thin suit, but so many other things had been attacking him, that he had hardly noticed....

In full flight, he had not wanted to think about what he had just done. He had not wanted to think about how many people he had just impacted by his desertion of it all. That was what had worn him down these last four years: the reality of how many lives he was impacting; and, worse yet: the reality of how many lives remained unchanged, no matter what he did. He had been walking for about an hour and a half; and now, at last, here he was in Harlem: in the ghetto, where all the easily discarded and broken things were thrown. His hands were numb from the cold, and his teeth were beginning to chatter, but none of that mattered when he looked up to find himself among the hectares of rubble that had once been his childhood neighborhood. The last time he had been here, was a year and a half ago, when he had ceremoniously razed the two city blocks to make way for new developments. Standing before the cheering crowd, he had promised that by the end of his term, it would be a thriving community, with businesses and new housing. But as he entered the blocks, he saw, with his own eyes, that it was still a wasteland; and since there was neither funding nor interest, it would remain so for some years still. There were few streetlights here, so the piles of rubble were only dull silhouettes, standing ominously in the cold night air. There was a horrible silence about this place, as if this were some void. Save for the sound of his chattering teeth, and the wind as it whizzed past his ears, there seemed to be nothing else.

He was getting ready to leave when, looking around, his attention was captured by a huge sign beneath one of the few streetlights. It read:

Your Tax Dollars Hard At Work
Making Our Community Safer and Stronger
Another Community Project
by Your Mayor, His Honor:
Alexander J. Randolph

Randolph stared at it for a long while, as if unable to get the meaning of the words and why he would be connected to them. Around the razed blocks, there were waist-high, wooden police blockades, lined up end-on-end. They were the quickly assembled kind, which were put together by the fitting of slots; and as he looked at it all, a searing need for permanence took hold of him. He just needed something that human hands couldn't destroy. On this strange day of destruction, with riots and murders and his desertion of it all, he just needed something real: some immutable pillar of strength to guide him. Indeed, the world was still changing—he could feel its violent rumblings beneath his feet. The enraged masses had been working themselves into a fit for years now; he had been hearing and seeing and *feeling* that rage for *years*, but the imminence of the eruption was breaking through his indifference; and finally heeding the danger signs, he was determined to be gone when the final eruption came.

But looking around, in the eerie quiet of the razed blocks, he just couldn't see the use. The world seemed to be full of too many contradictions for anyone to act decisively. There had been a *riot* today! People were dead and dying; and yet, a side of him, remembering the aftermath of the Brooklyn maniac's rampage—where the rage of the masses had fizzled away to nothing—wondered if the same thing might not happen again. Either the society was a volcano that was about to explode, or just a mountain that simply liked to "let off a little steam" every once in a while. Either they were building up to an eruption, or they were caught in a cycle of impotence. There seemed to be no way of discovering which it might be, until after the fact. The only certain thing was that his life, as he had known it, was finished. Like Roland, there was no going back. As such, his only guide was the nothingness into which he had fallen. Perhaps entranced by the pull of that nothingness, he pushed aside one of the police barricades and began to stumble through the dark piles of rubble.

His pace was slow now. He looked around intently, although the darkness made everything inarticulate. He couldn't understand it: how could this monochromatic world, with its amorphous shapes, have once been his home? Where were all of the colors and joyful sounds that he remembered? Too many things seemed too easily destroyed; and once again overcome by a need for permanence, he resolved to not forget his childhood—either as how he had fantasized it to be, or as it was. He would remember the families with whom he had once lived; he would remember the sweet sounds of their many voices; he would remember the fragrant smell of their freshly cooked food—

But just then, he stumbled over something soft. His feet had become used to the hardness of brick and concrete, but he almost fell to the ground upon encountering the softness. In the darkness, he looked down at the ground, trying to figure out what it was that he had stepped on. And then, when he finally realized what it was, a muffled shriek escaped from him and he backed away in horror: *It was a body*! Actually, it was Feingold's corpse, still lying where the bum had left it; and a few meters away, was the bum's corpse, lying where Kain had left it. Randolph took a terrified step backwards and encountered this second body. He froze! There were two dead men at his feet; and yet, in his state of mind, those two corpses weren't simply men that had been killed the day before, but the resurfacing spirits of the tens of thousands who had lived and died on these streets. This was a graveyard that he was in! It had once been sacred land, but his hand had set off the explosion that reduced these blocks to rubble; and all the restless spirits were emerging from their graves to take their vengeance. Randolph could still remember the faces of some of the people with whom he had once lived; and as he descended slowly into madness and delusion, he saw them standing before him. He saw himself as a child, playing childhood games; but now, instead of filling him with joy, those games seemed only to be a prelude to death. He saw his family; but now, they weren't the wonderful childhood construct that they had been before. His mother, who had succumbed to breast cancer two decades ago, was standing there in a tawdry outfit; his sister, who had met her end through an AIDS-infected heroin needle, reached up her hand, as though to claw out his eyes. Out of the abyss of his past, only his brother, Roger, was still alive; but he couldn't think about that now, because everywhere, hundreds of playmates and lovers and passing acquaintances, who had met their end through the streets, or in some war or through human frailties, were stumbling towards him like zombies. He had desecrated their graves, and they would drag him down into their hell and take revenge—

He turned and bolted for the sidewalk! Twice, he fell to the ground and scraped his legs on exposed metal rods, but nothing would stop him. He was running for his life, seized by the terror that only the insane knew. The world of men was somewhere out there—beyond the police barricade that held in all the restless spirits and demons. The ghosts were still hot on his heels; and now, it wasn't only the spirits of his past that had him fleeing: the din of the enraged masses was also a little louder in his mind. He felt the rumblings of the volcano all around him and the only thing that he could do, was run.

In his terrified haste, he tried to hurdle the barricade at the curb, but his trailing foot got caught and he found himself toppling through the air. He screamed out when he realized that he wasn't going to make it, then grunted as he fell heavily to the ground. He lay there for a moment, still trembling as he panted for air and winced from the pain…but there was silence again. Looking back confusedly at the rubble, he saw nothing but shapeless silhouettes; he heard nothing but the wind. He got slowly to his feet and looked around longingly. Eventually, he limped off, his mind numb….

On the next block, there were again streetlights and the tall, inhabited tenements that he had known from his youth. Nevertheless, there was nothing here for him. He walked on, still shivering—from the cold and the thought of spirits. He went on like this for about ten more minutes, letting himself get lost down the blocks of his former life. He was limping down the sidewalk, trembling from the reality of his utter homelessness, when, all of a sudden, sirens pierced the air and speeding police cars blasted past him. He almost fell to the ground as he whirled, staring gape-mouthed as they whizzed by. And then, just as suddenly and inexplicably, from the next block—which was Malcolm X Boulevard—there came the crisp pops of gunshots. From nowhere, color and sound and movement had come. Randolph's senses were being brutalized by all that was happening around him. The red and blue emergency lights of the passing cars blinded him—and their blaring sirens deafened him. Yet, the effect of all this chaos was strangely hypnotic, and the only thing that he could do, was stand there, staring at the speeding cars as they raced down the side street that he was currently on, and zoomed out, onto the wide boulevard.

Still hypnotized, he looked on as people on the next block suddenly began to empty out into the street. Some of them were almost run over by cars, which had to come to screeching halts. The people were in fact running for their lives, screaming and darting for cover as more gunshots sounded in the air. Police officers were fighting their way into the building, pushing past the fleeing youths. Everywhere, there was chaos; but still hypnotized, Randolph found himself slowly walking in that direction—still gape-mouthed...still staring and trying to make sense of it all. Some of the people were yelling and running in his direction—they were in fact running in *every* direction. Before he realized that the people were wearing Halloween costumes, it was as though a hole had been torn in reality, and fact and fiction were converging in one confusing, terrifying mess. He saw cowboys running next to toga-clad Greek philosophers; the products of human imaginations—their superheroes and monsters—all ran down the streets in terror, as if even they were no match for what was coming.

Randolph walked closer and closer. The people—kids, now that he looked at them—weren't running anymore; having gotten out of immediate danger, they were congregating in the street—which was now cut off by about 12 police cars anyway—talking excitedly amongst themselves. Some of those who had run out soon collapsed in the middle of the street, succumbing to gunshots. People gathered around them, yelling for help as police officers ran about. Randolph was standing shoulder-to-shoulder with the people now as they all watched the spectacle; and overhead, it seemed as if every windowpane framed an eager face or faces. There were probably two hundred people on the street with him now—and hundreds more were coming out from the surrounding buildings. Ambulances and more police cars were arriving, and he had to squint to protect his eyes from the glare of the swirling red and blue lights. There was death in the air, and it was both repellent and attractive to all. People were jostling for better views of the dead and dying now—even Randolph. Half a dozen bodies now lay on the pavement and in the street—several others were on ambulance stretchers, getting ready for departure. Some moved and cried out; others lay still, in positions that one only saw amongst the dead....Police officers were yelling for people to stand back. Paramedics moved quickly from one body to another, trying to discern which ones still had a chance at life. Then, all at once, a woman's voice pierced the air:

"Jimmy! *Jimmy*!"

People were moving out of the way; Randolph looked to see a voluptuous black woman about 35, who was dressed only in a pink bathrobe, slippers, and curlers. Her face seemed to be fresh with the shock and despair that was slowly draining from other people's faces.

"Where's my son!" the woman cried when she burst to the front of the crowd. She got no answer. Everyone was silent, including the policemen. But she was soon wailing, having to be held back by two policemen, because she finally discerned his corpse lying on the sidewalk—

"...*Oh, God*!" she cried hysterically. Gripped by the strangeness of the moment, she turned to the crowd, wiping her eyes with the wide sleeves of the robe. "He wasn't a bad child," she said; and right there on the bloody sidewalk, above the sirens and amid the flashing lights, she gave the eulogy, and everyone listened; and even those who didn't know the boy, stood solemnly and nodded along to her words.

Randolph was feeling the biting cold again. His fingers were fully numb, but he wasn't shaking anymore. Like everyone else, all he could do, was listen to the woman's words. An ambulance that had been loaded with the dying, took off suddenly; and as the siren blared in the air, the woman suddenly started crying, seeming on the verge of collapse. Randolph needed to leave this place. Once again, he wanted to leave. He went to walk away when the woman suddenly noticed him and frowned.

"*Mayor?*" she said in disbelief, her eyes wide.

Randolph froze, looking at the woman warily. There was a cascade of conversation as the presence of the Mayor was announced throughout the heretofore solemn crowd.

"Mayor, what's going on here!" the woman cried in despair. Randolph opened his mouth to speak, but nothing came out. "We thought you was gonna stop this kinda shit from happening!" the woman screamed.

There were people all around him now, he realized with a violent start. He tried to hide his fear with a nervous smile…but they were all around him now—there was nowhere to go! More voices cried out:

"...That nigga ain't done *shit* for us...What the hell *he* doing here...Probably looking for votes...!"

Harsh voices rang in Randolph's ears; then suddenly, he found himself being pushed, tugged and punched. He guarded his face with his numb hands, feeling himself being hit all over—in his ribs, in his thighs, in his back, in his neck; but all of the blows were dull, actually bring sensation back to his numb body. The voices waxed in the air, until he thought that there were *thousands* around him, all wanting a piece of his flesh to pummel. Here they were at last—the enraged masses. He dropped to his knees, feeling blows raining down on him as they had rained down on Andropov. But just then, he was pulled up gruffly. He thought that this would be the end for him, but the fervor of the voices was dying down, and the blows had stopped. He looked around confusedly, realizing that the police were leading him away now—

"Yea, you got the police to protect you, but who *we* got!" a defiant voice screeched. Randolph looked up to see the woman in the bathrobe, her tears gone. Her face was disfigured into a scowl, as were many others.

The half dozen policemen fought through the crowd and towards a patrol car, where they pushed Randolph into the back seat. Two white officers got in the front and drove off as quickly as they could. They inched their way through the sea of undulating bodies; the people outside the car glared and yelled and shook their fists....Even the living are ghosts, Randolph mused, closing his eyes in surrender. But even with his eyes closed, he kept seeing the angry faces of the people who were no longer his. He was fleeing from it all now, and was happy for it. He realized that he was hyperventilating, and consciously took some slow, deep breaths—

"Mr. Mayor?"

Randolph looked up, realizing that the young policeman in the passenger seat had been talking to him for some time now.

"Yea?" Randolph said, distractedly, as he looked out of the window again, seeing more angry faces appearing and disappearing from view.

"Do you want us to take you home, sir?"

Randolph stared at the man absentmindedly again. He nodded his head after a while, still taking deep, slow breaths. The car was finally free of the crowd now. The angry voices faded from the air, although they resounded in his mind. But then the young officer spoke up again:

"Where *is* your home, sir?" the man asked. He was only asking for directions, but Randolph stared at him for a long while before chuckling to himself and lying back in the hard, uncomfortable seat.

* * *

AS THEY RAN, Kain laughed at the chaos that they had left behind: Roland only ran. He was firmly in the grasp of something like drunkenness. He saw the world, but his reactions to it were sluggish; and as the drunkenness enveloped him, he found it more and more difficult to differentiate reality from the drug-induced delusion that his life had become. The world was coming apart, and he was somehow involved: somehow the *catalyst*—just as Kain had said. The ever-broadening scope of what was happening—and what seemed on the *verge* of happening—was so immense that a part of him was convinced that it was all a delusion. And when Kain opened a manhole cover and began to lead him down one dark, smelly sewer corridor after another, it was as though the man were some guardian angel in hell, there to meter out his sufferings. All those months ago, when Kain first accosted him at the banquet, Roland had thought that the man was some delusion cooked up by a mind that had long cracked; now, in a world of escalating chaos, the delusion seemed to be the world, itself. And yet, what could Roland do at this point? The thing about being in a dream was that, even if one realized that one was dreaming, one couldn't stop it. Accordingly, as Kain led him through the sewer, all he could do, was follow and wait for the end.

And then, while they were trudging through the muck, Kain laughed and looked over, saying, in a calm, menacing voice: "I'm not going to let you out of my sight, Micheaux. I want to be there when they put a bullet in your head."

When Roland shuddered, it only made Kain laugh louder, the sound echoing horribly down the corridors. But then:

"Don't worry, Micheaux," Kain said, patting the jumpy Roland on his shoulder, "they'll definitely want you alive—to show you around like some kind of freak at the carnival show. After all you've done, they'll have to make an example of you, boy: rape, murder, kidnapping…and now, inciting a riot!" His horrible cackling resounded down the corridor again, sounding like that of some second-rate cartoon villain. And yet, even then, Roland was so numb that all he could do, was follow….

Eventually, Kain led him to a side chamber, where he had his hideout. Roland looked about confusedly at the basement chamber.

The reality of the place—its *existence* in the sewers—was as surreal as everything else. The TV was still on; and as the volume was on mute, the bare images of the day's violence seemed more fantastic somehow. While Roland stood tentatively on the threshold, Kain walked over to the TV and turned up the volume. However, the first words that Maria Santos said were: "Roland Micheaux is a menace to society!" There was a split screen, with Maria Santos on one side, and one of her roving reporters on the other. The reporter was in front of the building that Kain and Roland had run through only 15 minutes ago.

"Two kids have been killed," the reporter cried, "and a dozen wounded, including police officers."

Maria Santos was so enraged that she shook as she declared: "We have to get Roland Micheaux behind bars as soon as possible—before he causes any more damage!"

Kain switched off the set; Roland, trembling from the weight of it all, managed to stumble over to the couch, where he sat down heavily. "...This can't go on," he whispered to himself; he looked around in a daze, as though seeing the events of the last 24 hours—of his entire life, in fact—playing themselves out before his eyes. "—I have to turn myself in—"

"*What*!" Kain said in disbelief.

"I'm turning myself in," Roland said, still battling with the numbness.

Kain looked at him in bewilderment, scrutinizing him with pursed lips. Finally shaking his head, he said: "You're no fun, Micheaux. You give up too easily—"

"This is a *game* to you?" he said, finally seeming to come to his senses. "People are *dead...kids*!"

But Kain only shook his head sorrowfully again: "You were just a fatalist all along," he lamented, "—waiting to be screwed. I should have seen that before—wouldn't have wasted so much time on you. You weren't worth it."

"Sorry to disappoint you," he mumbled under his breath.

But: "You *can't* turn yourself in, Micheaux—not yet."

"That's right: you haven't had your fun yet," he groaned sardonically.

"You just need time to clear your head—this is no way to go out, is it?"

"...All those kids at the party," he whispered, shaking his head as the reality of it hit him again. He sat back on the couch, staring at the ceiling. "I can't let anyone else die—"

"*Fuck* everyone else!" Kain roared, so that Roland instinctively cringed against the couch. "You're just like me, Micheaux," the man went on, "—driven by *hate*!"

"What the *hell* are you talking about!"

"You wanted to show them all, didn't you? The *world*, I mean—after they killed your father. That's why you were so driven to be successful—you wanted to show them that you weren't what they were saying: that you weren't what they were *implying* by saying that you were *his* son. All those years, studying hard with hate in the back of your mind, you only wanted to step above them and say: 'Fuck you all! I made it anyway!' There was no choice but to show them all—no matter the cost. All the self-sacrifice, the *drive*! There was a killer in you, Micheaux—you didn't care about nothing but winning: showing them all! You probably even hate your job, don't you?"

Roland couldn't think about that now: he shook his head wearily and looked away, sitting back in the soft cushions of the couch again.

But Kain went on: "You liked the money—the *status*; but at the end of the day, you hated the job and everything it represented: all those frivolous lawsuits—"

"*What difference does it make*!" he cried in frustration.

Kain's eyes had a strange gleam in them as he whispered: "Hate *is* everything—"

"I don't care anymore!" Roland said in desperation—he had needed to speak up: to do anything to drown out Kain's voice, but:

"That's right—one thing at a time," Kain cooed to him. "You need to think, don't you: to clear your head—"

"*Shut up*!" Roland begged. "Just keep quiet!" He got off the couch and began pacing nervously.

"Yes, I'll be quiet," Kain went on in a singsong voice. "But first, if I may, let me suggest that we both change our clothes—there's a bin over there with some extra clothes. We need something to throw the police off."

"I'm turning myself in, remember," he said, feebly, "—what do I need a disguise for!"

"That's right," Kain placated him, the way someone talked a raving lunatic off a ledge, "you're turning yourself in, but you want to do it on your own terms, don't you? You just don't want *anyone* to grab you off the street, holding you there like a criminal. You want to walk to the precinct house with some dignity: do it like a *man*!"

Roland stared at the man hopelessly, realizing how thoroughly the man knew him—and how easily he was manipulated by the man's will. It was at that moment that the two men locked in Kain's dungeon (no doubt roused by the loud voices) started banging on the door.

"—What's that!" Roland gasped, instinctively horrified. There was a terrible urgency to the banging; the door seemed like some supernatural barrier—

"Ah," Kain laughed as he turned towards the door in the corner, "how's that for perfect timing! I almost forgot." And then, to Roland: "Come over and I'll show you."

"What's in there!"

"The answer to all you questions, Micheaux," Kain laughed. "Behind this door [and he took Roland's trembling arm and led him up to the entrance] is everything you've been running from all your life." Roland was beginning to lose his will again, and this alarmed him. Torn apart by all the contradictions of his existence, he felt giddy and sick by the time they reached the door. Kain was just about to open it, when he laughed in a self-deprecating manner, as though he had forgotten something vital. "Oops," he said then, taking out Weiss's gun from the small of his back. [Roland looked on in horror!] "Can't be too careful," he said, winking at Roland.

When Kain pulled open the door, the effluvium of the place made Roland back away: he almost retched; and then, the two filthy white men scrambled out, onto the floor of the basement, their chests heaving.

"*What the hell…!*" Roland squealed.

"Let me handle this," Kain said, still with his disconcerting calmness. All Roland could do was stand there, feeling himself being devoured by the (un)reality of the two men on the ground—and of everything else—

"Okay," Kain started then, addressing the panting men, "have you figured out what madness is yet, Dr. Fishman? How about you,

Mr. Weiss?" But Weiss seemed even more out of sorts than Fishman. The latter was so thin and frail that he conjured images of Nazi death camps; but Weiss, while he still had his girth, had cracked in one night, and could now do little more than stare mutely, with the eyes of a dog that was both terrified of its master and willing to do whatever its master wanted.

"—Please…" Fishman begged, beginning to sob on the ground.

"You've had three weeks now to come up with an answer, Dr. Fishman—you're not proving to be a good student."

"We'll do whatever you want!" he begged again.

"All I want—all I've *ever* wanted—is for you to tell me what madness is. Do you want to live, Dr. Fishman? I'm beginning to think that you have some death wish—you definitely won't last much longer."

"*Please*!" Fishman cried again.

"Answer the question!" Kain raged, and he cocked the pistol and loomed over the sobbing doctor threateningly. "Do you want to live!"

"Yes!" cried the doctor.

"You desire to live, and yet you can't tell me what madness is? Do you want to live!" he demanded again.

"*Yes*!" Fishman cried.

"Then, what is madness!"

"I don't know!"

"I'm really losing patience with you, doctor!"

"There is no answer!" Fishman cried in desperation. "No matter what I tell you, you tell me I'm wrong. There is no answer!" he said through his sobs, "—you probably don't know yourself!"

Kain laughed at the assertion, shaking his head. "Then, you're saying that madness is unknowable?"

"…Yes," he said, unsure, willing to do anything to appease Kain.

"*Wrong*!" Kain ejaculated, cocking the gun again. Fishman screamed; the heretofore mute Weiss began mumbling something to himself. "Do you know that you want to live!" Kain demanded yet again.

"Of course I do!"

"Then how can you not know what madness is…!" Kain was silent for a while, then he took a deep, ominous breath. "*Last* time, doctor," he said, now bending down and squatting on his hams, so that the gun was practically touching the frail doctor's trembling head. "What is madness?"

Roland, who looked on over Kain's shoulder, wanted to do something, but he was frozen in place; he had the sudden and debilitating idea that all his substance had left him, and that even if he tried to tackle Kain, he would only fly past the man, like a vapor—

"*What is madness*!" Kain screamed.

Desperate, Fishman cried, "Wanting—wanting to live!" And as he said it, he closed his eyes tightly, averting his face, as though expecting the thundering report of the gun, but:

"Congratulations, Dr. Fishman," Kain laughed, standing back up slowly. "Madness is wanting what you can't have."

Fishman began crying uncontrollably, because the logic of the words told him that he was a dead man. Kain looked back at Roland then, and nodded; Roland, the vapor in search of his will, could only stare with an expression as desolate as his hopes and dreams. And while Fishman's cries filled the chamber, and both the meaning of madness and the reality of madness played itself out before him, Roland stood there, preparing himself for the inevitable. Kain turned back towards the doctor at that moment. They were all prepared for Kain to blow the man's brains out, but:

"You may go now, Doctor," he said in a calm, almost indifferent voice. "Take Mr. Weiss with you." Fishman looked up, unsure. Before the man could say anything, Kain walked up to Roland, who glanced uneasily at Kain's gun. But: "Come, Micheaux," Kain said as he walked past, gesturing for Roland to follow, "there is much work for us to do yet."

* * *

IF KAIN HAD kept the television on for five more seconds, he and Roland would have seen it all. Maria Santos's cameras had been on the faces of the crowd, showing one dark, brooding mass. They had all been standing beyond the police barrier, watching the policemen milling about as they detailed the crime scene. But in time, as the people stood there, what had been shock, turned to outrage. Someone started yelling about what had been done to the Thomases and Marenga. The same thing was happening! The police were killing their children—exterminating them like *rats*—and even the goddamn Mayor, a *black* man, didn't give a shit about them! The outrage grew until several people began yelling across the barrier at the police. Field commanders were consulted; and these cautious men advised their subordinates to break up the crowd—move them along before they became violent. But when the policemen began to tell the people to move on, the people only yelled back louder. One enterprising officer took out his baton; but in trying to goad a screaming black man into compliance, he only stoked the outrage of the crowd further. This officer got punched in the face; and then, a millisecond later, the whole angry mass ran through the police barrier....Sometimes people revolted because the injustice that had been done was so egregious that maintaining one's identity and humanity demanded action. Sometimes, when people revolted, the trigger, itself, was irrelevant—like the proverbial straw that broke the camel's back; sometimes people revolted because of what they had lost; sometimes people revolted because they had nothing to lose. There were those who made a conscious decision to revolt, and those who surrendered their wills to it, so that they could claim afterwards that they had had no choice. As for the people on the Harlem streets, who knows what their reasons were—who knows if there were even reasons. All that there was now, was a world of action—and Maria Santos's cameras were there to capture it all. Tomorrow, or the day after that, or the day after that...there would be consequences. But now, as cries and gunshots and the sounds of things being broken, rose in the air, there were only actions and reactions.

* * *

IT WAS ABOUT two hours after Marenga emerged from his coma and opened his pale, soulless eyes to the world, that he finally regained consciousness. Because of his corpse-like expression, those gathered around—doctors, policemen and Botswana Glade—thought that he had sustained brain damage. The chief doctor was in the process of checking Marenga's vital signs, when the latter's heretofore blank eyes looked up quizzically at the man. The doctor gasped.

"Do you know your name?" asked the doctor, an old white man with a benevolent face; and over the man's shoulders, Botswana

Glade and the police detective soon hovered, like relatives looking into a crib to hear a baby's first words.

Marenga wanted to curse the man—scream out that of course he could understand—but he was too weak. He barely managed to nod.

"What's the last thing you remember?" the man asked again.

Marenga went to say, *Wishing you all dead*! but curbed himself. "...Rally," he whispered.

The old man smiled, relieved; Marenga looked with further annoyance at the others, just as the doctor broke in again:

"The police are going to have to ask you some questions now, Mr. Marenga."

Marenga grunted.

The detective stepped up now. Maybe it was the residual effects of his heart attack, but the detective's face struck him as plate on which some repulsive dish was strewn. His lips were like greasy sausage links; his nose was like a half-eaten carrot; his eyes were like rotten eggs; and the entire dish was swarming with some nasty-looking gravy, which Marenga in time discerned to be the man's perspiration. The man walked up with a macho swagger and declared:

"I just want to fill you in on what has happened since your fainting spell at your little rally. [Marenga scowled at his tone.] First, a riot broke out, right in front of City Hall; then, some raping, murdering lunatic ran off with a little white girl; and when confronted by a cop, he shot him. In the resulting police chase through Harlem, there have been several other deaths—"

"Yea!" Botswana Glade exploded at the detective's mention of Harlem, "and you can bet your *last* dollar that we'll be organizing another rally tomorrow *in Harlem* for all those slain and wounded kids! And don't think we forgot about the Thomases, you bastards!"

The detective, fighting his every impulse in order to remain calm, went back to Marenga: "Look, Marenga," he continued, "things are *tense* out here, and something major's going to happen if all of this isn't resolved. There have been little skirmishes going on all over the city; and on top of everything, the *Mayor* quit!" At these last words, Marenga showed interest for the first time. But just then, Botswana Glade broke in:

"What do you expect him to do about it! You want him to sweep it all under the rug, don't you? Want him to make some stupid ass,

Rodney King, 'Why can't we all get along?' statement before the press? This is all *your* doing!" Botswana Glade roared, his horse teeth bared threateningly. "Don't try to make us responsible for your mess, you bastards!"

"Now wait a goddamn minute!" the detective yelled back at last. "You're the ones who started this mess, with your goddamn rallies!"

"You evil devils!" Botswana Glade squealed, "...always putting blame on somebody else!"

"—*Enough*!" the doctor yelled. "Both of you get the hell out of here! This is a hospital!"

Botswana Glade and the detective looked at the doctor confusedly, scowled as they looked back at one another, then left begrudgingly. The doctor nodded to Marenga and left as well; but when they were all gone, Marenga closed his eyes contentedly and chuckled to himself.

* * *

ALL THE MEDIA stars were out tonight.

Maria Santos was almost hoarse by now. The scenes of the riot—of *all* the riots—were before them now; and her screechy homily on the bestiality of their society was everywhere. Her homily encompassed Randolph's desertion, Roland Micheaux's murderous rampage, Marenga's irresponsibility, Botswana Glade's maniacal agenda...—everything and everybody, it seemed....

On another channel, Botswana Glade was standing outside of the hospital where Marenga was recuperating. "This should be seen as an attack on the black community!" The man shouted, his horse teeth bared to the cameras. "First the Thomas murders, and now this..."—he searched frantically for a word—"*Raid*...! *Yes*, the people are justified in rebelling against the police! Their raid on those young kids in that party was ill conceived and simply *racist* in origin! This kind of ambush—and it was exactly that—would *never* have happened in a *white* community. *Never* would you have police officers firing into a crowd of innocent *white* kids. But this kind of thing happens on a *daily* basis in our community!" he raged, waving his bony hand in the air. "Moreover," he continued, his eyes boring into the camera with new contempt, "were it not for the fact that reporters and policemen were searching desperately for a black man who had supposedly harmed some of their own—not only a cop, but *a rich white family*—and that our *weak*-minded Mayor happened to stumble into the mess left by the police's uncaring haste to punish that man, then we would not be hearing about *any* of this! It is time for us to forge a mandate for action! There will be a rally in Harlem tomorrow! It is time for us to mobilize and put an end to such attacks, by exercising our constitutional right to protect ourselves...!"

At the same time, in Brooklyn, Captain Miller, the man in charge of the entire Roland Micheaux manhunt, was on the air as well. He stood on the steps of the precinct where he was based, giving a statement to the press. About a dozen uniformed police officers stood in the background as he declared: "Recent events have not, in our opinion, shown a pattern of police brutality, but, on the contrary, a pattern of brutality *against* policemen. First," he went on, raising his hand threateningly in the air, "there was Officer Flanders's murder by that killer and rapist, Roland Micheaux; and now, once again, we have an incident, instigated by Roland Micheaux, where policemen trying to bring him to justice were attacked by a mob. That was the only reason they fired: they were defending themselves! And now, we have a riot, with people attacking the police directly! In view of these events, many officers have been contemplating going on strike to show this city our worth—"

"When?" yelled a reporter.

"We will decide that tomorrow—after the memorial for Officer Flanders and all the slain and wounded offers who have fallen over the last few days. [He looked into the camera ominously now.] One man, Roland Micheaux, has caused all of this—the quicker we get him off the streets, the better we will all be. Just ask Officer Mucelli here," he said, putting his arm around the young cop at his side. "He dealt with that killer firsthand. This is a *real* hero here!"—Mucelli looked as though he were in shock; his face seemed haggard—"Yes, here is a man who went out there and did his job!"

A reporter asked: "How are you feeling, Officer Mucelli?"

Mucelli leaned over to the microphone timidly: "Fine, sir."

Miller beamed; but then, another reporter asked, "If all the policemen go to Flanders's memorial, won't there be a shortage of officers to control the possible unrest tomorrow if Botswana Glade and his supporters get out of hand?"

Miller snorted in a sardonic manner, then went on: "If the choice is between paying homage to our fallen brothers, and putting out our necks for people who don't care about us, then we choose to pay homage…."

And of course, McPrice was there. She was back at her upper west side office, answering questions from the assembled reporters.

"What do you make of the latest events, Councilwoman?" a reporter asked.

"Well," she started with a sigh, "without a doubt, they call for change—especially in terms of leadership. The final result, in terms of innocent deaths, was unfortunate, but let us not forget the facts here. As I have been told, the police went to arrest that maniac, Roland Micheaux, who was even then running from them. A mob attacked the police officers, and they defended themselves. The final result of that pursuit is unfortunate—even *tragic*—but the thing is not to fight ourselves. We have to get that fugitive to justice—lock him behind bars with the other homicidal maniacs. In this instance, we might even get a chance to use the death penalty. After all, Roland Micheaux has killed twice; and, in the midst of all of this," she added in a pained voice, "let us not forget that Cindy Phelps is still in a coma from when he shot her in the head. Let us not forget that a scared little girl might have to grow up without her mother. No, Roland Micheaux, and misguided, self-absorbed men like Marenga—and now his lackey, Botswana Glade—are the cause of all of this strife. Combine that with weak leadership from the Mayor, and you have a dangerous situation. We cannot constantly go on blaming the police for everything. They are doing their job, which is fighting crime, and we must support them if we expect to have a lawful society…."

* * *

LIEUTENANT ERICSSON HAD watched the captain's press conference on the steps of police headquarters, then gone back to his office with a rising sense of alarm. While in Harlem, tear gas was being used to disperse the angry crowds, he sat in the darkness of his office by himself. The initial forensic report on the Flanders crime scene, and the murder weapon, had come back half an hour ago. Flanders had been shot in the *back*, which didn't make sense, since he and Micheaux had supposedly been fighting *hand-to-hand*. According to Mucelli's testimony, Micheaux had had Flanders up against the car, so how in the hell could he be shot in the back…! But the other, more troubling thing, was that there were no fingerprints on the gun—*not even Mucelli's*! It had obviously been wiped clean; and since Micheaux certainly hadn't wiped it before throwing it to the ground and running off, that left only one person: *Mucelli*!

Ericsson had said before that something was very wrong, but he was only now beginning to see how true that was. Just before the press conference, he had been reading the statement of the doorman at Micheaux's condominium. According to the man, Mindy Phelps, the little girl that Micheaux had supposedly kidnapped, had been brought in *the night before* by the nanny—something which had happened at least once before. Micheaux had left his house *with the little girl* the next morning, about 8 o'clock. Another report from a cabbie said that he had dropped them both off at the Phelps home about 8:45 that morning—five minutes before neighbors heard the gun shots and saw him running away with Mindy; but as the coroner had told him at the crime scene, Dallas had been dead for *hours*. Moreover, according to the doorman, Micheaux had been at home all night with his girlfriend; and before that, he had been at a news conference! Those were all practically air-tight alibis—unless there was something that Ericsson was missing. It was still possible that Micheaux had shot Cindy Phelps, but the gun had been in her hand when they found her; and as Micheaux had fled from the scene with such haste, it was doubtful that he had planted it on her! Yet another thing was that there were only two sets of prints on the gun—both belonging to the couple—so it was looking more like a murder-suicide all the time….But the fact that Micheaux had run, kept alive Ericsson's doubts. The man had run for some reason—run for *blocks*!—and in Ericsson's experience, innocent men didn't run like that….Maybe things would be clearer if they could only find the missing nanny—whom some were suggesting Micheaux had killed, or had been an accomplice. The doorman had mentioned that she was a mess—and had come in the middle of the night, as though running from something. They had found a cryptic letter back at Micheaux's condominium, written by the nanny, in which she said that she was leaving for Boston and that Micheaux could "handle the situation" any way he pleased. Obviously something had happened—but *what*?

Ericsson groaned in the darkness: he didn't like this at all! Only the final forensic report on the Phelps home was to be viewed: that was why he was still there. They were to call him when they were done. They had found semen all over the place: hopefully some of it was Micheaux's—or at least, not the husband's.... With all that had happened—and all that seemed on the verge of happening—Ericsson was almost *hoping* that Micheaux had done it!

* * *

THERE WERE STILL about half a dozen reporters at Charlotte McPrice's office. It had been a busy night, with the Mayor quitting and all the riots. Most had stood around to ask her follow-up questions and ingratiate themselves with the woman who was now, for all intents and purposes, the Mayor of New York City. Finally answering her last question, McPrice waved to them all and wandered off into her private office. They all watched her go, each one admiring the graceful precision of her movements.

I wonder where my husband is? she wondered when the door was closed behind her. It wasn't that she really cared: she was only concerned that he wasn't out somewhere, getting drunk. But even that might work for her at this point: portray her as a woman who could overcome her husband's weaknesses. And she certainly had! In time, she would have to divorce him, but she had plenty of time to think about that. As for now, nothing could stop her. In a matter of days, she was going to win the election and become the Mayor of New York City! She was just about to smile to herself when she heard a knock on the door. The prospect of another interview was loathsome to her, but she was a pragmatist.

"Come in!" she called, turning around just as two plain-clothed policemen entered the room.

The sight of their badges left her nonplused for moment, and there was a look on their faces that she couldn't quite gauge. Their expressions were a strange combination of respect and dread as they walked up to her. She frowned.

"Good night, ma'am," one started, bowing his head reverentially.

"Hello officers," she ventured, aware that this was just a polite prelude to something much more weighty and troubling.

"It's about your husband, ma'am," the other one put in.

What has he done now! she thought warily, just as the first policeman sighed sorrowfully, saying:

"He's dead, ma'am."

"*What*!" She was actually shaking; she took an unconscious step back and rested against her desk. Her mind was suddenly sluggish. She hadn't loved him—at least, not in the last few years—but still…! "*How*?" she demanded.

"He was shot ma'am—seems like a suicide, but it looks suspicious—we're still conducting an investigation."

"Where'd it happen…did anyone see?"

"He was found in his car—it was parked in an alley behind the bar where he was drinking. Nobody even heard a gun shot."

She nodded her head, but hadn't really heard.

"We're sorry about this, ma'am," one ventured.

"Yea," added the other. "The body is down at the morgue. Do you want to see it?"

"…Not tonight," she whispered.

"We liked what you said on the air—you always support cops: we need that right now."

She nodded to them as they bowed their heads and left. *Her husband was dead*! She didn't know what she was feeling. It wasn't exactly grief; still, there had been good times—before the man she had fallen in love with turned into a coward and a drunkard. Maybe that was the thing to be mourned. She sat down on a couch to think about it all, when someone knocked on the door again. Before she could say anything, the door opened. It was Wisinski. He stepped up to her quickly, excitement gleaming in his eyes; she rose to hug him.

"How are you doing? I guess you've heard the news?" he said when they disengaged, his eyes still gleaming with excitement.

She frowned unconsciously, but went on: "I'll be all right. I just can't believe that he's gone."

"Well," Wisinski said with contempt, "he *deserved* to die."

"Nobody deserves..." But she again looked at him, seeing the strange excitement in his eyes. They stared at one another then: she searching and he letting her see. Finally seeing, her breath got caught in her throat as a cold shiver went down her back. She went to sit back down, but Wisinski took her hand and pulled her up again. She was staring at him the way someone stared at a stranger—at a *killer*!

"Come now," he said, supporting her weight as he strode with her towards the door. "I told the press to stick around: you have another announcement to make."

—While all over the city, the rage and madness and senselessness of the day, set many dark possibilities in motion, McPrice shuddered; and then, while she stumbled along and stared at the man in horror, he exulted: "Now *nothing* can stop you!"

* * *

WHILE ALL OVER the city, the police dispersed the last of the crowds with tear gas and rubber bullets, and Botswana Glade palliated them into strategic retreat by vowing that tomorrow would be the day of reckoning, Randolph walked up to his brother's upper west side co-op. Out of the abyss that was Randolph's youth, only his brother was left. As he pressed the intercom button for his brother's apartment, he couldn't feel his fingers anymore. It had been a 20-minute walk from where the policemen had let him out, to here. Randolph had walked the blocks slowly, stiffly, feeling the frigid air in his bones. He did not exactly know *why* he had come here, just as he did not know why he had walked into the mob; but one thing was certain: whatever was leading him, was self-destructive. Or maybe it was only that that danger was everywhere....

He took his numb finger away from the button and waited. He was standing in front of a glass door, which had a cardboard cutout of Count Dracula with the caption: "Happy Halloween." The room beyond the glass had a rich quality about it. There was a plush couch and two antique armchairs, all situated on an exquisite oriental rug. The light from the lamps reflected off the tan upholstery, giving the room a golden quality. There were also some rubber plants and palms in the corners: a perfectly arranged scene. Yes, his brother,

Roger had done well for himself after his stint in prison. The man had gotten his life back on track and was now a CPA of all things. Maybe that, too, was why Randolph had come: to find out the secrets of his brother's magic. The man was happily married, with two beautiful kids—

Randolph looked at his watch. It was just past midnight. Maybe Roger was already sleeping; maybe Roger's wife and kids would be woken up as well; maybe Roger wouldn't be glad to see him after all...Where would he go now? He didn't want to be alone tonight—and he certainly couldn't go back to Gracie Mansion. He wasn't the Mayor anymore—he had given all of that up: had *fled* from it....He had felt the fists of spirits tonight: had heard their eerie voices more clearly than he had thought possible; and after a night out in the cold, he was desperate for even the illusion of safety that his brother could provide. In fact, on his walk over here, he had even thought about going back to his wife—

"Yes?" said a husky voice over the static of the intercom.

"Hello—Roger?—it's Alex!" he said, too loudly.

"*Alex*...! Thank God...! Come in!"

There was a loud, buzzing noise; Randolph pushed the door and stepped in cautiously, as though expecting something to break. The abundant heat of the chamber engulfed him at once. There was a momentary burning sensation on his exposed skin, which made him think that he was on fire. Still, he was relieved beyond reason to be out of the cold—and ostensibly away from ghosts. Only after he entered the elevator, did he find himself wondering what he was going to say to his brother. They were on good enough terms. They met for the big holidays: Thanksgiving, Christmas...birthdays. Still, since the summer that Randolph found out the truth about the world, there had been a certain stiffness between them. Randolph, distrustful of everything from that world, had never really accepted his brother back into his heart—even after the man began to make a success out of his life. In a sense, his temple had been destroyed that summer, and he had never been able to find another god. It seemed so obvious to him now—but the truth always was....

Roger was standing in the doorway of his apartment when Randolph emerged from the elevator. The man was in a bathrobe, gesturing for Randolph to come. His brother was a plump man of average height, who had just turned 45.

—While all over the city, people were being taken to hospitals and police stations by the droves, Randolph looked at his brother's concerned face, realizing that their positions had switched: that now his brother was the success, and he was the failure. Randolph walked towards his brother slowly, still arguing whether or not he should have come—

"I saw everything on TV," Roger said when Randolph was close enough.

"Lucky for me then," Randolph tried to joke. The men stared intently at one another for a weird moment.

"—Come in, come in," Roger said suddenly, as if coming out of a spell.

"Don't want to be seen in public with me, huh?" Randolph said, again trying to joke, but neither of them laughed.

They entered the living room. The lights were off, but the television was on, showing a news channel. Maria Santos was everywhere....

"Maybe I shouldn't have come over," Randolph found himself saying.

"Don't be ridiculous—"

"Did I wake you up?"

"Naw, I was watching television." But at that, Roger looked at his brother nervously; and then, seeming to need something to do, he turned and locked the front door. "I was just going to make some hot chocolate," he was saying now. "You want some?"

"Sure."

Roger gestured again, and they walked towards the kitchen. Just then, Roger's wife poked her head out of the bedroom, her hair in curlers.

"Is everything all right, honey?" she asked.

"Everything's fine, Mary," Roger answered; and then: "It's only Alex."

"Oh...Alex," she said, sounding unsure.

"Hi, Mary," Randolph greeted her.

"Hi—you all right?"

"Yea...I'm fine."

"Go back to sleep, honey," Roger said.

"I'm sorry if I woke you up, Mary," Randolph apologized.

"Oh, it's okay," she said, vaguely. "Good night."

"Pleasant dreams," Randolph said, and both men watched her head disappear. Randolph was feeling uneasy about intruding again, but Roger was gesturing him to the kitchen now.

Randolph sat down heavily at the kitchen table, while Roger put on the kettle.

"...So, you saw me give it all up, huh?" Randolph said sarcastically, smiling as he looked down at his fingernails.

"I saw lots of strange things tonight."

"Yea...me too."

Seemingly needing to preoccupy himself, Roger went to the cupboard to get some mugs.

And then, sitting down in the seat across from his brother: "What *happened* tonight?" he asked cautiously and uneasily. "I mean, what have you been going through? First the divorce, and now this. What's driving you?"

"That's a good question, brother?" Randolph said with another chuckle.

"...What are you going to do now?"

"What is there to do...? I won't starve, if that's what you mean."

"You *really* don't want to be Mayor anymore?" he asked incredulously.

"I don't know what the hell I want," he said in an offhand manner. "That's the most honest thing I can say to you. I just know that I'm sick of it all. It *sickens* me...I don't want any part of it."

"What *really* happened tonight?" Roger said again, this time in a more ominous tone.

"Death," Randolph returned. "Eventually everyone looks up and sees death standing there; and then, their only choices are surrendering to it, or running for dear life."

"And which did you choose?"

Once again Randolph chuckled to himself, while his brother looked on confusedly.

"...You need a break from everything, Alex," Roger started, now convinced that his brother was having a nervous breakdown. "...Look, I, myself know how hard you worked. I've *seen* you...all my life—"

"You happy Roger?" Randolph said abruptly, looking at his brother critically.

"What?"

"Are you happy? Are you *fulfilled* by your life?"

"...I suppose—yea....Why?"

"I just needed to know."

"Look," Roger started in a more determined tone, "we're not kids anymore, Alex."

"No, I guess we're not." And then: "I just came from our old neighborhood," he went on quickly, as if admitting some sin. "It's all in ruins now. There was going to be a development there, so I had it all destroyed. [He laughed strangely.] Maybe that's the only way...nothing was ever built on sterile ground—there was always something there before: something that had to be destroyed to make way for progress...."

Roger looked at him for a long while, a side of him terrified—either of his brother, or the world that could do this to the man who, for Roger's entire life, had been a kind of god—

But just then, the kettle began to boil; and a millisecond later, the kitchen door burst open as Roger's five-year-old daughter entered the room. "Daddy, I'm hungry," she moaned, rubbing her eyes; then, looking up and seeing Randolph, an astonished smile suddenly came to her face: "Hi, uncle Alex!" she said, giggling as he picked her up and put her on his knee.

"Worry no longer, my dear," Randolph said as he tickled her, "—feeding the hunger of little kids is what us grownups are for."

* * *

KAIN AND ROLAND snuck out of the sewers, emerging onto a dark, empty block. Roland could still hear Fishman's desperate cries in his mind; and with sirens blaring a few blocks away, it was as though the world were crying. Every once in a while, he would swear that he heard gunshots and people screaming—but who could tell anymore?

They walked along in silence, until Roland freed himself of enough of his drunkenness/numbness to look over at the man beside him and say: "Kain, where are we going?"

"We're going to turn ourselves in," Kain responded with his usual calmness. "Isn't that what you wanted, Micheaux?"

"...Yea," Roland said, surprised and confused. He looked over at Kain warily: "You're going to let me?" And he glanced uneasily at Kain's hand, because the man still held the handgun.

But Kain only laughed softly; he looked at the gun as though he had forgotten about it, then put it in his pocket. "There, Micheaux—feel safer now?" And then, still smiling in his inscrutable way, he went on: "I never have, nor will I *ever* force you to do anything against your will, Micheaux—except listen and look and draw conclusions from your observations. We all have free will—even the slaves among us. We all have power over that one vital thing: if we live or die. You have chosen to die."

Roland stared at him for a while. Kain was so self-assured, that Roland once again felt his will eroding. He was sick of going back and forth between life and death—between resolution and desolation. In frustration, he cried out: "What the hell do you expect me to do, Kain! You think I can go back home and act like none of this ever happened!"

"Here, Micheaux," Kain said, handing him the gun—

"I don't want it—"

"*Take* it!" Kain demanded, so that the desolate Roland held the thing tentatively, looking even more distraught.

"There, Micheaux," Kain said with a menacing look, "blow your fucking brains out! You want to die? *Die*!" While Roland stood there fidgeting, Kain grabbed his gun hand and began putting it to his temple. "*Do it*!" he demanded, while Roland instinctively tried to fight him off. "Do it!" Kain demanded, until Roland began to sob, like Fishman had sobbed.

"Look at you!" Kain raged. "Your head's so fucked up, you're rushing to be some goddamn martyr. *Look* at you!" he went on in disgust. "Dreaming about going out in some cinematic, 'Disney Movie of the Week,' 'I want to do what's best' scene. Be *real*, Micheaux! You're a *nigger*! [Roland shook his head feebly and unconsciously.] You were never nothing but a nigger to them! Let the world fuck itself if it wants! *Smell* the madness in the air now: people wanting all kind of things they'll never receive—things they can't even conceptualize: justice, revenge, order, peace...all of that.

Millions of fools are out there now, bandying about your life as if it were meaningless, and yet you have the *nerve* to think about them! You self-hating bastard, wanting to turn yourself in so that they can treat you like an animal—parade you like some freak! You think you'll be at peace if you turn yourself in, Micheaux? You think that all of a sudden everyone will start loving one another! *Fuck* society!

"Your life is nothing but a passing news blurb, to be forgotten in a week's time. You think you're at peace with turning yourself in, but what you're feeling now isn't peace: it's the resolution of a *suicidal* man! Always fight death, Micheaux—even if all you can manage is a couple of seconds. Make death take you like a *man*—don't let him trick you; because death is a lazy bastard, who will get you to do all of his work for him if he can!"

—But in that world of random violence, it was then that a young black man came up behind them. Actually, it was a youth, no older than 17. "Yo!" he called, and when Roland and Kain looked around, they saw that the youth had a revolver pointed at them.

"Gimmie all your shit!" he demanded. And then, seeing Roland holding the gun: "Drop it!"

Roland did as told, actually dropping it because his hands were trembling too violently. It seemed as if time had stopped, or as if time were going in some maddeningly convoluted loop. He was back at the parking garage again, being robbed by Lamar Smith—

"Back away from the gun!" the youth screamed again, and Roland and Kain complied. Roland's entire body throbbed with the pulse of his heart. Every time he thought that it was over, it was only just beginning! When Roland and Kain backed away far enough, the youth picked up the gun and put it in the small of his back; then, "Gimmie all your shit!" he screamed again.

"'Gimmie all your shit?'" Kain laughed with a frown. "Now is that any way to ask for something? Whatever happened to, 'Your money or your life?' At least that had some style—"

"Shut the fuck up!" the youth screamed, but was instinctively taken aback by something in Kain's eyes. "I ain't playing!" he said, maybe more to himself than them. "Gimmie all your shit!"

But Kain only laughed and turned to Roland, saying: "Here is a perfect specimen of society, Micheaux: a mind so corrupted by unattainable desires that—"

"*Shut the fuck up*!" the kid screamed hysterically. "I said give me everything you got!" But then, suddenly recognizing Roland, the kid's eyes bulged. "I *know* you! You're that nigger on TV! I bet I can get money for you!"

Kain snickered: "These are the fools you're trying to defend, Micheaux: a thief wanting to turn you in to the police for a reward."

"Keep quiet, old man!"

But Kain only shook his head and smiled to himself; and then, as though remembering something more relevant to his time: "Come on, Micheaux," he said, grabbing Roland's arm and leading him away, "we have work to do—"

"*Don't move*!" the kid screamed, pointing the gun with a trembling hand, but Kain continued to pull Roland along. "*Stop*!" the kid yelled, but Kain ignored him; and Roland, caught in a world of indecision and horror, was pulled along like a swimmer caught in the undertow. It was then that the kid's gun went off; a moment later, Kain fell to the ground, going through the death throes on the filthy sidewalk. The man died like that old, fat cop had died—*horribly*, and with an unexpectedness that was brutal to the senses. Yes, time was indeed following some maddeningly convoluted loop, because Roland and the kid stared down at Kain like Mucelli and him had looked at Flanders. Still, it was as though the kid had taken Roland's place in the loop, because he bolted then—like Roland had bolted. For a moment, the only thing that Roland could do, was stare at Kain's unmoving body; but soon, the madness of the night—*of his entire life*!—seemed to drop on Roland's head, both crushing him and freeing him in a way he had never thought possible. Whatever Kain had meant to him—had *become* to him in the last few hours—the emptiness left by his death sparked something in Roland that was raw evil.

From some terrible place within himself, the rage escaped and burst to the surface like an erupting volcano. The kid was halfway up the block, but as Roland took off after him, it was the power of hell that was fueling his muscles. The kid kept looking back in horror, because Roland was like some demon pursuing him. The kid ducked into a side street; looking over his shoulder, he saw that Roland was only a few steps away. He aimed the gun and pulled the trigger; but somehow, miraculously, it jammed. And then, seeing that Roland was upon him, he let out an involuntary yelp as he was tackled by the other man. There were no boundaries for Roland now; and so, he used all of his strength and will when he knocked the kid into a wall. The sound of the kid's head knocking the brick wall was blunt and horrible—*sickening*. But Roland couldn't hear. He was pummeling the kid's unmoving head with his fist now. "*Nigger*!" Roland yelled as he smashed the kid's front teeth and broke his nose. "*Motherfucker*!" he screamed as he began pounding the kid's unprotesting head into the pavement. But then, in the middle of picking up the kid's head to once again smash it into the pavement, he remembered Kain: remembered the strange bond that they had somehow managed to forge; he remembered his mother and grandmother, and all the people he had ever professed to love; he remembered his pride and hope, now unrecognizable and useless to him; and then, with the last ray of light provided by his sanity, he saw himself, perched over the kid's bloody corpse like a vulture. Still resounding in the air were the words that he had called the kid. With a shudder, he got up...The kid was dead—there was no doubt about it. His hatred of the kid had driven him like nothing had ever driven him—just like Kain had said; and for the second time in his life, he had killed a man with his bare hands! The hate had driven him and intoxicated him, but the high was fading away now. Like heroin passing out of his system, the drug which had brought him to ecstasy, was now, with its passing, rending his insides. He needed something to salve the pain. But that was all that addiction was: a desperate attempt to find some equilibrium between the highs and lows—between ecstasy and agony....*Kain*! Remembering the man, Roland backed away from the corpse and ran back the way he had come. How far he had fallen, that Kain was all that he had to stave off the pain! But a block away from where he had left Kain, he stopped. Hundreds of people were screaming, running down the block in terror! There was smoke in the air—tear gas—and four police riot vans were pursuing the people down the street, followed by police cruisers. Roland stared at it all, not knowing what to think. The world was chaos personified, and he was being sucked in by it! He was hurtling though a senseless, churning world; and within that abyss, the only thing he had to keep him company was the knowledge that he was a killer after all: that he was everything they were saying, and that he didn't care—*couldn't* care. He had once hoped to find his father an unrepentant nigger—just as bad as everyone was saying. Now, as he watched the people fleeing from the police, he knew that *he* was that super nigger, who would unite all the niggers behind him; and that together, they would rise up against the world in an orgy of self-destruction. He had killed, and he wanted to kill again—*needed* to kill again, in order to ward off the cries of his addiction. But then, no sooner had he succumbed to this thought, than the reality of the words reached his inner consciousness, and he scurried away, like a thief startled not by the light, but the darkness within.

7.

The Rutting Season

The world was awakening, but awakening to the nightmares of the previous day. Reports of death and madness and property damage would be with them for some time still—especially as the worst of it still lingered on the horizon—

Randolph awoke with a start. He was lost in more ways than one. He looked wildly around the strange room, then stared at the backs of the two children who were lying on the floor, watching TV. It was a while before Randolph remembered that he was in Roger's home—and went to lie back down; but as soon as he did, all that had happened the night before came back to him, so that he sat up abruptly on the couch—as though from a bad dream. The children, engrossed in other matters, didn't even acknowledge him. Randolph felt sick. From the grandfather clock, he saw that it was a little after seven o'clock. Roger's eight-year-old son was changing the channels, holding the remote control in an authoritarian manner. His sister, not yet fully cognizant of the inequality inherent in their relationship, sat patiently, more interested in her doll than the television.

Randolph glanced at the screen, just as there was a brief glimpse of hundreds of black people, their faces contorted by rage. Botswana Glade's face appeared for a millisecond; but then Joel, Roger's son, quickly changed the channel, so that now, two sweaty, entangled professional wrestlers were on the screen.

"Quick—change it back!" Randolph yelled from the couch. Both children bolted around, surprised to see him up. Joel changed the channel.

"—Yes," Botswana Glade was saying, already surrounded by *hundreds* of people, "we are going to march down the street, and *nobody's* going to stop us!"

Randolph cringed, just as the scene changed back to the studio. The anchorman, a white man who looked as though he had just come out of high school, looked into the camera in bewilderment and went over last night's riots. While the litany of madness continued, they showed images of all the damage, revealing how nine people had been killed, dozens of stores looted…Randolph started at it in a daze, breathing shallowly. Perhaps two minutes passed with Randolph sitting there like that; and then, the anchorman went on:

"Charles Marenga is out of his coma and alert, but we haven't been able to speak with him—"

I've got to get the hell out of here! Randolph thought as he sprang up from the couch, tossing aside the blanket that had been covering him. He was wearing his pants and undershirt; he got his shoes from under the couch, then grabbed his shirt and jacket, which had been placed on the love seat—

"What's going on!" Roger said, running out at the commotion.

"Everything's crazy!" Randolph said as he hastily buttoned his shirt. Now, the anchorman was talking about the police rally that was going to happen at City Hall.

Roger's wife came out then, dressed in only a housecoat. "Is everything all right?"

"No," Randolph said, grimly, "—not at all."

She too stared at the television in silence. There was a report on the death of McPrice's husband now…

"You got an extra coat for me, Roger?" Randolph asked, recalling that he had left his at the TV studio.

"Yea," Roger answered vaguely, going to the hall closet. But then he stopped, venturing: "Where are you going, Alex? Maybe I should come with you."

"No," Randolph said quickly. And then, in a lower voice as he looked back at the television: "Your family needs you."

* * *

DAWN HAD SEEMED a long time in coming, but time was still

meaningless to Roland. He had fallen asleep on a park bench for two hours or so, seeming like any other homeless man. It was a miracle that he hadn't frozen to death. He was numb in body and mind as he sluggishly emerged from his dream world. He felt trapped between times: suspended between the events of 20 years ago and those of today. And just like 20 years ago, he shuddered at thoughts of a man dying in the gas chamber. Back then, it had been his father; but now, it was he…strapped into the death chair, veins bulging from his neck as he tried futilely to hold his breath! On the other side of the glass, were all the cheering people—a cheering world, in fact—convinced that justice was being done.

…*Twenty years ago*: everything that he was, was back there….The morning after his father's execution, he had woken up in the Louisiana bayou. His mother had driven him there the very night of the execution. After he came home from the prison, crying and distraught, they had both known that they couldn't wait in the house, counting down the hours until the execution as though the death to come would be theirs. His mother had made him pack a few things, and they had headed down the highway. He had woken up to the sights and sounds and smells of the Louisiana bayou. The car had stopped, and the sun was just coming over the horizon, and there was a wonderful peacefulness in the air. Remembering his mother, his eyes had shot to the driver's seat, where she had been watching him quietly. He had opened his mouth, perhaps to betray some childish relief that she was still there; but as he recalled his father, all that he had been able to say was, "It's over…." Yes, it had all been over: his father had been dead by then—*way* dead. His mother had nodded sorrowfully to answer him; and as he looked away in that moment of uneasiness, he had all at once realized that they were near his paternal grandmother's house. He had visited the woman last summer, and memories of it had still been fresh in his mind. She had goats and pigs and chickens; and one morning, he had awoken to the sound of all the animals seeming to cry out at once—crying out as though their lives were about to end at the jaws of some wolf. He had rushed to awaken his grandmother, pulling the old woman outside so that they could save the animals. He remembered that there had been a strange kind of energy in the air. All the animals had seemed crazy. Even he, for a moment, had wanted to scream out and run about. But his grandmother had only laughed and said that it was the rutting season: that the pigs and goats were all in season, and that this was the way of nature. She had taken him over to the pen, where he had watched the pigs. Some of them had been fighting in the muck; some of them had seemed just as violent in their coitus. That was the way of all life, she had told him as they stood above the fray. That churning violence had been the way that generations begot generations and life went on....

Back then, all those years ago, while the young Roland Micheaux sat in the car, remembering his grandmother, he had still been jarred by images of his father's death in the gas chamber; images of the ease of rustic life on the bayou had been confronted by images of his father surrounded by brick and steel and glass: all the hard creations of man. He had looked around, lost and confused by the contradictions, but relieved beyond reason that his mother was there. He had abruptly turned back to the woman then, desperate for her company, but—

"I need to get right," she had cut him off. "I need to be alone for a while." And those words had hurt him more than anything she could have said, because the realization that she was all that he had in the world, had come anew. Still, he had nodded: had been unable to deny his mother anything. She had reached over and hugged him tightly, while he sat there stiffly, hoping that she wouldn't crack the thin shell that covered the furnace of emotions raging within him.

"Take this money," she had said as he got out and grabbed his bag. "I'll come back for you at the end of the summer...." She had said other things, but he had just stood there, trying to buttress himself against the thought that she would be leaving him in a matter of seconds....And then, he had been standing there limply, watching the car disappear around the bend in a cloud of dust.

When he regained enough of his faculties, he had started down the sinewy footpath that led to his grandmother's house. He had gotten a glimpse of the ocean through the foliage, but the footpath was taking him deep into the bayou. Part of him had always been terrified of the bayou—the creepy silence of it. And now that he thought about it, his grandmother had always seemed like an old witch to him. Why the hell did she live all the way out here? And he had always been unnerved by the fact that she ventured out into the bayou in the middle of the night by herself, without fear of snakes and crocodiles and all the monsters of a child's imagination. That apparent fearlessness had identified her as either a conduit or a *conjurer* of magic, so that even while it unnerved him, he was desperate to learn her spells....

In time, he had entered a foggy patch in the bayou, now unable to see 15 meters in front of him. The seeping water had been practically everywhere, making him have to hop on rocks and roots and fallen trees to keep from walking in the murky water. The stillness of the place, with the cries of far-off birds sounding like the insane pleas of the dying, had put an urgency in his steps. The moss-covered magnolia trees had now been everywhere; and as he looked at them, he had been convinced that they held angry spirits. The rancid-smelling water and the acrid smell of the earth, itself, had kindled thoughts of dead, rotting bodies; in fact, *all* around him, had been a place where one could disappear and be lost forever.

He had practically been running at full speed when he saw his grandmother's shack in the distance. The little house had been on stilts, to guard against the constant floods. The weathered boards of the structure had been partially covered by creeping vines, again striking him as some witch's hovel. The skein of smoke coming from the rickety chimney had been the only sign of life. He had stood there equivocally for a while, again uncertain of how to proceed; but just then, the scrawny black dog, Napoleon, had begun to bark from the front porch. The dog had first charged him threateningly, before stopping with an unsure yelp. Seeming unable to decide if it recognized him or not, Napoleon had then barked at him from the safe distance of few meters, while Roland stood there frozen. A few moments later, his grandmother, hearing the commotion, had finally come out. In the misty morning air, she had seemed older that time, itself; and yet, the woman had seemed as spry as she was fragile-looking. That incomprehensible mutability had always been her magic. It had been as though she could be anything; and at that moment, a side of him had desperately needed that. She had been wearing a long, billowy dress that danced around her thin figure and made her look even more like a conjure woman. As she approached, Napoleon had looked back at her for some clue of what to do; then, as she smiled and walked up, the dog had sniffed the air, scratched himself and trotted off into the mist, chasing some unknown quarry. She had walked up to Roland slowly, seeming to drift in the early morning air like a ghost. When she held him, and he smelt her sweet cinnamon scent in his nostrils, he had at last burst out crying—as uncontrollably as he had cried the night before. Wordlessly, his grandmother had taken him into the house….

He had slept again; and when he awoke in her immaculately clean house, it had been around noon. She had just been about to cook lunch; and seeing his eyes open, she had called him over with a gesture of her head. That taciturnity had always been her way—as it usually was with people who lived alone. When he went over to her, he had seen that she was holding a live chicken; and when he gleaned what it was she wanted him to do, he had shuddered, shaking his head. But she had been adamant—not with words, but with her stare. She had gestured to a heavy knife lying next to the sink and held the bird down against a board.

"Chop the neck cleanly," she had said, the intensity in her eyes making him tremble even more.

He had been numb as he rose the knife in the air; he had been about to close his eyes, but—

"Always look at what you're doing, son!" she had chastised him.

He had held the knife tremulously in mid air, waiting for his moment of courage—for whatever impetus would allow him to do the act. His hands had been trembling so badly that he had feared that the knife would fall out—

"*Now*!" she had screamed; and then, a millisecond later, a muffled squeak had escaped from his lips as, in mid swing, he realized that he was actually doing it! The sound of metal going through flesh and bone and hitting wood had resounded in his mind. Horrified, he had looked on as the chicken's head rolled off the board. And then, as the chicken's headless body squirmed macabrely beneath his grandmother's firm grasp, he had had to hold back the urge to vomit. He had looked over at his grandmother just in time to see her put her head back and laugh:

"You're a *killer*, son!"

A side of him, remembering his father, had wondered what kind of freakish childhood the man had had. But she had pat him on the back then, still chuckling to herself as she went on: "No, son, this ain't what your daddy done—ain't nothing natural about what he done. Don't worry, son," she went on with a reassuring smile, "you ain't your daddy. Sometimes evil grips you, but evil don't have to scheme. The Devil don't have to plant evil in men's hearts—to *trick* them into selling their souls. Men got to *want* the evil—to *choose* it. This is nature," she had said, pointing to the chicken's slowly twitching body, "and maybe she ain't always good, and she ain't always right, but she'll always tell you what you need to survive and grow strong. This," she had said, again pointing to the chicken, "is what we do to survive…."

Back then, the young Roland had been suddenly reassured about the world and all that had happened. But now, as the adult Roland looked about the park, there was no such peace in him. Then, the worst had been behind him; now, the worst lay ahead. And he had seen too much—*done* too much…! Cindy raped and bloody, Phelps shot to death, that cop blown away, Kain blown away, the kid that he, himself had murdered…! Death was everywhere, no match for his grandmother's eccentricities.

He got up from the park bench then, stretching and moaning. As blood began to flow to all of his numb parts, and sensation came back to his limbs, he looked about the park again, seeing how filthy it was. Dog droppings, food wrappers and broken bottles were everywhere. On the streets surrounding the park, were slums and abandoned buildings. What an ugly place! he thought to himself. Either the people who lived here were animals that had never attained their humanity, or, left abandoned in this wasteland, maybe they were simply reverting to the natural state and mindset of all humans. But then, he recalled how yesterday, he, himself, had been a man….

He was about to sit back down and brood on these thoughts, when he detected something in the air. He looked around confusedly, realizing that whatever it was, it reminded him of his grandmother. It was that sound again, infusing him with the sensation of the rutting season. He realized that it was coming from down the block, and walked out of the park in order to look down the street. And then, as he stood on the curb, the rumbling cry of many crazed voices grew louder. Still numb from the cold, he shuffled to the end of the block, and stood at the corner, looking to his left; and there, before him, was a tangled mass of black humanity—or black bestiality, it seemed. It was making its way up the middle of the street! Hundreds—no, *thousands* of them! He took an unconscious step backwards, but froze after that one step. They spoke with one voice, but that voice was animalistic in its intensity and madness. They seemed gripped by the same primal forces that had gripped the animals in his grandmother's sties. He was not able to make out their words: they just rumbled in the air, like inarticulate thunder; but like thunder, the important thing was that they told him that a storm was coming. The thing in the street was a multi-legged beast, lurching along, stepping over whatever was in its path. It was about 100 meters away from him now, and there was no stopping it; but for a strange moment, he exulted at that. Would it be so bad to destroy everything—to toss this entire mess into some cosmic wastebasket and start over! For a moment, standing there on the curb, he wanted to let his voice join with theirs: to join that great, inarticulate rumbling that now drowned out everything else, and be the unrepentant super nigger of last night—

But the police, he suddenly realized, were across the street, walking down the sidewalk. They were quietly stalking the beast: more policemen than he had ever seen in his life! And now, suddenly, every window seemed to frame some gaping black face that was mesmerized by the beast lurking below. Some people were coming out of their tenements, standing on their stoops; some were joining the tangled procession of angry bodies. This was how the beast grew, Roland realized with a shudder. It was almost upon him now! The beast was coming up the sidewalk on his side, and if he didn't move, he would be trampled. He could smell its scent in the air—as strong and acrid as the musk of bitches in heat. It was young and old, male and female: a huge hermaphroditic orgy. And as the beast grew closer, he suddenly realized that he could decipher its voice now. "Justice, peace, war: *decide*!" the thing chanted. He shivered suddenly—either with fear and loathing, or with great joy. Unable, in those few seconds, to figure out which it was, common sense told him to flee—to run as far away as his legs would carry him! But then, just as urgently, there came a voice that told him to surrender. He had been running since yesterday, and he was tired. He had been running all his life, in fact; and for once, instead of running away, he wanted to delve into the fire. He went to *leap* in—to join the great orgy before him—but at the last second, some unknown force held him back. He moved to the side, pressing his back against the rickety, chain-linked fence of the park, just as the beast came upon him. There were only centimeters between he and they; the smell of them was even more pungent in his nostrils now; the din of them was maddening...He trembled as the beast moved past him like a huge predator that, bent on some more substantial prey, was oblivious of his presence. He watched its anger and indignation; he listened to the relentless tramping of its many feet; and then, as though hypnotized and aroused by both—and no longer able to resist its pheromones—he found himself walking along with it, his legs feeling like rubber, his mind light and somnolent. He kept his mouth shut; he kept his arms limply at his side; his soul was still telling him to run, but the tramping and the shouting, and the waving of so many limbs, cast a spell on him and carried him along.

* * *

MARENGA HAD HIS hospital bed up on an incline, and was watching a Saturday morning cartoon as he ate his breakfast—some gelatinous swill that was supposed to return him to health. He felt more tired—more *exhausted*—than he had ever been in his life. He could barely move his arms up to his mouth to feed himself. The nurse had started to feed him, but he had been annoyed by her presence; and she, a white woman, had been resentful of having to attend to him, so they had reached an agreement between themselves. His chest still ached—after all, they had sliced him open to operate—but there was a strange kind of peace about him: perhaps a *horrible* kind of peace.

Suddenly, the door opened and a man entered. Marenga looked over at the man and smiled, saying, "I was wondering when you were going to come."

Randolph stepped in quickly; he was breathing deeply, as though he had run all the way there. "So you know why I'm here?" he said as he stepped up to Marenga's bed.

All of Marenga's movements were slow and deliberate: the movements of an old, wounded man. He lay there considering Randolph for a while; then, still speaking softly and hoarsely: "You want me to control Botswana Glade? [Randolph nodded.] I was watching him on the news this morning," Marenga went on, gesturing to the TV on the far wall. "I got sick of it," he laughed in an off-hand manner, "so I turned on cartoons."

"—Can you do it?" Randolph asked eagerly. "Can you stop Botswana Glade?"

But Marenga laughed at him, taking another spoonful of the swill as he said: "I couldn't stop him even if he *wanted* to be stopped—it's beyond even Botswana Glade now: the people want this....As it is," he went on, his voice getting hoarser, "I have no control over Botswana Glade anymore—especially now as he has tasted power."

"Yea, I suppose so," Randolph said vaguely.

"And you can't stop them either," Marenga warned, after clearing his throat. "They hate you now—want nothing more than to rip you to shreds. I've seen the news," he said, looking at Randolph intently, "—saw the end of the debate last night—"

"That doesn't matter," Randolph said quickly.

"Nevertheless," Marenga went on, "your words at the debate required courage. Hopefully they'll eventually come to understand what you meant."

"They understand enough to vote me out of office," Randolph returned, sardonically. And then, to get them back on track: "We have to do something, Marenga."

"Like what?" he said with a bemused smile. "The time when you and I could have stopped this has passed, Randolph."

"Look, Marenga, I know you're tired—you're *sick*—"

But Marenga laughed out then, saying: "You have no idea how sick I am."

"Stop being so melodramatic," Randolph jibed anxiously, "the doctors say you can make a full recovery."

Margenga looked up as though to show Randolph how drained he was: how dead his eyes were—how *soulless*. "...You know what I did when I heard about the riot after my rally? I *laughed*! I've never felt such peace before—*never*! You're here to try to get me to stop what's going to happen, when my only reason for living is to see it all come to pass—"

"You don't really believe that!" he said in alarm.

"Don't I?" Marenga returned with a laugh. "Not only do I

believe it, but so do you!"

"*What?*"

"This is the time for *revenge*," Marenga said with an insane gleam in his eyes. "They had the chance to do right, but didn't—now, fuck 'em!"

"...Marenga," Randolph whispered in bewilderment.

"It's down to the wire now, Randolph. Time to face reality. No more *illusions*!" But at that Marenga began to cough uncontrollably; there was a glass of water on the night stand, and Randolph picked it up and brought it to Marenga's lips. There was something strangely tender about that scene, with Randolph holding the back of Marenga's head as he helped the man to drink the water.

"Thanks," Marenga said at last.

They were both silent for a while, perhaps a little embarrassed by their strange intimacy. Whatever the case, Randolph sat down on the edge of bed, his back to Marenga. They sat like that for a while, both brooding in the silence, until:

"We have to do *something*," Randolph repeated, turning around and looking at Marenga imploringly.

Marenga looked over at him and shook his head in bewilderment. "...You still love them, don't you?"

"What?"

"The people out there—the ones who are killing you. They annoy the hell out of you—disappoint you, perhaps—but you still love them."

"*What*...? Of course not—that would be insane. Look," he went on, as if fighting to put his thoughts together, "we have to do something...We've got to stop them....No matter what has happened, we can't act out of hate: can't *surrender* to it. They are human beings, Marenga—"

Marenga was about to laugh sarcastically when he happened to glance at the television. A special report had come on during the cartoon. On the screen, a sea of black people—*perhaps tens of thousands of them*!—could be seen marching down one of the streets of Harlem. The point of view changed, and now a lanky white reporter was standing on a side street; and over her shoulder, one could see the passing mob. The reporter was holding a microphone tremulously as she looked over her shoulder. She was visibly shivering as her shrill voice fought to be heard above the chanting of the crowd. Randolph grabbed the remote control and turned up the volume.

"...This thing was both spontaneous and planned," the reporter continued, "—instigated by racial activist, Botswana Glade. As far as we know, they intend to march to the sight of last night's..."—she seemed to search frantically for the right word, her lower lip trembling—"*incident*. Botswana Glade said that this would happen, but nobody could have guessed the scope...."

The scene changed to a television studio, where a skinny black anchorman seemed oblivious of the fact that he was on the air. The stillness of the newsroom seemed abrupt and bombastic. The anchorman was looking off-stage, as if he were receiving some new information. He suddenly looked directly into the camera. "We now have a reporter within the march, itself, alongside its supposed leader, Botswana Glade."

The scene changed. Suddenly, the viewer had the sensation of being engulfed in a sea of writhing bodies. The camera kept bounding up and down, as though the cameraperson were running along. The loud voices could now be heard clearly, chanting: "Justice, peace, war: *decide*!" Their many fists were raised defiantly; their voices were thunderous. An athletic-looking white male reporter was holding a microphone before Botswana Glade's indignant face. Botswana Glade had been shouting to the reporter—no one could *just* talk anymore—before the scene switched to him. Randolph leaned in closer.

"...Injustice demands action!" Botswana Glade roared.

"What do you say to those who would say that this is nothing more than inciting a riot," the reporter yelled back.

Botswana Glade thought for a moment, then: "Maybe we *need* to have a riot every once in a while," he said in a voice that was almost peaceful. [Randolph looked at Marenga with alarm, but the man only shrugged his shoulders and took another spoonful of the swill.] We need justice *any* way we can get it," Botswana Glade went on. "The end justifies the means, as they say. If this society can only understand, and be moved by, the realities of war, then it is in those terms that we must speak! Justice, peace, war: *decide*!" he continued chanting, with the others.

The reporter was still running along, trying to keep up—trying,

Randolph considered, to keep from being trampled by those behind him. The reporter looked into the camera now: "There you have it," he said, out of breath. "Now, back to the studio...."

Randolph was nibbling his lower lip anxiously. The anchorman was talking over images of the scene, noting the disruption of the traffic, and how the police have so far tried to maintain their distance. The man kept repeating that the situation was tense and unstable—stating the obvious. He revealed that off-camera, many officers were saying that they were not going to risk their lives if a riot broke out; others seemed to want a confrontation to re-exert their authority after the weakness of Randolph. And then, the anchorman went over how, at that very moment, hundreds of police officers were gathering in front of City Hall to mourn all the fallen officers and protest the unsafe conditions that they have been forced to work under—

Randolph anxiously got up and started for the door.

"Where the hell are you going!" Marenga demanded.

"I have to stop this," Randolph said vaguely, looking suddenly haggard.

"Don't do anything stupid!" Marenga called after him, but Randolph was gone. Marenga shook his head.

* * *

SOMETHING BRUTAL AND ineluctable had happened to Charlotte McPrice. Having climbed to the apex of the mountain, she had taken a misstep and was now hurtling headlong into the depths. She had been sitting in front of the television all night; and yet, she had done so without seeing. Her husband was dead...and her campaign manager was somehow responsible for it. She had spent the first couple of hours in shock and panic; but about four in the morning, staring at an old episode of "Leave it to Beaver," it had occurred to her that she was panicking not simply because of her campaign manager's involvement in her husband's murder, but because, on some level, she was willing to live with that—could, in time, even *exult* at that. She had had a perfect soul before—unsoiled. Fighting her way to the top, there had been nothing that she couldn't have taken, save the idea of herself as soiled.

Now, as she sat on her couch and stared at the special report on the march she felt, for perhaps the first time in her life, indecisive. The thing that had happened to her was like a boulder in her belly, keeping her from moving. She needed to run—to act quickly and decisively—but she was trapped on the ground...*helpless*. There was a poison working its way through her system. A normal person would call it guilt; but for Charlotte McPrice, who had lived practically all her life without a sense of her wrongdoing—her *humanity*, in fact—this was like being tossed from Grace....Why wasn't she calling the police: telling them that she thought that her campaign manager was implicated? Again, she hadn't done it because, on some level, she approved—was in fact an accessory! The prospect that she was *guaranteed* to win the election, was another thorn in her side; and for the life of her, she didn't know which horrified her more: the fear of all of this coming out, and her being publicly ridiculed and punished, or the prospect of living her entire life with this thing in her gut. But were there any choices at this point? Would the police figure out that it hadn't been a suicide? And if so, would they be able to trace it back to her?

But even these thoughts mocked her! When had she ever thought about hiding! She had always been at the vanguard, sure in her purity and correctness. Now, she was like the rest of them: like all the people whom she had lampooned and chastised—like *Randolph*! All that lay before her was learning to live with it—going through life with this knowledge of herself—or telling the world and losing everything...But maybe she had already lost everything, and having lying as an option was the proof of it. She put her hands to her face, and, for the first time since she heard of her husband's death, cried. They were tears of mourning, but for *her*, not her husband.

She was so lost in her grief that she didn't know when the two policemen had entered her study. They were the same men from the previous night; she flinched when she saw them—

"We're sorry, ma'am," they quickly apologized in unison. Both men were in their dress uniforms now, and as she stared blankly at them, one of the officers explained:

"We were heading to the memorial service, ma'am...just wanted to tell you that we are almost convinced that your husband's death was a suicide—there is no evidence that it was a robbery or anything else, since all of his money was in his pocket. And since there haven't been any threats to his life ...well, it looks like suicide, sorry to say. We even found a note." They handed the hand-written letter over to her. It read:

"I'm not worthy of my wife. [McPrice almost screamed out hysterically: those words were so obviously Wisinski's!] I'm a sinner and I can't go on!"

When she looked up from the note, one of the officers ventured: "It *is* his handwriting, right?"

McPrice stared at it—believe it or not, it actually was his handwriting. Wisinski had probably made the man write it before killing him. McPrice looked back up at the officer and nodded her head.

The man ventured: "I know it's no consolation to you...."

But she only nodded her head. "Thanks, officers," she said then, her voice faint. Once again bowing to her, they left. She stared at their retreating forms, feeling sick to her stomach. Wisinski walked in then: he had spent the night in the guest bedroom. Seeing him, she knew that this was her last chance to do right: to call the policemen back and tell them all that had happened. But she realized, at once, that it wasn't in her—that her hurtling flight from the apex had come to the end, and that her broken corpse was now sprawled against the rocks at the base of the mountain.

Seeing her sitting there dejectedly, Wisinski came up quickly. He kneeled before her then—the way someone kneeled before a queen—grasping her hands. She cringed at the sight and touch of him, but he was so insane in his joy, that he didn't seem to notice or to care:

"Did they tell you the good news!" he exulted. "Now, *nothing* can touch you!" She looked at him with the same horror as last night; and like Andropov and Randolph and Roland and Marenga before her, she wondered how in the hell she had come to this place....

* * *

YOUNG OFFICER MUCELLI hadn't slept in 30 hours now—and didn't expect to sleep anytime soon. He kept seeing Flanders falling to the ground. That scene would haunt him forever...but it was too late to do anything about it now. He was getting dressed for the police rally/memorial service now, putting on his dress uniform. He just had to hold on a bit longer, then everything would blow over.

At the rally, Mucelli would be in the first row, of course—with the rest of the dignitaries. And nobody suspected him—or at least nobody that mattered. There was only that bastard, Ericsson. Still, even he was only one insignificant voice in a sea of supporters. Mucelli was booked for Maria Santos's show that night. She and hundreds of others were calling him a hero now. The sickening irony inherent in that left him somewhat queasy; but again, it was too late to do anything about it. He just had to keep going—

There was a knock on the door. That must be my ride, he thought, taking a deep breath to calm himself. "I'm coming!" he bellowed, glancing at himself one last time in the mirror before walking to the door. He had affected a calm, reverential expression before opening the door; but after he opened it, and looked into the eyes of the man standing on the other side, all of that fell away. Ericsson's eyes bored into him; Mucelli stood there in shock, fighting not to panic. He had a sudden impulse to rush at the man and beat his brains out...! He opened his mouth to say something—he didn't know what—but Ericsson stepped boldly past him then, and into the room.

Mucelli closed the door softly, seeming suddenly frail. When he turned to face the man, Ericsson was still staring at him the way someone stared at a piece of filth. Ericsson began by ceremoniously holding up a plain manila folder: "Let me tell you about the final forensic report I have in my hand here," he started, "—and some of the conclusions that I've come to. [Mucelli, as though losing his strength, moved over to the couch and sat down heavily; Ericsson walked over as well, but remained standing.] First of all," he continued, "the semen inside of Cindy Phelps was her husband's alone; second, Dallas Phelps was dead for *hours: way* before Micheaux got there—several people corroborate that. Dallas Phelps was in fact killed the night before—most likely by Cindy Phelps, whom *he* raped. And why do I say that? The only fingerprints on the murder weapon were hers and her husband's. They had fought over the gun...she won. Furthermore, it was his skin alone that we found beneath her fingernails: more evidence that they were the only ones involved in the struggle. As far as I can tell, they had fought the night before; frightened by this fight, the nanny had left with the little girl, and gone over to Roland Micheaux's house. They used to have a relationship, so this explains their connection, and why she would turn to him for help. But," he said, walking up and stopping before the blanched Mucelli, "there is still the question of who shot Cindy Phelps. Roland Micheaux, we've all been saying. However, the angle of the gunshot wound to Cindy Phelps's head is consistent with a self-inflicted wound, which is to say that after killing Dallas, and shooting at Micheaux, who had just then come to return their daughter, she tried to kill herself. When she fired at Micheaux, he ran away—was so traumatized by it, that he probably went into shock, neither realizing that he still held the little girl nor how far he was running. Now," he said with a dead smile, "does any of this make sense to you, Mucelli?"

Mucelli had been staring on in a daze, but now ventured: "I guess so, sir."

"You *guess* so?" Ericsson said with a smirk. "Since you have the answers, what do you suggest I tell the commissioner?"

Mucelli opened his mouth, but nothing came out. Ericsson went on: "From all this, it looks to me like we've been chasing an innocent man, Officer Mucelli. What do *your* keen senses tell you?"

Mucelli couldn't move—couldn't even manage to look up anymore—

"And then," Ericsson went on quickly, "there is the question of your partner. [Mucelli looked up in horror!] I was wondering if Micheaux did that either. What do you think about that, Officer Mucelli?"

Mucelli was breathing shallowly now, his face seeming drained of blood and life. Ericsson stepped up to him threateningly then, screaming:

"*You* did it, didn't you!"—Mucelli cringed against the couch, looking like a scared dog—"*You killed Flanders by mistake and were too frightened to admit it*!"

Suddenly, Mucelli burst into tears, hiding his face like a terrified child; Ericsson stared down at him, still hoping, somehow, that he had been wrong about it all, but Mucelli's tears forced him to put away those fragile hopes. All that he could do was stare at the man in horror.

* * *

"JUSTICE, PEACE, WAR: *decide*!"

Roland was pulled along with the rest of them. He was as terrified of those marching at his shoulders as a man who had just fallen into a serpent pit, would be terrified of the forms slithering in the darkness. It was as though his slightest movement might provoke a stinging bite—and death. He was unable to escape from them—to leave the mob. He walked along numbly and mutely, while tens of thousands of them screamed their demands, venting their hatred of the world. How long he went on like this, he couldn't say for sure. It seemed as though he had spent an eternity trying to keep ahead of those behind, yet just behind those ahead: trying desperately to maintain some unattainable homeostasis within the chaos of the mob. Every inadvertent touch had seemed to be a prelude to death. He had only survived by locking himself away: by ignoring the touch of death, the way the man in the serpent pit had to remain calm and still while the snakes slithered next to his warmth.

But eventually, when it was about 10 in the morning, the mob finally began to slow. Whoever or whatever was leading the mob, it was now making a right-hand turn onto Malcolm X Boulevard. Thousands of people were already there! Camera crews and speakers had been set up—as if it were a rock concert or something. Pushed along, Roland found himself on the left-hand side of that huge boulevard—and was content to stay where he was—when he all at once found himself being jostled again. Now, everyone seemed eager to get on the right-hand side of the street, where a dais had been erected. This block seemed to be their destination. Panicking, he suddenly realized that this was the block that he and Kain had fled down the night before. The police had chased them into that building over there! The realization brought a flood of memories and fears. *He had to get out of here*! The feeling came out of nowhere, but its voice was undeniable. He had ridden the crest of the wave as long as was possible: now, it was time to escape before he was thrown to the rocks....But the current was taking him to the right; people were amassing around the dais. Microphones and speakers had been set up, and everyone was desperate to get a good spot. As he was jostled about in the crowd, he felt like screaming out. He felt like the lone moth that understood the meaning of fire—yet who was compelled to enter the flames with the rest of them. He couldn't stay to the left—not with so many people fighting him. But he soon realized that while others tried to go from left to right, he could, with some degree of success, keep going straight—and that way, get free of them all and flee.

He was coming level with the dais now—a man had alighted it, and was now waving to the people below; the crowd, responding to the man's gestures, began cheering. The din of them was horrible in the air. Roland felt as if he were in a whirlwind; he was giddy and nauseous—but he had to keep fighting. There were cameras across the street from the dais—Roland passed beneath them as he fought his way down the block. Helicopters were hovering overhead—some from television stations, and some from the police. He imagined the scene from above—the *madness* of it. Tens of thousands of people, stretching along the length of the boulevard…The march was becoming a shuffle now; soon, they would all be locked in here like sardines, *suffocating*….!

But when Roland finally passed the dais and was about 5 meters from the end of the block, he realized, with a start, that there were *thousands* of police officers in riot gear amassing at the end of the block! With the crowd shuffling for space, Roland hadn't noticed the policemen until he was practically on top of them. He turned his back abruptly, his heart racing in his chest as he prayed that they hadn't noticed his face in the sea of enraged blackness. The police were, for all intents and purposes, making it a dead end block. They, too, had anticipated where the march was going to end, and were now taking up defensive positions. There was nowhere for Roland to go now: nothing for him to do but to wait…but wait for *what*? What was he to do after this? What were *any* of them to do? The old numbness was coming over him again. The air felt charged, as though lightning would strike at any moment. He looked around in bewilderment, looking at the thousands of people. Some were sitting on the cars parked on the curb—anywhere there was space…and thousands more were coming! So many people...the air was filthy with them. There were speakers on roofs—in open windows…Botswana Glade had prepared well, Roland thought, just as the man began gesturing for the crowd to be still and silent. Roland took a sneak peek over his shoulder: the police were still amassing, trapping them all like rats—

"Yes, we're here—we're *finally* here!" Botswana Glade's voice boomed over the loud speakers. The voice reverberated in Roland's chest...and then the cheers: *tens of thousands* of them...the noise left him trembling. It was a good two minutes before Botswana Glade could speak again. The cheering had a domino effect, spreading down the blocks, soon to reach people who were seven blocks away! They cheered, even though they couldn't possibly know what they were cheering for. Again, Roland nervously glanced over at the police. They were still amassing, with more blue and white cars pulling up all the time—

"We here," Botswana Glade roared when the cheers had died down, "and ain't *nobody* gon drive us away! We gon *stay* here"—he had to yell over their cheers—"till we good and ready to leave!" Once again, the deafening cheers spread down the blocks; the people looking out from their windows screamed and waved as well....

"Yes," Botswana Glade started in a more solemn voice, "right *here*, in front of this very stoop, *three* brothers and sisters—*children*—died; and four more are on the verge of death as we speak! Right *here*, this happened, but let us not be fooled into thinking that this is an isolated event! [The crowd groaned, feeling his words.] No, sir! That's what those devils like you to think. *Remember the Thomases*! [The crowd roared!] Every time these crackers get caught with their hands in the cookie jar, they cry out: 'It was only this one time!'" he mimicked them in an effeminate voice that made the crowd burst out in laughter. "Well," he continued, "we *ain't* fools! Yea, we caught you this *one* time, but how many cookies did you eat before I got here!" The applause rose and crested, like a wave, and Roland felt as though he would drown.

"Those devils *always* playing their tricks! Pacifying us like it ain't *nothing*! Well, devil," he screamed, "we will no longer be appeased by your silly lies! I've got God on my side, and got sense enough to know that the strength of God will always win out over the lies of the Devil!" The crowd was in a state of euphoria once again; Roland couldn't move....

"I'm not here to whip you into a fury!" Botswana Glade said, even while the cheering crested above his head. "I'm not here to instill the mob instinct in you, like the media are saying! [People laughed.] I'm here to *bore* you, because this event is nothing new! It has happened before—and it will happen again unless we do something to stop it! I'm not here to outrage you by pointing out the excessiveness of the force that was used by the police last night—and *every* time they come into our community! On the contrary, I don't have to say *anything*! I don't have to point *anything* out! We *all* know! Many of us have known for most of our lives! There will be an inquiry, a few cops will be punished…blah, blah, blah…This is nothing new! I don't have to whip you into a fury, because that fury has always been there, and will be there until this ceases once and for all! [The cheers roared in the air: roared like *thunder*!] You don't need *me* to tell you, brothers and sisters!" Botswana Glade went on. "*I* didn't drag you out of your homes! You came because you know what they are going to do; and you are here, finally and *totally*, to put an end to it!"

Botswana Glade barely managed to take a breath, when—

"*Please, stop this*!" a voice suddenly cried. Everyone was confused, because although it boomed in the air like Botswana Glade's, it hadn't come from him. It had come, Roland and thousands of others realized a millisecond later, from the police-blockaded side of the boulevard. Even down the blocks, the cheering had dwindled to almost nothing. The euphoria, as fragile as it was, scurried away, leaving only surprise and confusion. They all turned to see where the voice had come from; and there, standing on the hood of a heavily armored riot van, was Mayor Randolph! The van, fitted with huge speakers on its roof, was right on the edge of the crowd—actually, just a few meters away from Roland! Randolph was still holding the microphone that had allowed his voice to be heard above their cheers. "Botswana Glade!" he cried again as the stunned crowd looked on. "Please, I beg you, put an end to this craziness! This is the *last* thing that our people need!"

Botswana Glade, who had been taken off guard like everyone else, allowed himself to smile. He looked over the crowd with an exaggerated gaped mouth, and people laughed at his feigned disbelief. "Why, Mr. Mayor," he said, in a singsong voice, "what might *you* be doing here?"

The crowd laughed.

"Please, sir—"

"Yes!" Botswana Glade was shouting now. "We should have expected *this*! What was I just talking about? Pacification? Well, here is Mr. Uncle-Tom-House-Nigger, himself, here to tell all us field niggers that we shouldn't do nothing to harm dear old massa."

The crowd was laughing a mirthless kind of laughter.

"Look at this bastard," Botswana Glade went on, pointing a bony finger across the multitudes to Randolph, "...still got his police protecting him! If you're too scared to come in the black community without your mommy holding your hand, then go back home!"

The cheering became something even more vicious—

"Look, Mr. Glade, let's just talk about this!" Randolph begged again. "Let's *all* talk. I'm not here as the Mayor. I'm just a man now, here without the police—without the threat of violence—without *power*—"

"You here to talk?" Botswana Glade laughed with a bemused expression that made the crowd break out laughing once again. "Well, then, if you're here to talk, then that's a different matter. Come on up here, brother!" Botswana Glade laughed. "That's right: if you're a man like you say, leave those police and come up here—walk though this gathering of people you claim to represent, and come up here!"

"—All right," Randolph said at once, to everyone's surprise. People had just been about to break out laughing when Randolph got off the roof and pushed aside the barricade, so that he could make his way though the crowd. But there was a horrible kind of tension in the air. In the people's eyes, the hatred of the Mayor was clear: it contorted their faces into scowls; some were whispering to their neighbors, asking if "that nigger" was actually going to do it—

"Pardon me," the Mayor said to the first person in his path, who begrudgingly made way with a snarled lip and a grunt, and then he began to inch through the crowd. Soon, Randolph would come upon Roland; and for a moment, Roland panicked at the realization that the man—his mortal enemy of the last few years—would recognize him and turn him in—

"Yes," Botswana Glade laughed mordantly, "come right up, Mayor, we want to hear everything you have to say." He had tried to joke, but the laughter was suddenly flat and forced. There was a new intensity within the crowd now. They seemed restless; they seemed, thought Roland, like snakes about to strike; and just then, as Randolph was on the verge of coming upon him, a husky black man—who had practically been standing right beside Roland—

tackled Randolph and began raining blows on the man. Everyone cheered as Randolph was driven to the ground by the blows. Roland looked down at the thing that was literally happening at his feet, feeling a horrible emptiness opening up within him. As for the crowd, none but a few of the sickest of them wanted to cheer, but it was as though none of them could stop the thing growing in their souls. If Roland had had any faith in humanity left, it was gone now as he stood there watching the husky man pummeling the Mayor and the surrounding crowd cheering and whooping like animals.

"—Stop it!" Roland cried out then, but his words were lost in the cheers. He balled his hands into fists, gnashing his teeth in frustration and madness: "*Stop it!*" But still, he was ignored. In desperation, Roland tried to grip the man and throw him off the Mayor, but the crowd was inadvertently pushing him back as they clambered around the fight. In fact, with all the whooping, his efforts were easily lost in the chaos. It was then that something occurred to him: an idea born of madness—maybe not even an idea, but the old impulse to push everything to its conclusion and get everything over with; and without thought, he shoved some people out of the way and made haste to the police barricade—which he leapt over. Soon, he reached the riot van, grabbing the microphone that the Mayor had left on the hood. The riot police had actually retreated when the crowd began mauling the Mayor, so Roland had free access as he leapt onto the roof. It was then that he screamed at the top of his lungs:

"*It's me: Roland Micheaux!*" His voice was so forceful that those nearest to the speakers were literally blown back. The crowd, again thrown off track by a new voice, cut short their cheers and again looked up in confusion as Roland repeated: "It's me: Roland Micheaux! It's *me!*" he screamed as people gasped and whispered and frowned, trying to see from themselves. "...Roland Micheaux," he said again, "—the killer and rapist..!" Now, it was their whispers that had a domino effect throughout the crowd. Tens of thousands of people were asking their neighbors if it was really he: really Roland Micheaux. Even the police, who had maintained their distance when the husky man attacked the Mayor, were craning their necks now. Roland Micheaux—the cop killer: the cause of all of this! Even they couldn't believe it; but: "It's me, *the killer!*" Roland screamed, confirming it again.

And now, as though his name had hypnotized them, dozens of

riot policemen, seeing their chance, began to approach the van. The man on the roof was their quarry—they had been chasing him for over a day now; and here, of all places, they had finally found him. The people didn't know what to do—even Botswana Glade was in shock. As they looked up at Roland's face, there was something horrible there—an emptiness which was so vast that it seemed as if it would swallow them all—

"I'm Roland Micheaux," they heard the man say one last time, just before he began to laugh with a sick, empty kind of laughter that was like weeping. He laughed before cameras and all the gaping faces, realizing that his death was complete. And yet, despite his utter emptiness, a side of him was thankful that nobody he loved was there to see it. The world was something that he was indifferent to—there was no hatred left. He stood there limply, so that the microphone slipped from his fingers and tumbled off the roof—

But just then, the riot police, finding themselves close enough, grabbed Roland's ankles and pulled him off the roof. He hit his head on the roof as he fell; and then, after having the wind knocked out of him by the fall, he was swarmed by dozens of officers. People still stood about, stunned; but it was when the police began to club Roland, that a horrible scream erupted from within the crowd, breaking the trance that had kept them in check. Those policemen, hypnotized by the name of Roland Micheaux, had made a grave misstep: they had assumed that the mob's fire had gone out for good; when in truth, Roland had only distracted them. Outraged by the sight of the same brutality that they had come to protest, those thousands—or at least, those within sight of the outrage—rushed at the policemen. The fire that burned within the people was not only back, but increased tenfold by the sight of their devil. The eruption came at last; and as he lay on the ground, beneath the chaotic surge of thousands, Roland closed his eyes and listened to all the violent explosions. In their haste to rip the officers to shreds, the people were trampling Roland now. He could literally feel his bones breaking and his organs being crushed! His hurtling descent from the heavens came to an abrupt end, and he lay splattered against the filthy street. At that very moment, Officer Ericsson appeared on TV, relating the story of Roland Micheaux's innocence—and Mucelli's duplicity. But it was too late by then: both for Roland and the city.

Epilogue

Years seemed to pass; but years, to a child, were lifetimes. Roland found himself lost in the chaos that had been his life. One moment, he would be with his grandmother, then with his mother; then, he would be a man, working in the city—but filled, strangely enough, with all the carelessness of that child; and then, just as he seemed be on the brink of some breakthrough, he would be a toddler again, living with both of his parents, in that strange preconscious bliss known to all children. Reality didn't matter anymore—just as time didn't matter. Love and hate and all the other emotions and sensations blurred into one, so that the only thing that mattered, was that he kept marching on, continuing the meaningless circle of a life which had borne no fruit, and would never do so.

As the years passed by, strange, incomprehensible scenes began to filter into his consciousness: a nurse standing over him; strange men touching him; strange voices reverberating from the heavens…and then they would fade away, and he would be back with his relatives, breezing through the chaotic series of recollections that seemed to be his only respite.

But then, one day—ostensibly after centuries within the strange cycle of life—he found himself playing in the park with his mother. It was a sunny, wondrous day. She was holding his hands, and they were dancing in a circle together—going faster and faster, so that eventually, his legs left the ground, and he was *flying*, around and around, with the world as a blur, and only his mother's smiling, euphoric face as a reference point. And he was laughing too, having no thought but to hold onto his mother as they shared the wonder of giddiness and silliness—

But then, all of a sudden, a white man was peering into his eyes. Roland's first instinct was to flee, but it was as if he had been bound in lead. There was a horrible sluggishness about him. Everything seemed to be moving in slow motion—and *warped*. The white man's face was a misshapen oval—like reflections of faces in spoons; the man was saying something, but it was so resounding, that it only rumbled inarticulately in the air. And then, seemingly after more years had passed, the man stepped away; and there, before Roland, were some other men. Roland stared at them, hopelessly lost. They were saying something, but their words only resounded in the heavens once again. The original man—the doctor, it now occurred to him—was checking him again; Roland's eyes were pulled open; impromptu auscultation was performed on him. He lay there, staring up at the strange man—and at the three others, who seemed just as strange. Of the latter men, two were black, and one was white. The white man was in a police uniform; the two black men were in robes, as though they were patients. All were middle-aged and haggard—

Mayor Randolph! Roland finally recognized one of the men. What was *he* doing here? The man had a bandage around his head; his face was discolored and swollen, and his hand was in a sling. And the other black man was Marenga! The man was standing there with the help of one of those walkers used by old women who had broken their hips. The third man was…The Police Commissioner? Roland couldn't remember the guy's name, but he looked as though he hadn't slept in days. The doctor, who had just finished checking Roland's vital signs, was staring at him with concern. He loomed above Roland again, repeating some resounding gibberish several times before—

"…Can you understand me?"

Roland looked up excitedly when he deciphered the words.

"I think he's coming around!" the doctor said to the others. He looked back at Roland: "Can you understand me?" he asked again.

"Yes," Roland managed to say—even though his mouth felt horribly dry. He glanced down: both arms were in casts; his left leg was in traction; his neck, he realized as he tried to turn his head to look back at the men, was in a brace. As he emerged back into consciousness, all of his broken and bruised parts began to ache—or rather, he became aware of the pain. He grimaced. Nevertheless, the men before him suddenly seemed relieved; the doctor looked over his shoulder at the others and beamed. Then:

"You've been in a coma for two days now," the doctor said, turning back to Roland. "But you should make a complete recovery of your injuries—"

Roland had a sudden flashback to the rally—*all of those rampaging thousands...!*

The Police Commissioner stepped up now; Roland cringed at the sight of him, but the man quickly said, "We're not chasing you anymore, Mr. Micheaux. We realized that you weren't involved in any crimes—but too late."

Marenga chuckled sardonically; the Commissioner looked back at him nervously, then went on:

"There has been social unrest for two days now—riots, looting, fires...and in all five boroughs...It's even spread over to New Jersey, Connecticut and Long Island."

Roland smiled unconsciously: *Let it burn*! he thought.

Randolph stepped up now: "After the initial"—he seemed to search for the right word to describe Botswana Glade's rally—"...disturbance, when people found out that you were innocent, everything went crazy. Twenty policemen have been killed in the last two days; scores of people have been killed...hundreds wounded—"

"And they want you to put an end to it," Marenga said.

"Yes," Randolph went on, either ignoring Marenga's sarcasm, or not acknowledging it, "we need your help."

When Roland looked away and said nothing, the Police Commissioner went on: "The National Guard has been called out. Martial Law has been instituted. Thousands of people have been left homeless by the fires."

Let it burn! Roland thought again.

"You have a right to be angry," Randolph was saying now. "It's natural..." But his words died off when Roland continued to stare into the distance. Randolph stood staring at the man for a while, then said: "I know something that might change your mind."

Roland looked up to him in annoyance as Randolph went to the door and whispered something to whoever was standing outside. He then returned to Roland: "Like I was saying, you have a right to be angry—I was almost killed myself"—Marenga chuckled to himself—"but we need you—"

"You *need* me!" Roland screamed, his voice hoarse and horrible. He wanted to rant some more, to spring at all the men and claw their eyes out; but he was too weak, and just then, the door opened, and a police officer came in with a little girl that he at first didn't recognize.

Randolph started: "Cindy Phelps finally died of her injury. This little girl now has no one—she's been calling for you all these days."

Roland stared down at Mindy, and then looked at the men in the room with pure hatred. *What the hell was this*! What did they expect him to do about any of it! But the little girl...*damn* her, she was standing there looking wretched and unsure; then, seeming to recognize him, she ran up and jumped onto the bed, hugging him around the neck. Besides the sharp pain her grip caused (the doctor made her ease up a little bit after Roland gasped) her touch was disconcerting, setting off strange, contradictory feelings in him. A side of him wanted to wrench her from him and fling her away....For her, he had almost been killed—maybe not even for her, but for the social construct that she was: a little tow-headed, blue-eyed white girl....But then, something melted within him, and he lay there in a daze as she sobbed against his chest. It wasn't even that she was innocent, and innocent of all that he suddenly wanted to accuse her and her society of, but that even now, she still trusted him. It was not the loss of innocence that was the great evil, but the loss of trust. She was hardly innocent anymore, but she was still somehow trusting of the social contracts that seemed like so much shit to him now. The city was being torn apart because those social contracts had been thrown to the side. Without them, all that had been left was the same hate that he had fought against all his life. Hundreds of thousands of people were now either gripped by that madness or becoming victims of it: how could it possibly end, but with the end of the world...just as Kain had said. What was the use! he thought, just as the little girl disengaged from him a little to look at his face:

"You hurt bad, Uncle Roland?"

He stared at her a while, not knowing what to think; then: "I'll be fine"—he looked at the doctor—"...will make a full recovery."

"Maybe this might help," she said then, handing him her doll.

It was the same repulsive abomination that could spit up, burp and shit its panties; but for some reason, he was on the verge of tears. A side of him still wanted to fling her away—to revert to the simple joy of bestiality. He suddenly wanted to be out there with the rest of them, tearing the world apart…But the little girl was there, still trusting him, despite the demon in his chest. How horrible the world was! he thought. He held her closely then—which was to say he moved his cast over her—wishing that the world would end quickly and brutality; but then, at the same time, he found himself hoping that a precious few, like the child in his arms, would be spared that sterilizing brutality: that they might be the seeds for some more sane and forgiving world…just as Kain had said. He felt so very tired. Every time he thought it was over, it was only just beginning….

Randolph and the Police Commissioner were still staring down at him, hopefully. Watching them, Roland was again trapped between the urge to scream for the people to rip the world apart and the impetus to stop them; but at last, reaching a conclusion that seemed just as futile as its opposite, he looked up at the Mayor and whispered:

"What do you want me to do?"

"Just a quick statement to the press," Randolph said eagerly. "Just a few words, so that people see that you're alive—and are willing to go on."

Roland sighed; the Police Commissioner quickly went on: "The media are already waiting. They heard that you were coming out of the coma, and began to gather downstairs. Just the sight of you might help bring this to an end."

They stood there, looking at him eagerly; Roland nodded, even though he didn't believe that he could do anything.

"Thank you!" the Mayor began—

"Can I have a few moments alone," Roland cut him off….

All four men left the room solemnly, leaving Micheaux in the room with the little girl. When they had closed the door behind them, the Police Commissioner looked warily to the others and said:

"Do you think Micheaux will do it?"

"Will do *what*?" Marenga said in annoyance. "Look at what we're doing! The man is barely out of a coma and we're rushing him off to give a press conference! He can barely move"—Marenga looked at the doctor accusingly; the man looked away nervously—

"and yet we're pushing him out there to fight our battles."

"We're desperate," Randolph said at last.

"But what the hell can we expect Micheaux to do?" Marenga returned. "Bring peace and order? No one man can do that when people are bent on killing one another and scavenging the world. If we're brutal enough, we may be able to keep them from killing one another; but in the long run, only they have the power to bring peace and order."

"Then we'll settle for the short term," Randolph replied. "One day at a time…start over if we can."

"Start over with the same old lies?" Marenga said in bewilderment. "And what was the meaning of bringing in that little girl? You've got to put a guilt trip on him to get him to act, and yet you want him to get people to start behaving with dignity and respect. Come on!" Marenga said, looking pointedly at the others. "This is bullshit and we all know it!"

"What are we supposed to do!" Randolph said in frustration. "The city's falling apart, Marenga! When someone's bleeding to death you don't stand there moralizing, you get in and do something. Yes, it's short term, but at least the bleeding will stop. I'll do *whatever* it takes!"

Marenga sighed and stood looking at the man. There was no true antagonism between them: they were only two desperate men trying to make sense of the world. At this pause in their exchange, the Police Commissioner, preoccupied with his own thoughts, nodded and walked off, somehow looking even more haggard than before; the doctor, perhaps still smarting from Marenga's jibe about his ethics, bowed his head and walked off as well, leaving Marenga and Randolph standing there.

They were silent for a while, then: "I just hope this comes to an end," Randolph mused.

"It will never end," Marenga said, matter-of-factly. "People will always find some excuse to hate one another—and to kill one another. Justifications and foes change, but the actions remain the same."

Randolph sighed thoughtfully. "Maybe you're right, Marenga…"

"Being right doesn't matter anymore…" Then, seeming to remember something he had meant to ask, Marenga ventured: "You find out why McPrice dropped out of the mayoral race at the last moment?"

"No—it doesn't make sense to me or to *anyone*. Some say her husband's death was too much for her: that she loved him so much..."—he sighed—"Only McPrice seems to know."

"So then," Marenga laughed, "I guess that congratulations are in order."

"No," Randolph said, smiling at his friend's baiting. "I'll only be Mayor until another election can be staged. I still feel the way I felt when I walked out on that last debate. I'll do my duty until then, but I'll never hold office again."

"What happened?" Marenga laughed. "I thought you were willing to do 'whatever it takes'? Your generosity wear out?"

Randolph smiled at Marenga's jibe at first, then sighed, shaking his head. "I don't know Marenga," he said, pursing his lips, "—that's just the point. Something has changed in me. After the doctors bandaged me up and put my arm in a cast, there was this...excitement in me. I wanted the people to destroy one another: destroy *everything*...just like you said I did. [He glanced at Marenga ashamedly.] I don't know anymore. For a while, I wanted to see it all scrapped—like a painting that didn't come out the way I'd wished. I guess that's human nature: destroying the things we can't fix...but if you are going to be people's leader, you should at least know what you think about them....I look at them, and I cringe—but it's not fear, exactly: it's a reminder to be on my guard—*mistrust*."

"What do you expect? They almost *killed* you!"

"But it's more than a few bruises and broken bones, Marenga. I feel like some animal in the jungle. Is that what our society has come to? I want to *live*, Marenga—and live as a *man*, not as an animal." Laughing, he went on: "Maybe this would be a good chance for *you* to run for Mayor."

"No," Marenga chuckled, "...not me, my friend." And at that, he patted Randolph on the back and they walked down the corridor like two old men.

* * *

AN HOUR LATER, Roland was wheeled into the cafeteria on his bed. The bed was on an incline—which is to say that his torso was elevated—so he could see the hundreds of reporters and the three dozen or so camera crews that had gathered to hear his words. There had been excitement in the air, with those hundreds talking like school children at an assembly; but when Roland entered, a hush came over the room. The little girl, Mindy, held the cast over his right hand and walked by his side, while two orderlies wheeled him onto the dais. Roland didn't know why he had come—or what he would say. But what could possibly do it? What words could possibly put an end to the madness of thousands—of *millions*, in fact. With all that he had been through, he couldn't even be convinced of his own sanity, much less try to conjure sanity and peace in others.

Randolph, Marenga and the Commissioner were all sitting in the front row. They, along with everyone else, were staring at him expectantly and silently. But out of that silence, there now came the cacophony of camera shutters; flash bulbs made him squint; camera crews and sound men were maneuvering to get the best vantage points...Before him, on the dais, were *dozens* of microphones, each with the logo of a network. All was in readiness for the elusive words that would save them all. The orderlies pushed him up to the edge of the podium; a technician came up and affixed a small microphone to his gown, then they all left the stage, leaving him lying there with Mindy standing by his side—

Yes, they've planned this well! he thought with a renewed feeling of revulsion. He glanced over at Mindy then: yes, they had seen her as their secret weapon against him; and having her there with him was perfect: a brutalized black man and an orphaned little white girl, loving one another...what could be more cinematic! He suddenly felt sick to his stomach! Even Maria Santos was there, waiting to question him and boost her ratings. People were dead, thousands were homeless...the very society was tearing itself apart, and yet all it was, was a feeding frenzy: a *spectacle*! For the next few weeks, it would be the "hot" story around the world; and then, after the mandatory network specials asking how it had happened and why we weren't a peaceful nation, it would all fade away—until the next riot or whatever became "hot"; at which time, Americans would once again feel compelled to pretended that they were just discovering the problem, asking how it could possibly have happened, and why they didn't have a peaceful nation...*ad infinitum*! He had a sudden, violent impulse to curse them all: to leap up and yell, *Fuck you all*! But he knew that that wouldn't reach them: would only *add* to the spectacle. He sat there, trembling with rage and ineptitude, until, glancing at Maria Santos's expectant face, he saw something that made his breath get caught in his throat!

Right behind Maria Santos, was a man whose existence was impossible! *It was Jasper Kain*! The man was in a suit and tie, looking up at Roland with his usual calmness. All Roland could do, was stare. *Kain was alive*! Roland couldn't even begin to conceptualize it—had the man been wearing a bulletproof vest perhaps? Or maybe the man was a ghost, haunting Roland from hell—or just a lingering delusion from his coma…All the possibilities flared up in his mind, so that he knew at once that he was no match for them. And there was an inscrutable smile on Kain's face—a look of triumph, almost *transcendence*. The man was clean-shaven now; and with his suit and tie, and his stylish, wire-rimmed glasses, his existence was potent proof that the world was mad. Just then, inexplicably, the man winked at Roland; and, as though his only reason for being there had been to show Roland that he was still alive, Kain began navigating his way through the media and towards the exit.

Roland stared at Kain's retreating back in shock, already believing that he had imagined it all. And Kain looked so normal—so *sane*—especially in comparison to everyone else, that a side of Roland began to wonder if the entire thing hadn't been an act: all the supposed madness, all the rants…so that Roland could be put in the position where he would understand everything that was now so clear to him.

And presently, Kain stopped in the crowded exit (which was crammed with people who had come to get a glimpse at Roland) and turned back, nodding at Roland as if he had read his mind and approved. They stared at one another for a while, then Kain smiled and was gone—as if suddenly at peace—and there was again a horrible void left by his absence.

It seemed as though minutes had passed. Now that Kain was gone, Roland was overcome by a feeling of loneliness and isolation; and looking around—perhaps for someone or something to take Kain's place—he realized that the people were still waiting to hear his words: the elusive incantations which would make everything right. All those parasites and scavengers were still waiting for the meal that Roland was to provide, and the hatred began to grow in him again. But suddenly remembering Kain, and the man's lesson that madness was wanting the unattainable, Roland was suddenly buoyed by the realization of how easy it would be to thwart them all. *Yes*! he thought to himself, either fully in the throes of Kain's madness or his *sanity*. It was all so simple! The only hope for them—the only thing that might stun them into consciousness—was emptiness: the vast abyss that they all held within themselves. The emptiest of them were out on the streets now, deluded by thoughts of justice and right and wrong, when all that they were possessed by, was the chaos that was the human will. That will, fed by unattainable, self-destructive desires, was rising above their heads now, like a giant getting clumsily to his feet. And yet, all that was needed to knock that colossus off of his feet, was the brutal realization that there was in fact no justice—no right and wrong: that there were, in the final analysis, *no* pithy answers: *no* perfectly packaged thoughts and solutions. They had wheeled him out there in order to add to the chaos and keep the farce going, but he refused to perform: refused to be a harlequin at his own funeral! *Yes*, he thought with an inner smile: let them sit there in the wake of his silence and take him in; and realize, *for themselves*, without the safeguards that his rage and self-righteousness—or, for that matter, his *magnanimity*!—might provide, not *simply* that they had been wrong about him, for that was irrelevant in the face of all that had happened. On the contrary, he wanted them to look up at him in the uncomfortable silence that was even now wearing heavily on them all, and see for themselves that they had no power over him; and that despite everything, *he was still a man*!

About the Author

D.V. Bernard emigrated from the Caribbean to New York City when he was nine years old. After completing a BA degree in sociology at the University of Pittsburgh, he left graduate school at the University of Arizona in order to concentrate on writing. Over the past few years, he has made extended trips to Southern Africa and the Caribbean. He currently lives in New York City. This is his first published novel. Interested parties may contact the author at dvbernard@streborbooks.com.

STREBOR BOOKS INTERNATIONAL ORDER FORM

Use this form to order additional copies of *Strebor Books International* Bestselling titles as they become available.

Name: ______________________________

Company ______________________________

Address: ______________________________

____

City: ____________ *State* ________ *Zip* ________

Phone: (____)____________ *Fax:* (____)____________

E-mail: ______________________________

Credit Card: ☐ *Visa* ☐ *MC* ☐ *Amex* ☐ *Discover*

Number ______________________________

Exp Date: ____________ *Signature:* ______________________________

QTY	DESCRIPTION	PRICE	TOTAL
1.	*The Sex Chronicles*	*$ 15.00*	
2.	*Shame On It All*	*$ 15.00*	
3.	*Daughter by Spirit*	*$ 15.00*	
4.	*God's Bastard Sons*	*$ 15.00*	
		Subtotal	
		shipping	
		5% tax (MD)	
		Total	

SHIPPING INFORMATION		
Ground	one book	$ 3.00
each additional book		$ 1.00

Make checks or money orders payable to

Strebor Books International

Post Office Box 10127

Silver Spring, Maryland 20914

Books can be purchased at online booksellers

and A&B Distributors (718) 783-7808